...years of stifling her writers muse and acquiring various ...piring job-titles, **Victoria Parker** finally surrendered ...t persistent voice and penned her first Mills & Boon ...nce. Turns out, creating havoc for feisty heroines and ...sh heroes truly *is* the best job in the world. In her spare ...dabbles in interior design, loves discovering far flung ...ns and getting into mischief with her rather wonder-...mily.

...ard-winning author **Zuri Day** snuck her first Mills & Boon ...nce from her older sister's collection and was hooked ...page one. Knights in shining armour and happily-ever-...s spurred a lifelong love of reading. Zuri now creates these stories as a full-time author. Splitting her time between the stunning Caribbean islands and southern California, and always busy writing her next novel, Zuri still loves to connect with readers via Zuri@ZuriDay.com

Maya Blake's writing dream started at 13. She eventually realised her dream when she received *The Call* in 2012. Maya lives in England with her husband, kids and an endless supply of books.

Contact Maya:
www.mayabauthor.blogspot.com.
www.twitter.com/mayablake.
www.facebook.com/maya.blake.94

Becoming
the Boss

VICTORIA PARKER
ZURI DAY
MAYA BLAKE

MIX
Paper from
responsible sources
FSC C007454

This book is produced from independently certified FSC™
paper to ensure responsible forest management.

For more information visit: www.harpercollins.co.uk/green

Printed and bound in Spain
by CPI, Barcelona

MILLS & BOON

First Published in Great Britain 2019
by Mills & Boon, an imprint of HarperCollins*Publishers*
1 London Bridge Street, London, SE1 9GF

BECOMING THE BOSS © 2019 Harlequin Books S. A.

The Woman Sent to Tame Him © 2014 Victoria Parker
Diamond Dreams © 2012 Lutishia Hinton
The Price of Success © 2012 Maya Blake

ISBN: 978-0-263-27779-1

0919

THE WOMAN
SENT TO
TAME HIM

VICTORIA PARKER

For my Dad.
Always my anchor in the storm.
I love you.

CHAPTER ONE

Monte Carlo, May

Hold on to your hearts, ladies, because racing driver Lothario Finn St George is back in the playground of the rich and famous.

After sailing into the Port of Monaco with a bevy of beauties only last eve, the man titled Most Beautiful in the World donned a custom-fit tux and his signature crooked smile and swaggered into the Casino Grand with all the flair of James Bond. Armed with his loaded arsenal of charismatic charm, the six-times World Champion then proceeded to beguile his way through the enamoured throng—despite the owner of Scott Lansing advising the playboy to 'calm his wild partying and tone down adverse publicity'.

Seems Michael Scott is still battling with threats from sponsors, who are considering pulling out of over forty million pounds' worth of support for the team.

True, Finn St George has always danced on the devilish side of life, but of late he seems to be pushing some of the more family-orientated sponsors a fraction too far. Indeed, only last week he was pictured living it up with not one but four women in a club in Barcelona—apparently variety really is the spice of his life!

Though, with only two days to go until the Prince of

Monaco launches this year's race, we suspect Finn's wicked social life is the least of Scott Lansing's worries, because clearly our favourite racer is off his game.

While Australia was a washout, earning him third place, St George barely managed to scrape a win in Malaysia and Bahrain, leaving Scott Lansing standing neck and neck with fierce rivals Nemesis Hart. But when he crashed spectacularly in Spain last month, and failed to finish, racing enthusiasts not only dubbed him 'the death-defyer', but he slipped back several points, leaving Nemesis Hart the leader for the first time in years.

Has St George really lost his edge? Or has the tragic boating accident of last September, involving his teammate Tom Scott, affected him so severely?

Usually dominating the grid, it appears our much-loved philanderer needs to up his game and clean up his act, or Scott Lansing may just find themselves in serious financial straits. One thing is certain: while Monaco waits with bated breath for the big race tomorrow Michael Scott is sure to be pacing the floors, hoping for a miracle.

A MIRACLE...

With a flick of her wrist, Serena Scott tossed the crumpled newspaper across her father's desk. 'Well, she was wrong about one thing. You're not pacing the floors.'

On a slow spin the black and white blur landed in front of him, hitting the glass with a soft smack. Then the only sound in the luxurious office on the Scott Lansing yacht was Serena's choppy breathing and the foreboding thump of her heart.

'No pacing. Yet,' he grated, dipping his chin to lock his sharp graphite eyes on hers.

Well, now... She had the uncanny notion that after hours of musing over the true genesis of her three a.m. wake-up call she was about to discover exactly why she'd been dragged from her warm bed in London to globetrot to the Côte d'Azur. And if the suspicion snaking up her spine was anything to go by she wasn't going to like it.

'I have no idea what you're worried about,' she said, perfectly amiable as she folded her arms across the creased apple-green T shrouding her chest. 'Finn is performing to his usual sybaritic standards, if you ask me. Fraternising with God-knows-who while he parties the night away, drinks, gambles, beds a few starlets and crashes a car for the grand finale. Nothing out of the ordinary. You knew this two years ago, when you signed him.'

'Back then he wasn't this bad,' came the wry reply. 'It's not only that. He's…'

That familiar brow furrowed and Serena's followed suit. 'He's what?'

'I can't even explain it. He goes on like *nothing's* happened but it's like he's got a death wish.'

She coughed out an incredulous laugh. 'He hasn't got a death wish. He's just so supremely arrogant he thinks he's indestructible.'

'It's more than that. There's something…dark about him all of a sudden.'

Dark? A sinister shiver crept over her skin as the past scratched at her psyche, picking at the scab of a raw wound. Until she realised just *who* they were talking about.

'Maybe he's been overdoing it on the sun deck.'

'You're being deliberately obtuse,' he ground out.

Yes, well, unfortunately Finn St George brought out the worst in her—had done since the first moment she'd locked eyes with him four years ago…

Serena flung her brain into neutral before it hit reverse and kicked up the dirt on one of the most humiliating experiences of her life. Best to say lesson learned. After that, what with her engineering degree, working alongside the team's world-famous car designer in London and Finn's thirst for media scintillation—which she avoided like the bubonic plague—face-to-face contact between them had been gratifyingly rare.

Until—*just her rotten luck*—their formal 'welcome to the team' introduction, when he'd struck at every self-preservation instinct she possessed, oozing sexual gravitas, with challenge and mockery stamped all over his face. *Hateful* man. She didn't need reminding she was no *femme fatale*—especially by a Casanova as shallow as a puddle.

Add in the fact that his morals, or lack thereof, turned her stomach to ice, from the outset they'd snarled and sparked and butted heads—and that had been *before* he'd stolen the most precious thing in the world from her.

A fierce rush of grief flooded through her, drenching her bones with sorrow, and she swayed on her feet.

'Look,' her father began, tugging at the cuff of his high-neck white team shirt. 'I know you two don't really get along…'

Wow, wasn't *that* an understatement?

'But I need your help here, Serena.'

With an incredulous huff she narrowed her eyes on the whipcord figure of Michael Scott, also known as Slick Mick to the ladies and Dad when in private, or when she was feeling particularly daughterly, as he rocked back in his black leather chair.

Nearing fifty, the former racing champion reminded her of a movie icon, with his unkempt salt and pepper hair, surrounding a chiselled face even more handsome than it had been at the peak of his career. The guy was seriously good-looking. Not exactly a father figure, but they were friends of the best kind. At least they usually were.

'This is your idea of a joke, right?' It was hard to sound teasing and only mildly put out when there was such a great lump in her throat. 'Because, let me tell you, I have more of a chance to be Finn St George's worst nightmare than his supposed…*saviour.*'

The idea was ridiculous!

Visibly deflating, he shook his head tiredly. 'I know. But I find myself wondering if you have a better chance of getting through to him. Because, honestly, I'm running out of ideas. And drivers. And cars.' Up came his arm in a wave of exasperation and the pen in his hand soared over the toppling towers of paperwork. 'Did you watch that crash last month? Zero self-preservation. The guy is going to get himself killed.'

'Let him.' The words flew out of her mouth Serena-style—that was before she could think better of it or lessen the blow. One of her not-so-good traits that landed her in trouble more often than not…

'You don't mean that,' he said, with the curt ring of a reprimand.

Closing her eyes, she breathed through the maelstrom of emotions warring in her chest. No, she didn't mean that. She might not like the man, but she didn't want anything bad to happen to him. Much.

'What's more, I refuse to lose another boy in this lifetime.'

The hot air circling behind her ribs gushed past her lips and her shoulders slumped. Then, for the first time since she'd barged in here twenty minutes ago, she took a good look at Michael Scott—a real look. Her dad might be all kinds of a playboy himself, but she'd missed him terribly.

Inspecting the grey shadows beneath his eyes, Serena almost asked how he was coping with the loss of his only son. Almost asked if he'd missed *her* while she'd been gone. But Serena and her father didn't go deep. Never had, never would. So she stuffed the love and the hurt right back down, behind the invisible walls she'd designed and built with the fierce power of a youthful mind.

Yeah, she was the tough cookie in the brood. She didn't grieve from her sleeve or wail at the world for the unfairness of it all. Truly, what was the point? She was this man's daughter, raised as one of the pack. No room for mushy emotions or feminine sentimentality spilling all over the place.

So, even though she now had a Tom-sized hole in her heart, she had to deal with it like a man—get up, get busy, move on.

It was a pity that plan wasn't working out so well. Some days her heart ached so badly she was barely holding it together. *Don't be ridiculous, Serena, you can hold up the world with one hand. Snap out of it!*

'Anyway, you can't stay in London all season, fiddling with the prototype. I thought it was ready.'

'It is. We're just running through the final testing this week.'

'Good, because I need you here. The design team can finish the trials.'

I need you. Wily—that was what he was. He knew exactly what to say and when.

'No. You need me to try and control your wild boy. Problem is I have absolutely no wish to ever set eyes on him again.'

'It wasn't his fault, Serena,' he said wearily.

'So you keep saying.'

But exactly which part of Finn taking Tom to Singapore on a bender and Finn coming back first-class on his twenty-million-pound jet whilst her brother returned in a box wasn't his fault? Which part of Finn taking him out on a boat when Tom couldn't swim and subsequently drowned wasn't his fault? He hadn't even had the decency to attend the funeral!

But she didn't bother to rehash old arguments that only led her down the rocky road to nowhere.

'So you want me to…what? *Forgive* him? Not a chance in hell. Make him feel better? I don't. So why should he?'

'Because this team is going down. Do you really want that?'

She let loose a sigh. 'You know I don't.' Team Scott Lansing was her family. Her entire life. A colourful, vibrant rabble of friends and adoptive uncles and she'd missed them all. But the entire scene just brought back too many memories she was ill-equipped to handle right now.

'So think of the bigger picture. Read my lips when I say, for the final time, it wasn't Finn's fault. It was an accident. Let it go. You are doing no one any favours quibbling about it—least of all me.'

He pinched the bridge of his nose as if to stem one of his killer migraines and guilt fisted her heart.

He was suffering. They were all suffering. In silence. *Let it go...*

But why was it every time they spoke of that tragic day, when the phone had shrilled ominously through their trailer, she was slapped with the perfidious feeling she was being kept in the dark? And she *loathed* the dark.

It didn't matter how many times she asked her father to elucidate he was forever cutting her off.

'Tom wouldn't want to see you like this,' he said, irritation inching his volume a decibel higher. 'Blaming Finn. Doing your moonlit flit routine. Holing up in London. Burying your head in work. You've done all you can at base—now it's time to get back in the field. Quit running and stop hiding.'

'I haven't been hiding!'

He snorted in disbelief.

Okay, maybe she'd been hiding. Licking her wounds was best attempted in peace, as far as she was concerned. But honestly...? How far was solitude getting her on the heart-healing scale?

Serena's heavy lids shuttered. God, she was tired.

She'd lost her brother, her best friend, and she kept forgetting she was supposed to carry on regardless. This was tough love and she'd been reared on it. Admittedly the vast majority of the time she'd appreciated Michael Scott's particular method of parentage. You needed skin as thick as cowhide to trail the world for ten months of the year in the company of men. Not the best way to raise two children, but she'd genuinely loved her life. Honest.

If she'd often stared at other children with their mothers, wondering what it would be like to have one of her own, to live in a normal house and walk to an actual brick-built, other-children-present school every morning, she'd just reminded herself that her life was exciting. And if she'd prayed for a mum all those years ago when her adolescence had been shattered, leaving her broken and torn, she'd comforted herself that she had Tom. Tom had been her rock.

But now he was gone. Nothing was exciting any more and there was no one to hold her hand in the dead of night when the shadows loomed. *You don't need your hand held. You're stronger than that. Snap out of it!*

She swallowed around the lump in her throat, forcing the overwhelming knot of grief to plunge into her chest. Buried so deep her stomach ached.

'*If* what you say is true and there *is* a problem,' she said dubiously, 'how can *I* possibly help?'

'Get him to take an interest in the prototype or work on your latest designs… I don't know—just get him to focus on something other than women or the bottom of a bottle.'

Impossible.

'*I'm* a woman.'

'Only in the technical sense.'

'Gee, thanks.' As if she needed reminding.

Then again, the last thing she wanted was to be like one of Finn's regulars. They were the skirt to Serena's jeans. The buxom bombshells to Serena's boyish figure. The strappy sandals to Serena's biker boots. The super-soft, twice-conditioned spiralling blonde locks to Serena's wild mane of a hue so bizarre it defied all colour charts.

Which was wonderful. Inordinately satisfying. Exactly the way she liked it.

'The last thing he needs is another bedmate,' he muttered wryly. 'He needs a kick up the backside. A challenge. And, let's face it, you two create enough spark to fire a twin-stroke. Therefore I am asking—no, you know what…? I am *telling* you to help. You're on my payroll. You move back in here and you chip in.'

Tough love.

Then his graphite gaze turned speculative. Calculating. An expression she didn't care for that nailed her to the wall.

'Or you can kiss the Silverstone launch of your proto-type goodbye.'

A gasp of air hit the back of her throat. 'You wouldn't dare.'

'Wouldn't I?'

Yeah, he probably would. He didn't believe the racing car she'd designed would be anything special and she'd do anything to prove him wrong.

That prototype was her baby. Three years of hard work. Her and Tom's inspiration. Launching at Silverstone had been their dream. The only tangible thing she had left of him.

'Low, Dad,' she choked out. '*Really* low.'

Averting his eyes, he scrubbed a palm over his face. 'More like desperate.'

Serena sighed. Nailed. Every. Time.

'Fine. I'll try…something.'

Unease began to hammer at her heart—she had no idea how to handle the man. None.

'But I know Finn will make it up. He had a slow start last year. The sponsors will forgive and forget once he starts playing to his fans. Monaco is in the bag. He always wins here. What happened in qualifying sessions today? He's in pole position, right?'

Her father's expression turned thunderous—one that boded only ill. 'He screwed the engine.'

He blew the engine? 'So he's at the back tomorrow? In one of the slowest and hardest circuits in the world?'

'Yep.'

Pop! Up came a vision in her mind's eye—the scene she'd

bypassed as she'd hauled her motorbike along the harbour—and her stomach fired, anger swirling like a tornado. Sparking, ready to ignite.

Raising her arm, she pointed one trembling finger in the general direction of Finn's floating brothel. 'And he's along there, in that…that yacht of his. Engaging in some kind of… drunken debauched sex-fest to celebrate his latest cock-up?'

One weary hitch of those broad shoulders was all it took to light the fireball raging in the pit of her stomach.

'What in the blue blazes is he *doing*? Doesn't he care at all? In fact, don't answer that. I already know.'

The man cared for no one but himself! *And this was a newsflash?* Obligation and decency had clearly been disowned in that gene pool.

'I've had it with him.'

Bullet-like, Serena shot out through the door, her biker boots a clomp-clomp on the polished wooden floors as she raced through the galley. 'I'm gonna kill him. With my bare hands.'

'Serena! Watch your temper. I need him.'

Yeah, well, she needed her brother back—and that was about as impossible as keeping her mitts off Finn St George's pretty-boy face. She'd had enough of that man messing with her family. Her team. Her life. Her brother was dead, the championship was heading for the toilet, and her dad was aging by the second as Finn continued to yank at his fraying tether!

How selfish could one man be?

Well, she was stopping it all. She was taking control. Right now.

CHAPTER TWO

SERENA DUCKED AND dived around the loved-up couples milling on the harbour, her sole focus on the *Extasea*, rising from the water, formidable and majestic.

Even moored among some of the finest vessels in the world, Finn's super-yacht was in a class of her own—a one-hundred-and-sixty-foot, three-decker palace—reminding Serena of the resplendent seven-star hotels he favoured in Dubai and certainly more regal ocean liner than bordello.

Still, opulence aside, she had the acumen to know that appearances were deceptive, and the fact that she'd been lowered to this chafed her pride raw. But there was no backing out now. She was going to say her piece and he was going to listen.

The bravado felt wonderful. Freeing. Cleansing. She should have done this months ago, she realised—had it out with him instead of letting everyone sweep her under the carpet like some bothersome gnat, as if her feelings were of no importance. Her grief had been so all-consuming that she'd allowed it to happen. Well, not any more.

Closer to the yacht now, she felt the balmy air cling to her skin and the thud of her boots become drenched by the evocative beat of sultry music. As she marched up the gangway the splash of water from the hot tub on the sun deck followed by intimate squeals of sexual delight made her trip over her size fives.

Flailing, she gripped the rail on both sides. Then a tidal wave of apprehension crashed over her and she stood soaked with a keen embarrassment. She was about as comfortable with this scene as she would be treading water in the company of killer sharks.

You don't belong here, Serena. Surrounded by sex and women who exuded femininity. *Don't think about it. Just get in there, find Finn, and make him clean the decks himself!*

Hovering a few feet from the top, she inhaled a deep wave of saltwater air to reel back her bravado.

In every direction—whether it was left, towards the luxurious seating area abounding with plush gold chairs, or right, towards the outer dining suites—there were bodies, bodies and more bodies. Wearing as little clothing as possible.

She shivered, chilly just looking at them.

One step further and still no one seemed to notice the impromptu arrival of an uninvited guest. No ravaging lips ceased to kiss. No fervent hands slowed their bold caresses of sun-kissed flesh. No flutes of champagne paused on their way to open mouths and the laughter rolled on in barks of joyful humour that only served to remind her of the last time *she'd* laughed—which made a scream itch to peal up her throat.

Why should Finn and his entourage be laughing when she was still unable to cry? Unable to shed one solitary tear? *Because boys don't cry...*

Indignation launched her the final few feet and out of nowhere a sinister-looking figure loomed and grabbed her wrist in a manacled grip.

'Ow!' Pain shot up her arm and she flipped her hand in an attempt to dislodge the hold—even as she was flung back in time and any lingering panic was ramped up into bone-shattering fear. 'Get off me!'

Except the more she struggled, the tighter the hold became—until the knife-edge of terror scored her heart and her vision swam in the blackest waters...

A rough yet familiar voice shattered the obsidian glaze. 'Hey, let her go. She's okay.'

Mr Manacle released her so fast she stumbled backwards. Her only conscious thought was that she was taking up self-defence classes again. Pronto.

Righting her footing, she glanced at the owner of that masculine rumble.

'Thanks,' she murmured, her voice disgustingly fragile as she rubbed at her wrist to ease the throb of muscle and friction burn.

'You okay, Serena?'

Vision clearing, she focused on the handsome, boyish face of one uneasy chocolate-haired Jake Morgan. Scott Lansing protégé and an apparent star in the making. She'd never watched him drive. For some reason he always got a bit tongue-tied around her, and the fact that he was Tom's replacement gave her heart a pang every time she looked at him. *Not his fault, Serena. Let it go.*

'Peachy. Since when does Finn have security?'

'Had them on and off all season. Mainly for parties when there's a big crowd.'

Translation: when he needed to fend off gatecrashing bombshells.

'Where *is* your dissolute host?' she asked, somewhat surly and unable to care. She was shaking so hard she had to cross her arms over her chest to stop her bones rattling.

'Not sure.' Jake's Adam's apple bobbed and his eyes jerked to a door leading to what she guessed was the main salon. 'I haven't seen him for a while.'

Oh, wonderful. He was covering for Finn. 'Forget it. I'll find him myself.'

The sensation of copious eyes poring over her wild mane and crumpled clothing made her flesh crawl and she had to fight the instinct to race across the polished deck. Ironically, the door to the devil's lair suddenly seemed very appealing and she slipped inside with a bizarre sense of relief.

The lavishness of the place was staggering, and way too gold-filigree-and-fussy for her. She might have a DNA glitch but it didn't even suit Finn. Granted, he'd purchased the mega-yacht from some billionaire, but at least a year had passed since.

After ten minutes of being creeped out by cherub wall sconces she was standing in a corridor surrounded by more doors. It was all like a bad dream...

Moaning, purring, steamy and impassioned noises drifted from the room at the far end of the panelled hallway, licking her stomach into a slow, laborious roll.

Pound-pound went her heart as she edged further towards the sounds, her gaze locked on the source as if drawn by some powerful magnetic force.

Her hand to the handle now, a wisp of a thought passed through her brain: did she *really* want to catch Finn the notorious womaniser *in flagrante* with his recent squeeze? She had enough nightmares to contend with at the best of times. Except...she could hardly roam around here all night, could she? If he was in a drunken stupor she only had sixteen hours to clean him up, and she was *not* leaving this place without some answers!

Astounded at what she was about to do, she pressed her ear up against the door panel in an effort to decipher voices.

Rustle went the sheets and *creak* went the muffled bounce of springs, as if bodies were interlocked and undulating in an amorous embrace. Cries of rapturous passion bloomed in the air and her blood flushed hotly, madly, deeply, in an odd concoction of mortification, inquisitiveness and warmth.

Jeepers, what was *wrong* with her?

Focus.

Ignoring the anxious thump in her chest warning that exposure was imminent, she leaned further in and relished the cool brush of wood against her fevered flesh.

The woman, whoever she was, was clearly glorifying in what was being done to her. No subdued cries or awkward silences while she wished it were over. Just murmurs of encouragement in a deep velvet voice that made the damp softness between Serena's legs tighten.

Not Finn. She would recognise that seductive rasp of perfect Etonian English laced with the smattering of an American drawl any day. A distinct flavour from the time he spent in the off season, presenting a hugely popular car show in the States.

Not that she *liked* his testosterone-and-sex-drenched tone—not at all.

Edgy, she licked her arid lips and told herself to back away before she was nabbed. So why couldn't she move? Why did she strive to imagine what was happening behind this door? Wonder how, precisely, Mr Velvet Voice adored his lover's body for her to reach such hedonistic heights that she became paralysed, unable to do anything but scream in wanton pleasure and abandon—?

'Has she come yet?'

A voice, richly amused and lathered with sin, curled around her nape.

A squeak burst from her throat.

Her head shot upright.

Boom! Her heart vaulted from her chest and she pivoted clumsily, then spread herself against the door panel like strawberry jam on toast.

One look…

Oh. My. God. *No!*

Squeezing her eyes shut she began to pray. *This is not happening. Not again. I am not the unluckiest woman alive!*

'Good evening, Miss Seraphina Scott. Come to join the party?' he asked, with such unholy glee that she was fuelled with the urge to smack her head off the door. 'There's always room for one more.'

'When…' Oh, great—she couldn't even breathe. And her heart—God, her heart was still on the floor. 'When hell freezes.'

She wanted out of here. *Now.* Except the idea that she was

acting like a pansy made her root her feet to the floor like pesky weeds and she prised her eyes wide. Only to decide being a sissy wasn't so bad.

Leaning insolently against the polished panels, no more than two feet away, Finn St George smouldered like a banked fire and the heat spiralling through her veins burst into flames, seared through her blood. All she could think was that she must have done something atrocious in another life to deserve this.

After what he'd done, had it truly been too much to hope his mere presence would have stopped affecting her?

She hated him. *Hated* him! He hadn't changed one iota. Still the most debauched, moral-less creature on two legs. And clearly he intended to go on as if he *hadn't* taken a crowbar to her life and smashed it to smithereens. What had her father said? *'He goes on like nothing's happened...'*

Over her dead body.

Seraphina. No one was allowed to call her that. No one!

'This isn't a social call, I assure you,' she said, proud of her don't-mess-with-me voice as she restrained the urge to shiver before him. 'Any other time it would take an apocalypse to get me into this den of iniquity.'

His mouth—the very one that had been known to cause swooning and fever-pitch hysteria—kicked up into a crooked smile and one solitary indentation kissed his cheek. 'And yet here you are.'

Here she was. It was a pity, that for a moment, she couldn't remember why. All she could think was that that mouth of his was a loaded weapon.

'I do seem to find you in the most...*deliciously* compromising situations, Seraphina.' His prurient grin made his extraordinary eyes gleam in the dim light. 'Listening at doors? Bad, bad girl. I ought to take you over my knee.'

Thanking her lucky stars that she wasn't prone to blushing like a girl—because, let's face it, she'd never *been* one, and the fact that this man made her feel like one was probably the greatest insult on earth—she weighed up the intelligence of answering that symphony of innuendo. Meanwhile she returned his visual full-body inspection just as blatantly. Why he insisted on going through this rigmarole every time they met was a mystery. With one arching golden brow he arrogantly put her in her place—ensuring she understood that she was a duck among swans.

Unluckily for him intimidation didn't work on her. Not any more.

As she soaked up every inch of him she decided she didn't understand the man's appeal.

Obviously there had to be some basis for his being named the world's greatest lover, an erotic legend in the racing world. But, come on, plenty of men must be good in bed—right? Plenty had sexy dimples in lean jaws. Plenty had a mouth made for sin, lips that moved sensually and invitingly and downright suggestively, and eyes the colour of—

Ohhh, who was she kidding?

Finn St George was flat-out, drop-dead *insanely* gorgeous—an abundance of angelic male beauty.

Thick dirty-blond hair; cut short at the back and longer at the front to fall in a tousled tumble over his brow, gave him a sexy, roguish air. And that face…

Not only did he defy nature, he literally bent the laws of physics with his intriguingly wicked mouth and that downright depraved gleam in his cerulean eyes. Eyes that had catapulted him into the hearts and fantasies of women the world over.

Between his leading-man looks and his celebrated body—currently dressed in low-slung board shorts and an unbuttoned crisp white linen shirt, showcasing his magnificent torso—he was mouth-watering, picture-perfect in every single way.

It was a good thing she knew how well a polished chassis could hide an engine riddled with innumerable flaws.

'What do you think you're playing at, Lothario? Don't you

think drinking and partying the night away before a race is dangerous, even for you?'

'I have to find *some* way to work off the residual adrenaline rush from the qualifying session, Seraphina. Unless *you're* offering to relieve some of my more…physical tensions.'

Her lower abdomen clenched in reaction to that catastrophically sensual drawl, and as if he could sense it his lips twitched.

'I'd be quite happy to knock you out—would that help?'

There it was again. That smile. A dangerous and destructive weapon known to bring women to their knees. And the fact that it turned her own to hot rubber made her madder still. 'Then again,' she sniped, 'we wouldn't want to mar that *pretty-boy* face, would we?'

A trick of the light, maybe, but she'd swear he flinched, paled…before something dark and malevolent tightened the hard lines of his body until he positively seethed.

Whoa…

Her mind screaming, *Danger! Danger! Run!*, she backed up a step and nudged the door. She wanted to snarl and bite at him. It was as if her body knew he was the enemy and she was gearing up for a fight. The fight she'd once been incapable of.

Not any more.

Her blunt nails dug into her palms, but in the next breath he pursed that delectable mouth in suppressed amusement, as if it had all been some huge joke, and the change in him was so swift, so absolute, she floundered.

'There's something dark about him all of a sudden.' Or she could be hallucinating from an overdose of his pheromones.

'If you don't mind,' he drawled, 'I'd appreciate it if we kept my face out of it. After all, I wouldn't want to distress the ladies with some unsightly bruising.'

'Like you need any more ladies! Looks to me like you've had your fair share already this evening.'

He looked well-sexed, to be sure. Hair damp, with his glorious fresh water-mint scent flirting with her senses, she guessed he'd just stepped from beneath the assault of a shower.

'On the contrary, I was just about to indulge in a good workout.'

Disgust drove her tone wild. 'Yes, well, bedding the latest starlet or pit-lane queen is one thing—partying the night away before racing on the most dangerous circuit on the calendar is downright risky and inappropriate!'

He gave an elaborate sigh. 'Where is the fun in being *appropriate*? Even the word sounds dull, don't you agree?'

'No, I don't—and nor do our sponsors.' She rubbed her brow to pacify its exasperated throb. 'I swear to God, if you don't start pulling through for this team I will make you wish you'd never been born.'

'You know, I believe you would.'

'Good.'

He brushed the pad of his thumb from the corner of his mouth down over the soft flesh of his bottom lip. 'So if you haven't come to indulge in some heavy petting why are you here, beautiful?'

His voice, disturbingly low and smooth as cognac, was so potent she swayed, nigh on intoxicated.

For an infinitesimal moment his cerulean-blue eyes held hers and a riot of sensations tumbled down the length of her spine. Pooled. Pulled. Primal and magnetic. And she hated it. Hated it!

Beautiful?

'Don't mock me, Finn. I'm not in the mood for your games. I want this place cleared and you sober. How *dare* you party it up and put the team at risk while everyone sits around feeling sorry for your little soul?'

'You know as well as I do that sympathy is wasted on me.

Especially when there is a profusion of far more…*enjoyable* sensations to be experienced at my hands.'

Ugh.

Temper rising, implosion imminent, she felt her breasts begin to heave. 'For someone who blew up an engine this morning—and, hey, this is a *wild* idea—how about you start thinking of how to salvage the situation instead of screwing around? Have you been drinking? You could get banned from the race altogether!'

With a shake of his head he tsked at her. 'No drinking.'

'You swear?'

One blunt finger scraped over his honed left pec. 'Cross my heart.'

Time stilled as she walked headlong into another wall of grief and memories slammed into every corner of her mind. The games of two children. One voice: *'Cross my heart.'* The other: *'Hope to die.'*

There it was. The elephant in the room.

Tom.

Cold. Suddenly she was so very, very cold. Only wanting to leave. To get as far away from this man as she could before the emotion she'd balled up in her chest for months punched free and she screamed and railed and lashed out in a burst of feminine pique.

She'd tell her dad he was barking up the wrong tree. No way could she work with Finn. She felt unhinged, her body vibrating with conflicting emotions, all of them revving, striving for pole position. And that was nothing compared to the hot whirlpool of desire swirling like a dark storm inside of her. How was that even possible? How was that even fair?

Life isn't fair, Serena. You know that. But what doesn't kill you makes you stronger. Makes your heart beat harder and your will indestructible.

So before she left she was getting the answers she wanted if it was the last thing she did.

* * *

In all the times over the last eight months when Finn had imagined coming face-to-face with Seraphina Scott, he'd never once envisaged the tough, prickly and somewhat prissy tomboy with her ear smashed against a door panel, listening for the orgasmic finale sure to come.

How very...*intriguing.*

It had certainly made up his mind on how to handle her impromptu arrival. With one look his heart had paused and he'd stared at the sweet, subtle curve of her waist, battling with innumerable choices.

Apologise? Not here, not now. Wrong place, wrong time. The risk that his defences would splinter equalled the prospect that she wouldn't believe him.

Wrap her tight in his arms because for a fleeting moment he'd sensed a keen vulnerability in her? Far too risky. If he buried his face in that heavenly fall of fire he might never come up to breathe again.

Act the polite English gentleman? Despite popular opinion he was more than capable of executing that particular role. He could be anyone or anything any woman wanted, as long as it wasn't himself. The problem was that kind of outlandish behaviour would only make her suspicious and no doubt she'd hang around.

He might be responsible for the words *delectable, fickle* and *playboy* appearing in the dictionary, but he was far from stupid. Soon she'd start asking questions about her brother's death, and he had to ensure they never came to pass those gloriously full raspberry lips. Lips he'd become riveted upon. Lips he'd do anything to smother and crush. To make love to with every pent-up breath in his taut body until she yielded beneath his command.

Never.

So in the end he'd settled for their habitual sparring. The usual back and forth banter that was sure to spark her every nerve and induce the usual colourful dazzling firework display. Make her hate him even more. Followed by her departure, of course.

While a vast proportion of him had rebelled at the notion, some minuscule sensible part had won out. After all, if there were fairness and justice in the world *he* would be the man six feet under and not an innocent kid who'd always looked at him as if he were some kind of hero.

What a joke.

But death eluded him. No matter how many of life's obstacles he faced, and no matter how many cars he crashed. He was Finn St George—dashing, death-defying racing driver extraordinaire. Death took the good and left the bad to fester—he'd seen that time and time again. Not that he deserved any kind of peace. When it finally came and he met his maker he doubted he'd hear the sweet song of angels or bask in the pearly glow of heaven. No. What waited for him was far darker, far hotter. Far more suited to the true him.

Was he worried? Hell, no. Rather, he looked forward to heading down into fire and brimstone. It couldn't be much worse than what he'd lived with all day, every day, for the last eight months.

Ah, great. There he went again. Becoming ridiculously maudlin. Entirely too tedious. A crime in itself when faced with the delectable Miss Seraphina Scott, who never failed to coerce a rush of blood to speed past his ears.

Clink. The door behind her opened and a bikini-clad blonde shimmied past, trailing one French-tipped talon down Finn's bare forearm. A soap opera star, if he remembered correctly, and a welcome distraction that twisted his torso as he watched her saunter down the hall with a practised sway of her voluptuous hips.

What he couldn't quite discern was why his eyes were on one thing while his mind, his entire body, was attuned to another, riding another wavelength—one set on Seraphina's ultra-high frequency.

Typical. Because—come on—if there was ever a more

desirable time to regain some kind of sexual enthusiasm for his usual coterie of fanatics it was the precipitous return of Miss Scott.

'One of yours, I presume?'

Derision drizzled over that strawberry and cream voice making every word a tart, sweet bite.

'I don't believe I've had the pleasure.' Turning back to her, he licked his decadent mouth in a blatant taunt. 'Yet…'

Shunning her sneer of scorn, Finn gave an unconcerned shrug. Women had been flinging themselves in his direction since he'd hit puberty. What kind of man would he be to deny their every sensual wish? Anyway, he loved women—in all their soft, scented glory. Almost as much as he loved cars. It was a shame the current state of his healing body continued to deny him full access.

Not that he was concerned. It would fix itself. He just had to make sure he was a million miles away from *this* woman when it happened.

'Do you think you could refrain from thinking with your second head for one solitary minute?'

He pretended to think about that and in the silence of the hallway almost heard himself grin. 'I *could*. If you made it worth my while.'

Three. Two. One. *Snap.*

'You're a selfish bastard—you know that? Anyone else would try and focus on the good of the team after we lost Tom. Or should I say after *you* took Tom from us?'

Strike one. Straight to his heart.

'But not the consummate indestructible Finn St George. No, *no*. You think only of yourself and what slice of havoc you can cause next. If it isn't women, it's barely being able to keep a car horizontal.'

'While horizontal is one of my *preferred* positions, I admit it doesn't always work out that way.'

Grimacing, she moaned as if in pain. 'Don't you take

anything seriously? You crashed a multimillion-pound car last month. One I doubt will ever see the light of day again.'

He scrubbed a palm over a jaw that was in desperate need of a shave. 'That was unfortunate,' he drawled. 'I agree.'

'Is everything a joke to you?'

'Not in the least. I just find it tedious to focus on the depressing side of life. I'm more a cup half full kind of guy.'

'Unfortunately that cup of yours is going to run on vapour if you don't start winning some races.'

Yeah, well, he was having a teeny-tiny problem getting any shut-eye, thanks to the flashbacks visiting him far too often for his peace of mind. And, while his driving had always controlled the restless predator that lived and breathed inside him, of late that wildness had overtaken all else. Until even behind the wheel he felt outside of his own body. Detached. His famed control obliterated. Even as he wiped his mind he could still feel the tight scarred skin of his back rubbing against his driving suit—and then… *Hello, flashback.*

Luckily his body was healing. The memories would pass and he had all season to make it up to Michael Scott. Thirteen races to land the championship. Piece of cake.

'Don't worry about a thing, baby, the team is in safe hands with me.'

It was, of course, entirely possible Michael didn't think him capable of pulling them out of the quagmire. Hence this visit from Little Miss Spitfire.

'Now, why does that fail to ease my mind? Oh, yes—because these days, unlike Midas, everything you touch meets a rather gruelling end.'

Strike two, sending his heart crashing into the well of his stomach even as he managed to hide his wince with another kick of his lips. 'You need to trust me, baby.'

She snorted. 'When sheep fly and pigs bleat. I'm pretty sure the first step to trust is actually liking the person.'

He let his debauched mouth fire into a full-blown grin. Finally—someone who loathed him instead of walking on eggshells and spouting blatant lies to his face that it wasn't his fault. Michael Scott had a tendency to do just that. But Finn wasn't blind to the turmoil in the other man's eyes. The reality was his boss had a team to run and they were locked in a multimillion-pound contract, so Mick had no choice but to keep him around until the end of the season. The fact the man had to look at him every day left a bitter taste in Finn's mouth. Mick was a good guy. He deserved better.

After years of driving with the best teams in the world, constantly restless, his itchy feet begging to move on, he'd hoped he could settle with Scott Lansing for a while. It was more family than moneymaking machine, and respect ran both ways. Little chance of that now, but he'd win this season if it were the last thing he did.

As long as this woman stayed out of his way.

'Also, do me a favour, would you? Quit the *baby* thing. It suggests an intimacy I would rather die than pursue.'

Then again, he couldn't see close proximity being a problem, because—*oh, yeah*—she wanted to stamp on his foot good and proper. He could see it in those incredible eyes. Eyes that were a sensual feast of impossibly long dark lashes acting like a decadent frame around a mesmerising blend of the calmest grey with striations of yellow-gold as if to forewarn that there was no black and white with this woman—only mystifying shades of the unknown. Ensuring he was continually intrigued by her. Bewitched by her secrets. Yet at the same time they promised peace, true tranquillity—a stark, stunning contrast to that hair.

Her hair...

A shudder ripped through his body just from looking at it, inciting pure want to move through his bloodstream like a narcotic. Because that spectacular mane of fire told him she'd been burned and lived to tell the tale. A survivor.

Shameful, reprehensible; his eyes took a long, leisurely stroll down her lithe little body, soaking up her quirky ensemble.

Clumpy biker boots which, more often than not, made him instantly hard. Skin-tight denims and an apple-green T with the words 'It's All Good Under the Hood' stroking across her perfect C's.

Ohhh, yeah, she was delicious. Lickable. Biteable.

She leaned towards a serious tomboy bent and after multiple seasons of being faced with silicone inflation, Botoxed lips and an abundance of flesh on show, looking at Seraphina Scott was dangerous to say the least. Intrigue gave way to intoxication every time. Unfortunately he'd just have to suffer the side effects—because she was the one woman he could never, *ever* touch.

Not only was she the boss's daughter, and not only did that tough outer shell conceal an uncontrollable fiery response that lured the predator inside him to prowl to the surface and claw down those walls, but he'd also made a promise to her brother—and he'd stand by it even if it killed him…

'If I don't get out of this alive, Finn, promise me something?'

'Don't talk like that, kid. I'll get us out of here.'

'Whatever you do, don't tell Serena about this place. She's been through enough. She'll go looking for blood. You have to keep her safe. Promise me…'

His lungs drew up tight, crowding his chest until he could barely breathe. He would keep her safe. By getting her away from him.

Shuttering his eyes for a brief spell, he blocked her mesmeric pull. He'd dreaded this moment for months, he realised. Knowing she would come out fighting even as grief oozed from her very pores.

Where once she'd been a little bit curvy, now she was a little bit too thin. A stunning force of anger and sadness, beautiful and desolate. As if heartbreak had pulled the life force out of her and every morsel was tasteless.

Finn had done that to her.

Tom Scott…

Guilt lay like crude oil in the base of his stomach and every time he looked at her it churned violently, threatening to catch fire, making him ache. *Ache.* God, did she make him ache. Make the mourning suffocate his soul. As if it wasn't enough that the kid was still his constant companion even in death.

He didn't want her here. In fact he wanted her as far away from him as he could get her. Which begged the question: why was she back?

She who now eyed him expectantly and for the life of him he couldn't remember what she'd said.

Shifting gears, he asked, 'How's London?'

'Cold.'

'How's work?'

'Great. Thank you for asking,' she said, with such a guileless expression he didn't even see the freight train barrelling down the hallway. 'Why didn't you come to Tom's funeral? He worshipped you.'

His stomach gave a sickening twist.

'Sick.' He needed off this topic. *Right. Now.* 'How's the prototype?'

'Spectacular. Sick how?'

'Boring story. Is it finished?'

Say no.

Fuming at his attempt at derailing the conversation, she breathed slow and deep. 'Maybe. Did you know he couldn't swim?'

Crap. 'No.' *Not at the time.* 'Are you staying?'

'Possibly.'

Dammit. This was getting too close for comfort. 'I think you could do with more time off,' he said. 'Take a holiday.'

Suspicion narrowed her glare. 'Is that right?'

'Sure. How about a nice sojourn round the Caribbean? All that sun, sea and sex would do you good. Loosen you up a little.'

She raised one delicate dark brow. 'Why, Finn, I didn't know you cared.'

'There's a lot you don't know about me.'

'Funny, I was just thinking the exact same thing.'

Now he remembered why he couldn't stand the woman. 'Anyway, I was saying. A holiday is just what you need.'

'Are you saying I don't look so good?'

'Well, now you come to mention it you *are* a little on the thin side.' True, most women would consider that a compliment, but Miss Scott wasn't like other women.

As predicted, she prickled like a porcupine. But at least she wasn't musing about funerals and swimming any more.

'Trading insults, Finn? I wouldn't advise it. You've buried yourself in so much dirt over the years I'll always come out on top.'

A growl ripped up his throat. 'Mmm… You on top. Now, *that* is something I would love to see,' he said, sending his voice into a silken lazy caress, frankly astonished at how much effort he was expending to keep this up. For the first time in history one of their sparring sessions was stealing great chunks of his sanity.

'Liar. Furthermore, I'm not one of your fans or bits of fluff, so do me a favour and keep those blues above neck level. If you're trying to intimidate me you'll have to do a better job than feigning interest and eying me up.'

'But it's so much fun watching you prickle.'

'Some of us have a deeper meaning in life than having fun, and fickle playboys don't bring out the best in me.'

'Oh, I'm not so sure about that.'

Fired up, she was a whole lot of beautiful. Which he supposed was why he'd always tumbled into the thrust and parry of verbal swords with her. Sparks truly did fly when he was duelling with Miss Scott.

Now she was breathing in short, aggravated bursts, her breasts pushing against her rumpled T, and his fingers itched to climb beneath the hem. She'd be *sooo* lusciously soft, one hundred per cent organic and berry-like delicious against his tongue as he sucked her nipple between his lips...

Heat scrambled up his legs, heading straight for his groin... Until she crossed her arms over her chest, jerking his attention to the red blotches that marred her delicate wrist.

'What are those marks?' Closing the gap, he leaned in for a better look. 'What *is* that?'

'That is a gift from your security detail, keeping the hordes at bay.'

Hordes at bay? 'Let me see.'

'No!' Tucking her hands tighter into the creases of her underarms, she regarded him as if he were ten kinds of crazy.

'Come on. Stop being a girl. It doesn't suit you.'

'You know, that's the first truth you've uttered since I got here.'

As he gently tugged her hand free his knuckles brushed over her soft breast. *Holy...* More heat raced south, pleasure and pain moving through him at full throttle.

Oh, man, the last thing he needed was his first hard-on in almost a year to be for this woman. It was an inconceivable prospect that was swiftly overtaken by the dark bruising marring her wrist, and his insides shook with anger as he remembered the sight and sensation of torn wrists, shredded skin, blood dripping from shackles.

'Finn?' she breathed. 'What are you...?'

With deliberate and infinite care he brushed the backs of his fingers down one side of her forearm and up the other. 'I...' *I'm sorry he hurt you. I'll make him pay. I swear it.*

'Finn?'

Tilting her head, she frowned. Cutely. The action softened the often harsh yet no less cataclysmic impact of her beauty.

Seraphina Scott wasn't pretty in the normal sense of the word. She was no delicate English rose. No, no. She was a wild flower. Tempestuous and striking. Made in technicolour. Hardy, tough. Weathering every storm, only to survive more beautiful than ever before.

And she was clearly waiting for him to expand. Trying to work him out.

Such a small thing, that softening. It made her appear vulnerable. From nowhere more words sped through his brain. *I'm sorry...I'm sorry. So very sorry I took Tom away from you. I would do anything. Anything to bring him back.*

How he wished he could tell everyone the truth. Let the world know what had truly gone down in Singapore. But with an ongoing investigation and a sense that he'd meet his adversary again one day it was impossible. Business hadn't been settled. Too many men roamed free. So if there was to be a next time he was going in alone.

As if she knew the direction of his thoughts, she shaped her lips for speech—no doubt to ask more questions he would never answer, couldn't even bear to hear. Tension throbbed like a living force, so heavy he could taste it, feel the weight of it pressing on his shoulders.

What was it going to take for him to get rid of her? He didn't want Serena near him. Hell, he felt dangerous at the best of times. Around her he felt positively deadly. The need to charge upstairs and throttle the security guy's neck roiled inside him, toxic and deadly, and surely he had enough blood on his hands.

Speaking of hands... For some reason he couldn't let hers go. She was trembling. It couldn't possibly be him. Finn required a large hit of G-force to feel moved.

Holding her wrist in the cradle of his palm, he reached up with his other hand to touch the wild mass of her hair. Hair the deepest darkest red, reminding him of ripe black cherries.

How long had he resisted the temptation of her? It felt like a thousand years.

Almost there and her eyes caught the movement, flared before she jerked backwards.

'Finn. Let go of me. Right now.'

Distantly he heard the words, the quiver in her command,

and knew they held no heat. Control slipped from his grasp and he fingered the stray lock tumbling over her shoulder.

Pure silk. Hot enough to singe. Fire burning on a dangerous scale.

Ignoring her sharp gasp, he corkscrewed the thick wave and tugged. Hard. Being rough. Too rough. But that was what she did to him. Severed his control. Fed his wildness. Even as the thought of hurting her fisted his heart.

'Fiiiinn...' she warned, as her chest rose and fell in rapid, mesmerising waves.

Familiarity rattled her. Always had. After the last time he'd touched her, however innocently, she'd avoided him for four years. Clever girl, she was.

Not once had he seen her embrace her father and he'd never noticed her with a lover. It couldn't possibly be through lack of interest. Whether they would admit it or not, every guy on every team wanted a piece of her, Jake Morgan in particular carried a huge crush. But they always kept their distance. Prewarned? he wondered. Or did none of them have the courage to take her on?

There was a story there. One he'd pay any price to discover. One he would never know.

And that, he realised, was his answer. Or at least he told himself it was.

The charm he'd been born with, the charismatic beauty he'd wielded like a golden gun since he'd been old enough to deduce the fact that it got him out of many a sticky situation, would be the one thing—the only thing—to drive her away. Back to London. Out of sight. Out of mind. Free from the claws of temptation.

It wasn't as if he could do any harm. Despite every word that fell from her delectable pout, she felt the same exquisite thrill of attraction he did. Hated it just as much as he did.

Decision made. It was bye-bye, Miss Seraphina Scott.

May the gods forgive him for what he was about to do.

He unleashed his desire and went in for the kill.

CHAPTER THREE

LIKE A RABBIT caught in the headlights, Serena's heart seized, and her eyes flared as the world's most beautiful man brushed the back of his knuckles up the curve of her jawline.

Weakness spread through her limbs and she started to shake as if she'd been injected with something deadly. And when he skimmed the super-sensitive skin beneath her ear and sank his fingers into the fall of her hair to anchor her head in place dark spots danced behind her eyes.

'Don't you dare,' she barked. Or at least she intended to. Bizarrely, it came out as more of a panting plea.

'You should know better than to challenge me, Miss Scott. Especially in that gorgeous husky voice of yours.'

'Honestly, Finn, will you stop that for just one minute?'

'What?'

'The lies.' She loathed them. Not only did they torment the girl beneath, desperate to believe him, they also whispered of a long-ago web of deceit, a dark betrayal that haunted her soul.

'I'm not lying, baby,' he murmured.

The crackle of energy sizzling between them turned sharper—a sense of anticipation much like the coiled silence before the boom of thunder.

Surely he wasn't going to...? He'd be crazy even to contemplate...

His body came up flush against hers—all hard lines,

latent strength and super-hot heat—sending shock waves straight through her. Then his free hand splayed over her waist, swept around the small of her back and tugged her closer still, until every inch of their bodies—her soft curves and his hard-muscled form—were fused together with need and sweat and fire.

Need? No, no, no. *Impossible.*

'*Wow*, you really do have a death wish, don't you? You're on a collision course for total bodily destruction here, Finn.' Bending her knee, she aimed it to jerk upwards into his groin. Or maybe from this angle she could hook her foot around his ankle and send him off balance...

Kiss.

His lips pressed against the corner of her mouth, then brushed across the seam of her lips.

Ohhh, not good—not good at all. Especially when he moaned low in his throat and started to...well, to nuzzle his way over her cheek, then flick the tip of her nose with his to coerce her head back. And whatever had taken over her body answered his every command.

A heated ache bloomed between her legs, and when he nibbled on her lips to prise them apart the electric touch of his tongue was like a shot of high-octane fuel surging through her.

Don't respond. Don't you dare kiss him back.

'No...' she breathed, hating him. Hating herself even more for wanting. Flailing...

Serena reached up to push him away but ended up grabbing fistfuls of his shirt, holding on for dear life, powerless to sever the warm, moist crush of his mouth against hers as he moved with a consummate and inexorable seductive ease to find the perfect slick fit for their mouths.

Oh, my life. His kiss was slow and lazy, not meant to enflame but to enrapture, and before she knew it she was whirling in the epicentre of the fiercest storm, bringing her own force of nature into play.

She shivered and arched into him. *Never* had she felt anything like it. That warm, damp place between her legs throbbed together with her heartbeat and she wriggled closer, pushing her breasts into his chest to relieve the heavy, needy ache.

Tender and fiercely intimate, he didn't take her will, he invited. He didn't invade her body, he lured. He didn't punish her for her internal struggle, he tempted and teased with an amorous touch.

The pure sensual pleasure of it all was enthralling, making her feel feminine in a way she'd never dreamed possible. A way no man had made her feel before.

He deepened the kiss—the languorous thrust of his tongue a velvet lash of tormenting pleasure. It poured through her veins, heated her bones and weakened her limbs. It blasted all thought from her head until her most basic sexual instincts screamed for him to be inside her. Instincts she'd never known she possessed...

There were reasons for that, of course. She—

Whether it was the rush of unwanted memories or the gentle touch of his hand deviating on a feral bent to roughly fist and yank at the hem of her T, she wasn't sure, but—*oh, God*—he might as well have dunked her in an ice bath.

Emotion was a burning ball at the base of her ribs—embarrassment, humiliation and a heart-rending vulnerability that brought tears to her eyes. *No! No tears.* But all of it, all at once, was so overpowering that her mind began to shrill.

Flattening her palms, she shoved at his chest. Finn instantly let go and took a large pace backwards, that awesome chest heaving as he held both hands in the air in a show of surrender.

Intelligent guy.

The walls of the hallway began to close in on her as she gulped hot air. 'What the blazes are you doing?'

Taut silence pulsated off every surface as Finn blinked

dazedly and scrubbed his palms down his face, playing the role of slightly rattled, wholly astonished, guiltless gent! He belonged on the stage—he really did.

He gave his head a good shake. 'Seeing if your lips taste as good as they look.'

'What?'

He must think her dense. A fool. She was so far removed from his usual entourage she might as well derive from another planet, and for months he'd poked and prodded at her blatant lack of femininity. Now he expected her to believe his impetuous come-on was legitimate?

He was messing with her and she knew it.

And how could she have forgotten Tom? The part this man had played in her brother's death?

Guilt climbed into her chest and sat behind her ribs like a heavy weight. It crushed her lungs, making her breath shallow, her voice high-pitched. 'Answer me, Finn! What was that about?'

His lips parting to speak, he faltered yet again.

Why did she feel as if he wanted to tell her something? Something vital. Something she desperately wanted to hear. Nothing but the truth.

Rightly or wrongly—more than the next race, more than his success or the victory of Team Scott Lansing—the promise of that truth was the only thing tempting her to hover in his orbit.

Hold on…

'Are you trying to get rid of me? Is that your game?'

Wow, it seemed the heights of her humiliation knew no bounds.

Finn blinked several times in rapid succession and with every flutter of those ridiculously gorgeous thick lashes his expression smoothed into unreadable impassivity, until once more she was looking at Lothario.

'Is it working?' he drawled.

'Yes!'

'Good,' he said, those legendary dimples winking at her. 'Then you'll be pleased to know the door is that way.'

With a swift finger towards said exit, he pushed open a panel to her left. One he strolled through before it closed behind him, leaving her standing there, jaw slack, twitching in temper. The nerve of the man!

Fury grounded her flight instinct.

He wanted rid of her? He could go to the devil! This was *her* family, *her* life, and she was staying put. Her team was in trouble because of him and he needed to pay his dues. Not forgetting the fact he was hiding something and she wanted to know *exactly* what. Maybe then she could start to repair her broken heart and let Tom go. Move on. Find some peace. Remember what it was like to enjoy life—although she often wondered if she ever had.

Two steps forward, she pushed at the panel of what appeared to be a secret doorway. If it hadn't budged an inch and then rebounded back with a slam she would have thought it locked. Was he leaning on the other side, trying to regulate his breathing like she was? *Don't be a gullible fool, Serena.* He'd be grinning like the feckless charmer he was, delighted that he'd got the better of her.

The second time she put all her weight behind the oak, pushed and stumbled into a room, tripping over her feet with as much elegance as a battering ram.

A zillion things hit her at once—mainly gratitude for the fact that her ungainly entrance was witnessed only by Finn's back as he swaggered towards the bed and the sheer extravagance of the room.

'Wow.'

Infinite shades of midnight blue, the decor was a pulse-revving epitome of dark sensuality and masculine drama, and about the only thing on this floating bordello that fitted the man himself. As if, after purchasing the mega-yacht, Finn had only stamped ownership on this one room.

'Did you run out of money before the renovations were

complete?' she asked, tongue in cheek, knowing full well he was one of the highest earning sportsmen in the world.

For a beat he paused at the side of the bed. 'Let's just say I decided the yacht didn't suit. She's on the market.'

'Now, that *is* a shame.' If he restored the rest of the yacht in the same vein it promised to be spectacular.

'Do you like my bedroom, Seraphina?'

His voice was a pleasured, suggestive moan as he flung himself atop a gargantuan carved bed covered in black silk sheets and propped his back against a huge mound of textured pillows.

'I love it,' she said, unable to hide her awe and trying her hardest to look anywhere but at him. 'Present company excluded.'

Black wood furniture lined walls of the deepest red, with the spaces in between splashed with priceless evocative art to create a picture of virile potency and sophisticated class. It was visually breathtaking. Until the intimacy of the dim lighting set her right back on edge.

Searching the darkened shadows behind her, she cleared her throat, 'Lights?' she said, and hoped she didn't sound as jittery as she felt.

Bending at the waist, he leaned sideways to press a button on the tall glass nightstand and the opaque ceiling flickered for one, two, three beats of her thundering heart before the night sky shone down upon the room, ablaze with a million twinkling stars.

The sheer magnificence pulled her eyes wide. 'Seriously?'

He plucked a large red apple from the colourful mound of ripe delicacies toppling from a crystal bowl, then straightened up and raised one of his heart-stopping smiles.

Just like that her unease drifted, melted like a chilled snowflake on a new spring breeze.

Moonlight frosted his body, from the open white linen draping his sides to the wide bronzed strip of naked torso in between, taking his powerful beauty from angelic to supernatural. Otherworldly. Dazzling, magical and utterly surreal.

And she forgot all about not looking at him, suddenly entranced.

He tucked one hand beneath his head, tossed the glistening red fruit up into the air with the other and his honed six-pack flexed and bunched—the sight bringing a mist of perspiration to her skin.

'So. Come back for more, Miss Scott?'

His sinful rasp shattered the spell he wove so effortlessly and she gave herself a good shake. The man was *lethal*.

'I have heard my mouth is highly addictive.'

Serena raised a brow and hoped she looked suitably unimpressed. She had no desire to stroke his ego or any other part of him ever again. 'Such a…tempting offer, Mr St George, but I think I'll pass. Your reputation has been highly exaggerated.'

Apple to his lips, he sank his teeth into the crisp flesh with a loud *crunch* and she dredged the taste of tart flesh from her memory banks, making her mouth water.

'Ah. Must have been the champagne, then.'

'What must have been the champagne?' she murmured, distracted by the rhythmic working of his lean jaw. It truly was *not* good form to be so sexy even when eating. 'The champagne, incidentally, that I did not drink.'

'The weakening of your knees,' he drawled, with a wicked satisfaction that rolled over her in hot waves before he let loose an irrepressible grin that seared her nerves.

One day… She thought. One day she was going to wipe that smirk off his face once and for all. The thought that today was as good a day as any made her let loose a smile of her very own.

Strangely, he froze mid-bite. As if her smile affected him just as much as his did her. The mere notion that he had the power to make her believe such a thing made her temper spike.

'Speaking of knees—I'm going to bring you down on yours, pretty boy.'

A curious tension drew the magnificent lines of his body taut, precisely as before, and she racked her brain to figure out the trigger. All she could think was that there was more to this man than met the eye.

In the next instant he relaxed. 'I do hope that's a promise, Seraphina. I'd be more than happy to oblige.'

Blowing out a pent-up breath, she deliberated over how long she could ride this roller coaster of emotion with Finn at the helm before she plunged to her doom.

Especially when he licked his lips hungrily and dropped his feral blue eyes to the seam of her jeans, to the zipper leading down to the tight curve of her femininity. From nowhere an image of Finn on his knees before her as she stood bathed in moonlight slammed into her mind's eye. *Oh, God.*

Ribbons of heat spun in her veins, moving through her blood in an erotic dance. Her skin was suddenly supersensitive, and her nipples chafed seductively against the soft fabric of her plain white bra. The shockingly carnal expression on his face made her wonder if he'd visualised the very same.

As if. He's just trying to distract you again and you're letting him!

She stiffened her spine and ordered her voice to sweet. 'Oh, I'm so glad. In that case, let me be the first to tell you the good news.'

Crossing one bare foot over the other, he leaned back with more of the insolence he'd doubtless been born with. 'Somehow I don't believe you mean *good* in the literal sense.'

'Oh, I don't know. We could learn a lot from each other, you and I.'

The true meaning of that statement lay between them, gathering momentum with every passing second. It would take time, of course. To get him to talk. To unearth his secrets. To make him crack. Thankfully she had all the time in the world.

Another flash of perfect teeth sinking into white flesh. Another lazy crunch. Another sexy swallow gliding down his throat. 'I doubt that.'

The lack of innuendo suffused her with pleasure and a heady sense of power. It seemed she was finally getting somewhere.

'Why don't you enlighten me, Miss Scott? Your excitement is palpable and I find I can barely stand the suspense.'

She deflected that sarcasm with a breezy flick of her hair off her shoulder. 'I would *love* to enlighten you, Mr St. George. Me and you? We're about to be stuck like glue.'

A shadow of trepidation passed over his face before he cocked an arrogant brow. 'And the punchline is…?'

Musing that the word *babysitter* didn't quite have the right ring to it, she let her impetuous mouth stretch the truth, not really giving a stuff.

'You're looking at your new boss.'

CHAPTER FOUR

FANS DESCENDED ON Monaco in their droves and celebrities flocked to the world's most glamorous sporting event of the year for the exhilarating rush of lethal speed and intoxicating danger. So it didn't bode well that Finn stood in the shade of the Scott Lansing garage, his temples thudding with a messy blend of sleep-deprivation and toxic emotional clatter.

He had to get it together. Get that little minx out of his head.

Hauling in air, he rolled his neck, searching for the equilibrium he needed, knowing full well the smallest of errors in these narrow streets were fatal. Overtaking almost impossible... And didn't that just make him smile? Feel infinitely better as a fuel injection of hazardous adrenaline shot through his bloodstream?

Monaco was hands down his favourite circuit in the world: the greatest challenge on the racing calendar. It never failed to feed his wildness and remind him that life was for living. A master at shutting off fear and anxiety, he was a man who existed in the moment. Life was too short.

Seize the day.

Finn closed his eyes, tried to block the memory those words always evoked. But of late, since he'd touched hell itself, his past refused to stay buried.

Thirteen years old and he'd watched his Glamma—the woman who'd been a second mother to him—die a slow, agonising death. *'Glamma, because I'm far too young and vivacious to be Gran,'* the award-winning actress would declare.

Even when she'd been sick and he'd sworn his heart was breaking—*'Carpe diem, Finn, seize the day,'* she'd say theatrically, with a glint in her eye that had never failed to make him smile. *'That's better. Always remember: frown and you frown alone, smile and the whole world smiles with you.'*

Yeah, he remembered. How could he possibly forget a legend who had been far too young and vibrant for her passage to the heavens. Then, when the cancer had seeped into the next generation and his mother's time had come—spreading more grief and heartache through his family, much like the stain of her disease, destroying her beauty, her vitality, her life—he'd vowed to live every day as if it were his last. And, considering the way Finn had handled her demise, he owed his mother nothing less.

His heart achingly heavy, he left the technical chatter of the engineers behind and stepped towards the slash of sunlight cutting across the tarmac, shoving the pain and guilt back down inside him.

Enthusiasts spilled over balconies and crammed rooftops as far as the eye could reach. The grandstands were chock-full, the area where the die-hard fans had camped from the night before roared with impatience, and huge TV screens placed for optimal viewing flickered to life. It was a scene that usually enthralled him, excited his blood. And it would. Any second now. It had to.

His attention veered to the starting grid, cluttered with pit crew and paddock girls flaunting their wares, and then muttered a curse when not one of them managed to catch his eye. No, no. The only woman who monopolised his thoughts was his ruby red-headed *boss*!

Talk about a simple meeting of mouths backfiring with stunning ferocity. Instead of pushing her away, he'd stoked her curiosity—and how the devil he'd managed to step away, not to devour her, he'd never know.

Good thing he was an expert at disposing of the opposite sex. He'd just have to try harder, wouldn't he? With a touch of St George luck, Serena would make herself scarce today.

He snorted in self-irritation. Now he was lying to himself. He might *need* her at the far ends of the earth but he *wanted* her here, didn't he? Why was that? She was sarcastic, she had a sharp, spiky temper, and she was beautiful but not *that* beautiful—he'd dated catwalk models, for God's sake. *Yeah, and found them dull as dishwater.* And on top of all that just looking at her made him feel guilty.

Self-castigation, he decided. Penitence dictating that he had to make himself suffer by hanging around with a woman who wanted him dead.

He rubbed at his temple and thrust the same hand through his damp hair. Where on earth was she? Some boss she was turning out to be—

He chuffed out a breath. Boss? Doubtful. Babysitter, more like. She had spunk—he'd give her that.

Suddenly the crowd erupted and in the nick of time he realised he'd stepped into the blazing sunlight. Up came his arm in the customary St George wave as the pandemonium reached fever pitch. On cue, he whipped out his legendary smile, even as the movement of his torso pulled his driver's suit to chafe against his scarred back and black despair churned in his stomach with a sickening revolt.

Keep it together, Finn.

'There you are. Playing to your adoring audience, I see.'

Whoa—instantaneous body meltdown. The woman held more firepower than the midday sun.

'How nice of you to turn up, Miss Scott,' he drawled, keeping his focus on the crowd for a few seconds longer. Let her think he was inflating his ego—the worse she thought of him the better—but Finn knew how far his fans had travelled, the huge expense. He'd spoken to hundreds of them over time after all.

'I would've been here sooner if I hadn't detoured to that

floating bordello of yours, looking for you. I much prefer today's security man, by the way. New shift?'

He shrugged. Made it indolent, couldn't-care-less. 'Probably.'

Alternatively Finn might have shown the other man the error of his ways the minute Miss Scott had stepped off his... What did she call it? Oh, yes—his *floating bordello*. Naturally Finn would have used his most amiable, charming voice. The one he used to express how tedious a situation had become, how boredom had set in. The very one which ensured that people made the terrible mistake of underestimating him. Shame, that.

If that *had* happened the man in question might have been escorted from the premises in a not so dignified manner, with a reference that not so subtly informed the world that he'd never work in the industry again. Together with the unequivocal, downright irrefutable notion that to meet Finn in a dark alley any time soon would be a very, *very* bad idea.

Would he tell her any of this highly amusing tale? God, no.

Why ruin a perfectly good reputation as a callous, no-good heartbreaker when it was security money couldn't buy. Women had more sense than to expect more than he could give, so there was no fear of broken hearts or letting anyone down. What you saw was what you got.

And Miss Scott was no exception. Not now. Not ever.

Rousing a nonchalance he really didn't feel, he glanced to where she stood beside him; hands stuffed into the back pockets of her skin-tight jeans, the action up-tilting her perky breasts, and his pulse thrashed against his cuffs.

Then his heart turned over, roaring to life as he checked out her white T-shirt, embellished with a woman clad in a slinky black catsuit and the words 'This Kitty Has Claws' stroking across her perfect C's.

How beautifully apt.

'Lucky kitty,' he drawled, stretching the word as if it had six syllables. 'Can I stroke it?'

A shiver rustled over her sweet body and his smile warmed, became bona fide, as she slicked her lips with moisture. 'If you need all ten fingers to drive I wouldn't advise it.'

'I love it when you get all mean and tough. It turns me on.' It was that survivor air about her. Did strange things to him.

'Forgive me if I don't take that as a compliment. Seems to me that anything with the necessary appendage flicks *your* switch.'

'You'd be amazed at how discerning my sexual palate is, Miss Scott.'

Very true, that. After a few disturbing front-page splashes in his misbegotten youth he'd vowed to take more care in his liaisons. Absolute honesty with women who read from the same manual. Short, sweet interludes. No emotions. No commitment. Ever.

The mere word *relationship* caused a grave distress to his respiratory rate.

Not only had he started to see himself as some kind of bad luck charm—a grim reaper for those he cared for—but he was also inherently selfish. Driving was his entire life. Women were simply the spice that flavoured it.

Existing in the moment wasn't exactly conducive to family ties when he travelled endlessly, partied hard, and there was every possibility there would be no tomorrow.

She snorted. 'Discerning? Yeah, right.' And she brought those incredible grey eyes his way, arching one brow derisively. 'Let's take this conversation in a safer and more honest direction, shall we? Where's your helmet and gloves?'

'Not sure. Be a good little girl and go get them for me, would you?' he drawled, his amusement now wholly legit.

She puckered those luscious lips at him and a layer of sweat dampened his nape.

'Don't push it, Finn. I promise you, you don't want to get on the wrong side of me today.'

He dipped his head closer to her ear and relished the way her breathing hitched. 'I would *love* to get on any side of you, Seraphina. Especially now I've tasted that delicious mouth of yours.'

Easing back, he licked his lips to taunt her with the memory. It certainly wasn't to try and remember her unique flavour—that tart strawberry bite sparking his taste buds to life. Incredible.

'In your dreams.'

'Always,' he said, knowing she wouldn't believe him. Odd that it made him feel safe enough to drop his guard, tell her the unvarnished truth—which was a danger in itself.

With an elaborate sigh she stormed into the shadows of the garage, her voice trailing off to a murmur as she spoke to the mechanics and engineers. *Yes, go—get as far away from me as you can.*

From the corner of his eye he noticed a news crew focusing on him with the ferocity of an eagle spotting its prey and his chest grew tight. *No chance.*

Feigning ignorance, he ducked his head and strode back into the shade. Where he ran smack-bang into a helmet.

'Here,' Serena said, slapping a pair of gloves in his other hand.

A shaft of shock rendered him speechless. She used to bring Tom his helmet and gloves. She used to murmur something too. At one time Finn had tried to eavesdrop, but he'd quickly decided he was being ridiculous and didn't care what she'd said.

Then she'd always run to meet her brother after the finish, whether he'd won or not. She'd run out and hug him warmly, affectionately, with admiration in her smile and trust in her heart.

Instead of the usual envy the memory evoked, he battled with another surge of guilt that she couldn't run to Tom any longer. Then called himself fifty kinds of fool for toying with the idea that she could run to him if she needed to. *As if.*

'Hey, are you with me?' She clicked her fingers in front of his face. 'You're phasing out, there. Something I should be worried about?'

Out came his signature smile. 'You worried about me, baby?'

'No. I'm worried about the multimillion-pound car you're likely to crash to lose the championship! Did you get some sleep?'

Strangely enough, the couple of hours he'd managed had been demon-free, with his new boss the star of the show. Which was typical of him—wanting something he could never have just to make the challenge more interesting. The win more gratifying. Because, let's face it, while he fed off the rush of success, it never seemed to be enough. He was always restless. Always wanting something elusive, out of reach.

So, no, he did not trust himself around her. 'I did catch a few hours, thank you. It's amazing what the presence of a sexy spitfire can achieve.'

Her delicate jaw dropped as she grimaced. 'You mean after I left you actually...?'

Finn shook his head in disbelief. She thought he was talking about someone else.

Why was it that she'd grown up surrounded by men and yet had no conception of her unique brand of sexuality? It was as if she lacked self-confidence. If so, he wished she'd start believing him. Wished he could show her what she did to him.

Too dangerous, Finn. Just get in the car, win the race, show her you're a fixed man and get her back off to London out of harm's way.

The pep talk didn't work a jot. And, come on, she might fancy the pants off him but it wasn't as if she would ever answer to this overwhelming burn of desire. One, she was an intelligent little thing and she had more sense. And, two, she hated his guts.

'After *you*—sexy spitfire that *you* are—left, I slept. Alone.'

Her mouth a pensive moue, she simply stared at him.

Finn watched the soft shimmer of daylight dance through the shadows to cast the lustre of her skin with a golden radiance, enriching the heavy swathe of her hair until the strands glittered with the brilliance of rubies. A shudder pinballed off every vertebra in his spine.

'Why do you do that?' she asked, more than a little frustrated.

'What?' Shudder?

'Say things you don't mean.'

'Who says I don't mean them?'

She gave a little huff. 'Past experience. You've always delighted in ensuring I know you see me as nothing more than a tomboy.'

'Tomboys can't be sexy?' She was the sexiest woman he'd ever laid eyes on. And that was before she wrapped that incredible body in leathers to straddle her motorbike or—*give him mercy*—put on a driver's suit. Then it was, *Hello, hardon; bye-bye sanity.*

He had no right to slide his gaze over her body in a slow, seductive caress, trying to remember the sight.

The boots moulded to her calves shuffled uneasily. 'Stop it!'

'You don't like it.'

Statement. Fact.

'No. I don't.'

Why? Because the extraordinary chemistry bothered her? Or because she was experiencing it with the man who'd stolen her happiness?

While the reminder punched him in the heart, it didn't stop him from saying, 'So why don't you take the compliment for what it is, baby? The truth.'

Crossing her arms over her chest, she hiked her chin up. 'But I don't want practised compliments from your repertoire. They mean nothing to me. I merely want you to do your job.'

Knife to his gut. Fully deserved. For the first time in his life he rued his reputation.

The smooth skin of her brow nipped and he realised his emotions must be seeping through the cracks in his façade. He schooled his expression with ruthless speed as his guts twisted in anger. One false move with this woman and he'd be finished.

'Look, Finn….' She sighed softly. 'I know you want to win this race and you've held the title for four years, but positioned at the back…? It's too risky an endeavour for even *you* to try and take the lead. I don't think anyone has ever done it before.'

If that wasn't a red rag to a bull he didn't know what was. He was also *pretty* sure being careful wasn't the name of the game.

'So just try and get a decent finish and come back here with the car in one piece, okay?'

For a second he thought he saw fear blanch her flawless complexion. Fear for him. And something warm and heavenly unfurled in his guts. Until he realised she merely wanted the car back in one piece. *Idiot.*

'Yes, boss,' he said, with a cheeky salute as he sealed up the front of his suit.

'Good,' she said, and the word belied the cynicism in her eyes. 'Now, get your backside in that car and let's see some St George magic.'

Walk away. Finn. Walk away and stop playing with her like this. You cannot have her!

'You think I'm magic?'

'I think you display a certain amount of talent on the track, yes.'

'My talents—

'If what is about to come about of your mouth has any reference to bedroom antics I will knock your block off.'

Finn cocked a mocking brow. 'I wasn't about to say anything of the sort. My, my—haven't we got a dirty mind?'

'Liar,' she growled, long and low, like a little tigress, and he almost lost his footing as he backed out of the garage.

How did the woman do it? Make him feel alive for the first time in months. Make his smile feel mischievous and his body raw and sexual when no other woman could.

Narrowing her glare, she lifted one finger and shook it. 'I don't like that smile, Finn. I really don't. Whatever you're thinking, whatever stunt you're about to pull…'

The scorching rays hit his nape, the crowds chanted his name and he unloaded his charismatic arsenal and licked his lips. 'Trust me, baby.' Slanting her a wink that made her blink, he veered towards the Scott Lansing race car. 'Trust me.'

Finn was sure she muttered something like, *Not in this millennia*, and he smiled ruefully. If she had any sense she'd remember that.

Inhaling long and deep, he infused his mind with the addictive scents of hot rubber and potent fumes that stroked the air—as addictive and scintillating as the warm, delicious redhead he'd left back at the garage.

Within ten minutes he was packed tight behind the wheel, the circuit a dribble of glistening molasses ahead of him, pushing his foot to the floor until the groans and grunts of the powerful machine electrified his flesh. Oh, yeah, he was a predator, with a thirst for the high-octane side of life, the thrill of the chase. One goal—to win.

Pole position. Middle or back. Dangerous or not. Didn't matter to him.

This race was his.

Trust him. *Trust him?*

'What the blazes is he doing?' It was, quite literally, like waiting for the inevitable car crash.

One of the engineers whistled through his teeth. 'Look at that guy go. Phenomenal, isn't he?'

'Crazy, more like,' she muttered. Zero self-preservation. *Zero!*

More than once she heard the pit-lane channel go silent and probably wouldn't have thought anything of it—*if* she hadn't noticed him do that thing last night and this morning. Almost phasing out as some kind of darkness haunted his gaze. It was disturbing since he was renowned for his awesome ability to concentrate with such focus that nothing else existed but his car hugging the tarmac.

A battalion of bugs crawled up her spine and she glanced back at the shaded screen hanging in the garage.

'Grand Hotel Hairpin. Just ahead of him. Holy Toledo! It's a pile-up.'

Her heart careening into cardiac arrest, she held her breath, waiting for the iconic red Scott Lansing car to clear the haze of dust and debris. *Come on, come on. Stuff the car. Don't you dare kill yourself. I will never forgive you.*

Serena wondered at that. Decided it was because she hadn't managed to coax the truth about Tom's death out of him yet. Tom, who should be here. Racing in this race. Doing what he'd loved best.

A fist of sorrow gripped her heart. Too young. He'd been just too young to die. And despite everything Finn was too young to be chasing death too.

She had to swallow in order to speak. 'Where is Jake?' With a bit of luck *he* had more sense.

'Still holding fifth.'

A cackle of relieved laughter hit her eardrum as Finn's car flew past the devastation to take third place.

'I don't believe it,' she said, breathless and more than a bit dizzy.

'I do.' Her dad stood alongside her now, his attention fixed on the same screen. 'Whatever you said to him has obviously worked, Serena. What *did* you say?'

'That I was his new boss.'

Michael Scott's head whipped round with comical speed. *'What?'*

'Worked, hasn't it?' she said, knowing full well that her impulsive mouth had nothing to do with it.

Finn danced to his own tune, had his own agenda front and foremost. Moreover, just watching him race like this—with the ultimate skill and talent—made her even more certain there was more to his crashes and sporadic losses than met the eye. But for some reason today he was *mostly* focused.

'He's taking second place with one lap to go! It's gonna be tight, though.'

She snorted. 'He doesn't want to lose the Monaco title.' Then she squeezed her eyes shut as he almost rammed into the Nemesis Hart driver, swerved to avoid a crash and clipped his front wing off instead.

'Whoa—there goes the car coming back in one piece.'

Stomach turning over, she shoved her hands into her back pockets to watch the last minute on screen.

Heck's teeth, he was going to do it…

Admiration and awe prised their way through the hate locked in her chest. The man was *amazing*.

'Half a second. Unbelievable!' someone yelled.

A warm shower of relief rained down from her nape and her entire body went lax.

The crowd erupted with a tremendous roar and chanted his name: *'Fi-in Fi-in Fi-in.'* Every mechanic and engineer ran out into the scorching rays and Michael Scott—who hadn't hugged her since she was fourteen years old, when she'd been broken and torn and his face had been etched with fury and pain—turned round, picked her up and spun her around the floor.

She imagined it was how a ballerina felt—spinning, twirling, dancing on air. Her beauty delicate, feminine. Nothing like *her*.

Before she even had a chance to wrap her arms around his neck, to bask in this inconceivable show of affection, to actually *feel* his love, he abruptly let go and jogged into the pit lane.

Swaying on her feet, she swallowed hard—told herself for the millionth time in her life not to be upset. That she mustn't be angry with him for not wanting to be close to her. It was just the way he was. He only knew how to deal with boys.

'*Come on, Serena, get a grip, get busy, move on,*' he'd say. '*Boys don't cry.*'

Okay, then. Get busy. Move on.

Except alone now, with the dark shadows creeping over her skin like poison ivy, she felt…lost. Grappling with the annoying sense that she was forgetting something.

Oh.

This was the part where she ran out to Tom.

Cupping her hand, she covered her mouth, gritted her teeth and tensed her midriff to stop the sob threatening to rip past her throat. *No. No!*

She should never have come back here. Should have stayed away—

Footsteps bounded from the pit lane and she sucked great, humongous lungfuls of air through her nose, then blew out quick breaths. Over and over.

It was a good job too, because Finn strode into the shadows—and the intense magnetism he exuded was a tangible, vibrant combination of devil-may-care and decadent sin.

Blond hair now dark with sweat tumbled over his brow and he wore an indecipherable expression on his over-warm face, almost as if he knew exactly what she'd been thinking. *Impossible.*

Bolstering her reserves, she stood tall as he drew near and threw his arms wide.

'What did you think, baby?'

'I think that by the end of the season I'll be on a whole

lot of medication. Good God, you're a liability.' A very expensive, scorching hot, stunning liability.

'So you don't wanna hang around with me any more?' He clapped a hand over his left pec. 'I think my heart's broken.'

'Come on, Finn, you and I both know you don't have one. You take direction from another body part entirely.'

Standing there, smouldering with testosterone, he sneaked his tongue out to moisten his lips. When it came, his voice was a low groan. 'You think about my body parts?'

That was it. Later she'd have no idea how she could veer from abject misery to munching on the inside of her cheek to stifle a snort of laughter. He was incorrigible. She hated him. *Hated* him!

'I think about many of your body parts. Your neck, especially—the very one I'd like to wrap my hands around.'

She reminded herself that to be turned on by that cocksure smile was a gross dereliction of self-preservation.

'Did you need something?' she asked, thoroughly confused. 'You've left your fans wailing for your return.'

'No, I just wanted…' He lifted his hand and scratched the side of his jaw in an uneasy, somewhat boyish manner.

'What?' she murmured, distracted by a small scar she'd never noticed before—a thin white slash scoring his hairline. How on earth had he got that?

'I wanted you to say how awesome I am.'

'Don't be silly. You can barely fit your head through the open cockpit as it is. Keep dreaming.'

'Oh, don't worry. I will,' he drawled suggestively. And just like that she was transported back to his yacht, his kiss. Then came the heat, curling low in her abdomen, licking her insides, making her shiver.

Honestly, she was certifiable. Without a doubt.

Much as earlier, he began to back out of the garage, taking his dizzying pheromones with him, and within a nanosecond fury overtook her. For the playful banter. For the way she'd allowed him to affect her so utterly.

'By the way, I want to speak to you tonight,' she said sharply.

Before he hit the bright light his feet froze mid-step. 'Saying goodbye already?'

Tilting her head, Serena frowned. 'Now, why would I do that?'

'I won the race. I'll charm the sponsors at dinner. Disaster averted.'

That was why he was so focused on winning? To get rid of her? Surely not. His need to win overruled all else. Unless what he was hiding was of far more importance.

Her heart flapping like a bird's wings against a cage, she said, 'I'm not going anywhere, Finn. I promise you that.'

Gazes locked, they engaged in some sort of battle of wills—one she had no intention of losing. She was here to stay.

'Unfortunately, Miss Scott, I have a date this evening. With my good friend Black Jack. Unless you'd care to join us...?'

'*The Casino?* I wouldn't be seen dead there.'

And the smirk on his face told her he knew it!

'Then I guess you'll just have to catch me some other time, beautiful.'

Not if she could help it. The man had to get dressed on that den of iniquity, so she'd just have to corner him before he stepped foot on the harbour. There was no way on this earth she was going up to that swanky Casino, where the dress code pronounced that all women had to dress as if they were for sale. Not for love nor money. She didn't even own a dress, for heaven's sake.

Nope. She'd just have to catch him first.

CHAPTER FIVE

FINN DIDN'T WASTE any time calling in a favour and landing a suite at the most exclusive Casino in town—where all the glitz and glamour that made the city famous came together in a fairy-tale fantasyland of opulence and high-flyers—and ordering a tuxedo from one of the exclusive concessions in the marble and bronze foyer.

Strict dress code aside, at times he luxuriated in his debonair façade. Playing Casanova was generally more interesting than being himself. Also, as it turned out, his penthouse here had evolved into a necessity. Not only did he need somewhere to sleep with no lingering residue of the demons haunting him in the dead of night, but a gratifyingly quick sale had gone through that very afternoon. One of the members of a minor royal family reviving his Swiss bank account very nicely.

The fact he was Seraphina-free for the evening was also an added boon.

The plan was, he'd grab a couple of girls, lavish money on a few gaming tables, dance until the wee hours and then sleep. Great plan. The fact that he lacked enthusiasm…? Not so great.

Her fault. It's all her fault.

Had he actually stormed into the garage to check on her? According to his memory banks, yes, he had.

Since when had he left the hullabaloo of the roaring crowd for a woman? Never before in his life!

Do not panic—it's the guilt.

Knowing she missed her brother and veiled the ache with her beautiful bravado was killing him. The pain that lurked behind those incredible grey eyes was a fist to his gut. Her strength was formidable, but he couldn't help wondering what it cost her. Of late, holding his own façade in place came at an extortionate price, but the alternative fall out would be catastrophic. As soon as he opened the door to his emotional vault the contents of Pandora's box would be unleashed and all hell would break loose.

Now, sitting in the prestigious lounge known as the throbbing heart of the Casino, he palmed a tall glass of tequila and raised it to his lips, hopeful that the sharp kick and bite would burn the dull edges off his dark mood. For some reason the suave, elegant cut of his suit wasn't working tonight. He felt dangerous enough to burst out of his skin.

The sensation of black eyes staring into his soul reminded him of dark, agonising days and he downed the liquor—his first drink in a week—and it slid down his throat, trailing a blaze of fire to his gut.

Gradually the muted *whoosh* of spinning roulette wheels, the mumble of inane chatter and the evocative beat from a small band filtered through his mind.

The singer was a stunning blend of French beauty and passionate sultry vocals, and when he felt her eyes slither over him in blatant invitation the crystal in his fist cracked with a soft clink. What was he *doing* here? He'd sell his soul to be someone else for one day, one night—

Between one heartbeat and the next the hair on his nape tingled, shifting his pulse into gear.

Easing his totalled glass onto the low-slung mahogany table, he glanced covertly around the room—from the impressive plaster of Paris inlays and priceless art to each and every table in between. By the time he reached the archway leading to the main gambling hall every cell in his body was on red alert and his heart had roared to life.

It was the kind of stupefying feeling he'd used to get on the starting grid. The very one he'd lost what felt like aeons ago, leaving a dull imitation in its place.

Now the cause of that incredible sensation shoved heat through his veins as he caught a flash of ruby-red hair flowing across the foyer.

Within seconds he was on his feet. What *was* Miss Spitfire doing in here? Looking for him? She was a determined little thing.

In the main lobby he glanced left, towards the wide entryway—seeing the line of supercars curling around the fountain beyond—and then right, to fall beneath her spell as she disappeared around a darkened corner.

By the time he caught up she was facing a door, her hand in mid-air—

'You've come to the Casino to use the bathroom, Seraphina? Do you have a problem with the plumbing on your father's yacht?'

She froze, palm flat against the hardwood panel, and Finn watched her decadent long lashes flutter downwards to whisper over her satiny cheeks. No make-up, he mused, and her natural beauty was really quite breathtaking.

With a swift inhale she spun on her feet and then crossed her arms over her knee-length black coat. She arched one delicate brow. 'When a girl needs to go, a girl needs to go.'

'How right you are.' He needed to be rid of her just as badly. Because she was angry—no, she was furious—and he wanted to kiss that mulish line right off her lips.

'You could have told me you'd sold your bordello *before* I stormed the place looking for you.'

Ah.

'I would have if I'd known you were coming to visit, baby. You know how much I look forward to our little…assignations.' He felt a smile tug at his lips. Stretching wider as her gaze loitered over his attire and a shiver racked her svelte frame.

'Am I doing it for you tonight, Miss Scott?' he asked, his voice a decadent purr.

She grimaced as if she were in pain. 'If by "it" you mean making me regret the moment I ever laid eyes on you, then, yes, strangely enough you are.'

Aw, man, she was delicious. 'How do you feel about dinner?' It was a horrendous idea, but he suddenly had the urge to feed her. Fill out those over-slight curves.

'You mean *together*?'

'That's a bit forward, don't you think? But, yes, okay. I accept.'

Mouth agape, she slowly shook her head, clearly questioning his sanity. Oddly enough, that made two of them. 'Did you attend some school specialising in becoming the most annoying and arrogant person ever?'

'As a matter of fact—'

A tall blonde, dressed to the nines in a slinky red number, appeared from nowhere and motioned to the bathroom door. Finn stifled his irritation at her giving him the once-over and zeroed in on Serena as she clammed up, took a step back, and dipped her head until that glorious fall of hair veiled her face.

Unsure why it could be, but loathing the way she threw out distress signals, he curled his fingers around her upper arm and tugged her further along the hall to where the dim light imparted privacy.

Except every muscle in her arm tensed beneath his fingers and her gaze bounced off every surface until even *he* half expected someone to pounce.

'Hey, are you okay?'

'Peachy.'

She wrenched free and wrapped both arms across her chest. It was like watching someone erect guard rails.

Okay, so she didn't want to be alone with him. Yet she'd

been fine last night in his bedroom. What had she asked him for? Lights.

'You don't like the dark?' For some reason it made him think back to that odd ramble of Tom's—*'Protect her for me...she's been through enough...'*—and his fists tightened into hard balls of menace.

She bristled with an adorable blend of embarrassment and pique.

'Hey, so you don't like the dark? So what? Neither do I. When I was a kid I used to crawl into bed with my mum during power cuts, for Pete's sake. Some hard-ass Spider-Man I was.'

She blinked over and over, until the fine lines creasing her brow smoothed. 'Spider-Man, huh? Did you have the blue and red outfit too?'

'Sure I did. And the cool web-maker.'

Her small smile lit the corners of the hall. Finn wanted it stronger, brighter.

'Did you have a tutu or a Snow White dress? My baby sister had all that crap.'

She snorted. 'I doubt Snow White wielded a wrench, and I don't expect engine oil would wash out of a tutu very well.'

His every thought slammed to a halt.

Reared by men in a man's world. No mother—he knew from Michael Scott that Serena's mum had died giving birth to her. No sisters.

'Have there been *any* women in your life?'

She gave a blithe shrug but he didn't miss the scowl that pinched her mouth. 'Only my dad's playthings.'

'Ah. I get it.' The narcissistic variety. Or maybe weak, fawning versions Serena would have recoiled from. So naturally she'd kept with the boys, until, 'You feel uncomfortable around women.'

'No!' She kicked her chin up defensively.

Finn cocked one brow and a long sigh poured from her lips.

'I don't know what to say to them, that's all, okay? We have nothing in common.'

'You've never had any girlfriends *at all*?' The notion was so bizarre he couldn't wrap his head around it.

'Not really, no. Tom and I had long-distance schooling, and it was pretty rare to see girls hanging around the circuit.'

Finn kept his expression neutral, conscious that empathy wouldn't sit well with her. Yet all he could think of was his sister, surrounded by girlfriends, and she'd had their mother through her formative years. He dreaded to think what Serena's adolescence had been like. No shopping trips or coming-of-age chats, nor any of that female pampering stuff he'd used to roll his eyes at but which had made Eva fizz with excitement.

He was astonished that Serena had managed without a woman in her life. Had she been allowed to be a girl at all? And why exactly did that make anger contort his guts? They were nothing to one another; only hate coloured her world when she looked at him.

'So you have a sister?' she asked quietly, almost longingly, and his chest cramped with guilt. It didn't seem fair, somehow, that he still had Eva and Serena had no one.

'Yes, I do. Eva.'

Eva—who had suffered greatly from the demise of Libby St George. And what had he done? Turned his back on her, on both of them, and walked away to chase his dreams, his big break. Knowing what they'd go through because he'd seen it all before. He'd left Eva to cope, to watch their beautiful mother slowly fade away.

Finn had let them down. Badly. And, what was worse, he hadn't been the only one. His father, the great Nicky St George, eighties pop-star legend, had left to find solace in many a warm bed. Looking back, Finn still found it hard to believe he'd watched a good man—his childhood hero—break so irrevocably under the weight of heartache. And, while he felt bitterly angry towards his father to this day, he could hardly hate the man when he'd felt the same pain. When he'd let them down too.

Yet still his baby sister loved him. She was all goodness while he was inherently selfish.

Eva. His mind raced around its mental track. Eva would be perfect for Serena. A great introduction to the best kind of women…

Finn stomped on the brakes of his runaway thoughts.

It would be dangerous to take Serena to Eva. Eva might get the wrong idea. Serena might get the wrong idea. *He* might get the wrong idea. He was supposed to be getting rid of her, not fixing her and finding ways to keep her around! What was *wrong* with him?

'Through here.' He beckoned her towards another door. One he pushed wide and held as she warily followed him into one of the small lounges where the private games of the high-flyers were often held.

'Why do I half expect the Monte Carlo Symphony Orchestra to strike up any second?'

'It's the grandeur of the place. It's pretty spectacular.' Oppressive at times, but spectacular nonetheless.

'If you like that kind of thing,' she muttered, with a slick manoeuvre that brought her back flush against another wall.

Musing on why she'd cornered herself again, Finn lounged against the arm of an emerald antique sofa a few feet away and faced her. 'So, what do you fancy for dinner?'

She sniffed, the action wrinkling her little nose. 'I'd rather starve.'

'You've changed your tune pretty quick. Is it a habit of yours? It was only this afternoon you said, "I wouldn't be seen dead" in reference to this very establishment. What changed your mind?'

Pouting those luscious lips, she weighed him up from top to toe, her gaze burning holes in his ten-thousand-pound tux. He felt all but cauterised.

'First off, why don't you tell me why you're avoiding me?'

Because I can't tell you what you want to hear.

'Because every time I look at you I want to make love to that beautiful mouth of yours. It's addictive.' She was like a drug—the prime source of some very intense highs. 'But you don't want that, do you, Seraphina?' he asked, rich and smooth, with a sinful tone he couldn't quell even if he tried.

Up came her stubborn chin. 'No, I don't.'

'Then I would advise you to stay away. Because sooner or later we'll have another repeat of last night.'

It was only a matter of time. Whether she wanted to believe it or not.

From the way her pulse throbbed wildly at the base of her throat and a soft flush feathered her skin he knew she was thinking about their kiss. Was she still tasting him as he could her?

'I don't intend to make the same mistake twice. I know a car crash when I see one,' she said tartly. Then gave herself away by licking her raspberry pout.

She could taste him, all right. He'd also bet she wanted more and loathed herself for it.

Cursing inwardly, he allowed himself the luxury of drinking her in before he made his excuses and left.

Covered in a thin black trench coat, with a high, stiff collar and a straight no-nonsense hem just above the knee, she reminded him of a prissy professor. Though her perfectly sexy knees and her shapely bare calves smothered in luscious ivory skin ruined the imagery. As for her feet…

Finn clenched his jaw and breathed past the grin begging to be let loose.

Oh, man, did he want to see under that coat. More than his next breath.

'Do you like to gamble, Miss Scott? Try your chances with Lady Luck?'

'Not particularly. I'm not so sure I believe in luck.'

Her admission was a prelude to a charge in the air as secrets and lies swirled around them in an electrical storm.

'I'll make a deal with you,' he drawled. *Risky, Finn*—and didn't that just rouse his desire? He chose his next words very, *very* carefully. 'If you do something for me I may grant you one wish. As long as it's in my power to give.'

Up came her chin once more, her grey gaze narrow with scepticism as her need fought hand in hand with obvious discomfort. 'Deal.'

'Show me what you're wearing beneath that coat.'

'Wh…*what*?'

'You heard. Untie that sash, undo those buttons, pull that coat wide and show me.'

Chaotic emotion and energy writhed around inside him.

What he was doing he had no idea. All he knew was that common sense and control took a back seat when he was within five feet of her.

Closing her eyes, she took a deep breath, and the sultry swell of her breasts made heat, fast and furious, speed through his body.

Ah, hell, he should stop her.

Right now.

'A deal is a deal, Miss Scott. You don't strike me as the type to renege.'

She tapped her hands against the ruffle of material at her thigh and slowly, provocatively, tiptoed her fingers up to the knot of her sash.

Finn gritted his teeth as the ribbon-like belt sank to each side of her hips.

Every pop of every button was magnified, the sound echoing off the silk-covered walls, until she gripped the sides of the soft black fabric.

Then she heaved a bashful sigh, rolled her eyes, and pulled the lapels wide, giving him exactly what he was looking for.

'Happy now?' she snapped.

'Ecstatic.' Only Serena would storm into one of the most exclusive casinos in the world wearing a pair of frayed denims cut high on her toned thighs and another quirky

T-shirt—this one ocean blue, with two scuba divers and the words 'Keep Your Friends Close and Your Anemones Closer' riding across her taut stomach.

With no effort whatsoever, she lit up his dark, dark soul.

'What gave me away?' she asked, a hint of petulance smoking her tone.

He pointed his index south. 'Your feet.'

Her gaze followed the direction of his finger. 'What's wrong with my feet?' Her brow furrowed, her head shot back up, eyes slamming into his. 'And what's with that wicked gleam and that grin?'

'I've just never seen you in anything other than biker boots.'

'So?' she snarked. 'One of my dad's ex-lovers gave them to me, I think. This is the first time I've had them on.'

Light crept over marble-grey and Finn hurtled towards lucidity. The reason she wouldn't be seen dead here. The reason she'd shied away from the glamour puss outside the bathroom. Not only did she feel uncomfortable around women, she felt horridly out of place—and yet she'd come here to find him.

Beautiful *and* brave. He'd never wanted her more. And didn't that spell trouble?

'So I'll ask you again,' she groused. 'What's wrong with my feet?'

'Nothing, baby, they're cute.' The last thing he wanted to do was make her feel worse. She didn't have a clue.

'Cute?' she spat. 'Kittens are cute. I am *not* cute. And cut it out with the *baby*. It's driving me nuts!'

'Tell the truth—you love it. Every time I say it you careen into some kind of delightful fluster.'

The nuts part was that she *was* beginning to like it, and she didn't want to like anything he said to her.

'Don't be ridiculous,' she snapped. 'Now it's my turn. I want my wi…'

Her voice trailed off, eyes widening, as he pushed himself

off the sofa-arm and sauntered towards her. While he had every intention of playing fair, it wouldn't hurt to distract her, now, would it? If he tried to kiss her again she would either hit him or bolt. Either exit was fine with him.

When he was up close and personal she raised her head, and Finn caught sight of the wild flutter at the base of her throat.

'I bet you don't even realise you have the most beautiful, elegant décolletage.' He trailed one fingertip down the side of her neck. 'And this skin of yours is a perfectly gorgeous peach colour.' *Yeah, like peaches and cream, to go with that strawberries and cream voice.*

'St…stop saying stuff like that, Finn.'

No.

'Love the T,' he murmured as he brushed down between her breasts with the backs of his fingers, over the creased transfer of frothy waves in a blue ocean—'Keep Your Anemones Closer'. *Sorry, beautiful, not going to happen.*

Down, down he stroked—with fire unfurling at the tops of his thighs—and when he reached her navel—

He growled. Snatched his fingers away and slammed both hands against the wall on either side of her head.

'Wha…what's wrong?'

Finn closed his eyes. 'I need to look.'

'A…at what?'

'You know what. On your stomach.'

A tremble shook her voice. 'Only if you tell me what's wrong with my…my feet.'

Prising his eyes open, he focused on the perpetrators. 'Nothing is wrong. Nothing at all. They're pretty little… ballerina pumps. I think that's what they're called.'

'Do you know you pause when you lie?'

Great.

'Okay, okay. They're slippers.'

Her gorgeous face fell in horror and if she'd been any

other woman he suspected she would have burst into tears. Not Serena.

'They *are*?'

'Cute ones,' he said quickly. 'With little leopard spots on.'

Dismay vaulted into pique and she visibly vibrated before him. 'I refuse to feel stupid just because you know more about women's stuff than I do, considering how many you've had.'

He divined that any figure she could engineer would be highly exaggerated, but still… 'Agreed.' If she felt stupid she wouldn't let him take a peek at her belly button, now, would she?

'Fine. Go on, then. Get it over with. Take a look. But know this: I couldn't care less for your opinion.'

'Liar.' He brushed the pad of his thumb from the corner of his mouth across his bottom lip, eking out the suspense of the moment, then bent his knees and lowered himself into an elegant crouch.

Serena raised the fabric of her T-shirt with an innate feminine sensuality she wasn't even aware she possessed and vicious need clawed at his gut.

One look and he cursed softly.

All the will in the world couldn't have stopped him. Out sneaked his tongue and he licked the small loop and diamond-studded ball.

Cool was the silver against the tip of his tongue, and her soft flesh was a welcome splash of warmth as an aftertaste. *Holy*…

She tasted of passion fruit and coconut and something else he couldn't quite catch, so he knew it would torment him.

That was it. He was a goner. He even felt his eyes roll into the back of his head. Wondered if hers were doing the same.

'You got any more?' he asked thickly, nuzzling her navel with the tip of his nose. All the while he was commanding his legs to stand up and back the *hell* away.

'M…more?' she said, or at least she tried to.

The way her midriff quivered he could tell her breathing was as bad as his.

'Piercings.'

'Piercings?'

What was she? A parrot?

'Yes!'

'No. No more…piercings.'

He moaned low in his throat. 'But something else, right?'

Silence. Only the staccato wisp of a desperate moan from her lips.

'Tell me,' he demanded.

So of course she said, 'No.'

'Oh, man, you're killing me, Serena.' Up he came, standing tall to press closer. To crush those gorgeous breasts against his chest.

When was the last time he'd felt like this? Like his old self but astoundingly better because his ever-present guard was low. Risky. *So* risky.

But when was the last time he'd thought about anything but Singapore? In one way it physically hurt to be near her, aware that he caused her pain. But in the next second he was a man again and there was heat. So much heat. Scorching his blood in a rush of need and pure want. Never had he felt anything like it.

Selfish as always, he wanted—no, *needed* one more taste.

'I warned you, baby. You should've left when you had the chance.'

Desperate to savour as much of her as he could, he dived into the heavy fall of her hair and closed the gap until they were nose-tip to nose-tip.

'This is crazy, but—do you *feel* this?' he asked, unable to hide the awe in his voice.

Fighting to keep her eyes open, she shook her head, rubbing his nose with her own. 'No…' she breathed on a hot little pant.

'Good. Me neither.'

Softly, languidly, he brushed his lips over her velvety pink flesh and the pounding of his heart jacked out of rhythm. Then the need that continually clawed at him grew steel-tipped talons and slashed through his gut, demanding he mark her, take her, glut himself on her.

And she was melting. There was no other word for it.

'I'm…' *Hard. So hard.* For the first time in almost a year.

Thought obliterated, he crushed her body into the wall, then slanted his head and deepened his kiss. Like dynamite they ignited, and when she responded with a tentative stroke of her tongue his hands began to shake.

Her mouth was heaven—warm and wet, with the slip and slide of passionate lips—but, greedy as he was, he wanted more. A deeper connection. He longed for her to move, to touch him properly, covet his body with her small hands, be skin-to-skin. *Claim* him. Brand him as her own. Which was not only bizarre but hellishly scary.

Still the need went on. Because he wanted her to feel how hard he was for her, to know what she did to him, how sexy and desirable she was—

Whoosh! The door swung open with a bellow of male voices and they were flung apart as if electrocuted. It was comical in a way. Serena was visibly rattled and he doubted he looked much better. And since when had *that* ever happened?

She whipped the black fabric around her waist, veiling her body, and fumbled with the sash—her jerky movements made his heart thunder in a fiercely savage urge to protect.

'We leave *now*,' he commanded, livid that he'd placed her in this position.

They were halfway to the door when one of the men broke into laughter as he settled at a gaming table.

Serena crashed to a halt. Stared at the man's back. Paled to a ghostly white. And Finn's guts twisted, tying him into knots. 'Hey, baby?' he murmured. 'What's wrong?'

In response she bolted past one of the other guests like a

mare from the starting gate, almost knocking that man off his feet as she virtually ran out the door.

What the…?

By the time he caught up she was galloping down the hallway.

'Serena, stop. *Stop!*'

Edging his way to stand in front of her, before she trampled over half the Casino members, he slipped his finger under her chin and lifted it gently.

'Look at me. Speak to me. Do you know that guy?'

'No.' Hands trembling, she gripped the lapels of his jacket and leaned into him.

Finn could feel her warm breath through his shirt as she burrowed as if starved of affection, and he instinctively pulled her into the tight circle of his arms.

Holding her was like a chorus of pleasure and pain that struck at his guilt but sang a sweet note of solace, and he luxuriated in the feel of her.

'No!' She twisted and rolled her shoulders to wrench free. 'Get off me, Finn. Right now.'

Feet leaden, he took a step back, fists plunging to his sides.

Remorse and mortification darkened the grey hue of her eyes and he swallowed hard, knowing. It was Finn who was the issue here. She was ashamed of wanting him, crestfallen at her reaction to him, horrified she'd kissed him back at all.

Well, then… Considering the destruction he'd caused in his life, it was highly indicative and somewhat poignant that he'd never hated himself more.

CHAPTER SIX

SHE WAS HEARING voices, seeing things. She *must* be. That laugh was dead and buried but still it crawled through her veins like venom.

Gorging on air, she calmed the violent crash of her heart before she completely lost her mind and tried to snuggle into Finn again. *Come on, Serena. Snuggle?* Being weak and needy was not a condition she'd ever aspired to.

Honestly, this night couldn't get any worse. Charging up here to confront him hadn't been the brightest idea, but she'd had an entirely different kind of tongue-lashing in mind.

Forget lethal weapon—the man was a nuclear bomb. And his kiss… *Holy moly.* There she'd been, quite content to pretend their last lip-lock had been an apparition. Why bother to remember when it couldn't possibly have been *that* shockingly good?

Except it *was* that shockingly good. And bad all at the same time.

Her reactions to him were ridiculously extreme. It was as if he flipped a two-way switch inside her—hate or lust. Which just made no sense. She'd kissed men she'd actually liked before and been slammed in a freezer, yet one touch from Lothario here and she burst into flames!

Sheer panic had her scrambling for perspective. Truthfully, she shouldn't feel so disgusted with herself, so humiliated for succumbing to him. Not when the entire female race swooned at those extraordinary cerulean eyes. Expired at that sinful, sensual mouth. And that was before he backed it up with a truckload of charismatic charm.

Serena was just one of many.

Ugh. The idea that she was turning into a woman like one of her dad's playthings made her feel physically sick.

And of course the dirty deed *had* to transpire with her wearing slippers, of all things—just her rotten luck. And Finn knew what they were. Of course he did. He'd probably tugged billions of the things off perfectly feminine feet.

How. Utterly. Mortifying.

At the risk of garnering attention, she whispered furiously, 'Don't you *ever* touch me again. Your hands are not welcome on me.' She was being unfair, she knew she was, but she despised herself for that momentary lapse.

'Noted,' he bit out, his jaw tight enough to crack, and she fancied his broad frame seethed with self-loathing.

Clearly she was losing it.

Serena edged around his broad frame, determined not to notice how he filled out his sinfully suave tuxedo to perfection. 'I have to go. I'll see you in the morning.'

She didn't slow her pace until she was free of the oppressive glitz and glamour, her feet step-step-stepping down the stone slabs of the wide front entrance.

'I'll walk you down to the harbour.'

Finn fell into place beside her, hands stuffed into his trouser pockets, and as if he sensed she was spooked he ground out, 'No arguments.'

It was the second time he'd brandished that arrogant, masculine tone like a swordsman in protective stance and it did something strange to her insides. Made her go all warm and gooey. Which naturally made her every self-defence instinct kick into gear. She wanted to tell him to get lost—preferably on Mars. But something stopped her.

It was that frigid, ominous laughter. Playing in her mind. An endless loop of pain and vulnerability. Vehement enough for her to say, 'Okay...' because in truth she felt infinitely safer with him beside her.

Down the cobbled streets they went, the only sound the *clickety-clack* of his highly polished shoes and the sensual whispers of couples strolling by hand in hand.

As always, the sight made her heart ache. Ache for something she'd never have. Relationship material she was *not*.

Suddenly cold, she wrapped her arms across her chest, and by the time the tang of seawater filled her lungs and the harbour was a glittering stretch before them she was waging an internal war against asking him to stay.

'Thanks for walking with me. I'll be fine from here.'

'Are you sure you'll be okay? Is there anything I can do? Anything you want, Serena?'

Cruel—she was being cruel. The last few months had turned her into a horrible, horrible person but she couldn't curb the truth.

'The only thing I want right now is Tom. He was more than my brother—he was my friend.' And she didn't want to be alone.

But you are alone, Serena, and you always will be. What doesn't kill you makes you stronger.

'I know,' he said, his voice deep and low, tainted with sombre darkness. 'Believe me, I know.'

It was a voice she'd never heard before. One that made her stop. Pause. Wonder at the torment engulfing his beautiful blue eyes.

'I would do anything to turn back the clock. Anything to change the words I said. If only I'd just told him no when he asked to come out with me. Countless times I've wished for just that.'

As if he'd hit her with a curveball, she swayed on her feet.

The way he'd phrased it, so simply, had brought it all down to choices. Tom's choice in asking to follow his hero. Finn's choice in allowing him to.

Strange to think how the twists of fate intertwined with free will.

Every day they lived a voyage of discovery, moved through life based on choices like forks in the road. They peered down all the options, considered, weighed the risks, finally made a choice—some good, some bad. Some affecting no one but themselves. The worst affecting those they loved. But all of them defining. Forging who they were.

She'd made hundreds of choices in her lifetime and had one major regret. A choice that had affected her dad's life, Tom's life too, until the day he'd died. One made when she'd been naïve about her place in the world, no more than a girl, but a disastrous choice even so.

'I would do anything to turn back the clock.'

Serena would too.

Instead she lived with the guilt, struggled with it, controlled it. Recognised it when she saw it in others. This time she saw it in Finn—such depth of emotion—her first glimpse in…forever.

First? No. She'd been struck with shards of his shattering façade since last night.

Glimpse? No. He looked *devastated*. Seething with a darkness she truly believed was pain.

'Finn?' Who *was* this man? Thawing the ice and hate she'd packed in her chest. 'Oh, Finn, you really liked him, didn't you?' He was grieving too.

Punching his fists deep into his trouser pockets, he cast his gaze over the moonlit ripple of the ocean. 'He was a good kid.'

Knowing this was her chance, she begged him, 'Tell me what happened that night. Your version. Please. My dad just keeps saying there was a storm and he fell overboard during the night, but when I checked there were no weather warnings, no reports.'

His brow etched in torment, he closed his eyes momentarily. 'It was…' His throat convulsed. 'Unexpected. There is nothing more to tell.'

His tone was as raw as an open wound and she ached for him, but— 'Why do I think there is?'

'Because you need to let go.' He shoved frustrated hands through his thick blond hair. 'Otherwise you'll find no peace, Serena. I promise you.'

A cool rush of sea air washed over her in a great wave and she crossed her arms over her chest, then curled her fingers around her upper arms and rubbed at the sudden prickle of gooseflesh.

'Peace? I don't know what that feels like. I never have.'

Finn stilled, watching her, predator-like. Then anger crept across his face, dark and deadly, and her pulse surged erratically at her wrist.

'Have you been hurt? In the past?' he asked, almost savagely.

It was as if his genetic make-up had been irrevocably altered and she could feel the ferocious fury of an animal growling through him. Not to harm—no, no. To protect.

She shouldn't like that. She really shouldn't.

'Serena?'

'I… Well…' She bit her top lip to stem the spill of her secrets.

Ridiculous idea. It had to be the way he visibly swelled beneath his suave attire as if to shield her. It made her heart soften and she couldn't afford that. Just the thought rebooted her self-preservation instincts and she dodged.

'To be honest, Finn, I'm not one for dwelling on the past.' She didn't want to remember being naïve and weak and broken. Didn't want Finn to suspect she was any of those things. She refused to be vulnerable to him. To any man ever again.

More importantly, she was over it. She'd made a life for herself. A good life. True, being initiated into the dark realms the world had to offer at fourteen years old was not conducive to relationships and all the messy complexities that came with them.

It was hard to trust, to let go. And, while she'd vowed her past wouldn't define her, or cripple her life with fear, any attempts she'd made at intimacy had been a dishearteningly dismal experience. She'd chosen a wonderfully sweet safe guy but she'd felt distanced somehow. Detached. Compounded by her blatant lack of femininity, no doubt. But she had her work, which she loved, and her team kept her from touching the very depths of loneliness. And if the tormented shadows still haunted her once in a while she fought them with all her might.

Feeling that infusion of bravado, she lifted her chin. 'Anyway, do I look like the kind of woman someone could easily mess with?' She hoped not. She'd spent years building her defences after all.

Finn slowly shook his head and his fierce scowl was tempered into a decadent curve of his lips as he murmured what sounded like, 'That's my girl.'

Their eyes caught…held…and Serena would have sworn she actually felt the odd dynamic of their relationship take a profound twist.

Before she knew it more words flooded over her tongue— a chaotic, unravelling rush she couldn't seem to stop.

'When I look at you I want to blame you, hate you.' And hadn't it been easier to blame Finn instead of just accepting it as a tragic accident from which no justice could be reaped? 'But on the back of those thoughts comes the guilt, the self-censure, because he asked *me* to go out with him that night and I wouldn't.'

She'd been horribly selfish, hating the social scene, knowing she didn't fit in, so she'd told him to go, to have fun.

'If I'd gone out with him he wouldn't have asked *you*.' Misery poured from her heart. 'I was such a coward.' Oh, God, could it have been her fault?

Finn surged forward, raised his arm and brushed a lock of hair from her brow so tenderly her heart throbbed.

'You can't take responsibility for someone else's actions, baby. He was old enough to make his own decisions.'

'Well, then I should've persuaded him to take professional swimming lessons—' Her voice cracked. 'Something. Anything.'

'Again, you can't make people do what they don't want to. You think he'd honestly want you to blame yourself like this?'

'No,' she whispered. Tom would go crazy if he saw her right now.

Crazy? She gave a little huff. If Tom knew she was being cruel to Finn he would go berserk. Finn had been his hero. He'd talked about him constantly. And hadn't *that* driven her insane too? Ensuring he was never far from her mind. Taunting her. Creating more anger. Powering more hate. But that wasn't Finn's fault. It was hers. Because she'd never understood her unruly all-consuming reactions to such a wild player. He was anything *but* safe.

'How did it happen?' she asked, suddenly weary. 'Were you there? All I want to know is that he didn't suffer.'

A muscle ticked in his jaw and he took a large step back, filching her heat. 'I was…asleep. It was the middle of the night.'

A black blend of torment and bone-wrenching guilt stole the colour from his beautiful face and from nowhere she wanted to throw her arms around him. He was hurting so badly. Like a wounded animal. It was like being tossed back in time, staring at her own reflection. She couldn't bear it.

Trembling, she reached for his hand, the despair and loneliness she'd suffered in the last months calling to her—reaching out for his, to share it. To comfort and be comforted. A craving she'd stifled for months.

All the torment. The guilt suffocating her. Suffocating him. When she'd thought he didn't care she'd wanted to punish him endlessly. Yet he'd buried it just as she had. And where was it getting them? Fate had dealt them a cruel card and unless they moved on all she could see lining the road ahead was endless misery.

Let it go...

Her fingers met his skin and as if she'd zapped him with three thousand volts he jolted backwards.

'I've already warned you once tonight, Serena,' he said roughly. 'You touch me right now and I'll lose it. Won't be able to stop myself from wanting more.'

The memory of him crouched before her, his hot gaze locked on her lower abdomen, his warm breath teasing over her flesh, sprang up in her mind's eye and heat drenched her body like a deluge of tropical rain.

'I...I don't understand you. Are you still trying to distract me or something? Because you're wasting your time, Finn, I'm not going anywhere.'

He rubbed at his temple as if she was giving him a migraine. 'I'm beginning to realise that.'

'Good. But I still can't fathom why you want more from me. I'm not—'

His turbulent gaze crashed into her. 'Not beautiful? Yes, you are. Sexy? More than anyone I've ever met.'

Yeah, right. 'I meant I'm not a woman. Not feminine—stuff like that.'

'Of course you are—'

'Er...hello? Slippers?' While *he* looked wicked and gorgeous in his devilish tux.

'In your own unique way.'

'No. I'm not.' *Was she?* 'Nor do I want to be.' Unveiling that secret part of her would only bring more vulnerabilities. Weakness.

Finn shook his head, his mouth shaping for speech. Then he seemed to think better of it. 'Listen; while the best place for you is far away from me, we have to work together, *boss-lady.* At least until the end of the season.'

Was he saying he wasn't staying with the team? He must know her dad would want him to.

'I know that.' The strike of her conscience made her wince. 'About the boss thing...'

The ghost of a smile softened his sinful mouth. 'A slight exaggeration on your part, Miss Scott?'

'Could've been,' she posed lightly.

'You've got balls, Serena, I'll give you that.'

Their eyes locked once more and she held her breath. Wishing she could read him better. Hating her lack of experience. By the time he tore his eyes free she felt dizzy from the lack of oxygen.

'Regardless, we'll still be seeing a lot of each other, so I suggest we endeavour not to end up alone. Unless...'

'Unless?'

He shifted on his glossy feet. 'Unless you ever need...a friend.' He scrubbed his nape with the palm of his hand. A bit uneasy. A whole lot handsome. 'That's what you said, wasn't it? That you'd lost a friend too? So if you ever need one I'll be there.'

Oh, great. Now he was being all thoughtful. A little bit wonderful. The *last* thing she needed.

Friendship was a terrible idea. They clashed like titans. But she wasn't about to throw his offer in his face. She didn't have the heart. 'Okay. It's a deal.'

With a brief nod he turned to walk away.

'Finn?'

'Yeah?'

Am I truly beautiful to you? Did you mean it?

'Don't forget,' she said. 'You owe me a wish.'

Finn stripped his jacket from his body, yanked the black tie from his collar and slung them across the caliginous suite. Then he flopped atop the bed, face down, his insides raw and aching from being clawed to shreds.

Withholding the truth hammered at his conscience, making his temples pound until his vision blurred and he prayed for peaceful slumber. Not that he deserved it. The past was catching up with him, slowly but surely.

He'd been so close to telling her everything. Battling with a promise made, an investigation that could blow wide any day, and an insight that she'd been through her own version of hell.

What had happened to his brave little tigress? She'd cleverly derailed him and he'd never met anyone who'd managed that feat. Were they talking emotional or physical hurt, here? Though in reality maybe it was best he didn't know.

The imagery taunting his mind made him want to snarl and lash out—vicious, savage with the need for revenge. It made his guts ache with a peculiar primal need to take her in his arms and hold her to him, protect her. Kiss her tenderly, passionately, over and over—make her feel like a real woman.

How was he going to keep his hands off her if she took his offer of friendship?

Exhaustion pulsed through his bones and darkness called to him like an old friend, dragging him into the depths where only nightmares pulsed to life…

Singapore, September, eight months earlier

'Wakey-wakey, pretty boy.'

Derision leaked from the hoarse oriental twang as the sound of heavy boots clomping over concrete, cracking the grit and filth beneath inch-thick soles, penetrated the lethargic smaze in which his mind wandered.

Hair like the heart of a ruby…fire in its most dangerous form…

The twang grew louder. 'How are we feeling today?' But it was the jangle of a loaded key ring slapping against a military toned thigh that finally roused his head from its cushioned spot on the exposed brick wall.

His backside numb from sitting on the damp floor for hours on end, he conspicuously flexed the legs outstretched in front of him, knowing what was to come.

After all, he could set his watch by these guys—if he still had it. As it was, the rare platinum timepiece now graced one of the guard's thick, brawny wrists.

Four and a half million he'd been paid to wear that watch—to have his face plastered on every billboard from here to Timbuktu.

Easy money.

Exactly what these men wanted from him. He could have coped with that if it wasn't for the kid in the next cell. If that kid hadn't been in the wrong place at the wrong time and got dragged into this godforsaken mess.

He smacked his head off the pitted brick, wondering once again if they'd get out of here alive. Wherever 'here' was. Some place near the ocean, if the sporadic bites of salt water were anything to go by.

He craved a glance at the skyline. Light. Space. Or, better yet, an endless track to drive down, to escape from reality. As it was, he had too many hours to think—an overrated and highly dangerous pastime. If he wasn't imagining the peaceful waters of stunning grey eyes regrets suffocated him as they shadowed his mind like tormented souls.

The mistakes he'd made in his life. The hearts he'd broken in his youth. The way he'd abandoned his mother and Eva. What if he never had the chance to say sorry?

Chest so tight he could scarcely breathe, he stuffed the lot to the back of his mind, where all the other emotional garbage was, and let it fester. Concentrated on what he was capable of dealing with—Mr Happy in the khaki combats, who seemed to be snarling at him.

'There is something wrong with your tongue?'

Yeah, as a matter of fact there was. It hadn't tasted water for two days. But he'd guess Brutus, here, just wanted his answer.

How was he feeling? As if he'd had his insides scooped out and then shoved back in. With a blunt spoon.

'Great. Never felt better. Your hospitality is second to none.'

The you'll-pay-for-that smirk should have made him regret his smart mouth, but he had to keep their focus on *him*. *Always* on him.

'I am pleased to hear it.' The guard paused outside the kid's cell and Finn felt the familiar toxic churn of foreboding right in the pit of his empty stomach. 'And your friend?'

Already halfway up from his cosy spot on the floor, Finn almost lost his precarious stance. 'He's sick. Can't even walk. So leave him alone.' Then he smoothed the edge off his harsh tone and kicked up his lips, offering the legendary St George smile as he straightened to his full height. 'It's me you want, anyway. Isn't that right?'

Another smirk. Another churn of unease and sickening revolt in his stomach.

'Boring when they don't fight back.'

'There you go, then. Let me out of here.' He jerked his chin towards the kid. 'The view is depressing.' Or it would be for the kid pretty soon.

'Finn?' Tom croaked. 'Let me—'

'Shut up, kid.' Every muscle in his body protested as he coerced his legs forward as if two of his ribs *weren't* cracked and his shoulder *wasn't* dislocated. Piece of cake. 'I'm feeling cooped up in here.' His door swung wide. 'Give him some water, would you?'

The guard grinned, flashing a less than stellar set of teeth, eyes brimming with calculation. As if he knew something Finn didn't. As if the last four days had been foreplay to the main event.

Darkness seeped through the cracks in his mind and threatened to rise like some ugly menacing storm. 'You leave the kid alone—you hear me? Or no money.'

The laugh that spilled from those blood-red lips made his guts wrench tighter.

'Boss says the only thing I leave alone is your pretty face,' the guard said, and slapped said face with enough force to sting. 'Get moving.'

'Speaking of my generous host, I want to talk to him again.'

'Your wish is my command.'

Somehow he doubted that. Nevertheless, ten minutes later a big palm pushed on his shoulder—the dislocated one, thank you very much—and he fought the wince as he was slammed down into a black plastic chair in the corner of a room that looked like an interrogation hotspot out of a gritty cop show. But, nope, this was no TV set. Proof of which sat in the chair opposite, with a rickety steel-framed table separating them.

Face-to-face with his captor, it wasn't in Finn's nature to beat around the proverbial bush, so he kicked off today's festivities.

'Let's barter,' he managed to say through a throat that felt serrated with sticks. 'I'll trade you another five million if you let him go. *Now*.'

Eyes as black as his soul and sunk into a battered, rock-hewn face stared back at him. 'That's quite an offer, Mr St George. But I was thinking of a different kind of bartering altogether.'

'I'm getting tired of these games. What exactly is it you want?'

'Right now I want you to make a choice, racer-boy. The first of many.'

Behind him, the iron door ground open with a chilling squeal and a frigid bite swept through the room—so cold his bones turned to ice. The kid was behind him. He knew it.

'Forget choices. Make it another ten mill and let. Him. Go.'

'You don't like him being touched, do you, pretty boy?' he said silkily—in striking contrast to the sharp crack of knuckles that caromed around the room. 'So shall I play with him? Or will you?'

Finn's breath sawed in and out of his lungs. 'Twenty. That will be sixty million, transferred from my Swiss bank account within the hour. You can do what the hell you like with me. Deal?'

CHAPTER SEVEN

MONTREAL BASKED IN the warmth of a glorious dusk, the sky a canvas of fluffy spiralling ribbons tinged with orange and red, with only a blaze of yellow on the curve of the earth, where the sun kissed the horizon.

Its beauty failed miserably to improve her ugly mood.

'You'd better be in, Finn,' Serena muttered as she stormed across the endless blanket of tarmac towards his glossy black motor home.

Never mind the prescient darkness that had clung to her skin for two weeks since Monaco, like some kind of impending doom, Michael Scott—aka *dear old Dad*—had just pulled a number on her! As if the day hadn't been enough of a stress-fest.

The day? Who was she kidding? The last two weeks, working with Mr Death-Defyer, had been a roller coaster named persecution; emotions had dipped and dived all over the place, to stretch her patience endlessly. Was it any wonder she could hear the clang of looming disaster?

Still, she'd never forget this afternoon as long as she lived.

Another close shave as Finn scraped second place after going silent on the pit-lane channel for over two minutes. Heart in her throat, she'd snatched the headset from the chief engineer in the end. Not exactly the done thing, but she'd had to snap him out of it somehow.

He was getting worse. Darker. Harder. Taking unnecessary risks no other man would dare to chance. Why? She couldn't understand it. Unless… Unless Serena had made him worse. By storming into his life and throwing Tom's death in his face when he'd been trying to deal with the loss in his own way. Burying it. Just as she had.

It boggled the mind to think they had something in common.

God, she felt sick.

But had *he* been worried when he'd nearly obliterated himself? Heavens, no. While she'd popped migraine pills like chocolate drops he'd supplicated and beguiled the masses with his glib tongue and legendary rakish smile, standing atop the podium as if life was a fun park and darker emotions were aberrant to him. When she knew they were anything but!

Then—*then* he'd swaggered into the Scott Lansing garage, again, and drawled in that sinfully rich, amused voice, 'What do you think, baby? Was I awesome?'

As if he *hadn't* just phased out while driving at over two hundred miles per hour!

Fist balled, she stomped up the metal steps and rapped on his door until her knuckles stung.

If she was an ace at burying pain and masking it with a brave face he was a pro—a grand virtuoso. But now Serena could see it. Feel his darkness more acutely.

Oftentimes behind the charming, irrepressible smile lurked a guilt-drenched agony she still couldn't bear.

Last night hadn't helped matters either. Bored—okay, plain nosey—she'd searched the internet for a peek of his sister and got a lot more than she'd bargained for. Not only was Eva Vitale the most beautiful woman she'd ever seen, but together with Finn she ran a huge charity for breast cancer in honour of their mother. Another death that must have crippled him.

By the time she'd trawled through all the articles and spotted the Silverstone driving day he held every year for sick and disabled children she'd cringed at all the heartless, dishonourable comments she'd perpetually tossed in his face.

The thought that she'd been so prejudiced against his type, his Casanova proclivities—enough to use him as an easy scapegoat for Tom's death—was making her seriously dislike herself.

The door opened on a soft swish to reveal the man himself, wearing a deep red polo shirt—*yum*—and a pair of washed-out stomach-curling jeans riding low on his lean hips.

As her gaze touched his bare toes that delicious drawl rumbled over her. 'Do I meet with your approval this evening, Miss Scott?'

Her heart thundered like a freight train through her chest and she crossed her arms over her breasts before it burst through her skin. 'You'll do.'

The ghost of a smile softened his sinful mouth—only to veer into a scowl as he searched her face. 'What's wrong? Has something happened?'

Yeah, I feel wretched.

This was a stupid, stupid idea, she thought for the millionth time. Fair enough doing practice laps and talking designs, but to come to his trailer? She was making their awkward truce personal and she knew it.

'Can I come in?'

His eyes said, *Do you have to?* His mouth said, 'Sure.'

Unconvinced, she battled with the urge to turn around and flee. But he'd offered, hadn't he? To be a friend if she needed one? And maybe, just maybe, he needed one too.

She was worried about him. Her conscience pleaded with her to help him before he well and truly did some harm. She just didn't know how. While she knew tons of men, she hadn't felt ready to spontaneously combust with any of them as she did with Finn. *So just ignore it, like you have for the last four years!*

Sucking in a courageous breath, Serena followed him into

the spanking new motor home—all sharp lines of glass and steel alongside huge cushy leather sofas.

'Nice place. Biggest and best on the lot. If I hadn't heard the endless man-muck around the pits—' she was *not* about to admit he was dubbed the world's greatest lover '—I would think your penchant for size compensated for some kind of deficiency.'

He flashed his sexy suggestive smile and her knees turned to hot rubber. 'Nothing lacking in that department, I promise you.'

'I'll take your word for it,' she muttered. Meaning it. Only to curse blue when her traitorous mind provided her with an image of the first time she'd ever seen him in the flesh, bar-boxer-shorts-naked, strolling into his bathroom. Where Serena had been... *Oh, God.*

A tingling flush crept up her neck until she felt impossibly hot. And the idea that she looked like some gauche ninny made her vibrate with pique.

'Uh-oh. I sense trouble.' Finn leaned against the slash of the kitchen bench, gripped the ledge on either side of his hips and crossed one ankle over the other. 'Okay, baby, spill it.'

Baby. *Baby.* She had to stop dissolving in a long, slow melt when he called her that!

'I'm...' Shifting on her feet, she eyed the door. South America was wonderful at this time of year. Maybe—

'Enraged? Incensed? Hopping mad? Splenetic? Thoroughly bent out of shape?'

'You swallowed a thesaurus, or something?'

'Nah, it's that school I went to. You know—the one that specialises in breeding the most arrogant and annoying people ever?' he said, flinging her words back at her.

'As you can see, I'm rolling around the floor laughing.'

He grinned.

She sighed. Glanced at the door again. Wondered why she felt hideously exposed. Sharing woes and asking for help wasn't weak or too feminine, was it? She didn't enjoy giving men the impression she was weak—it was like hand-delivering an invitation to be messed with.

Oh, to hell with it. 'My dad just decided not to launch the prototype at Silverstone.'

'Why not?'

A tinge of anger fired in his eyes. One that made her feel infinitely better. Even though her bad funk was technically *his* fault.

Because Finn here had officially earned the title 'too wild and problematic' to handle her multimillion-pound proto-type. And she was angry. Noooo. She was upset. There—she'd admitted it, and miraculously the sky hadn't caved in.

'Doesn't matter the reason. His decision is final.'

Next year wasn't so far away. *It felt like forever.* It wasn't as if it would never happen. There was really no need for her to be so…devastated. 'Point is, he has a brunette over there, and I refuse to play nice when I feel—'

'Like someone peed in your biker boots?'

'Exactly.'

One side of his mouth kicked up ruefully before his focus drifted to the window, far into the distance, as if he'd virtu-ally left the room.

Angst crawled through her stomach and Serena gnawed her top lip.

Yes, she was crushed, but she could easily have gone to a hotel. It was a convenient excuse and she knew it. Some-how she had to slide him back on track.

Letting go of a long, soft sigh, she sprinkled some can-dour on her remorse.

If she'd been courageous enough to look into her heart, to face her own fears, she would have accepted that culpa-bility lay with fate. Otherwise she couldn't possibly have kissed Finn with everything she was. And, if she wanted to be brutally, painfully honest, blaming him had been a grand excuse to hate him even more. Since the moment she'd laid eyes on him he'd stirred a hornets' nest of inadequacies to sting her pride and spawn desires that defied logic. Reason.

Inadequacies she'd been slammed up against from when she was nine years old—ribbed for being 'too girly' to play—and had stolen a pair of blunt scissors to hack off her hair.

Desires she'd always had to force, coerce, to do her bidding. Determined her past would not define her.

Disaster.

Until Finn. Who had never failed to spark every female cell in her body to ignite. The sexual pull of his velvet gaze roving over her when he thought she wasn't looking jacked her pulse. Made her dream about the firm, sinful stroke of his hands moving over her skin and the hot drive of his tongue between her lips. Then came the heat, spearing through her veins like arrows of fire.

She didn't want her heart to thump when he was near or for weakness to spread through her limbs. He was still a Casanova. A prolific player.

He took a long, sensual pull of water from a tall glass bottle and she watched his smooth jaw work, his sexy throat convulse, and knew this was a stupid, stupid idea. *Tough.*

'So, can I stay here?'

'No!' he choked. A distressed noise followed by a splutter. A cough. A hard swallow and watering eyes. 'I don't do sleepovers.'

Her mouth going slack, she wasn't sure which to process first. The fact that he didn't do sleepovers with his women or the fact he thought she wanted to 'sleep' with him!

'I didn't ask you if you did. I asked you if I could hang out here while you go out and do your Lothario thing.' Okay, she was digging for info, but right now she didn't care. 'You know—borrow your place. Like friends do.'

Wincing inwardly, she hung on his reaction as she played the friend card, unsure if the tight knot in her stomach wanted him to pick it up or discard it.

'I was planning on staying in most of the night.'

'Oh.'

Come to think of it, of late there'd been no kiss-and-tell stories. No rumours of orgies or nightclub antics. Half of her gloried in the idea that he was abstaining from his playboy shenanigans and the other half hated the suspicion that he was becoming reclusive, withdrawing from the world even more.

For pity's sake, the man had her tearing herself apart!

Finn scrubbed a palm over the back of his neck. 'Fine. You can hang out here. For a little while.'

'I've never seen a "fine" such as yours right now, Finn.' At his quizzical expression, she elaborated. 'Like I'm sticking hot needles down your fingernails.'

His knuckles bleached white as they gripped the lip of the bench. 'Probably because that's what it feels like trying to keep my hands off you.'

A loaded pause sparked in the air. 'Seriously?'

'Oh, you're happy now?'

Maybe. It wasn't so bad resisting him if he felt the same. Maybe he hadn't been lying to her. Maybe he did find her beautiful after all.

Her heart smiled. 'I'll be even happier if you feed me and let me beat you on your games console.' *Friend stuff.*

He snorted. 'In your dreams, baby.'

She had the feeling that was exactly where he'd be tonight. In her dreams. Centre stage. Just as he had been last night. And every other night she could remember.

'You have until ten o'clock to triumph and prove your console supremacy, then I'm going out.'

'Oh.' That was *not* disappointment in her voice. Certainly not.

Finn cocked an arrogant brow and tilted his head, as if she'd presented him with a puzzle he couldn't quite figure out. 'I'll make you a deal.'

'I'm not keen on your deals. Last time I ended up—' *Ohh*, there it went. Stomach flipping over…

'Getting your belly button piercing licked?'

Hello, heatwave—blasting her from all angles as the incredible sensation of his hot mouth on her skin flicked over her on replay.

'It wasn't the most disgusting experience in the world.' *So you can do it again if you like.* No—no, he could *not*. It was a terrible idea. Crazy to think she was hurtling towards a lack of self-preservation as diabolical as his.

That legendary beautiful smile touched his lips and he raised one hand to scratch at his jawline. 'Deal is—if you beat me I'll take you with me.'

His grin said he was perfectly safe. That she didn't have a hope in hell of winning. Obviously he didn't want her going with him at all. Which naturally flipped every one of her excitable curiosity switches.

Poor guy. She almost felt sorry for him.

He'd been thrashed. By a girl.

Totally and utterly thrashed at supercars, tennis, football and loaded weapons—repeatedly. Then he'd fed her and fetched her soft drinks. Before she'd zonked out on the sofa in an alluring puddle of colour and vulnerability—the latter hitting him smack-bang in the solar plexus.

Seraphina Scott was extraordinary in every single way, and if he didn't give her a good shake pronto he was liable to kiss her awake like Sleeping Beauty. If he was any kind of prince material he would. As it was he'd lied to her repeatedly and lusted after her repeatedly.

Unfortunately some idiot had suggested he was friend material, and though it scared the crap out of him—because he wasn't the most reliable bloke on the planet, and his own sister could vouch for that—he fully intended to stick by his word. It was the least he could do after he'd caused her so much pain, despite the fact it was the equivalent of flinging himself onto the track lane mid-race.

The fact was, she fed his wildness. Unearthed all kinds of

feral, animalistic instincts until need was a constant claw that slashed his insides. Not just craving the heat of her sweet, supple body, but wanting to protect her at all cost, to touch that desolate tinge in her grey gaze.

She was a lonely soul right now.

It took one to know one. He'd been surrounded by people all his life, and yet soaked in a bone-deep loneliness he found impossible to shake.

Yeah, and impossible to understand too.

Easily bored, he relished variety. *Every day with Serena would be as unique as she was*, a little voice whispered. He told that little voice to shut up. It was being controlled by his libido and for once he wasn't listening.

Finn stared at her for a long moment, curling a strand of her hair around his finger. How could anyone even resist her? How long was it going to take before he snapped and crossed the bridge from friends to lovers? *An eternity*, his conscience told him, *because it's never going to happen. You're supposed to be keeping her safe, remember?*

'Hey, Sleeping Beauty.' He flipped his hand over to check his watch. 'It's nine-thirty and we have a date.'

With her sinuous stretch and a sultry writhe her T-shirt inched upwards until that sexy-as-hell diamond piercing winked at him.

Just like that an airlock cinched his chest. 'Come on, spitfire, get a shake on.' *Before I take that silver loop between my lips, flick it with my tongue and suck it into my mouth. Then I'll tear those jeans off and lick all the way down to your clit. Damn.*

'Or maybe I'll just go by myself.' *Way better idea.*

'I'm coming, I'm coming,' she murmured, in that gorgeous, husky sleep-drenched voice.

He growled long and low. This was such a bad idea. What had possessed him to gamble with her? No one had ever beaten him. Ever. He should've known this minx would throw him for a loop—which only made him want her even more! *So cancel. Tell her something. Anything.*

The problem was he was already living one lie, and the thought of customising another pierced his guts as if they were twisted in barbed wire. Add in the suspicion that today's racing blip—courtesy of a flashback like no other—had totalled her aspirations of launching her prototype at Silverstone and he could never tolerate it.

'Where are we going?' She swung her legs off the leather couch, sat upright and shook out her hair until those spectacular ruby-red flames blazed down her back.

'Here,' he croaked, grabbing two caps from the marble bench and tossing one in her lap. 'Put this on.'

'Incognito?' Her grey eyes bolted to his, sparkled with excitement.

It was an effervescence that wasn't going to last long. Or was it? Continually she threw him, and this little jaunt might be just what she needed.

In a sudden burst of self-honesty he acknowledged that the temptation to take her had arrived shortly after the tickets. But the subject matter had made him pause. She was prudish at times, yet inquisitive at others—the delightful memory of her ear crushed against the bedroom door on his yacht came to mind—and he'd flirted with the idea that her past experiences were slim and less than stellar.

Meanwhile here he was, a veritable connoisseur in the erotic arts of passion and seduction, impervious to being knocked off his feet, suddenly disturbed—no, downright daunted—because this woman could easily take his legs from under him.

It took him five minutes to lock up, usher Serena round to the storage compound and heft the double doors wide.

Click went the automatic lights, flooding the space with fluorescence, blinding him momentarily as he waited for...

Her swift inhalation. A deep, rapturous moan. One that nearly brought him to his knees.

Did she *have* to be the hottest woman on the planet?

'*Ohhh*, yeah,' she breathed, her sultry voice loaded with salacious hunger for his latest toy. 'Your taste is impeccable, Finn. All that horsepower makes me twitchy. I think I'm about to have the ride of my life.'

Finn closed his eyes. He was doomed.

CHAPTER EIGHT

SERENA WAS DOOMED.

Finn had driven her across the city behind the wheel of his high-spec, custom-made, invitation-only sports car, slamming her to the edge of the hot zone. Her hormones were frantic as she imagined him making love with the same intensity—with an inordinate skill and a passionate appreciation for the machine in his hands.

The way he smoothed the leather of the steering wheel with an amorous touch, curled his long fingers around the gearstick with a firm, sensual grip… She'd shuddered with pleasure just watching him.

Now, seated in a super-comfy armchair in a magnificent tent in the middle of Montreal, she was right back on edge. A thrumming mass of expectation.

From the outside the structure appeared like a giant theatrical dome, with multiple conical peaks that soared into the sky in a colourful array of blue and yellow stripes—reminiscent of Arabian nights. And inside the capacious space rivalled the outside's awe factor with a distinct flare of class and luxury. It was the type Serena liked—more avant-garde than ostentatious, cast by the heights of technology for performers to achieve mind-boggling feats. It was exciting and thrill seeking. Definitely her thing.

Something awesome was about to happen, and anticipation fired through her veins like gasoline sparking to ignite.

The dark-haired man sitting on the other side of Finn suddenly turned to face him. 'You're real familiar. Have we met before?'

Serena stifled a smile. She'd expected to lounge in some VIP suite, and being one of the masses was more scintillating than ever. Adding a kick of danger that they'd be discovered.

With the black caps pulled low on their foreheads and dressed in T-shirts and jeans—Finn in a yummy buttery black leather jacket, collar flipped high, and Serena in a dark blue hoodie—they created a perfect image of friends out for kicks.

Finn smiled, all charismatic charm, and held out his hand for an old-boy shake. 'I'm sure I would have remembered you if I had, sir. It's a pleasure.'

It struck her then. In many ways he was a showman himself. Although he blended seamless confidence and ease in any situation, she fancied he adapted to his surroundings, even altered his accent to fit. A veritable chameleon.

It was a talent she could only marvel at with no small amount of envy. Yet she couldn't quite figure out why he felt the need. Why not just be himself?

She could only presume, from the way he blocked his emotions, it was some kind of survival technique—and, let's face it, they'd both been reared on fame and fortune so she knew all about those. Except where she'd shunned it he'd danced beneath the limelight, albeit somewhat distanced by not being his true self. It was as if he preferred to be untouched by everyone around him. Now, *that* was something she definitely understood. Opening up wasn't easy. It invited all sorts of pain, disappointment and heartache.

But, more profoundly, what seriously blew her mind was the stranger who came into view when Finn ditched his façades. *That* man was the most fascinating of all.

It was the man who'd made her spaghetti in his kitchen—the one who'd tucked her unruly hair behind her ear, pouted when he'd lost at the video games, the one who seemed perfectly happy to hang out with 'normal' folk and swig cola.

As for the secretive girly smile on her face—that was down to the way he seemed more content. Not so restless and edgy. No dark pain in his eyes tonight. So any regret she'd harboured about going to him earlier in the evening had flown by the wayside.

'Hey!' the man next to him said. 'I know where I've seen you before. On the TV. You're that guy.'

Serena bit down on her lips and held her breath, curious to see if he'd protect his privacy, give them this one night. Craving the real him for a bit longer.

Finn raised his chin, his bewildered expression worthy of an Oscar-winning actor. 'Who?'

'The one who races them fast cars.'

Frowning, Finn turned to face her, his voice thick and deep enough to carry a perfect American drawl. 'Hey, baby, do I look like that race-car driver?'

Suddenly slap-happy, as if she'd had one too many beers, Serena glanced past Finn to the stranger. 'That British guy?' she asked incredulously.

With a dubious flush, the other man shrugged. 'He could be.'

'No way.' Shaking her head, she leaned back against the pad of her chair. 'He's weird-looking. And his eyes…' She deliberately pulled a shudder up her spine.

Finn cocked one dark blond brow, excused himself graciously, then twisted his mighty fine torso and leaned into her.

'What's wrong with his eyes?'

'They're weird. Cerulean blue and yet sometimes…' She left him dangling for a few blissful seconds in an effort to get him back for all the times he'd toyed with her.

'Sometimes…?' he demanded.

'They change colour. Gleam in a feral kind of way. Hypnotic.'

'Hypnotic?' he murmured silkily, his skin flushed beneath the shadowy peak of his cap. 'Maybe it depends what he's looking at.'

Their gazes caught, held in timeless suspension, and the pull tugged at the base of her abdomen until warmth flooded her knickers.

A groan ripped from his throat as if he knew. Could smell the scent of her arousal.

'And…' She smothered her lips with moisture. 'He has this serious animalistic vibe going on. He *growls*.'

Sculpted in black leather, his broad shoulders rose and fell as the tempo of his breathing escalated. 'Do you like it?'

'I love it.' She'd been lured, ensnared, and now she wanted to be caught—

No. *No!* God, what was going on with her? She had to cut this out. Think *friends*.

The hand that lay on his muscular thigh fisted and he pulled back an inch or three. 'Do you know what Seraphina means, Miss Scott?'

She gave a little shake of her head and he elaborated.

'The fiery one.'

Right now that made perfect sense.

'So be careful that you don't get set ablaze. You don't want to get burned, do you, Seraphina?'

'You *burn* women?' she whispered, sounding more intrigued than appalled—and how ridiculous was that? Of course the man burned women. He had a much-publicised trail of ashes in his wake to prove it.

'Badly,' he murmured, his voice tinged with regret. 'Hence my rules.'

Throat swollen, she had to squeeze out the words. 'What rules are they, Finn?'

'No commitment. No emotional ties. Just pleasure beyond your wildest imagination.'

'That sounds…'

'*Good*. It's good, baby. For as long as it lasts. A few hours at the most. Then there's nothing but emptiness. So believe me when I say keep safe and don't be lured by your inner fire. Especially when it ignites for me.'

A ten-bell siren blared through her head, silenced her desire. He was only being brutally honest. No flippant innuendo from this man. No play on words. No clever retort. She liked the real Finn St George, she realised. Very much. He was an arrogant, seductive, sexy blend of bad-boy meets boy-next-door.

Keep safe. Good advice. Not that commitment interested her. Emotional ties made her blood run cold. She'd just lost one man she'd loved, and being obsessed with a player who rapped on death's door with alarming frequency wasn't her idea of a rollicking good time.

Still, what if Finn was the only man she'd ever want sexually? Was she crazy to want to experience such pleasure once in her life? She knew the game, the rote, had been a spectator all her life. She could play by the rules, couldn't she?

Serena fancied he could see the internal battle warring inside her, because he raised his hand and swept a strand of hair from her brow with a shiver-inducing graze.

'Trust me, beautiful. It's a bad idea.'

The main lights dimmed and what remained was a black canvas ceiling dotted with tiny pricks of light. It was like sitting beneath a million twinkling stars. So romantic that yearning pulled at her soul.

Finn eased back into his own chair, leaving her oddly bereft. Until the music struck an almighty beat and she felt the punch of power deep in the pit of her stomach. Then the full instrumental peeled from the band, the sound caroming around the vast expanse to infuse the atmosphere with what she could only describe as a seriously evocative sensual bent.

'Oh, my life.'

The thought slammed into her psyche within seconds. Finn hadn't intended bringing her here at all. So who…?

As if he could hear her mental meanderings, he murmured, 'I was coming by myself. This is a new cabaret-style show directed by a friend of mine and he sent some tickets over last night. He knows I like to blend occasionally, and they often debut in Montreal. I've no idea what to expect.'

She was pretty sure he had a better idea than she did.

'All I know is that it's strictly over eighteens and it explores human sexuality.'

Okay-dokey, then. Right up her street. *Not.*

The risqué undertone of the music was a prelude to a stage lifting from beneath the floor, bringing the performers into view, still as statues. Until the Moulin-Rouge-type beat peaked with an almighty crescendo...

The cushioned pad beneath her bottom quaked, sending a vibration straight to her core, making the hair on her arms stand on end.

And then the artists came to life.

Heat that had nothing to do with the amount of bodies packed in one space and all to do with the hedonistic bent of the performance shot through her bloodstream, growing ever hotter when the stage became a writhing mass of mind-boggling feats of flexibility and synchronicity.

Bodies were bending, stroking, touching. Hands glissaded over painted flesh, the vivid colours of their skin alive with sensuous beauty.

Hanging from the dollies above the plinth were three massive chandeliers from which acrobats were suspended, and they too began to move in a series of gyrations, spinning and twisting as they swung from one bar to another in a dizzying spectacle.

Oh. And they were all half naked. Half naked and—

She sucked in a sharp breath and Finn leaned over.

'You okay?'

'Mmm...' It came out like a groan, because where Finn had made her hot and bothered seconds before the show, now she was burning up. *The fiery one.*

'You want to leave?'

'Absolutely—' She had to take another breath as one of the female performers wrapped her legs around her partner, locked groins tight and bent backwards to the floor, as if he were sliding inside her, as if…

'Okay, let's go.'

'—not. No, I'm not leaving. I'm staying right here. A tornado whipping through the room wouldn't move me as much as this. It's… They…they're *beautiful*.'

Dancing, whirling, bending—the women were incredible acrobats, so much femininity and strength all rolled into one stunning blend.

'So strong,' she whispered in awe.

'They have to be. Strong-willed to train so gruellingly. Strong-minded to hold their positions, trust in their abilities. Believe in their talent. But elegant and graceful at the same time.'

Yes, and all the while remaining strong of heart, body and soul. No shame, only dazzling radiance.

Still staring at the stage, her mind spun. 'What are you getting at, Finn?'

'Maybe I'm just pointing out that being a woman doesn't render you weak, and being strong or unique doesn't make you less feminine.'

She didn't see all women as weak. Did she? Then again, she'd never known many women. Only her dad's bits of fluff, and they all seemed desperate somehow. Serena had watched them, thinking how bizarre they all were, flitting to and fro, trying to make her dad happy, in the idiotic assumption he would keep them. Desperate. Weak. But wholly feminine. Had she subconsciously knitted the two together?

Finn had told her she was feminine. His words, *'Of course you are… In your own unique way…'* came back to her. She'd taken them as a kind of insult, but at the same time had longed for him to mean it. Despite or perhaps because of the shoe-slipper debacle.

Finn saw far more than what met the eye. Behind the celebrity persona he had a depth of intensity and an intelligence that astounded and intrigued her.

'People underestimate you, Finn,' she murmured, and the show continued all around them, just as the world still spun, ignorant of the seismic shift inside of her.

Seismic since she suspected that he was not only right but that her issues ran far deeper. Too deep for her to delve into that gorge right now.

'Always a bad idea,' he said, with an arrogance that made her smile.

With her gaze glued to the sinuous, serpentine movements on stage, she could feel him staring at her.

'It's enthralling, don't you think?'

'Absolutely mesmerising,' he said, still watching her.

'Provocative,' she whispered.

'A unique kind of sensuality.'

Her heart did a trapeze artist flip in her chest. In Monaco he'd said similar words to her.

Unable to resist a moment longer, she turned to look at him.

Face flushed, he licked his lips, as if his mouth was over-dry.

'Finn…?' she breathed. 'Aren't you going to watch?'

'I am watching, baby. The only thing worth looking at.'

Whoosh. Her heart did another flip. Three somersaults and a free fall. And just like that she struggled to breathe.

Before she knew it her eyes had closed and she leaned forward, needing his mouth on hers so badly her entire body ached—and that was *nothing* compared to the flood of moisture low in her pelvis, the incessant clench demanding satisfaction.

French vocals drifted on the air—a sultry line that enhanced the suggestive notes pluming around them:

Would you like to sleep with me tonight?

Another Serena might have asked—a braver version, one who was confident enough to know she could satisfy a man like him, one who knew she'd feel no regrets in the morning. The real Serena couldn't guarantee any of that.

His warm breath trickled over her lips, yet intuition told her he wouldn't close the ever-so-small gap—a virtual Grand Canyon, considering the past that lay between them and all the reasons for them to rebuff this weird and wonderful attraction and simply walk away.

Just the thought that he might take the decision from her kicked her doubts to the kerb and she prised her eyes wide.

His eyes were as dark as midnight, glittering like the stars above, and from nowhere she found the strength to move in, close that gap, lick over his full bottom lip and then bite down to tease with a gentle tug.

Lust...

Finn growled.

Heat...

'Back off, Serena.'

More. Another lick. Another soft suck. Another tender bite. He returned it with sharp yet gentle teeth, then kissed away the sting, causing her to shiver and the deep ache in her body to spike.

'You really want me to take you right here?' he rasped.

That stopped her.

Visibly shaken, her hand trembled as she brushed the hair from her sticky nape and leaned back in her seat. Her sensitive breasts chafed against the cotton of her plain bra and she had to stifle a whimper.

Who knew how long she sat there, her lower body contracting around thin air, while a surge of mortification because she couldn't control her own body inched her anger levels up the charts?

Intermission hit and, unknowing what to say, what to do, feeling seven kinds of stupid that she couldn't make light of the fact that she was teetering on the edge of an orgasm or handle it in some practised feminine way, she launched to her feet.

'I'm going to the Ladies'.'

And she shot through the crowd at a fast clip.

She had to cool off and there was only one way to do it. As far away from Finn St George as she could possibly get.

CHAPTER NINE

'DON'T GET A fright,' Finn murmured, taking a tentative step closer to where she stood in the dark corridor that led to the plush offices at the rear of the tent. How she'd found her way around here he wasn't sure, but for the six minutes it had taken to find her he'd never felt so ill in his life.

Seemingly ignorant of the shadows enveloping her, Serena faced the wall, her head bent forward, brow kissing the evocative red plaster, as her supple body shook violently.

His heart hammering, his insides writhing in a chaotic mess, Finn braced his hands on either side of her head, then buried his face in her neck and inhaled a sweet burst of summer fruits—a scent that pacified, a taste that he'd come to associate with her. One he would never forget. One he wanted to lap right up.

He nuzzled up to her ear. 'Let me take the edge off, baby.'

He shouldn't have brought her here. She was burning. He'd never seen anything like it. Or felt anything like it. He was going insane with lust. Yet he had no intention of taking his pleasure from her. For once in his life he was going to be unselfish. Give instead of take. Douse her fire well and good.

For a second he thought she'd refuse, and despite knowing it was probably for the best he felt his guts twist tight. And then she turned and, *bam*, her mouth was on his, and she was twining her arms around his neck and thrusting into his mouth.

Just like that his largesse slipped a gear. *Aw, man*, this was not good. This was going to be harder than he'd thought. Much, *much* harder if the erection that strained against his zipper was anything to go by.

Grateful that she'd found her way round to this section of the tent, Finn picked her up, wrapped her legs round his waist and carried her straight into his friend Zane's office, thanking fate that he'd passed the man only moments ago and orchestrated thirty minutes of privacy.

He kicked the door shut behind them and braced her against it, his lips never leaving her mouth as he rolled his hips against her heat to create the friction she needed.

His little tigress moaned and purred around his lips, thrust her hands into his hair and held on while he took her on the ride of her life.

'Finn, Finn, Finn…'

'It's okay, baby. It's okay. I'll get you over.'

'I don't like this. I've never felt like this before. It's never been this way before.'

The words poured out on a rush but he got the general gist. Sex didn't usually flip her switch. Bastard that he was, he revelled in that.

'This doesn't feel normal,' she whimpered.

'I know, beautiful.' *Nowhere near normal.*

Which was the entire problem. He was *feeling* things. Desperation, need, a want like no other. A bone-deep fervour to protect, to satisfy her every craving, her every wish, to make her come over and over until her cries of ecstasy filled his mouth. To give her the world and the stars beyond. Too much. It was all just too damn much.

Holding her up with one hand, he smoothed around her small waist, then un-popped the button of her jeans. Her piercing teased and tormented his fingers and he growled as his flesh turned to granite. *Keep it together…keep it together. What are you? A virgin?*

He wanted *in*, and the angle was all wrong, so with a light squeeze of her deliciously pert rear he loosened his hold and splayed his hand beneath the T-shirt on her back to keep her close. The touch of her fevered skin was like an electrical charge up his arm.

What he wouldn't do to have a good, *long* look at the body that had featured so prominently in his dreams. To claw at her clothes and tear her panties off with his teeth.

Serena shimmied to the floor, snatching kisses as if she never wanted to leave his mouth, and burrowed under his polo shirt, making him sweat.

Okay, then. She wasn't the patient type. Which was dangerous with a capital D because *he* was—it was the only way to stay in control.

'Slow—slow down, baby.'

She had to slow down. Before he buried himself in her dewy heat and lost himself inside her.

'Oh, God, this is so good,' she moaned.

'You knew I would be.'

'Arrogant man.'

With great pains he managed to focus on her luscious mouth and devour her, trying his hardest to focus as he slowly but surely eased the waistband of her jeans down her hips and encountered some lacy girly version of boxer shorts.

Oh, man, he was a goner. 'I have to look.'

'Now, where have I heard that before?' she panted.

Finn pulled back and ripped her hoodie and her T-shirt over her head; his temples were pounding, his blood was pounding, his erection was pounding. Everything was pounding.

Her jeans were rucked around mid-thigh, her biker boots sculpted her calves and those subtle curves were making his vision swim. Then he was seeing red... *Red?* Bra and panties. Closet girl, that was what she was.

'Red,' he growled.

His first thought was, *She's perfect.* His second thought was, *Oh, hell, she's perfect.*

Lamplight spilled over the room and he could just make out the lustrous tone of her ivory skin dusted with freckles. He wanted to lie her down and count them all, give them names and kiss every one. He wanted to crush her to him and hold on tight. And from nowhere came the senseless idea that he could be a one-woman-forever man, that she could trust him always.

With defcon speed he ruthlessly shut the notion down. He was *never* taking the risk of hurting her. He'd already done too much of that already and she didn't know half of it.

'Stop staring at me!'

'No chance.' He was looking and she was going to learn to like it, to know how seriously sexy she was.

He cursed blue to get his point across. Lots of the F-word and *gorgeous*es and *sexy*s flying out of his mouth at two hundred miles per hour.

Then he kissed her hard, to back up every word with a truckload of ardour just in case she wasn't getting the point. And with each thrust of his tongue and every swivel of his hips desire mounted, until her rapture created a cloud of erotic fervour and her rich arousal plumed in the air.

Oh, man, he wanted to bite her, mark her, brand her like the animal he was inside.

Hand splayed, he rubbed his palm over her piercing and sank it beneath her shorts, delving to touch her hot heat.

A tortured moan filled the air. His. Hers. Theirs.

She was slick and swollen with want, and when her hips bucked, moisture trickled down his finger.

'Serena...' he groaned, tormenting her with a good dose of exquisite friction.

Gingerly he peeled one shoulder strap down her upper arm, and when her perfect C's popped free the room spun as if he was on a whirly top. They were like works of art. Firm but soft. Each underswell lush and round and topped with a dusky rose nipple.

'You're so beautiful, Serena.'

Taste—he simply *had* to taste her.

Finn cupped her breast and trailed his mouth down her neck. The anticipation of reaching her tight nipple thrummed through his blood, and when he flicked his tongue over the taut peak and simultaneously pushed one finger deep inside of her, a keening cry ripped from her throat.

This was agonising. He wanted her. All of her.

Hot little pants escaped her mouth and the sight of her teeth buried in her bottom lip sent another jolt through him. When he closed his lips over her puckered flesh and sucked, the scent of her arousal filled his nostrils, making him hard enough to penetrate steel.

As if she'd lost the ability to hold her head high, Serena tipped it back to smack the wall. 'Oh. My. Life. Finn…!'

He sank his finger deeper inside her body, this time a little harder, and felt her tight walls close in, grab onto him.

He had a big problem here—a huge problem. And if he wasn't careful he would explode in his hipsters. She was so tight.

'Been a long time baby?'

'Mmm-hmm.'

She was petite to start with, and the way he was sized he would snap her in two. *Not an issue. You're not going there.* It still didn't stop him from imagining the sensation, the hedonistic pleasure, of spreading her across Zane's desk and licking her from head to foot before he plunged deep inside her slick channel.

Her hips pivoted in time to his rhythm and she grabbed his shoulders and arched her back, seeking deeper penetration.

'More?' He pushed a second finger to join the first and she spasmed around him, saying his name over and over with soft, heated, anguished cries of ecstasy.

Keep it together. Don't lose it. Don't you dare.

With one last light squeeze of her breast Finn skimmed up and over her collarbone to rub her bottom lip, back and forth. Then he pushed his index finger inside her hot moist mouth at the same time as he thrust his two fingers deep and thumbed her sweet spot to tease out her pleasure.

Plunge and stroke, here and there, until she writhed and swirled her tongue around his finger. *Holy...* And when he touched her nipple with a nice long lave of his tongue...

She *broke*, splintered, shattered, coming long and hard, spasm after spasm racking her body. The walls of her femininity closed in, squeezing his fingers as she flew apart at the seams, clamping violently in a stunning erotic symphony.

Sweat trickled down his spine, making the tight, scarred skin of his back itch. *Hold it together. Hold it.*

As she tumbled from the heights of bliss, rolling in wonder and passion and exhilaration, Finn leaned his forehead against hers, jaw locked, his total focus on willing the erection bursting out of the top of his jeans to chill out. Willing his body not to come just from watching her orgasm.

He needed air. *Now.* He was shaking from head to foot and his teeth were clamped so tight he nearly cracked a molar.

'Finn?' she breathed.

'Give me a minute.' He squeezed his eyes shut.

Her small hand slipped off his shoulder, smoothed down his chest, and didn't stop until she cupped his erection through his jeans.

He hissed out a choice curse. 'Careful, beautiful.' He placed his hand over hers to lift it to his mouth and kiss her palm. 'This can't happen between us, Serena. For starters, I haven't got a condom.' He sounded a hoarse, desperate man. Very true, that.

'It's already started, Finn.' Back down she went, fingering his jeans. 'I'm safe. You're clean, right?' She began to rip his belt buckle free.

Once more he tugged her hand away, knowing he'd never make it a third time.

'Serena, I've never had sex without a condom in my life.'

This could *not* happen. He needed a condom. It would be too close. Too intimate. Too everything.

Without a barrier he'd lose it. Lose himself. Inside her. He would mark her. Brand her. Have real trouble letting her go.

'We're stopping before we go too far.' *There. That should do it.* He sounded forceful and arrogant and domineering. And just so he could cut off the screenplay in his head he hitched up her bra strap and veiled her gorgeous breasts.

'Don't you *want* to sleep with me, Finn? Be inside me?'

He groaned long and low, never having wanted anything more in his entire life. Right now an endless reel played in his head. She was so utterly perfect for him. But he was *not* the man for her.

In another life he would think he'd finally found The One. If he'd been a different man. If he'd made different choices and hadn't caused so much pain. Pain he knew he'd eventually cause her again. He was too selfish. Unreliable.

He was also taking too long to answer, because she'd tugged her jeans into place and wriggled back into her T. All the while trying to school an expression made up of dejection and embarrassment.

'I don't do it for you, do I?'

Finn cupped her face and kissed her softly on the mouth. 'One look and you do it for me, beautiful. You always have. But, like I told you before, it's a bad idea. You'll wake up in the morning and hate me even more. Regret every minute. Feel only emptiness. It's a stone-cold feeling, Serena, I promise you.'

She stared into his eyes. 'So what was that? Friends with benefits?'

'Sure—why not? You needed me.'

'You need *me* too.' She dipped her head to where he was straining against denim and licked her lips in bashful invitation. 'At least let me…?'

Finn reared back, creating some space. *Hell, no.* If she

knelt before him, took him into her mouth, he would never get the picture out of his head.

'I won't take pleasure from you. That was for you, just this once. Never to be repeated.'

If they reached this point again he'd be powerless to stop.

The only reason he had this encounter under control was because they were in Zane's office, with no condoms, flanked by secrets and lies.

Here she was, beginning to trust him, and she couldn't. It was insane. She was forgiving him, tumbling into his arms under the influence of deceit, and he could not sink into her body, look into her eyes as he came inside her, without her knowing the full truth.

'There are many things I'm not proud of in my life. If I take from you, if I use you, it will be one too many. Do you want a friend, Serena? Or a one-night stand that leaves you frozen? We can't have both.'

For long moments she stared at her feet, drew patterns with the toe of her boot.

Then she glanced up and gave him a small, indecipherable smile. 'Then I guess…a friend.'

Finn swallowed. Hard. 'Good. Friends it is.'

Satisfied he'd taken the hard edge off his need, he grabbed her hand. 'Come hither, Miss Scott, the night is young.'

Halfway out the door she crashed to a halt, and Finn followed her line of sight to their entwined fingers, dangling between them.

Well, what do you know? He hadn't even realised. 'What's up, baby? You never held hands with someone before?'

Brow nipped, she gave a little shake of her head. 'No.'

Finn shrugged, made it easy. 'Me neither.' And before she could make more of it he hauled her out of the room. 'Now, let's get out of here. Don't know about you, but I'm starving.'

For a woman he could never have.

CHAPTER TEN

'WHAT'S GOING ON?' Serena tucked her bike helmet under one arm, shook the damp kinks out of her hair with the splayed fingers of her free hand and closed in on the small crowd gathered at the pits. 'What's the SL1 doing down here?'

One glance at her big beauty, squatting on the Silverstone circuit, looking every inch the sleek, glorious feline she was, and Serena felt her heart swell up with pride.

It wasn't until the silence stretched that she realised several pairs of peepers were soaking in the sight of her going all goo-goo—over a *car*, for heaven's sake. *Sometimes you're such a girl, Serena.*

Tearing her eyes away, she glanced up at Finn and thought, *Oh, great, here we go again.*

The early-morning sun picked out the bronze and golden tones of his hair and his deep cerulean eyes twinkled knowingly.

'Good morning, Little Miss Designer, how nice of you to roll out of bed to join us.'

His voice was deep and devastating, richly amused and lathered in sin. Then his delicious fresh scent whispered on the breeze to douse her body with scads of heat.

'While you've been getting your beauty sleep I've driven fifty laps in your pride and joy.'

Tensing, she felt the hard lip of her helmet dig into her

hip. 'I don't understand.' The only reason he would practise in her racer was if her dad had changed his mind—

Her stomach began to fizz—which was absurd. Serena knew the kind of miracle *that* would take, and she didn't think Finn had demolished every car on the fleet. Yet.

Saying that, she'd rarely seen those dark clouds of guilt overshadowing him during the two weeks since Montreal. And the thought that she'd succeeded in finagling his attention long enough for him to move on made her soul smile.

Finn swiftly dispersed the group with an arrogant jerk of his head and leaned against the car's lustrous patina. Then he crossed his arms over a delicious cerise polo shirt and ran his tongue over his supremely sensual mouth.

A mouth she shouldn't be staring at, hungering for. The problem was, her new BF had taken her to the heights of ecstasy, and every time she looked his way every blissful, shattering moment came back on a scalding rush.

Car, Serena. Focus.

'So what did you think? Of my car?' A sudden swoop of nervy fireflies initiated a frenzy behind her ribs.

'She's much like the woman who designed her. A fiery bolt of lightning.'

Okay, then. A few happiness bugs decided to join the midriff party. 'She handles well?'

'Unbe-frickin-lievebly. She pulls more G's than a space shuttle. Her curves are divine and she worships the tarmac. She's a dream, Serena. You've done an amazing job.'

The world vanished behind her eyelids as she tried to calm the internal flurry and take a breath. All the hard work, the late nights, the testing and retesting over and over, and *still* she waited for her dad to tell her she'd done well. But the admiration and respect in Finn's gaze, from a man who'd driven the greatest cars in the world, was even better.

Oh, who was she kidding? It was awesome. She felt like flying. Having a real girly moment and jumping and whooping. Which was just silly.

'Good. I'm glad.'

Finn leaned towards her and Serena was lured by his sheer magnetism. She drew forward until his husky breath tickled her ear.

'You can squeal if you want to, baby, I won't tell anyone.' *She jerked backwards.* 'Don't be ridiculous.'

That fever-pitch-inducing smile widened and one solitary indentation kissed his cheek. Despicable, infuriating, *gorgeous* man.

'So how did this happen, anyway? My dad said—'

'We had it out last night. Talked long enough for him to see sense.'

From nowhere a great thick lump swelled in her throat.

Oh, honestly, he had to stop doing stuff like this. Because every time he did, another teeny slice of her heart tore free and vaulted into his hand. Serena couldn't recall the last time someone had pushed for what *she* wanted. Even Tom had tended to side with their dad.

'You'll soon learn,' he began, his voice teasing and darkly sensual, 'that it's always best to leave business down to the men, Serena.'

The blissful feeling vanished. 'You only say that stuff to pee me off.'

A devilish glint entered his eyes…

'When I tell you my condition you'll be even more so.'

'I don't like that look.' A little bit shrewd. A whole lot devious.

'You have to attend the Silverstone Ball tonight. That's the deal.'

There it went. In point five of a second. '*It*' being her stomach, hitting ground level with a sickening thud.

'No way. You know that's not my scene.'

Black-tie extravaganza to kick off the weekend of racing with VIP clientele and the usual coterie, sipping champagne, dressed up to the nines in…? No.

Just no!

'Hold up there, handsome. Your *condition*? What do you need *me* there for?'

Never mind the dresses and the shoes and the dancing and the mind-numbing chit-chat, if he thought she was suffering that soiree only to watch him portray Lothario he had another think coming!

'Your car needs to be unveiled and it's the perfect venue. You *have* to be there. This is your big moment. You need to revel in it, enjoy it. Come on, Serena, I dare you.'

'Ooh. Low, Finn, real low.' The beast knew exactly how to get a rise out of her.

Huffing out a breath, she stared unseeingly at her car while a war raged inside her. As far as big moments went this was pretty huge.

She chose her words carefully. 'On my own?'

If he was taking a woman she wanted to know so she could prepare herself. It was crucifying, waiting for him to choose a new starlet.

True, she'd been batting away the sneaking suspicion that he'd already done so for days. What with the odd phone calls he refused to answer in front of her. The ones that made his jaw set to granite as his gaze locked on the screen before he glanced at her with something close to remorse.

If not a woman, who else?

Then again, she doubted he'd had the time to wield his charm elsewhere. More often than not they were together. Which brought on a whole new set of problems. Because while she liked having him as a friend—a pretty cool friend, as it turned out, who'd sneaked her into the premiere of the latest action flick last night—it was getting harder and harder to keep her hands off him.

All in all, since Montreal her sanity was slowly being fed through a shredder.

'You'll hardly be on your own, Serena. The entire team is going and you'll be walking in there with me.' He gave her a wink that made her feel dizzy. 'I get first dance.'

Oh. Well, then. Those fireflies started doing an Irish jig. He was taking *her*, not some flashy starlet. He was going to dance with *her*, not the latest paddock beauty. As friends, of course. Unless he'd changed his mind...

Suddenly *her* mind made the oddest leap, to a vision of her biker leathers, and a groan ripped from her chest. 'And what exactly would I *wear*?'

He chuckled at that. Actually laughed.

'What's funny?'

'And she says she's not a woman.'

Serena threw him a few daggers, wholly unamused.

'Don't worry, okay?' A smile seeped through his voice. 'We'll find something.'

'*We?* Are you worried I'll turn up in T-shirt and jeans and embarrass you?'

Fully expecting some wisecrack, she was unprepared for the way he reached up and tenderly brushed a lock of damp hair from her brow. Only to melt when he stroked down her cheek with the side of his index finger.

'Listen to me. I would dance all night with you wearing a driver's suit—I wouldn't change you for the world. But what I *don't* want is for you to feel uncomfortable or out of place. Why don't you think of it as an adventure? If you have the time of your life, that's great. If you don't, nothing lost. At least you'll have tried. For you. And you'll have given the SL1 the launch she deserves. Come on, it'll be fun.'

The only thing she heard were his words *I wouldn't change you for the world*. And she knew he meant every single one.

'Know what I tell every rookie when he faces the fast lane? Fear is a choice. Don't choose it, Serena.'

In some sort of Finn-induced trance, she murmured, 'Okay.'

She could do this. Launch her car. Dance with Finn. Keep it friendly.

If he still wanted that. She wasn't so sure any more. In

truth she had no idea why they were still fighting it. *Stone-cold morning-after, full of regrets about being one of many.*

'Good.' He delved into his pocket and whipped out his mobile. 'I'll go make some calls and we'll head back to the Country Club. Within two hours you'll have half a boutique in your suite.'

Another wink as he backed towards the garage and her insides went gooey.

'Trust me, baby.'

Trust him.

Why did he always say that? Because he wanted her to trust him so badly? Or was he transmitting some kind of subconscious warning that she shouldn't? The problem was, his warnings were now falling on deaf ears.

Especially since his predicted 'stone-cold emptiness' had evolved regardless. Wherever they went, whatever they did, when the time came to part, stone-cold was exactly what she felt—right down to her bones.

Until her sheets twisted with hot longing and her mind saw an evocative cabaret with her and Finn centre stage. Her only thought: *I want that man. I always have and I'm going to have him.*

To hell with it all.

It was becoming harder and harder to control that voice, to silence the woman inside.

Serena ambled across the tarmac towards the perimeter, enticed by the serenity of lush green meadows—an endless landscape of possibilities. She struggled to remember if she'd ever seen her life that way. As an adventure. Always the pragmatist, she'd never been a dreamer.

There was Finn, with his rich and wondrous, albeit debauched past, but at least he'd lived life to the full. While she'd been fighting that voice, the woman she was inside, since she was thirteen years old, having just rolled onto her stomach in bed, only to wince as the sensitive mounds of flesh on her chest crushed against the mattress. Then a few days later the stomach pain had come, to signal an even bigger humiliation—how to buy panty liners surrounded by men. And that had been nothing on the hormonal avalanche making her feel confused, wishing more than ever that she had a mum of her own. She'd been lost—like a stranger in her own skin. Trapped in someone else's body.

Looking back, it was all so clear to her now. Raised a tomboy, she'd hastened to repress her nature. Yet slowly, secretly, she'd begun harbouring fantasies of more. Dreaming. Easily beguiled by a man who'd lured her with lies and deceit, making the temptation to be all things feminine a compulsion she couldn't resist.

Tipping her face skyward, she let the sun warm her face and breathed through the hurt in her heart. The sinister backlash would stay with her always.

Ever since Finn had made her realise she saw women as weak the idea had rubbed her raw, like a scratch to her psyche.

The naked truth? She was petrified of being a woman. It led her to make bad choices. To walk headlong into betrayal. Pain. Weakness. It led her to lack-lustre sexual encounters as her body fought her will.

So here she was. Twenty-six years old. Still trapped.

Until Finn touched her and she threatened to burst out of her own skin.

Serena knew it was foolhardy but she wanted a good long look at the woman beneath. The person she'd stifled and ignored. And she trusted him.

Fear is a choice.

So hours later, when rails upon rails of dresses in every shape and hue lined her rooms, she duelled with the bouts of anxiety and doubt and managed to conquer each and every one.

For years she'd vowed that her past would not define her. Yet it had. All along. Well, no more.

A strong woman would pursue what she desired. If Finn

was prowling for some female company to take to his bed tonight Serena wanted to be it.

They could still be friends afterwards. She'd just have to prove it to him.

'I'm in the cocktail bar. Come for me?'

Finn strolled into the bar of the swanky Country Club and made a quick sweep of the softly lit circular lounge.

Designed in a sinuous art nouveau style, the architecture was a showcase for curvy lines where no shadows could lurk and deep furniture made from exotic woods, lending a warmth that pervaded his bones. A warmth that grew hotter as his eyes snagged on his prey, her back facing him, perched on a high stool at a central island bar made of iridescent glass.

Whoosh. His blood surged through his veins, drowning out a soft croon.

For one, two, three beats he stared. Because something was different and he certainty had faltered. Then she leaned towards the barman as if she hung on his every word…tipped her head back with infectious laughter and graced him with her exquisite profile.

'Holy…'

Confidence. She was incandescent with it.

His heart cramped, stopped and started again, as if he were crashed out on a gurney in need of some chest paddle action.

Commanding his feet to move, he ordered himself to be calm—not to pick her up, twirl her around the floor, tell her she looked every inch the stunning beauty she was. Not to kiss her hard on the mouth before taking her upstairs to slake this crazy lust and devour her gorgeous body for days.

Instead he scoured his mind for an appropriate Finn St George comment that would do the job whilst ensuring they slept between separate sheets—because his control was as treacherous as an oil slick.

This thing, this friendship between them, was taking on a dangerous bent, and losing the precarious hold on his sanity wouldn't be pretty.

The dilemma being, he couldn't disengage himself from her heavenly pull.

When the moon rose so too did his demons, and there he lay, tormented, although adamant that his endless procrastinating would cease with the rising sun. Then she appeared, all fire and dazzle, with her snarky wit and her beautiful smile, dragging him from the darkness into the light more magnificently than any sunrise could ever do. Leaving him torn asunder once more, frustrated and infuriated with the ugly little corner he'd found himself in.

Keeping her in the dark had been an easy enough decision to make after Singapore, when he'd still been able to taste the metallic tang of blood and they hadn't been face-to-face. All black and white, his reasoning had been crystal clear. Protect her at all costs. No harm done.

But as one day had overtaken another *simple* had accelerated to *beyond complicated.*

Now Finn was loath to tamper with her contentment, to substitute the happiness in her eyes with hate and betrayal. At the same time he was selfish enough to want her to look at him that way a while longer. As if he was a good man. As if he *hadn't* led her brother to his death. As if his day of reckoning *wasn't* hurtling towards him.

Before he even reached her side she stilled. Curled her fingers around the beaded purse on the glass bar-top. Closed her eyes and just…breathed.

Honest to God, what they did to each other defied logic. It was a car bomb waiting to detonate if he didn't defuse it somehow.

Gripping the back rail of her stool, he became enraptured by her fiery river of hair—the way the sides were loosely pinned back to create a cascade of soft, decadent curls down her back.

Thought fled and he dipped his head to kiss her bare shoulder. But he slammed on the brakes in the nick of time, making do with a long, deep inhale. In place of her usual fruity undertones there was an evocative note of something dark and distinctly passionate, reminiscent of her arousal.

His body quaked as that scent registered in his brain like a Class A narcotic and he growled in her ear, 'Looking good, baby.'

A slight tremble passed over her before she swivelled on her bottom and slipped off the stool. Then he got a really good look, and his heart started doing that palpitation thing again. *Wow*, she was filling out. That over-thin look of Monaco was being replaced with subtle curves.

Her pewter dress was snug, held up by one heavily beaded shoulder strap which trailed down the side of a boned bodice, cupping her breasts, moving down to a small bustle at her hip. Her skirts were frothily layered, plunging to the floor in swathes of a lighter toned silver, the hue turning darker by degrees to charcoal and finally edged in ebony. It was a sexy version of rock-chick princess, with Serena lending it her own unique kick.

He was left with the ludicrous urge to lift the froth and take a peek at her feet.

A small smile teased her lips. 'Don't tell me. You need to look.'

Finn shrugged, feeling oddly boyish. He'd never been obsessed with a woman, and the hunch that obsession was definitely the evil he was up against made him recoil, take a step back.

Serena, however, took that as an invitation to show off, and she slowly, seductively, inched her skirts up her calves, then lifted her dainty little foot and flexed her ankle this way and that.

The diamond-studded sandals twinkled in the light, sending prisms of colour to dance across the walnut floor.

'You're very pleased with yourself, there, Miss Scott.'

Smoky sultry make-up enhanced the colour of her grey gaze as she sparkled up at him. Lips glossed, pink and full taunted him as she spoke in a rush. 'I am. No boots, no slippers, and I can actually walk. Who knew wedge sandals actually existed?'

The way she was looking at him—confident, serene, enchanting…

Dammit. How was he going to get through this night? Need was a ferocious claw in his gut, slicing deeper with every second.

'You look sensational, baby.'

'Why, thank you, Finn. But do you know what's really scary?'

'What?'

Her brow nipped, as if she were controlling her emotions. 'I think I do too.'

'That's my girl.' His voice cracked under pressure. 'Let's get this show on the road. The helicopter awaits.' He held out his arm and shut down every possessive instinct in his body. 'Shall we go to the ball, Miss Scott?'

She slipped under the crook of his arm, pressed her breast in tight to his side and his pulse shot through the roof.

'Why, yes, I believe we shall, Mr St George. I have a feeling this is going to be a night to remember.'

Finn tried to swallow around a lifetime of regrets. 'Curiously enough, so do I.'

CHAPTER ELEVEN

'CONGRATULATIONS, SERENA, she's a beauty.'

'Thanks!' she said for the hundredth time as she cut through the swathe of racing drivers, TV pundits and VIP celebrities littering the champagne reception.

Despite her stomach doing a really good impression of a cocktail shaker, she'd slipped free of Finn's arm an hour earlier. Half of her was adamant not to appear clingy and her other half was determined to venture out on her own. An endeavour that had whipped her into a whirlwind of team chit-chat, photos and promo for the SL1 until she felt high as a proverbial kite.

It couldn't possibly be the champagne. Truthfully, she thought it was a disgusting blend of wince-worthy tartness and bubbles exploding up her nose. She'd do anything for a beer.

Spotting a familiar face in a bunch of footballers, she pulled up alongside her dad, waited for a lull and then tugged at his sleeve. 'Have you seen Finn anywhere? We're supposed to be heading into the marquee for dinner.'

'Not lately. Good God, you look stunning, sweetheart. I had to pick my jaw up off the floor when you walked in.'

'That makes two of us.' Jake Morgan sidled up to join them, his chocolate gaze liquid with warmth. 'You look fantastic, Serena.'

'Oh, stop, now you're making me blush.' She gave a small

smile to soften the brush-off—she still wasn't used to compliments. She kept expecting someone to shout *Impostor! Fraud!* Even if she felt...well, beautiful for the first time in her life. All giddy and girly.

And if that aroused an anxious tremble in her stomach she ignored it. There'd be no dark shadows tonight.

She took a deep, fortifying breath and switched gears. 'I can't wait to see my baby whizz around Silverstone tomorrow.'

'She'll win for sure,' someone said.

'Too right she will.' *As long as Finn kept his mind on the game.*

'Can I get you a drink before we head over?' Jake asked.

Inwardly cringing at the thought that she'd end up with another glass of fizz, she said, 'Actually, Jake, I'll come with you.'

The bar was the traditional mahogany type: deep and framed with brass rails. Serena gripped the cold metal as they deliberated over the mirrored wall of various optics.

'What does gin taste like?' she mused.

'Not sure, but it used to put my mother in a crying jag.'

Serena snorted a laugh, turned round. 'Really?'

And *that* was when she caught a glimpse of dirty blond hair in the mirror's reflection and twisted to see Finn laughing in that charming, charismatic way of his.

'You pick, Jake. I'll be back in a tick.'

Off she went, diving through the throng and popping out at the 'Finn cluster' planted at the top of some stone steps leading to the vast lawn—a lush green blanket saturated with an array of iconic racing cars from past to present, as well as supercars, helicopters and yachts in a huge luxury showcase.

As if Finn sensed her behind him he reached round, grabbed for her hand, then pulled her into the fray and introduced her with practised ease and a pulse-thrumming smile. A smile she tried to emulate as he assaulted her senses, rubbing his thumb over the ball of her hand, making her bones liquefy and then leaning in until his dark scent fired heat through her veins.

'You enjoying yourself?'

'Yeah, I am. Surprise!' she said, only to cringe at the quiver in her voice, musing that she might be a league too deep with this man who effortlessly consumed her. 'Are you coming in for dinner? We're being seated any minute.'

'We?'

'Jake is at the bar, ordering drinks. He's waiting for me.'

Finn glanced towards that very spot, staring with an enigmatic hardness that turned pensive. Then he squeezed her hand until she flinched. *What the—?*

Jerkily he released her. 'Sorry, beautiful.'

If she didn't know better she would think he'd shocked himself.

'Sure, I'll follow. You go ahead,' he said, with an austere jerk of his head and a dark note to his drawl that she couldn't grasp.

As it was, they were halfway through their appetizers when he finally deigned to join the highly sophisticated mix, whipping out all the weapons in his loaded arsenal to schmooze his tardiness away.

And while every man and woman fell beneath his spell Serena stared at those tight shoulders, filling out his suave custom-made tux, and fought with disquiet. He appeared ruffled. As if he'd been thrusting his fingers through his hair. Or someone else had. *Stop. Just stop. You're being ridiculous.*

Soon, she told herself. As soon as the first band came on he would come for her to dance. Although the anticipation was a killer. Especially when she could feel his eyes burning into her flesh when he thought she wasn't looking.

What he failed to grasp was that her every sense was attuned to his high frequency. Every word from his lips dusted over her skin like the petals of the wild orchids that trailed from the crystal centrepiece, and every deep, sinful chuckle tightened the flesh between her legs. The waiting, waiting, slowly drove her insane, until at one point his gaze was so intense a tornado whipping through the room couldn't have stopped her meeting it across the table.

Finn placed his palm on his chest, as if his heart ached, and, *oh,* her own thumped in response. But then he pulled his phone from the breast pocket and she realised it must have been on vibrate. *Idiot.*

Her stomach hit the velvet seat with a disheartened thump even as she tensed with the chill of suspense.

Much as he had on another few occasions, he stared at the screen, then glanced back up, his demeanour fierce, indecipherable, his jaw locked tight, something dark and portentous swirling in his eyes.

Guilt. Another woman. It had to be.

Throat thick, she had to swallow hard. 'Aren't you going to answer it?'

It was the same question she'd previously voiced, and for the first time she *wanted* him to say no. Not to spoil the moment. Their night.

Except this time he stood. 'Yes. I've been waiting for a call. It's…important.'

'Is that right?' She sounded snarky, but right now she couldn't care.

One of the black-and-white-garbed waiters lowered a gold-trimmed plate in front of her and the sweet aroma of salmon and asparagus hit her stomach like battery acid even as she told herself she could be leaping to conclusions. But why act so guilty if it was innocent? Either way, she had no right to be upset, no claim on him whatsoever. *Exactly.* She was not furiously jealous. Absolutely not. That would mean she was far more emotionally involved with him than good sense allowed.

'I'll be back in a while.'

Mutely she nodded. Forty minutes later she was still calling herself fifty kinds of fool. He'd left. He must have. And while an orchestra of pain and hurt struck a beat inside—

directed at herself for believing she had a shot with him—she refused to let him take her pride from her tonight.

The bolt of fortitude was like taking a match to gasoline, and fury hit her in an explosion of fire. Once again she'd set herself up for a fall. But she wasn't going down. Not this time.

'Serena? The band is striking up. Would you do me the honour?'

Glancing up to Jake's handsome face, she felt her throat pulse, raw and scratchy. Was she seriously going to sit here all night like a fool, waiting for a man who might never come back? Was she really that desperate?

'Sure, Jake,' she said, ignoring the forlorn thump behind her breast telling her that this felt very, very wrong. 'That'd be great.'

It was like being confronted with his nemesis. The antithesis of everything he was.

Guts writhing in a chaotic mess, Finn leaned against the wall at the rear of the dimly lit ballroom, thinking how poignant it was to be enveloped by shadows—everything Serena feared—as he watched Jake Morgan enfold her hand and beckon her to the dance floor.

His body jerked on a visceral instinct to go over there, stop the other man from taking her in his arms. But, dammit, he could be honourable for once in his life. Step aside. Let the guy make his move. It was a thought he'd battled with all night. Would have surrendered to if it weren't for the undesirable, inexplicable, violent primal instincts that demanded he protect her. Possess her. Take her. Make her his.

But Finn knew the fall out from such selfishness. It had chased his career, fed off the high-octane rush of success, abandoned his mother when she'd needed him, left Eva to the heart-wrenching fate of watching her die. It had cost this woman her brother. So this, he assured himself, was an argument he would win. He wanted her to be happy.

One of the country's top bands struck out with a Rat-Pack number and when Serena offered Jake a small smile and moved into his embrace, white-hot lightning shot up his forearms, tearing through muscle. He had to shake his fists loose. What was wrong with him? He had to get a grip.

Jake was a good guy. Reliable. Honourable. Chances were *he* could remember the names of every woman he'd slept with.

Jake was trustworthy. What was more he hadn't just ended a call to the Chief of the Singapore Police, who'd discovered a new lead and was about to make an arrest.

Insides shaking, he blanked his mind. *Back away, Finn. Back the hell away.*

She could have a relationship with this guy. Finn knew nothing about those apart from the fact that the mere word spawned ramifications that were bad for his respiratory rate.

Across the room Jake fitted his hand to Serena's dainty waist, tugged her close, whispered in her ear, and Finn felt the first fissure *crack* in his sanity. His every possessive, protective instinct kicked and clawed with steel-tipped talons, tearing his insides to shreds, until he was back in that cell, fists balled, ready to protect what was his. And had it worked? No!

The dark licked around the edges of his life.

'Finn?'

Sweat trickled down his spine, making the skin on his back itch as violence poured through his veins. He'd been a stranger to brutality before Singapore and now, like then, it coated his tongue with vile bitterness.

Pain shot up his temples.

'Finn? You okay, my man?'

Michael Scott.

'Gotta go,' Finn said. 'Something's come up. Can you tell Serena…?'

Any response was lost as he shoved through the double doors, commanding his body to stay in control before darkness engulfed him and his demons wreaked havoc on his soul.

Serena waltzed across the marble foyer of the Country Club as if her squished feet *weren't* throbbing and her legs *didn't* feel as if they'd been chewed by a Doberman.

Heart weary, her only thought a hot bath and some sleep, she rode the elevator to the top floor, then slipped through the yawning metal doors—and stumbled to a halt.

A maid shuffled on her feet outside Finn's suite, biting on a torn fingernail.

Unease coiled through Serena's midriff. 'Is there a problem?'

The brunette jerked upright, wide-eyed. 'I...I'm sorry, Miss Scott, I heard a crash as I was passing so I knocked to check everything was all right.' She gave a tremulous smile. 'He isn't answering. You're with Mr St George, yes?'

Serena frowned, then realised the maid must have seen her in his suite earlier, put two and two together and came up with six.

A crash? Oh, God. What if he was hurt? Had had some kind of accident?

Chin up, she lied through her teeth. 'Yes, we're together. Don't worry—I'm sure everything is fine. But, while you're here, I've lost my room card. Could you switch me in, please?'

Antsy, suddenly slapped with the suspicion that he could be having sex in there—which would seriously be one humiliation too many—Serena tap-tap-tapped one diamanté toe on the floor.

As soon as the maid dipped into a curtsey and turned to walk away Serena slipped into the room. A room filled with dark shadows. She blinked rapidly to adjust her vision and when the scene crystallised, she sucked in air at the sight before her. One surely from her nightmares.

Trashed. His room was completely and utterly trashed.

Clothes were strewn all over the floor, as if his luggage had been overturned from the stand. A floor lamp was lying drunkenly on one side and the bed was stripped; dark silver satin pouring over the sides. The notion that he'd just had frenzied sex all over them crushed her heart.

It wasn't until she spotted the man himself, hands braced on the curved walnut bar, head bowed, white dress shirt damp and clinging to his back, that a portentous sensation crept up her arms. This didn't look like a seduction scene. It looked like—

'Oh, my God, Finn, has your room been ransacked? You have to call Security!'

Spotting the phone on the bedside table, she dashed over to call Reception.

'You know,' he said easily, 'that would be a very good idea. Perhaps they could take me away and lock me up.'

Reaching for the phone, her hand froze in mid-air. '*You* did this?'

She took his silence as a yes and shivered right down to her toes.

The atmosphere had turned thick with danger. She could virtually *feel* his darkness, blacker than ever before. And the urge to turn, to leave, was so strong she had to push her feet to the floor until they rooted—she would *never* be frightened of this man.

'But why?'

'Get out, Serena. Now. Before I break.'

Break? What was he talking about?

He swiped a bottle of tequila from the marble bar-top and poured the liquid into a crystal tumbler.

'Finn?' she said, panicking as he raised the glass to his lips and took a long swallow. 'What are you doing? You're driving tomorrow!'

'Nagging, Miss Scott? Now, that is a typical female trait.

One unbelievably hot dress and you're halfway there already.'

'You were the one who dressed me up! Only to disappear on a booty call and leave me there.'

A humourless laugh broke past his lips. 'A booty call? Is that what you thought?'

'What else was I supposed to think?'

With a severe kind of control, completely at odds with the state of the room, he turned to face her and air hit the back of her throat. His beautiful blue eyes were black with guilt, devastation and fury. So much fury it poured off him in waves. Great tidal waves of anguish.

'Hold up there, Lothario. What are you angry with *me* for?'

Slam went the glass to the marble and liquid sloshed over the crystal rim. 'No booty call. But it didn't take *you* long to fall into the arms of another man, did it?'

Serena flinched at the scathing lash of his tongue, the cut biting deep.

She'd messed up. Royally.

Raising one arm, Finn pointed due west and emotion gushed on a voice thick and unsteady. 'Do you have *any* idea how hard that was for me? To see his arms around you, holding you close? To walk away thinking you were better off with him?!'

Words blasted from him like bullets—*bang, bang*—until she rocked where she stood. Then she cursed for thinking the worst of him.

'I'm sorry. I waited and he asked me to dance. That's all we did—dance. I...' Her heart was beating so hard and loud she could barely think. But never mind her pride. She owed him this much. 'I only want you, Finn.'

Serena held her breath, waited. She didn't think it was possible for him to look even more tortured, but he did.

'You have to leave.' He stabbed his fingers through his

damp hair, then pawed down his face. 'Please, Serena, just go. I don't know how long I can hold on.'

Realisation hit and her entire world narrowed to this point. This man. 'So don't. Let go.'

Though her insides trembled, she commanded her feet to move deeper into the shadows and reached up to grip the zipper hook at the side of her dress. Slowly she tugged downward.

Fists clenching, he shook his head. 'Stop. Just stop. I'm on the edge here, Serena, and I can't control myself with you. I don't think you'll like that.'

As if he'd tossed her into a bramble bush, her skin prickled all over with the flash replay of violent hands gripping her throat, twisting her wrists, pinning her down—

No. *No!* This man was Finn. Granted, she'd never seen him so dark before, and it made her wonder if she was missing something, but still… 'I can handle it. I can handle you. I'm stronger than that, Finn.' Clearly he lacked faith in himself but she trusted him. Completely. Utterly.

She dragged the single beaded shoulder strap down her arm and teased the satin past her plunge bra to her waist.

His throat convulsed. 'Don't you dare, Serena. Don't you *dare.*'

She hurled his words from the yacht in Monaco so long ago back at him, amazed at how far they'd come, how far they'd travelled. 'Oh, Finn, you should know better than to challenge me. Especially in that gorgeous husky voice of yours.'

Shimmying, she eased the rucked material past her hips and the pewter satin rustled to the floor to pool at her feet. Leaving her standing in a black plunge bra, tiny lace panties and studded heels. Now, if she could just breathe she might get through this.

With his shirt agape, she could see his chest heave and the way he looked at her—with such heat. Such fierce desire and molten need.

A look so hot she melted beneath his gaze, pooling like gasoline, brandishing her earthy colours. Raw, elemental and utterly flammable.

'Serena,' he growled. 'I'm hanging on by a thread here, baby girl.'

'You know what, Finn? I love it when you call me that.' To think this man could have any women in the world and yet wanted her intimately, with such desperation, made her feel invincible. Confident. Beautiful. A real woman for the first time in her life.

He pointed at the door. 'You've got three seconds to run. Three.'

Up came her chin as she walked towards him with a sway in her hips she'd never before possessed, and then she pressed her hand to his hot flesh, felt the rapid thump of his heart beneath her palm.

'Two,' he bit out. Sweat glimmered on his skin and his broad shoulders quaked as he fought the immense power of his body. 'I can't promise I won't hurt you.'

'I *know* you won't.'

No more waiting. Avoiding. If this signalled the end of them, the end of their friendship, so be it. She didn't want another friend. She wanted a lover—the only man she'd ever truly desired.

'The fight is over, Finn.'

'One,' he said fiercely. 'You're making the biggest mistake of your life here, baby.'

'Then so be it.'

Snap.

CHAPTER TWELVE

FAST AND FRENZIED, as if he were lost beneath an unseen power, entranced by a dark, feral spell, Finn simultaneously crashed his mouth over hers, gripped the front fastening of her bra and tore it wide.

'Skin,' he commanded around her mouth as he tugged the straps down her arms and tossed the black scrap across the room. 'I want nothing between us.'

'Whatever you want.' Her voice was as shaky as the rest of her and for a second her inner voice whispered that she was mad. Totally out of her league. With no idea of how to give such an intensely passionate man what he needed.

Following her instincts, she placed her hands on his honed chest, then swept them up and over his shoulders, taking his shirt with her until it bunched and locked around his thick upper arms.

Finn shucked it off the rest of the way and grappled with the fastening at the front of his waist.

She'd never seen him like this. Ever. No practised seduction. He was uncoordinated. Lost. And to think she was the inducement made her blood surge with elation and fear and an excitement so intense she ached with it.

A sharp hiss whistled through his teeth as he fought with his tuxedo trousers and she simultaneously pushed his hands away and broke their lip-lock. 'Let me do it.'

Not easy when he sank his hands into the fall of her hair,

tilted his head and crushed his lips over hers, banishing every thought from her brain. He ravished her with a kiss that was desperate and messy but she loved it. Loved the way he thrust his tongue into her mouth and groaned with need and contentment. A sound of soul-wrenching solace.

Now she was the one who fumbled with the rotten button. Heavens, he was bursting past the satin waistband, and when she thumbed the velvet head of his erection and encountered slick moisture her knees refashioned themselves into rubber.

A deep groan rumbled up his chest and he simply...tore the trousers off, buttons pinging, material shredding—the sounds of patience evaporating in the sultry air.

Then his long, thick length was in her hand and she couldn't even close her fingers around it. *Oh, my life.* She stroked up and down his erection as best she could and a sharp tug at the base of her abdomen made her insides clench. It felt as if she was contracting around thin air.

'Finn,' she whimpered. 'I need you inside me so bad.'

With an agonised moan, he jerked from her grasp. 'Soon. We need to slow this down or it will be over before it's even started.'

A sob of frustrated need broke from her throat. 'Finn, *please.*'

'That's it. Say my name. Tell me you want this. Want me.'

'I do. I do.' A wave of dizziness hit her and when she realised she wasn't breathing she gasped in air.

He nuzzled deliciously across her jaw, scraped her neck with his teeth, and somehow she knew exactly what he wanted.

'Go ahead—do it,' she demanded, frantic for his mark, and he sucked on her skin until her eyes rolled into the back of her head. She had to clutch his wide shoulders to stop dissolving in a puddle at his feet.

Beneath her palms she felt his tight muscles relax, as if he was slowly relinquishing the image of someone else and staking his claim on her. Branding her. And she loved it. Loved his sublime body too. From the lean ridges of his washboard abs to his sculpted arms—arms that made her feel gloriously safe, protected, coveted. Girly needs, but she was too far gone to care. She was tired of fighting them, weary of the constant struggle to stay strong. She only wanted him to hold her tight. For just a little while.

'You're so beautiful, Serena.'

Wherever his lips touched his urgent breath left heat—all the way down to her breast, where his hand cupped, where his thumb brushed over her tight nipple.

Her flesh ached for more, puckering when he took it into his mouth to swirl it and tongue it and suck it in a way she felt deep inside her pelvis.

She started to cry out but his mouth came right back, covered hers again, his fierce kiss silencing her until she surrendered to the sheer bliss of it all.

Finn splayed his hand over her stomach, rubbed her piercing with his palm, and his erection jerked against her bare thigh. Oh, that definitely did it for him. She wondered, then, what he'd think of the base of her spine…

'As divine as these panties are,' he said hoarsely, wrapping his fingers around the lace, 'you're even more so.' And he tore them clean off.

'*Ohh*, my life.'

Then he cupped her intimately, possessively, wickedly. 'Wet…*sooo* unbelievably wet and hot.'

The deep rasp of his voice, the seductive touch of his fingers against her slick and swollen folds, made her move to create the friction she craved, and within seconds her knees gave out.

'I've got you, baby.' Curving his arm around her waist to hold her upright, he thrust a finger inside her.

'Finn… Finn.' Needing his lips back on hers, his taste on her tongue, she pushed into his mouth with a boldness she'd never before dared, mimicking what he was doing with his hand as she rode his finger to completion.

The vibrations gathered force like a flock of birds sprouting wings and flying up into the sky, taking her with them far up and away as her body flew apart at the seams.

Flailing, she clutched his tight shoulders—shoulders that shifted in a delicious pattern as he gently tumbled her atop the bed.

Shivering, tingling with aftershocks, she writhed on the cool satin as he crawled over her.

'*Aw, man*, you are so incredibly, amazingly perfect. You drive me crazy, Serena. From the first moment I saw you I wanted you in my hands.'

Those very hands were shaking, but no more than hers, as he stroked up her waist and teased her ripe nipples in an unrelenting current of pleasure.

'You…you did?' Arching her back, she silently pleaded, then opened her legs wide to coax him into settling between her thighs.

He did too. Lowering his delicious weight until she could feel his hardness where she wanted him most.

'Oh, yeah. And know what else?'

'What?'

'I wanted to know how you would taste. Not only here…' He laved her nipple and gently sucked the peak into his mouth, stoking the internal fires he'd just doused. Then he shifted further down, gave the silver loop a quick lick. 'And here…' Another shift. 'But especially…here.'

Before she even knew what he was about he was at the juncture of her thighs and taking a long, leisurely cat-like lick up her still swollen folds, which still beat a tattoo of lingering pleasure. She couldn't possibly…

Serena bucked off the bed. Okay, this was really new to her, and she wasn't so sure, and it was a raw, open feeling.

'Finn?' she breathed, with vulnerability lacing her voice, making it almost inaudible.

'You taste so good, baby. I'll never get enough of you.'

Oh. His words were intoxicating, making her feel giddy,

making her heart soar. Which was just silly—she knew full well she needed to keep her heart out of this.

'Trust me. Relax. You'll love it.' He trailed lush, moist kisses across her inner thighs and she could feel his hot breath dusting her flesh. 'Heaven. I'm in sweet, delicious heaven. I love how good you taste. I knew you would.'

Gently, he sucked her clit into his mouth, pushed his tongue inside her, and every rational thought evaporated as he devoured her body and mind.

Within seconds she was writhing, fisting the trillion-count sheets. 'Finn! I can't take much more.'

'I want you mindless. Desperate. Needing me as much as I need you.' His gasped words were threaded with a hint of delicious agony. 'Able to take all of me.'

'Finn, please. I'm going out of my mind here. I'll do anything. Just give it to me, for heaven's sake—'

With a primitive sound that rumbled from his chest he crawled back up her body, prowling like a starved animal, his eyes dark as midnight, his body shaking with the strain of holding back.

'Anything?'

'Anything,' she said, softly panting, her gaze fastened on his delectable mouth.

'Beg me for it.'

Time stilled together with her heartbeat.

Power play. Control, she realised. Dominance. Her effect on him scared him. Made him feel out of control. And he wanted it back.

Yet how many times had *she* felt that way? Vulnerable, desperate to regain command of her life after the attack.

With no hesitation she reached up, cupped his gorgeous face, brought his mouth down to hers and kissed and begged and pleaded, told him exactly what she wanted him to do, using every uncouth word she could think of, until his eyes sparked electric blue and the arms that braced either side of her were shaking. And then—*thank you, God*—he thrust inside her in one powerful lunge, filling her huge and hard, covering her body with his, his possession so total she ceased breathing.

'Bliss. Sheer…bliss.'

Her lashes fluttered downward as his solid flesh pulsed inside her, making her feel exquisitely stretched. He felt *shockingly* good.

Pausing, perhaps as stunned as she was, he held still, his lips against the throbbing vein in her neck where he inhaled deeply.

A sharp arrow of unease burst through the rapture. 'Finn…?'

'Shhh, baby. I'm listening to your heartbeat, deep and hard and true. I'm soaking in your scent, rich with your arousal for *me*. Knowing…'

'Knowing?' she whispered.

'This is the closest I'll ever get to heaven.'

Oh. Her heart filled to bursting for him.

Serena sank her fingers into his damp hair and held him tightly to her. All the while fighting a punch of panic. This shouldn't be so intimate.

A chord of vulnerability sang to her heart and she squeezed her eyes shut. She didn't understand any of this. Not her body's reaction to him nor the emotions swirling inside her.

Finn finally raised his head and began to move tentatively. 'Look at me,' he ordered.

Serena opened her eyes to see him braced above her, his expression dark and fierce, so intense she trembled beneath him. Then, with their gazes locked, he began to move faster, pumping long and deep and hard, sweeping her up in a vortex of sensation so strong, so powerful, she cried out once more.

Finn captured her mouth with his—his tongue a tormenting lash of pleasure—and sank one of his hands under her bottom, lifting her, the better to meet his powerful thrusts, and grinding against her.

'Oh, *yessss*,' she moaned, raising her legs and wrapping

them around his lean hips. Her head tossed back and forth on the comforter as she fought to hold back the waves that threatened to crash over her. Almost sobbing with the fierceness of her need.

'Look at me,' he ordered again, louder this time. Heightening the sharpness of her desire. As if he didn't want her to forget who was inside her, dominating her, loving her body with his.

As if Serena could ever forget. Impossible.

She hastened to focus on his flushed face, where a thin sheen of sweat glistened on his forehead. His breath was hot and fast on her cheek; his erection throbbed inside her…then he suddenly crashed to a halt.

After a quick pause, in which he possessively gripped her waist, he pulled back. 'I want you with me when I fall. I don't want to be alone. Come with me.'

She tried, she really tried to push a *yes* past her lips, but at that moment he pushed so deep inside her that she felt him in every cell of her body and nothing came out but a high-pitched moan as she surrendered, let herself be dragged towards a climax the likes of which she'd never known.

'Finn…' she said brokenly, panicked that she wouldn't survive—that she'd die from pleasure, break after having him and losing him, shatter beneath his searing intensity.

'I know…I know.' He smoothed her damp hair back from her face. 'I'm here, baby, right here. Not going anywhere.'

She began to ride the shuddering crest. All-powerful, potent, almost violent as it ripped its way through her.

'That's it. Come for me.' He caught her small frantic cries with his mouth, tangled his tongue with hers as he upped the pace and pushed her higher than ever before.

'Finn!'

Climax was a blinding white-hot rush and she broke from his mouth as convulsions racked her body, making her spine arch violently.

Finn gave a final lunge, his dark-as-midnight eyes locked on hers, and at that moment she'd swear he touched her soul.

He stiffened, then came on a silent shudder that went on and on and on…

'Yessss…' she breathed, riveted on his gorgeous face, ravaged with pleasure, as he poured himself into her, giving her it all, and she'd never felt so strong, so powerful in all her life. She was a woman who'd just shattered this man. This beautiful, wonderful, amazing man.

A man who gave a convulsive thrust before he collapsed on top of her with a low sound of feral ecstasy. Then he wrapped her in his arms as if he never wanted to let go and nuzzled her neck, pressed a lingering kiss to the sensitive skin beneath her ear.

Serena stroked his damp hair from his brow and revelled in the feel of his body—heavy, slick and replete against hers.

Voice gruff, he murmured against her neck, 'You okay, beautiful?' with such tenderness that her chest ached.

'More than okay. That was…outrageously good.'

'Unbelievable.' He lifted his head, caught her gaze. 'Incredible.'

As if unable to stop himself he dipped his head to kiss her again—a kiss so sweet and tender that a lump pulsed in her throat and all she could think was that she didn't want to leave. She wanted to lie here forever and ever. With him.

Gently, he rolled onto his back, taking her with him, his hardness still locked inside her body, holding her tight as though fearful she would vanish into thin air.

'You'll stay here. All night. I can't let you go yet.'

'I'll stay.' Serena buried her face in his neck, tasting the musky scent of their passion and the remnants of his dark cologne. Desperately trying not to overanalyse his every touch, his every word.

He didn't do sleepovers. He'd told her that before. So maybe she was different from all the others—special enough to hold his attention. *Careful, Serena, you know better than that.* '*Yet*' implied that he would let her go come morning.

Fighting the hollow emptiness in her stomach, she snuggled closer, until they clung to one another as though braced for a turbulent storm.

For now she'd just enjoy him. Take what she could. Nothing would stop her. Not even the sound of her heart cracking wide open.

Selfish. He was so selfish craving the entire night with her. No doubt he would go to hell for it. So what was new? At least he'd have tasted heaven on the way.

Self-loathing gnarled and twisted in his guts like thorny branches as the tight skin on his lower back nipped, reminding him of what lay between them. And although it was wrong to hide, he was grateful for the shadows. The only light came courtesy of the thin slice of moon shining eerily through the leaded windows, ensuring he languished in the grim certainty that his world would come crashing down with the dawn—and if this was all he had of her he was taking it. Taking it all.

Spooned into the delicate delineation of her back, with her soft skin whispering over his chest, he toyed with a lock of her ruby-red hair; corkscrewing a silken strand and watching it bounce like a loaded spring.

Aw, man, he had it bad. Knew she could steal his heart as it lay vulnerable outside his chest.

Something close to panic clutched his throat and he felt driven to lighten the mood, to lift the portentous silence, fall back on the charm that never failed to smother his emotions.

'I do find you in the most delicious compromising positions, Miss Scott,' he said, his voice a decadent purr as he kissed the graceful slope of her shoulder.

She groaned. 'Don't remind me.'

'You never did tell me why you broke into my trailer through the bathroom window four years ago.'

'I…I didn't know it was your trailer! It was identical to ours. It was pitch-black, I was tired, I'd just come back from London and my key wouldn't work.'

He trailed one fingertip down her upper arm and a quiver took hold of her svelte body, ruining the indignant tone she was aiming for. He smiled mischievously.

'Yeah, whatever. You just wanted to see me in the shower.'

'I didn't even know you!'

'Hey, no need for panty-twisting. On the scale of women trying to get my attention it veered towards the tame side. It was quite the introduction. I was the perfect gentleman too—caught you before you went splat on the floor.'

'*Gentleman*? You said my boots were the sexiest things you'd ever seen and if I wanted your body I had to leave them on!'

'Ohh, yeah! Go get them and I'll prove how serious I was.'

He'd been deadly serious—until he'd locked onto that stunning gaze of hers and his world had tipped upside down. Then his only thought had been how quickly he could shove her back out through the window and transport her to another planet. Which didn't quite explain why, at this moment, she was gloriously naked in his bed.

She coughed out an incredulous laugh. 'You're insatiable.'

'Only for you,' he said. Meaning it. She'd ruined him. No other woman in the world seemed real any more—just mere cheap imitations that might as well not exist.

Crap, he was in big trouble here. And when she canted her head and peeked up at him, brow nipped, gauging his sincerity, his stomach hollowed out.

This was getting too deep. He knew it. She knew it. He could tell by the way she turned away, scissored her legs out of the silk sheets and moved to perch on the edge of the bed.

'I should go. Let you get some sleep. You have to race in the morning and…'

And he didn't care, he realised. He would rather she stayed. Which was scarier still.

'Serena—'

That was when he saw it, in the ivory glow of the moon shimmering over her back. Artwork, moving across the base of her spine.

'Aw, baby' he growled. 'That is one hot splay of ink.'

Her spine flexed as she stiffened for a beat, then she murmured, 'Thought you might like it.'

With one touch her body softened and he traced the design with the tip of his finger, skimmed the garland of tiny pink and purple flowers outlined in black, curling into a circle to form the traditional peace symbol and then swooping outward in an elegant trail to each side of her back. But it was the small butterflies at either side, fluttering at her hip bones as if poised to fly from their captivity, that cinched his chest.

'It's beautiful, Serena.'

Intuition told him there was more to this than met the eye, but before he could pry she said, 'Finn…?' with such vulnerability that he was powerless to do anything but nuzzle closer and worship the ink with lush, moist kisses, smoothing his hands over every inch of skin he could reach, caressing her, loving her.

Until she tumbled into his arms and he made love to a woman for the very first time. Took them both soaring to the euphoric heights of nirvana, where life as he knew it ceased to exist.

When reality knocked at the temporal door of his mind Finn was half sprawled over her, one leg flung over her thighs, one arm tucked around her waist, his head cushioned on her soft breasts. Even in slumber she cradled him close, her affectionate fingers toying with and stroking his hair.

Longing nearly shattered him.

It was like coming home. An indefinable precious feeling of utter peace he wanted to wake to every morning. She felt perfect in his arms. All soft, warm woman. *His* woman.

He wasn't letting her go. He was *never* letting her go. He—

He froze. Something foreign slammed into his chest as reality hit and his life skewed dangerously.

No. No, she could never be his, he told himself, fighting the crush of what felt suspiciously like panic. Fear. He had no choice but to let her go. Watch her walk away, powerless, as her endearing affection hardened to hate.

This was what he'd been afraid of all along, he realised. Losing himself. Relinquishing his hold on the reins of his life, allowing his emotions to rule until he wanted it all. Needed a woman he could never have.

Gingerly he eased back and cool air slapped his sweat-drenched body with lucidity.

It was all for the best, right? Yes. Absolutely. He'd only cause her pain in the end, with his uncanny knack of hurting people. Eventually he'd let her down as he had Eva. He didn't trust himself not to.

Yeah, he shouldn't forget the notion that he was some kind of bad luck charm for those he cared for. Had he been able to save his mother? Tom? No. Well he'd be damned if he took Serena down too.

Curling up on her side, Serena snuggled into the pillow, subconsciously reached for him. His heart kicked with the demand to pull her into his arms. Hold her tight. Adore her. Never let her go...

Finn launched off the bed, stumbled to the bathroom and with a quick flick of his wrist at the controls turned the shower spray to fast, hard and mind-numbingly cold.

There he stood, hands braced on the sandstone tiles, head bowed, while the water pounded his scalp and shoulders and he commanded his heart to stop beating for her. He shoved common sense down his throat until he nigh on choked on it, oblivious to time or place... Until bright light slashed through the room and a sharp, pained cry rent the air—

'Oh, my God, Finn! Your back. Baby, your back.'

Slam went his heart against the wall of his chest and he cursed inwardly. How could he have forgotten even for a moment? *Idiot.* This was what she did to him—banished thought until he operated like a loose cannon. Out of control. He hadn't wanted her seeing him like this, finding out this way.

Drenching his lungs with fortifying air, he commanded his heart to calm and relished the sanity that rained over him, bringing with it relief. So much relief it punctured his nape and made his head tip back until he stared at the white-wash on the ceiling.

It was over.

Now she'd loathe him. Just as he deserved. Hate him. Run. Far, far away from him. Before he hurt her, ruined her life beyond repair.

Slowly, inexorably, he allowed the cold to bleed into his veins, into his soul, until he was frozen to his emotional core. Braced for the highway to hell.

CHAPTER THIRTEEN

SCARS. SCARS ALL over his back. And she was shaking from head to foot, going all female crazy on him, her heart a searing fireball, acidic tears splashing the backs of her eyes— which was the wake-up call she needed to give herself a good shake. Careening into an emotional abyss wouldn't help anyone here, least of all him. But—*oh, God*—she could virtually feel his pain, as if the sensations of brutality had been exhumed from the Stygian depths of her memories. And her heart ached. *Ached* for him.

Serena snatched a thick warm towel from the rail, shut the water off and stepped behind the curved glass screen, striving to avert her gaze and failing miserably.

'You've been beaten,' she breathed, her throat clotted with anger and grief, because although time had endeavoured to heal him he'd been whipped and burned and— *Oh, my God...* 'When, Finn? When? How? Why?'

How could she not have known? Why hadn't he told her?

His torso swelled on a deep inhalation before his shoulders hardened to steel and he turned with excruciating slowness. Dark blond hair plastered his brow, falling into glacier-blue eyes as cold as the frigid droplets that clung to his naked skin.

A shiver shook her spine. Never had she seen him cold. Wouldn't have thought it possible from the man who beguiled the masses with his stunning smile and charismatic charm. It was the equivalent of dunking her in the Arctic.

'Singapore.'

One word, delivered in a voice so cool and sharp she knew it was just the tip of an iceberg.

'S…Singapore?' The floor tilted and her arm shot out to brace her weight; her palm slipped on a cool trickle of condensation as her brain was flooded with implications.

'Yes,' he said, devoid of emotion as he snagged the towel from her hand and wrapped it around his lean hips.

Singapore.

'Tell me…this has nothing to do with Tom,' she said, her voice barely audible as her mind whirled faster than the room. 'Tell me there's no connection. Because that would mean—'

Oh, no. Please, no.

'I've lied to you all along,' he admitted. Detached. Hateful.

Serena closed her eyes. 'I…I trusted you.'

She waited for the hot, pungent wash of anger and anguish to weave hotly through her veins, but all she kept envisaging were those barbaric scars marring his golden skin and all she felt was numb.

'No, you didn't, Serena. And if you were starting to it was against your better judgement, I'm sure.'

He was right, of course. She hadn't trusted him at all in the beginning. Amazing what the onslaught of sexual attraction could achieve. Gradually blinding her until a thick, dense veil of molten desire shrouded her eyes to what she'd suspected all along.

The truth she'd been waiting for all these months.

The truth this man had told her didn't exist.

Damn him. And damn her cursed heart too. How could she have been so naïve?

'I want the truth, Finn. And don't you dare lie to me again.'

'Put something on,' he ordered.

That chilly tone simultaneously made her shiver and feel bemused. Why was he being this way? So closed off. Aloof. Poles apart from the adoring, affectionate man she'd given her body to—as if he simply didn't care any more. The snaking suspicion that he never truly had coiled in her chest, constricting her lungs until her breath hissed past her throat.

No, wait. She would not think the worst of him again—not until she'd heard him out. There could be a perfectly good explanation for all this. Right? *Oh, God.*

'Here.'

He unhooked a white robe from the back of the door and she shoved her arms into the soft cotton, then tied the sash and nipped the lapels at her throat.

With an austere jerk of his head he motioned her towards the lounge area, where two cushy emerald-green armchairs sat at angles on either side of the marble fireplace. 'Have a seat. I just need a minute to dress.'

'I'd rather stand,' she said, altogether too jittery, needing the succulent warmth of the honey-coloured carpet brushing the soles of her feet to ground her somehow.

Every second was an endless stretch as her brain worked overtime. Then he reappeared, wearing a black T-shirt, low-slung jeans and a hardened façade that made her stomach tighten in response.

Just who *was* this man?

No daredevil swagger this night.

Gait stiff, body taut, he braced his forearm on the marble mantel and stared into the lifeless grate.

'We were taken from a private club in Singapore after our drinks were drugged. Out cold for about twelve hours. We woke up in an old wartime holding cell near the port.'

'You were…' *Breathe, Serena, breathe.* 'Taken? Like, for ransom?'

'Thirty million was the starting bid.'

Down she went, collapsing onto the nearest chair, while her thoughts tripped over one another. But when his meaning hit and collided with the imagery of his horrific scars the juxtaposition struck like a bolt of lightning and she began to shake. All over.

'Was…was Tom beaten like that?'

The hand at his hip balled into a tight fist and his legs flexed as he forced himself into the ground. For a split second she allowed herself the fantasy that he wanted to come to her, hold her.

'No,' he said, as black and hard as the mound of coal he was fixated on. 'He didn't suffer in that way.' Glancing up, he met her eyes, and for the first time she saw a frisson of emotion warm those ice-blue depths—sincerity. 'That's the absolute truth. So don't even picture it in your head. Didn't happen. Promise me you will remember that.'

She frowned, unsure what to believe. 'I don't understand. How come he wasn't touched when you were? It doesn't make sense.'

He held still, willing her to trust him—at least in this. It was important to him, she realised.

'Let's just say they had far more interest in me.'

What? Even that failed to compute. Why would criminals be partial to Finn—?

Air hit the back of her throat, where a great lump began to swell, and she bit down on her lips.

Panic flitted across his face. 'Hey, Serena, are you listening to me? Did you hear what I said?'

She swallowed thickly. 'You *made* them more interested in you.' He had an astonishing flair for it after all. 'You took the brunt of it, didn't you?' she asked, a little bit shocked, a whole lot awed.

Yet he merely hitched one shoulder in blatant insouciance as if it were nothing. *Nothing?* What? Did he think he'd deserved it, or something?

Switzerland… Sick…

'You were beaten so brutally that you spent months recovering in Switzerland, didn't you?' *In hiding.* 'And that is why you didn't come to Tom's funeral.' While she'd cursed and berated him, blind to it all.

'Yes,' he admitted.

Curse her throbbing heart, because the thought of him being alone, broken and torn, all that time in such pain…

His cerulean-blue eyes darkened dangerously as they narrowed on her face. 'Do not look at me with pity, Serena. I took your brother into that club. A club I knew was notorious. He *trusted* me.' Anger spewed from him, driven by the self-loathing that contorted his face. 'I led him into that hellhole and don't you forget it!'

Slapped with his fury, she rocked where she sat. Then she prompted her lungs to function properly as she sieved and scrutinised his way of thinking, only to recall their conversation on a harbour many moons ago.

'You didn't lead him, Finn. It was his choice. *His* choice. Back at Monaco you told me I wasn't responsible for the decisions he made. That I shouldn't feel guilt because he wouldn't want that. Are you going to tell me you lied about that too?'

Please don't. Because I'm already confused, wondering what has been real, and I'm afraid that every word from your mouth has been a lie.

'No, but—' His brow crunched for a beat. 'This is different.' Pushing off the mantel, he swung away and began to pace. 'I came out alive. He didn't.'

Now, *that* was a fact she couldn't dispute. To think that all this time she'd never known, had been kept in the dark—

'My God, Finn, did he even drown at all? What happened to him?'

Flinging himself down onto the opposite chair, he let the clasped ball of his white-knuckled hands dangle in the space between his open legs and met her gaze.

'Long story short: it was a get-rich-quick scheme run by some highly intelligent brains who had a perverted opinion of hospitality.'

He grimaced, as if the memories tasted vile on his tongue, and her heart thrashed for him.

'After about four days the bartering began, and on the fifth day they brought Tom in. Threatened him. Gave me the choice to do him over or they would.' A mirthless huff burst past his lips. 'The kid always looked at me like I was some kind of hero and there I was, inclined to knock him unconscious rather than allow the guards to maul him.'

The space behind her ribs inflated with his pain and her stomach gave a sickening twist. Because it was sick. Twisted. Perverted. 'Oh, Finn.' What a decision to have to make. It must have been torture for him—for them both.

'They knew fine and well he was my weakness, and I couldn't stand the lack of control.' With a rueful shake of his head he glanced towards the wide double doors leading to the balcony, where the strokes of dawn painted the sky in amber and gold. As if he searched for peace and beauty in the midst of such horror. 'To wrench some of it back I threw more money in the pot, and within two hours sixty million had been transferred from my Swiss bank account into one on the Cayman Islands.'

Self-derision twisted his full lips and her back crushed the downy cushions as she braced herself.

'It was a long shot, so I wasn't particularly surprised when two days later we were moved to an abandoned liner off the coast. I knew then we weren't getting out of there alive.' He jabbed his fingers through his hair. 'Tom was getting weak, losing his will. I got desperate. Bribed one of the guards to get him out. He could only take one of us for risk of getting caught. I didn't bother telling Tom. Didn't want him objecting to leaving me behind. He was an honourable kid.'

His voice cracked and the fissure streaked through her heart.

'Courageous too. You'd have been proud of him, Serena.'

Her trembling fingers slapped over her mouth to capture the sob that gathered force in her chest and burned the base of her throat. After all they'd been through together she was *not* going to break in front of Finn. She was not going to be weak.

'Next night, as planned, the guard smuggled him out. Whether he was anxious to get back before his absence was noticed or whether there was a struggle, I don't know, but he decided to drop him close to the port...'

His devastating gaze locked on hers, filled with pain, such heart-wrenching pain, that she sank her blunt nails into her palms, trying to stay motionless...

'So he could swim the half-mile to the shore.'

'Oh, no,' she breathed.

'Serena, I didn't know—or I would've warned the guard. I didn't know he could barely swim and I sent him to his death.'

The walls of her chest clamped vice-like as she shook with the effort not to crack. She had to stay strong for both of them. It was all so tragic. So heartbreakingly unfair.

Swallowing thickly, she prayed her voice wouldn't rupture. 'You couldn't have known unless he'd told you. He was really embarrassed about it.'

He'd been petrified of deep water too, but there was no way she was telling Finn that; he had enough to carry on his conscience. *Oh, Tom, I'm so sorry I wasn't there for you.*

Back she went, hurtling towards the emotional precipice, her eyes pooling with moisture. God, how did she make them stop? Averting her face, she blinked rapidly as her defences began to splinter.

Apparently she wasn't the only one, because in a flash Finn was striding across the floor and plunging to his knees in front of her. *Her* Finn.

Moving in between her legs, he brushed a lock of hair from her temple in a tender graze and pressed his lips to her cheek. 'I'm sorry. I'm sorry. So sorry I took him from you.'

The sound of his voice, so broken and desolate, slapped some strength into her spine and she cupped his face with a firm, warm touch and hardened her voice.

'You didn't take him from me. *They* took him from me. It was not your fault.'

'How can you say that? I am the sole reason he is gone. They wanted my money, Serena.'

'No. If that were true they would have taken just you. They saw an opportunity and they took it. Don't you see? You were both in the wrong place at the wrong time.'

His jaw tight enough to crack a filling, he frowned deeply. 'I sent him out there.'

'You were trying to save his life. It was a tragedy borne from their actions, not yours.'

A sense of *déjà vu* flirted with her mind. How many times had someone said that to *her* after the attack? Yet had she ever truly believed them? No. Since Finn had come into her world she'd realised her life was built on shaky foundations and she'd never truly moved on.

She didn't want that for him. To be trapped in some kind of stasis, haunted by the past.

She swept his damp hair back from his brow and his eyelids grew heavy. 'This is going to ruin you, Finn. This guilt that is driving you. I want it to stop. Tom wouldn't want this.'

Finn's frustration ignited and he jerked from her grasp, bolted to his feet and veered away from her. 'That's your emotions talking after sharing a bed with a born seducer. Sooner or later it will pass and you'll blame me—hate me as you should.'

'I'll never hate you, Finn. Ever. Nor will I blame you. You need to accept that.'

For an infinitesimal moment he simply stared at her. His expression was pinched with pain, but it was the intense flare in his cerulean eyes that lifted her spirits. Hope was reflected there…faith that slowly diminished as if the lights were going out in his soul.

'Serena, don't you see what you're doing? You're allowing good sex to drive your emotions and cloud your judgement. Already you've forgotten that I've lied to you for months.'

Unwilling even to consider how easily incredible sex could be downgraded to 'good' within hours—she wasn't ready for that reality just yet—she felt a burst of unease fire through her stomach. Nothing had been forgotten. But some sixth sense beat an ominous warning that his answers would never suffice. Only hurt. Badly.

Ignoring the tumultuous roil inside her, she lifted her chin. 'First off, don't speak to me like I'm some female and I don't know my own mind. I promise you it's not misted by desire up there. But maybe now is a good time to tell me why. Why you lied to me. Why, almost a year later, I would still be in the dark if I hadn't walked in on you tonight.'

The more she considered it, the more bewildered she became. And, if she were honest, there was a good dose of humiliation in there at her naïvety too. Once again she'd fallen into the hands of deceit, and the fact that those hands belonged to Finn was a bitter pill to swallow.

Finn flung the double doors wide, inviting the bite of British morning air to swirl around her ankles. Then he braced his hands on the overhead frame and looked out onto the green acreage surrounding the Country Club, the golden wash of dawn warming his pale complexion.

'Fact is Tom's drowning ruffled the rogue guard and he tipped off the Singapore police to my whereabouts.'

It wasn't difficult to comprehend the acrid tinge to his dark voice—Tom's death had likely saved Finn from a worse fate and *that* was anathema to him.

'The brains behind the operation disappeared—the ransom too, through laundering. There have been a few leads but it's slow going. We didn't want you in any danger, getting caught up in the ongoing investigation. I suggested you were told the same story as everyone else. Your dad agreed. He didn't want you hurting any more than you already were.'

'Wow, tough love must have gone by the wayside that day.' Then again, Michael Scott couldn't handle her at the best of times. Showing his love didn't come naturally or easily.

'Plus,' he began warily, his arms plunging to his sides, 'I kind of promised Tom I would look out for you. Make sure you didn't go looking for blood.'

The rush of anger drained away as quickly as it had come, leaving a numb sensation bleeding into every inch of her. Yeah, that was exactly what Tom would have done. But that wasn't the reason she crossed her arms over her chest to calm the dark storm brewing behind her ribs.

'Would this promise to look out for me be the reason you offered to be my friend weeks ago?' *Say no. Say no.*

Keeping his gaze averted, he shoved his hands into deep denim pockets. 'You could say that, yes.'

Whack. His words punched her midriff, making her flinch. 'That's very...*noble* of you, Finn.' Was that really her voice? That cracked melody of sarcasm and bitterness? A portrayal of a heart betrayed.

There she'd been, blissfully ignorant, revelling in the idea that he wanted to spend time with her. God, she'd even luxuriated in the way his guilt had eased, making him more content—had rejoiced in the sanguine expectation that *she* was the reason for it. And all the while he'd been keeping a promise. While she could grasp his need to, as far as she was concerned as soon as their friendship had developed into more they'd gone way beyond that. Why not just tell her before they slept together? It felt like dishonesty.

'You know what really gets to me?' she said, pleading with her strength not to abandon her now. 'Every day you omitted to tell me the truth, and every night I came closer to...' *To falling for you.* 'To trusting you. To sharing your bed. How could you do that, Finn? Lie with me...' *Make love to me with such intensity.* 'While keeping something so huge, so important to me a secret?' *Give me a good reason, please.*

When he finally turned to face her, one corner of his

mouth lifted ruefully. 'I've never pretended to be a saint, Serena. The sinner in me simply couldn't resist you.'

Their eyes caught…held…and she told herself she was misreading the fierce fervour in his gaze. That all along she'd imagined the emotional pull. If he'd felt more for her he would have had the decency to tell her the truth well before he'd taken her body. *What had you been secretly hoping for, Serena? That he was falling like you were? You're a fool.*

'I warned you, baby. That you were making the biggest mistake of your life.'

Yes, he had. *'So be it,'* she'd said, and here she was.

The cyclone of torment in her chest picked up pace and the strain of keeping her head high wrought a deep throb in the muscle of her nape.

It was a foolish heart and a fledgling female pride that spoke. 'Tell me something, Finn. Is every woman your *baby* too?' *Please say no.* In truth, she wished the words right back. Didn't want to hear she'd meant nothing to him. A silly, stupid girly part of her wanted to keep hoping she'd been different from all the others. Special in some way. As unique as he'd frequently told her.

A muscle ticked in his jaw and his brow pinched for one, two, three beats of her thundering heart. Then he hitched one broad shoulder in insouciance.

'Naturally.'

And just like that her stomach hollowed and she felt emptier than she ever had before.

'Naturally,' she repeated, with all the blasé indifference she could muster as she fought the anguished throb of her body.

Lashes weighted, she allowed them to fall until he disappeared.

Serena Scott—one of many. Like all the nameless faces that had wandered through his life. Her father's too. A woman she'd sworn she'd never become.

Anger hit her like an explosion of fire. At him, yes, but

equally at herself. For opening up once again. Being susceptible, vulnerable to a man.

Why did unlocking your heart, daring to dream, have to hurt so much? Have to end in crushing heartbreak and pain? There she'd been, lying blissfully in his arms, believing every word from his lips. Sure he was coming to feel more for her, that she was enough to hold his attention. Teasing her mind's eye with more blissful nights, more exciting wonderful days. A future.

Enough.

On a long sigh she opened her eyes. Literally and figuratively.

Thank God she'd discovered the truth before she'd fallen in love with him. It was petrifying to think how close she'd come to doing just that.

'Serena?'

That deep voice, now perturbed, laced with concern, brought her attention back to where he stood.

Ah. Worried he'd hurt her, was he? Well, admittedly she'd love to rail and scream at him, but the little pride she had left was too precious. When she walked out of this suite it would be with her head high and dignity roiling inside her.

In fairness, he'd never pretended to be honourable with regards to women, and he'd warned her over and over. It was hardly his fault she'd strived to be a player, convinced she knew the rules, adamant that she'd come out unscathed. Instead she'd believed every expertly practised word. Misread every artful amorous touch.

How could she have been so naïve? Again! Lesson learned.

Moreover, right now the man teetered on the edge of a black abyss and she refused to be the one to push him over—she'd vacationed in hell before, and the view wasn't pretty.

Fear. Flashbacks. Nightmares. Menace surrounding you, burrowing into your soul. It didn't take a genius to figure out his erratic behaviour on and off the track in the last few months now either. Even his own survival was anathema to him. He wished he'd died too. Or more likely instead of Tom.

Come to think of it—dread curdled with her pique, making her stomach churn violently—it was entirely plausible that he was suffering from some kind of survivor's guilt. She'd read about that somewhere—probably a pamphlet in some clinic. And if that were true he needed help.

Somewhat reluctant to bathe in those beautiful eyes, she met them regardless. 'Forget about you and me. We both knew it was just sex and now it's over.' His throat convulsed but she was determined not to read anything into it. Bad enough that she'd imagined he flinched. 'I'll never be ashes in your wake, Finn. You know me better than that.'

'Good. That's good.' Relief soothed his taut features and he padded out onto the balcony and gripped the iron railing—white knuckles stark over black.

Why could she still feel his pain as if it was a living, breathing entity inside her, melding with her own? As if they were bonded somehow? Heavens, it *hurt*.

Serena glanced at the door leading to her suite and escape beckoned like an old friend. Her feet itched to run until she was too exhausted to feel anything. 'I should go,' she said abruptly. 'We both need some sleep.' If she felt battered and bruised from riding an emotional roller coaster he had to feel just as bad.

Which was likely why she couldn't move. Found herself ensnared in a vicious primal pull. Honestly, it was like turning her back on a wounded animal. She couldn't do it. Despite everything, she couldn't leave without trying one last time.

The problem was no matter what she said no words were going to convince him he wasn't to blame.

Frustration ate at her.

Leaving her angry aching heart indoors, she followed him onto the balcony. A crazy notion stirred up a hornets' nest inside her even as she winced at the risk, at how he'd react, and wondered if she could even manage it without shattering.

Easy, she came up behind him. 'Don't get a fright,' she said softly, echoing his sentiment from the cabaret at Montreal. A night from her dreams… With deft speed she slammed the door on her reminiscing. *Focus.*

His honed frame tensed.

'Finn, it's okay.' She laid her hands on his back, as gentle and calming as if he were a skittish colt. She smoothed them around his waist, wrapped her arms about him and pressed her cheek to the soft, freshly laundered fabric of his T-shirt.

'Serena,' he choked out, muscles flexing as his grip tightened on the rail.

After a *'Shh…'* that ripped her soul, his shoulders dropped and he began to ease.

'Let me?' she asked, tiptoeing her fingers beneath the hem of his T and tentatively inching the material upwards before she pulled back.

One look at the deep white criss-cross lines that marred the centre of his back, the puckered skin between his shoulder blades, and her chest ached viciously. Tears pooled, brimmed once more, and this time she let them fall. Unable to stop the rain. Surely she owed Tom nothing less.

Boys don't cry, Serena.

Well, this *girl* did.

Silent tears seared her swollen throat—for him, for Tom— as she leaned forward and tenderly kissed his back once, twice, before she rubbed her cheek against him gingerly, affectionately.

'Thank you,' she whispered, her voice as raw as her heart. 'Thank you for making his last days bearable. For protecting him for me. For trying to save his life.'

'Serena…' he breathed, almost longingly, as his big body trembled.

'Please don't let his death be for nothing. You have your entire life ahead of you. He'd want you to live it.'

Torso convulsing, he hung his head.

Enough. No more. It was all over now.

Serena let the fabric fall and trailed her fingers down his sides in goodbye. Then she turned and walked away with her head held high. Ready to fight another day.

CHAPTER FOURTEEN

THE SILVERSTONE CIRCUIT was an almighty roar and the chant of Finn's name from his fiercest homeland supporters rang in his ears as he stepped off the winner's podium with a farewell wave and shot through the crowd. He hadn't seen Serena since dawn, and the perpetual torment from his heart and conscience had him hurtling towards insanity.

He had to see her. Check she was okay. In truth he'd swear he could feel her pain, and his arms ached to hold her—hell, his entire body ached for her. Had done since the moment she'd vanished from his suite. Since she'd ripped his heart out by pleading with him to live his life. The way she'd touched him so affectionately, forgivingly, would stay with him always.

It had taken every ounce of strength he possessed to keep his hands fisted on the iron rail, not to turn around and reach for her. But no matter how hard he tried he couldn't believe for one second that she could forgive him. He was convinced the only reason she hadn't looked at him with hate in her eyes was because of the incredible night they'd shared. Or maybe he'd taken Tom's place in her world. A rebounding kind of need.

Eventually, when she realised that, she'd walk away—and he'd be in so deep it would kill him. He'd lose her. Just as he lost everyone he cared for. It was inevitable.

So, while it had torn him apart to sever their connection, he knew it was for the best. For both of them.

In and out of the Scott Lansing garage he went—his guts twisting at the barren space—before he jogged round to the back of the pits, where a myriad of luxurious motor homes were parked.

Smooth tarmac gave way to the crunch of gravel beneath his boots and dark shadows crawled eerily over the dirt, up over the high-gloss black paintwork of the fleet, as if thick, ominous clouds slowly usurped the sun. He shuddered...

Then crashed to a halt.

There stood Michael Scott, at the bottom of the steps to Finn's motor home, wearing an expression that weakened his knees.

Skin clammy, he clutched at his chest, felt the thrash of his heart against his palm. 'Wha...what's happened?' *No, please God no. Please let her be okay.*

'What you've got to understand about Serena, my boy, is that when her emotions get too big for her she runs. Always has, since she was a little girl.' Regret deepened his voice. 'Don't suppose it helped that she never had a mother in her life. I take it you told her everything?'

Finn tried to swallow as relief and heartache vied for space behind his ribs. She'd left him. 'Yes. Everything.' Then he remembered the phone call he'd taken before the race. 'The police in Singapore have just made an arrest.'

The older man took one step forward and laid a heavy hand on Finn's shoulder. 'Good. Now we'll get some justice. I know you tried to do right by my son.'

Finn locked on to Mick's sincere gaze, desperate to believe him.

'Serena must know it too, considering all your body parts are intact. Time to move on, Finn. Let it go.'

Maybe he nodded; he was too numb to be sure.

'Can't guarantee she'll come back in a hurry. Last time,

after the funeral, she was away months. She's not going to London. I know that much. But she did leave you this.'

Michael passed him a white envelope, with Finn's name a messy scrawl across the front, then patted his shoulder and sidestepped to walk past.

'By the way, she watched the race—asked me to say you were awesome out there and that you'll know what she means.'

A ghost of a smile touched his lips. Finally the woman uttered the words he'd tried to tease out of her for months. *Aw, man*, was it any wonder he adored her?

'Yeah, I do. Thanks, Mick.'

Bones weighted with dread, he plonked down on the top rung of his steps and thumbed the sticky flap of the envelope. Patience wasn't his strong suit and after two seconds he tore it apart, until her letter was in his hands.

On a long exhale he unfolded the crisp sheet and stared for a long moment, watching a fine drizzle dust the page.

Despite the chaotic churning of emotions inside him, her messy handwriting brought another smile to his lips. He missed her already.

Dear Finn,

I've never been one for goodbyes, but in the last few weeks you've helped me say another kind of good-bye—to Tom, so I could lay him to rest. Despite how our friendship came about you've been a friend to me in many ways, shown me much about my life, and I'd like to return the favour. So I'm calling in the wish you owe me.

Now, I know what you're thinking: my logic is a bit backward—how can my favour be your wish? But hear me out, okay?

It dawned on me earlier, when I left, that it doesn't matter if you never believe my word or believe in my forgiveness. What truly matters is that you learn to forgive yourself. Otherwise, and trust me when I say this, you'll never truly move on. Which is why I'm about to tell you something very few people know and I'm asking you to keep it close to your chest.

Long story short, as you would say, my first naïve crush was with one of Tom's friends. One who quickly turned hostile. And for a long time I blamed myself for what happened afterwards.

I should probably explain that I was young, with no women around, and not really sure how to handle boys. I figured I'd rather be one of them, and that was fine until I came to that awkward age where they began to treat me differently. Anyway, I was fourteen, and let's just say I liked this much older boy—or should I say man? He was Tom's age: nineteen.

He weaved his web, spun his lies, told me anything and everything—'I want you, Serena, I love you. Come meet me, Serena, I won't hurt you'—until I fell for him. I started to dress up—girly stuff—flirted a little, sneaked out with him, but I wasn't prepared for what came back at me.

Turns out 'no' didn't mean no with him.

The first time he tried to force me I managed to get away, and he persuaded me not to tell Tom or he would hurt him. Foolish, I know, but I think it's easy to believe anything at that age. Spider-Man comes to mind...

Anyway, he began to follow me, watch me from the shadows, and I was frightened for a long time. Then one night, during a huge party downstairs, he came up to my bedroom. He'd been drinking. He overpowered me. I was beaten up pretty bad, among other things, and I'm sure he would've gone all the way if Tom hadn't come in.

There was a huge fight and Tom got seriously

hurt—we thought he'd never drive again—but he pulled through. Of course he blamed himself for not reading the signs sooner, so you see I'm not surprised he asked you to watch out for me. He became very protective.

I saw a counsellor for many months and she tried to help me past it. In many ways she did. She made me accept that I didn't ask for it. I didn't deserve to be beaten. She certainly helped me to stand tall, but in reality I never truly moved on. I didn't completely let go of the blame. Of the thought that if I'd been braver, stronger, told someone sooner, Tom's health and career wouldn't have hung in the balance for so long.

I didn't let go of the idea that my behaviour was at fault. Because if I had I wouldn't have suppressed the woman I am inside.

You've shown me that, Finn. Helped me see so many things. But watching you struggle this morning I realised I'm still searching for peace.

Choices.

I'm choosing to let go, Finn. To forgive myself. I wish you would too.

At the bottom of this note is the number of the counsellor I saw, and my wish is that you go and see her, even if it's just the once. She can help you if you'll let her. It's strange, but I used to resent my dad for sending me—just thought he was palming me off on someone else. But I can see now. He was too close to the situation. Too emotionally involved. Which is why I think you need to speak to someone who isn't personally connected, you know?

You're a survivor. We both are. Let's make the most of this life we have. If not for us, for Tom.

Well, that's it, I guess. Take care of yourself and try not to crash my car, okay? Look after her. She

*may be a fiery bolt of lightning with a tough outer
shell but underneath...she's still just a girl.
Serena.*

The paper fluttered to the dirt as Finn leaned his elbows
on his knees and pressed the heels of his hands to his eyes.
Moisture smothered his palms as his shoulders shook in the
suffocating silence.

Underneath...she's still just a girl.

Idiot. He was such an idiot. He hadn't just hurt her; he'd
caused more damage than he'd ever dreamed possible.

Was it any wonder she'd stifled her femininity? And what
had he done? Given her confidence, told her she was unique
in every way, encouraged her to open up to him. And in the
next breath, fuelled by his own fears, he'd insinuated that
she was just another good-time girl who meant nothing to
him, expecting her to take it like the tough cookie she was—
and succeeded in stripping her raw. Forgetting for one moment that *underneath she's still just a girl.* One who'd been
tampered with when she'd been merely fourteen years old.

Against all the odds, no matter what life threw at her, she
came out fighting.

'You have no idea how proud I am of you,' he murmured,
to no one but himself, wishing she was here and he could
hold her. 'How brave and beautiful and strong and amazing you are to me.'

Finn rubbed his eyes, then clawed down his face.

Why did he keep hurting people? He knew not to let his
emotions engage. Knew he was like a loose cannon, made
bad choices. He'd left Eva to suffer, sent Tom to his death.
Now he'd hurt Serena too.

What was more she'd been betrayed barely out of adolescence and now Finn had done it a second time. She'd never
trust him again—not in a million years.

Any last vestige of hope died in his soul as she disappeared with his heart.

He needed more than some shrink. He needed a miracle.

One perfectly beautiful little miracle.

Every cell in his body screamed for him to go and find her, make it all better somehow. But what would he say? *I'm sorry* didn't sound anywhere near what she deserved. And that was all he had to offer. Apart from more hurt in the long run. He was messed up and he knew it. He also knew he was far better off alone.

He just had to hope she found the peace and happiness she deserved.

As for him, he had a wish to take care of.

He owed his girl nothing less.

CHAPTER FIFTEEN

Five weeks and two days later...

THE MONZA POST-RACE party was the epitome of Italian style and elegance, held in the vast courtyard of a lavish hotel. But the midnight sky, twinkling with diamanté brilliance, acted as the perfect ceiling and only served to remind Serena of a magnificent tent in Montreal.

Champagne spurted from a towering ice sculpture like an ivory waterfall, to pool and froth at the base. But the bubbly effervescence only struck a chord of the Silverstone Ball.

Closing her eyes momentarily, she breathed in the sweet calming scent of the wisteria draping the balconies overhead and turned to her dad. 'I have no idea how you talked me into this. I've only been back a few hours. I could be in my PJs, eating nachos and watching a movie right now.'

Instead she was a nausea-inducing swarm of anticipation in killer heels, trying to perfect a smile that said she was having a ball. All the while wondering if he would come, who he would bring, what she would say to him. So much for the blasé *oh-hi-how-are-you?* she'd been hoping for at tomorrow's meeting.

'Yes, well, frankly I was getting sick and tired of the "I *vhant* to be alone" Greta Garbo routine. I'll only let you hide for so long, Serena.'

'I wasn't trying to hide,' she hissed.

'Whatever you say, sweetheart.'

Serena sighed. She'd just wanted their first hello to be on equal ground, and she refused to think less of herself for that. Not after she'd spent weeks trying to get over the man she'd purged her soul for. Writing that letter had taken her back, splintered her defences, but the thought of him hurting, being in so much pain, had somehow outweighed her survival instincts. And if the tabloids were to be believed he was back on top form, oozing charisma with that legendary smile of his, so it was worth it to see him happy. Moving on.

True, seeing him with another woman had been…hard, but she'd needed that push to move on. Now she was just… peachy.

Which didn't really explain why the sight of her dad smiling devilishly at some curvy blonde sparked her off. 'I don't get this "variety is the spice of life" business. What exactly is so wonderful about variety when they all look the same? There's something cold about it. About them.'

She couldn't understand the appeal. Not compared to the hours of scorching bliss she'd experienced in Finn's arms— all the more intense for the way she'd felt, she was sure.

'That's the point. It doesn't mean anything. It's safe.'

'That's like going on a ghost train with your eyes shut. Going through the motions—'

'With none of the emotions. Exactly. For me, it's because I'll always love your mother. She was The One for me. All the others since were just flash and no substance. Safe. A way to ease the loneliness, I guess.'

Serena frowned up at him as the floor did a funny little tilt. When she'd been a little girl she'd often asked about her mum. He'd tried to talk about her, but as she'd got older she'd thought his struggle and avoidance meant he hadn't truly loved her. But clearly he'd loved her intensely.

A pang of bittersweet happiness eased the ache in her chest. To think it had been *her mother* who'd had the power to win his heart. It explained so much about him. She almost asked him for more, but this wasn't the time or the place. Instead she murmured, 'Never thought of it that way.'

Safe. Untouched. That suited Finn to perfection too, didn't it? The showman who wore his charming façade to veil the tortured man beneath. But, unlike her mum, Serena hadn't been enough to win his heart.

'Don't suppose you're thinking about Finn right now?'

'I'm doing nothing of the sort,' she said, casting him a dour look before she did something stupid like burst into tears. When she was supposed to be peachy!

His graphite eyes twinkled knowingly before his handsome face took on a contemplative look etched with remorse.

'I doubt I've given you much decent advice in your life. I was ill-equipped to deal with two young kids—especially you. That's something I'll always be sorry for, Serena. But when I lost her I had to...'

Her voice as raw as her throat, Serena quietly finished for him. 'Get up. Get busy. Move on.' For all their sakes.

He gave her a rueful smile. 'But let me tell you this. If you're anything like me, or all the Scotts before you, you'll get one shot at true happiness. If you think Finn's The One don't let him go without a fight.'

Serena bit her bottom lip to stop it trembling. 'I'm not interested.' It didn't matter how much she hurt, how much she wanted, she was never opening up again. 'Anyway, he's already moved on.'

'You sure about that? Because the man who came to see me yesterday, asking for some time off so he could go gallivanting to find...' he made inverted comma actions with his fingers '..."his girl" didn't look like he'd moved on to me.'

A paralysing ball of hope bounced in her chest and she swiftly batted it away. No more foolish daydreaming. 'He has "girls" on every continent. He's moved on, I'm telling you.'

'Positive? Because that same guy, who's just walked through the archway, clapped eyes on you and looks like he's been hit with a semi-truck, is on his way over.'

'Oh, my life.' She wasn't ready—nowhere near ready.

'So you might want to get rid of that deer-in-the-headlights look and bear in mind another of Garbo's sayings.'

Huh? 'Which is?'

'Anyone who has a continuous smile on his face conceals a toughness that is almost frightening.'

'And why should that affect me?'

'No smile tonight. I get the feeling the shackles are off. I hope you're ready for this sweetheart.'

Right now the only thing she was ready for was to launch herself over the twelve-foot stone wall encircling the courtyard. She would have done if she hadn't been wandering around Europe aimlessly for the last month, only to find herself in some café in Paris, nursing a lacklustre cappuccino and the realisation that it didn't matter how far she ran, her aching heart still lay inside her chest and the memories lingered. Peace was nowhere to be found and solitude just made the emptiness deeper. She had to face him. Prove to herself she was over him.

'How far?' Appalled by her serious case of the jitters, she nailed her feet to the paved slabs. *'How far?'*

An unholy glee lit up her father's graphite eyes. 'Thirty feet and closing.'

She stifled the urge to smooth her riotous mane, insanely grateful that she'd developed a fetish for dresses, and silently chanted an endless loop of, *He will not affect me. I am completely over him. He will not affect—*

'Good evening, Miss Seraphina Scott.'

Ohh, this was not good. 'This' being the hellish swarm of fireflies lighting up her midriff in a mad, wild rush at the mere sound of his rich, sinful drawl.

More than a little woozy, she focused on turning gracefully, determined not to fall at his feet. She took a deep breath, raised her chin, then pivoted on her entirely too adventurous heels…

And went up in flames.

Doomed. She was totally and utterly doomed.

Dressed in a sharp black custom-fit suit and a thin silk tie, as if he'd just stepped off a movie set, Finn St George struck a stunning pose of insolent flair. All potent masculinity and devilish panache.

Confident as ever. A little arrogant. A whole lot bold.

Pure joy lapped at her senses—she'd missed him so much.

All that deliberately unkempt dirty blond hair was now long enough to curl over the collar of his crisp white shirt and that face… *Oh, my life*, he was so amazingly beautiful.

No depraved gleam in those cerulean blues tonight. Fantastical as the idea was, she fancied those eyes were darkly intense, savagely focused on her—a hunter stalking the ultimate prey. After weeks of living a dull, aching existence her body came alive, as if it recognised its mate, and her heart fluttered, trying to break free from the confines of her chest—

Serena slammed the cage shut and stamped on the brakes of her speeding thoughts. She would *not* misread those practised looks or his artful words. Not ever again.

He made her vulnerable to him with a click of his übertalented fingers, but demons would dance with angels before he stole more of her heart or her pride. So she dug out the biggest smile in *her* arsenal and directed her voice to super-sweet.

'Hey, Lothario, miss me?'

He wanted her now. *Now!* Fiercely. Possessively. Permanently.

When Mick Scott had texted him twenty minutes ago— *Guess whose girl is here?*—Finn hadn't trusted his luck but had tossed some clothes on nonetheless.

Now if he could just get over the shattering bodily impact of his first sight of her in weeks maybe he could think straight. As it was he had claws digging into his guts, demanding he haul her into his arms, delve into those fiery locks and slash his mouth over hers. But he reckoned since he'd messed up so catastrophically that winning her heart was going to require some finesse.

Mick eased by, patted Finn's shoulder and murmured, 'Try not to mess it up this time.'

Finn swallowed. Hard. Then told himself to forget about his boss and focus on his future. His entire life wrapped in a sensational electric-blue sheath. If she'd have him. Forgive him. Let him love her. Because that was all he had—his love.

This was it. The greatest risk of all. Because nothing came close to the potent charge of adrenaline that barrelled through his system when he was within ten feet of her. Fifty championships wouldn't even come close.

Had he missed her?

'I certainly have, Miss Scott. In fact I can easily say I've been miserable since the moment you left.'

He'd been plunged back into another hellhole, this one definitely of his own making, and he was determined to rectify that, no matter how long it took.

Granted, his admission hadn't worked the way he'd hoped—not if the stunned flash of incredulity in her sparkling grey gaze was anything to go by. Even the two feet separating them was a hot whirlpool that snap, crackled and popped with her pique.

Aw, man, maybe he was playing this all wrong. But the truth was he was nervous. *Him.* The man who flirted with death and had practically invented the word *reckless*.

'Yeah, okay, which is why you've already moved on and couldn't even spare me a phone call.'

Finn shoved his hands into his trouser pockets in case he lost his tenuous grip and just kissed the living daylights out of her. 'I wanted to give you some time to figure out how you feel. It hasn't been easy for me, Serena. It's been bloody agonising. You have no idea how many times I drove to the airport—'

'Going on holiday, were you?'

If his guts weren't writhing in a chaotic mess he would smile. That sassy mouth drove him crazy. Always had. And clearly she'd re-erected those barriers of hers. Well, he'd just have to pull them down all over again. He was fighting to win, and Finn St George always won.

'Dance with me?' He held out his hand. 'Give me your first dance—the one we didn't share back at Silverstone. Please?'

The truth was he just wanted to hold her. If he could make her remember what they were like together maybe she'd give him a chance.

She took so long to make her decision—her flawless brow nipped as she scrutinised his face—that Finn was headed for an aneurysm by the time her dubious voice, said, 'Okay. One dance.'

Before she changed her mind he grabbed her hand and practically dragged her across the courtyard—weaving around tables to a space right at the back of the dance floor, dimly lit, semi-private and leading to the gardens beyond.

Then he wrapped his hands around her dainty waist and hauled her into the tight circle of his arms to sway to an Italian love ballad. *Perfect.* She felt amazing, and when her deliciously evocative scent wrapped around his senses the ice in his veins started to melt.

'Finn,' she squeaked. 'I can hardly breathe.'

'Breathing is highly overrated. Do you really need to?' This was bliss for him and, selfish as it was, he was taking what he could while he could. *To hell with that. You're gonna win her back—she isn't leaving you again.*

'Yes, I do. I...'

She softened against him, twined her arms around his neck, and that glorious frisson of pleasure and pain jolted his heart.

When he pulled her closer still, crushing her soft breasts to his chest, a moan slipped past her lips—the kind she made when she was naked and sprawled all over him. Blood rushed to his head, making him simultaneously dizzy and hard. Not to mention astoundingly possessive—which he figured must be the reason he put his big fat foot in it.

'Have you been…seeing anyone?'

The spark of her ire crackled in the air and she stiffened in his arms.

Seriously? Could he be making a worse job of this? Where was his famed charm and charisma? Gone. Obliterated. By a five-foot-four spectacular bundle of fire.

'You've got some nerve,' she whispered furiously. 'Spouting rubbish about missing me, accusing me of seeing someone else, holding me as if you're petrified I'm going to vanish into thin air when you couldn't even last three weeks!'

Reluctantly he pulled back a touch. 'Three weeks before what?'

'Quenching your carnal appetites,' she hissed.

Finn just shook his head. 'You've lost me, beautiful.'

'Does Hungary ring any bells? Your much publicised photographs with some flashy starlet were all over the front page, so don't give me any bull crap.'

He couldn't help it. He grinned for the first time in aeons. 'You're jealous, baby.' *Aw, man,* he was definitely in with a chance. She had to feel something for him. *Had* to.

Her gorgeous face got madder still. 'I am not jealous at all. I don't give a flying fig who you dance the horizontal tango with—and don't you *dare* call me baby.'

Damn. What had possessed him to suggest she was one of many? A woman who'd witnessed her own father go through women like rice puffs.

'I never touched that actress, beautiful. It just so happens that was the only gig I went to and the woman couldn't take the hint so I left. There's been no one since you. In fact, you're the only woman I've slept with in well over a year.'

Those impossibly long sooty lashes fluttered over and over.

'Oh…'

And when she softened once more victory was a balmy rush, blooming out all over his skin.

Needing her taste in his mouth, he stole a lush, moist kiss from her lips. 'What's more I've never called anyone baby but you, Serena. And I never will. Because you're mine.' Another kiss. Then another. 'All mine. Unique in every single way—'

Suddenly she wrenched from his hold, took a step back.

'You've never called anyone baby but me, Finn? So you either lied to me then or you're lying now. Either way, I'm not interested. I...I can't do this again with you.'

The pain darkening her grey gaze punched him in the heart.

'I don't know if I can trust anything you say. I don't even know if your touch is real.'

The blood drained to his toes and a cold sweat chased it. 'You can. I'll prove it to you—

'Look, I just flew in a few hours ago and I could do with some sleep. I'll see you tomorrow, okay?'

Before he could say a word she darted off, swerving around the other couples on the dance floor.

Finn scrubbed a hand over his face. Okay. Maybe he should give her more time. The problem was, he couldn't abide her thinking she meant nothing to him. He was beginning to realise he'd made another huge mistake in not going after her sooner. But he'd been broken and he'd wanted to be whole. For her.

Oh, to hell with it.

Finn caught her up halfway to the exit, mid-throng.

'Oh, no you don't,' he said, swerving to block her path. She looked up, all flushed cheeks and wide eyes. Yet he couldn't decide if she was astonished that he'd chased her or that he was garnering them an audience.

'I'll follow you to the far ends of the earth, Serena.'

As for the onlookers—if he had to unveil the real Finn

St George to the world, show them the vulnerable man beneath to win her back, so be it.

'You're not getting away from me this time. I let you run once because I was scared, but I won't make the same mistake twice. I've made too many mistakes with you and I'll be damned if I make another.'

Finn would swear he could have heard a pin drop.

Until she breathed, 'Scared?'

'Terrified. But I'm not any more. I love you. You hear that, baby? I. Love. You.' Then, in front of hundreds of guests, he cupped her astounded face in his palms and kissed her with everything he was. With all the love in his heart and the need roiling inside him. Until neither of them could breathe and her shock gave way to desire. To the incredible bond he could feel pulling at his soul.

'Tell me you feel this,' he whispered over her lips.

'I…I feel this.'

'This has never been a lie, beautiful.'

Now came the hard part, he acknowledged. Convincing her that he meant every single word.

Dazed and disorientated, Serena suddenly found herself being lowered to her feet beneath a secluded pergola in gardens enchanted by moonlight. The wolf whistles and the roar of the crowd still rang in her ears and her lips were swollen from the wild crush of his ardour…

'Did you really just do that?' He'd kissed her in front of everyone. She was sure he had. Then he'd carried her out of there. He must have.

Sucking in air, she inhaled the minty scent of dew-drenched leaves as Finn took a step back, his eyes dark with desire, gleaming with intent.

Heat skittered through her veins. She felt hunted, and it was the most sensational, awesome, stupendous feeling in the world. If only her pesky inner voice would cease whispering doubt because she'd been seduced by his charm before.

'Finn? You do realise that come tomorrow morning the whole world will know you've just told me...' She still wasn't sure she'd heard him right. Or perhaps the truth of it was she couldn't bear to hope. To dream.

'That I love you? Good. It's about time. Then everyone will know that you're off limits.'

His voice was thick and possessive and dominating and it made her shiver. 'And you too!'

'That's the point, Serena.' Tenderly, he stroked his knuckles down her cheek. 'Because until you start believing that I'm yours and you're mine we're going nowhere. Until you believe that you're the only woman in the world for me there'll always be doubt. I've lost your trust, and I need to win it back before it's too late and I lose you forever.'

The impact of his words, his touch, his closeness, was earth-shattering. 'Just be honest with me, Finn. That's all I want.'

'And that's what you're going to get. Always.' His chest swelled as he inhaled deeply. 'I let you believe our friendship had been because of a promise I made to Tom, but that was just an excuse I gave myself to be with you. To spend time with you. Truth is, I've always wanted you, Serena. Since the first moment I saw you. And when I was in that cell thoughts of you kept me going. Looking back, if you hadn't come to Monaco and burst into my life again I would be dead right now. Because I was headed that way. I thought it should've been me. Not Tom. I wished I'd died instead. Until you.'

He cupped one side of her face and she nuzzled into his touch. Insanely grateful that he was still here.

'And that made me feel guilty, because suddenly I wanted to live and I thought I didn't deserve it. Then I was falling for you, and I wanted your love and I knew I'd never have it. You asked me a question that morning: why I'd waited and waited to tell you the truth, all the while digging myself into a deeper hole, until it was too late.'

She gave him a little nod.

'I was scared. Scared out of my mind. Of losing any chance I'd ever have with you. Try telling the woman you love that you were responsible for her brother's death.'

Her defences splintered as her heart swelled and beat so hard she feared it would burst from her chest. He loved her. He really loved her.

'Oh, Finn, why didn't you just tell me that? Why make out that I meant nothing to you? You hurt me.'

'I know, and I'm sorry. But I was messed up. Just wanted to push you away. Didn't believe for one second you could forgive me, let alone feel the same. The guilt and pain was crippling me, Serena. It wasn't until I read your letter. Oh, baby, your letter.' He wrapped one hand around her nape and gently kissed her forehead. 'I'm so sorry you went through that. But the more I read it the more I realised that for you to trust me with your past you had to genuinely believe Tom's death wasn't my fault. It gave me hope you had feelings for me too. And when I thought about what you went through… I've never met anyone like you. You're so beautiful and brave and strong. You make me want to fight. Be a survivor. For *you*.'

She could barely speak past the enormous lump in her throat. 'I was so worried about you. Once I realised you had some kind of survivor's guilt I thought, *I'm going to lose him too*. I would've done anything to prove that I didn't blame you.'

He frowned pensively and brushed his thumb across his bottom lip in that boyish way he did sometimes. Uneasy. As if he wanted to ask her something.

Serena laid her hands on his chest, felt his heart pound beneath her palm. 'Finn?' God, she wished she was better at this man-woman thing.

He seemed to think better of it and said, 'I owed my girl a wish, so I went to meet this shrink.'

Serena smiled up at him. She knew she was beaming but she was so proud of him.

'We do this thing…the shrink and me…where I have to come up with worse outcomes. She said it was really difficult, except I had an answer in a nanosecond.'

'What did you say?'

'*You* could have been there too. *You* could've been taken from me too.'

'Oh, Finn.'

'So I've started being grateful for that, you know?'

That was it. Moisture flooded her eyes.

'Aw, baby, I'm sorry. I keep making you cry.' Leaning down, he kissed away her tears, dusting his lips over her cheeks.

'Anything makes me cry these days. It's not natural!'

'Don't tell me. Boys don't cry, right? *Wrong.* I cried on and off for days when my mum died. Couldn't understand the injustice of it all. She was the most loving, self-sacrificing woman you'd ever meet. The good people always die.'

'That's not true. *You* didn't die, Finn, and every day I'm grateful for it.'

'You are?' he asked, with that pensive stare she couldn't quite grasp. There was something oddly endearingly vulnerable about him.

'Every day,' she assured him.

'Let it go, you said. Make a choice. Forgive myself. And I am. I'm trying. But the fact is it isn't only Tom I have regrets over. I've carried guilt for years over abandoning Eva when my mother was diagnosed. I was so selfish. Only thinking about the next race. But when I look back, the truth was I couldn't take watching her die. Seeing pain and heartbreak tear through my family again. I went to see Eva a couple weeks back, to say sorry. She doesn't blame me, Serena, not one bit. She said I had to let it go, that life was too short.'

'I like her already.'

'You'll love her. Her and Dante. They've just had a baby boy and he's amazing, and when I watched the three of them—a perfect little family—all I could think of was you and how I wanted that with you. How I could easily give up everything—the racing, the risks—to have that with you. Only you.'

She gripped the lapels of his jacket in order to stay upright. 'You want me and you to…have a family? A home? Like…together?'

He gave a somewhat sheepish shrug. 'Well, yeah, a family would be nice—but only if you want to. I'll be happy just to make you mine. Okay, you look horrified. It's too soon. I'm jumping the gun—'

'No. No. You're not. I've just never thought that far ahead before. What was the point of hoping for something I'd never have? Guess I didn't think I was wife material.'

That, she realised, had been the problem all along. Her insecurities. If she was honest she'd never been able to wrap her head around Finn wanting her. So it had been easy to think his every word and every touch was a lie. To avoid the pain of disillusionment. Heartache. So she'd run before she'd got too deep. Though in reality it had been too late. She'd already fallen.

And now—now she could have it all. And she felt like dancing and skipping and whooping and being really girly.

She bounced on her toes. 'What does a wife do, anyway?'

'She designs spectacular cars and wears biker boots and funky T-shirts. At least *my* wife will. I love you just the way you are, baby girl. You're The One for me.'

Ohh, here came the tears again. 'I am?'

'Sure you are.' He speared his fingers into her hair, rubbed the tip of her nose with his. 'I won't lie to you. I'm still scared of something happening to you. Of giving you my heart without ever holding yours in return. But if you give me a chance to prove my love, to prove that we could be good together, that I won't let you down, I can win it. I can win your heart. Just give me a chance.'

That shadowed gaze was back and she gasped, realising how intensely vulnerable he felt. 'Oh, Finn, I'm sorry. I'm such an idiot. You don't have to win it. It's yours. I'm madly, insanely in love with you.'

His head jerked so fast she reckoned he'd have whiplash in the morning. '*What?* That's impossible.'

'I promise you it is completely, utterly, absolutely possible.' She sank her fingers into the hair at his nape and pulled him down for a kiss. 'I literally fell for you when I tumbled in your window all those years ago. But you were a virtual carbon copy of my dad and I knew the rote. A boatload of broken hearts and weakened women in your wake. I hated you for making me vulnerable to that. But deep down I've always wanted you. Me all awkward and tomboyish, you all confident and sinfully beautiful—and, as it turns out, wild and honourable, with the ability to be completely and utterly selfless.'

'Hell, Serena, you scare the crap out of me when you say stuff like that. Then again, you always have.' He nuzzled into her neck. Breathed her in. 'Are you sure you…love me?'

'One billion per cent sure. Only you can make me feel like a woman. Only you can make me feel amazing. I love who I am with you. You're everything to me. I'm not saying it's going to be easy—life never is. We have millions of choices to make and sometimes we'll trip and fall and make mistakes. But we'll get through it all. We'll make it work. Together.'

Lifting his head, he ensnared her with a fierce, ardent gaze. 'You were designed especially for me—you know that? All my life I've taken risks on the track, but never with my heart. I never wanted to get close to anyone just to lose them. I didn't want to be touched—' He took her hand and laid it over his heart. 'In here. But you do more than touch me, Serena. You *own* me.'

Trust and love, hope and joy filled the warm air between them and she jumped into his arms. 'I'm yours. Take me home. Now. Please.'

With a sexy smile that made her insides gooey, he coaxed

her legs around his waist. 'That would be my place,' he said, with a hint of delicious possessiveness that promised a night to remember.

'That's what I said. I've never known what home felt like. What it was. I've been searching for it for years. Peace. Perfect blissful peace. I've finally found it, and it's in your arms.'

Finn tightened his hold and began to walk her into a future she couldn't wait to begin.

'And that's where you'll always be. Forever.'

* * * * *

DIAMOND DREAMS

ZURI DAY

To the wine country of Temecula, and especially winemaker David Vergari and media director Linda Kissam of Thornton Winery. The private tour and detail-laden interview were great, the wine…even better! And to my editor, Glenda Howard, who helped make this novel such a pleasure to write. La'Chaim!

Chapter 1

"I'm proud of you, Diamond," Donald Drake said as he continued to flip through the latest report that she had provided. "The sketches are fantastic, and your attention to detail continues to be impressive. These innovative interior-design ideas are going to make ours one of the best resorts in California."

"One of the best resorts, period," Diamond corrected. "I told you that I could do it, Dad. I'm glad you trusted me with such a major aspect of our expansion." Diamond beamed from her father's words of praise. She considered herself the ultimate daddy's girl and never wanted to disappoint. And being the only girl in the family made her quite competitive with her two brothers for their father's attention.

"I don't know how much trust had to do with it," Dexter Drake drawled. Diamond's always lovable yet sometimes annoying younger brother reared back in his chair and placed his interlocked fingers behind his head. "I think it was all of that whining and begging you did that finally wore him down."

"I believe the correct verb is *negotiated,* dear brother. Mine was the best proposal submitted, period." Even as she said this, Diamond knew that there was a thread of truth to Dexter's statement. Her older brother, Donovan, handled most of the construction projects and had overseen the first phase of this one. It had taken a lot of research, idea submissions and—okay, maybe a little whining and begging—to convince Donald, the company's founder, board president and chief operating officer, that when it came to the interior-design work and final stages of construction for Drake Wines Resort & Spa, Diamond was the woman to oversee the job.

Dexter continued his needling. "Was it the best proposal? Or just the only one submitted twenty times?"

"Ha! Come on, Diamond. Fess up," Donovan said with a chuckle. "You did send that thing in several times."

"I sent in several addendums to keep everyone up-to-date on the evolving ideas and projections," Diamond retorted, with a tilt of her chin. "Which you would know, Mr. VP of Sales, if you pulled your head out of the books long enough to see what's happening with the rest of the company."

Donovan calmly rubbed his goatee. "I don't miss a thing that happens around here, baby sis. Believe that."

"How could you," Dexter queried, "with those Dumbo-size ears on the side of your head?"

Diamond laughed as Donald frowned. "Watch yourself," he said, his narrowed eyes fixed on Dexter. "Donovan's ears are shaped like mine."

"Dad, I'm not sure that is something I'd be pointing out," Diamond said, still laughing.

"Sister, it's something that he has no *need* to point out." Dexter's dark brown eyes twinkled and his brow wriggled as he looked pointedly at his father's ears and then at the replicas on his big brother.

Donald couldn't keep the frown on his face any longer. He burst out laughing. It had always been this way among his children: friendly teasing and healthy competition all held together with huge doses of love. From the beginning, he and his stay-at-home wife, Genevieve Drake, had raised their children to be a part of the business and had involved them in every aspect of their award-winning vineyard almost from the time they could walk. And while each person had their specific job title, theirs was a working knowledge of the business as a whole, and they were encouraged to multitask along those lines. This is how Diamond, the director of marketing and public relations, was now overseeing the major expansion project of turning Drake Vineyard into Drake Wines Resort & Spa.

Donovan was the most serious among the siblings, and no one was surprised when he steered the conversation back to business. "Do you believe the job will stay within the latest budget you've presented?"

"I'll have a better answer for you after I meet with the interior designer—" she looked at her watch "—which is happening very shortly. So if there are no more questions, gentlemen, I need to go."

A few minutes later, Diamond sat at her desk, speaking with her assistant before heading out of the office. "Kat, I'm going to the site to check out the construction, not the *candy*," she chided, though a smile belied Diamond's sternly delivered words. "Man candy" is what Kathleen Fitzpatrick had deemed the construction workers who'd invaded their space. For months, a crew of around fifty men had been hard at work building the five-star facility that upon completion would include restaurants, a bar, lounge, day spa, gym, expanded gift store, executive offices and boutique hotel.

"Besides," Diamond continued, "I'm not into candy right now. I'm watching my wait, spelled *W-A-I-T*." Kathleen fixed Diamond with a chagrined look. "I'm just not ready to jump back into the dating game." She reached for a batch of drawings and placed them in her briefcase. "And even if I were… there's no time for that. Duty continuously calls."

"Pretty good speech but that's hogwash and you know it." At fifty-six years old, Kathleen was not only Diamond's assistant, but sometimes she felt like a second mother to the woman who was twenty-plus years her junior. And after many years as a dedicated Drake employee, she felt comfortable speaking exactly what was on her mind. "It's been two years, girl. How long are you going to let that jerk of an ex-boyfriend run your life? Oh, my, did I say *run?* I meant *ruin!*"

"Ha! Stop exaggerating, Kat, before you set that Irish blood to boiling. My ex, whose name is no longer worthy of being uttered from my lips, has not ruined my life. He just helped to enhance my search skills and made me very selective. Right now, my man's first name is Resort and his last name is Spa."

"Go ahead. Hide behind your pesky professional obligations."

"You call a thirty-million-dollar renovation pesky? You go, girl!"

"But just remember," Kat continued, not missing a beat or taking the bait. "You're not getting any younger. You may have pushed it to the back of your mind, but I remember a young woman who not so long ago was eagerly looking forward to marriage and motherhood. The right man to make that happen is still out there."

"Amid the glass, bricks and plywood that currently litter our vineyard?"

"No, sweetie, perhaps amid the blood, sweat and mass of

muscles moving that stuff around! I'm not saying you should marry one of the workers, but you should at least take a look. I have and let me tell you…there's some honeys in the bunch."

Diamond's phone rang. It was just as well that the conversation end and that she take her mind off men—her sore spot—and put it back on work—her salvation. Besides, when it came to those particular M&Ms—men and marriage—there was no use arguing with her trusty assistant. Kathleen had wed at eighteen and borne five children. In her mind one hadn't lived until they'd snagged a man, had a child, adopted a dog and got a house surrounded by a white picket fence. She'd been married longer than Diamond had been alive. So when it came to heartbreak and breakups, what did she know?

"That was the designer," Diamond said after completing the call. "She's at the site. I'll be back in less than an hour."

The clicking of Diamond's four-inch heels punctuated the air as she walked to her parking space. She unlocked the door of her shiny sports coupe and slid inside. Belatedly realizing that the heat index in sunny Temecula, California, had risen, she shed her suit jacket, grabbed a pen in the cup holder and hastily placed her shoulder-length dark auburn hair into a chignon. The construction site was less than a mile away from Drake Wines' executive offices. As she drove down the picturesque lane lined with colorful maple trees boasting red, orange and yellow leaves in the autumn sun, Diamond knew her focus should be on windows, tiles and color swatches and making sure that every aspect of the job to which she'd been entrusted was being executed to perfection. Instead, it was on man candy.

Chapter 2

Jackson "Boss" Wright leaned back in his large black executive chair with a satisfied smile. He and his team had done it again—outsmarted and outbid the big boys. Boss Construction had just won a lucrative contract for a downtown development in Chicago, Illinois. He couldn't wait to sit down with his team and fine-tune the plans, but first he needed to fly to Chicago for another meeting with the executives behind this combination shopping mall and office complex that would include a soaring edifice rivaling the Willis Tower. Jackson turned on his electronic calendar even as he reached for the speaker button on his office phone. At the same time, his office door opened and his assistant walked in. She was not smiling.

"We got another one," she said without preamble.

Jackson heaved a heavy sigh. Without asking, he knew what she meant. "Let me see it."

Marissa Hayes, Jackson's loyal assistant of six years, approached his desk, her outstretched hand containing a single sheet of paper. Jackson scanned it quickly. The note was short and succinct—as had been all the others.

The bigger they are, the harder they fall. You think you've gotten pretty big, huh? Mr. Big-Time Construction, Mr. Millionaire Business Owner. Enjoy it while you can. Because your days at the top are numbered...just like the days of your life.

Jackson casually tossed the piece of paper aside. He remained purposefully nonchalant, not wanting to upset Marissa more than this and the previous letters already had. "This is, what, the third or fourth one?"

"Fifth," Marissa somberly responded.

"Place it in the file with the others." Jackson scrolled the electronic calendar with his finger. "I need you to schedule meetings with all relevant parties of the Chicago project, including the mayor, if he's available. Then book a flight for the evening before."

"Returning when?"

"Either the evening of the last meeting or, if it's a dinner meeting, the next day's first flight." Jackson placed his iPad aside and walked over to a drafting table.

"So that's it?"

"What else is there? You already know to book me at the Ritz-Carlton Chicago, rent the car from—"

"Not the trip, Boss. I'm talking about the letter."

"What about it?"

"How long are you going to let these threats come before you do something about it?"

"What do you propose I do?"

Marissa worked hard not to let the exasperation she felt come out in her voice. "Call the police, hire an investigator, I don't know...but something!" So much for masking frustration. Even a blind man could have seen her chagrin.

Jackson noted the fear in Marissa's eyes. He didn't share it, but he didn't blame her. The first letter had arrived approximately two months ago, right after he'd ended a short-term affair. To say that the woman had been less than pleased was putting it mildly. She'd all but told him—in fact, she'd *actually* told him—that he'd regret the day he let her go. At first, he'd thought the letters were from her. But then again, it could be a former worker or subcontractor. He'd had to fire a few bad apples over the years. Maybe someone was still smarting from their termination—or being left off a job. He'd even considered the competition he'd beat out for the past few contracts. While the idea seemed highly unlikely, the construction business was a very competitive one. Boss Construction had landed several sweet deals in the past five years, outmaneuvering some pretty heavy hitters along the way. When billions of dollars were at stake and the national economy still shaky at best, who knew what companies were capable of? And finally there was Marissa's observation: that the letters began arriving shortly after he'd been featured in *Black Enterprise* magazine. The article, not to mention the accompanying photos, had resulted in a deluge of extra publicity—and fan mail. Maybe someone from his past had read it. Maybe someone from the life and the lifestyle he'd worked so hard to leave behind was trying to drag him back into it. But he wondered who would want to do that. And why? He'd left his old life more than a decade ago. Jackson wasn't so much concerned for himself as he was for those around him. For the first time, he fully acknowledged the potential extent of the threats. Damage could not only be done to him but to anyone in his offices. Marissa was right. It was time to take action.

"Call Abe," Jackson said, removing his jacket as he walked toward the walk-in closet at the back of the room. Abe Swartz was not only Jackson's attorney but a longtime friend. "Tell him we need a private investigator."

"Should I tell him why?" Marissa asked.

"Yes."

A moment later, Jackson stepped out of his office dressed in jeans, a T-shirt and work boots.

Marissa smiled as she eyed her supervisor's confident strides. She knew this routine. Jackson played the tough guy, and he was a typical alpha male. But he also had a huge heart, one that worried about those around him, those for whom he felt personally responsible. The anonymous threats were bothering him more than he let on. "Going to burn off some nervous energy?"

Jackson stopped at the outer office door, his hand on the knob. "Nervous? Do I look nervous? I'm going to engage in one of my favorite pastimes…working alongside my men."

Chapter 3

Man candy. These were the words that came to mind as soon as she saw him. They'd exited a small building and now stood outside. *Who is he?* quickly followed that thought. As Diamond and the interior-design team had walked the floors of what would become the freestanding wine shop, she'd casually eyed the hardworking men. A couple she'd seen were buffed and toned, but others had average bodies and equally average looks. One or two had smiled and waved, but none had dared approach her. She'd smiled when she saw one worker nudge another after he'd surreptitiously winked at her. She figured her brothers had been their usually overprotective selves, warning the men to stay away from their little sister—no matter that she was the middle child or that said "little" sister stood five foot nine in stocking feet, with a full Beyoncé-like build and curves in all the right places. Growing up, she'd gone toe-to-toe with her brothers more than once, and until height and muscle replaced scraped knees and baby teeth, she'd pretty much held her own. Yet when it came to her and the opposite sex, the Drake line of defense was legendary. Every man she'd dated since the age of sixteen had come under intense and biased scrutiny. But she wasn't interested in dating.

No interest. Too busy. I'm hardly even aware of these sweaty, shirtless, sexy men. Or of the gorgeous man now eyeing her openly. Yeah. Right. And Mona Lisa was a man.

"Jackson Wright," Taylor said, when she noticed her last two sentences spoken to Diamond had gone unheard. There was a reason Taylor Stevens was one of the country's top interior designers. She had an uncanny eye for detail that missed nothing.

"I'm sorry?"

"The man you're totally aware of while trying hard to act as though you're not noticing him? His name is Jackson Wright."

Diamond tried for a quick recovery. "I don't know what you're talking about."

"If you mean you don't know about the stone foyer I was speaking of, you're right. Or the major design change I just mentioned. You haven't heard a word I've said. But don't worry. It's totally understandable. The first time I saw him my reaction was the same. But fair warning. I've heard that he's known for leaving women speechless and taking their breath away…among other things."

Other things like what? Heart, soul, virginity? Diamond did not voice these questions. She didn't want to appear interested in something that for her held absolutely no interest. Like human gods and whatnot. Diamond's appearances in and around the construction site had been rare. But one thing was for sure: she'd never seen this god, uh, guy before. He had a face—not to mention a body—that one would not forget.

She shifted her eyes away from the tall, commanding stranger. It was the only way she could refocus on the task at hand. *What is he...six-three, six-four?* She frowned, surprised that her thoughts had not shifted along with her body. So much for out of sight, out of mind. In less than two minutes, this man had gotten under her skin, and truth be told... Diamond wanted to get under him.

This surprised her. Diamond Nicole Drake was a strong, powerful woman, healthy enough but not normally given to forceful, almost primal, sexual urges. She knew how to focus; *discombobulated* would rarely if ever be used to describe her. As a high-powered executive in the multimillion-dollar dynasty her dad had created, she was a woman used to being in control and demanding respect. Well, she wanted to demand something, all right, and didn't care if it seemed the least bit disrespectful: a little rendezvous with Mr. Muscles. Private meeting. After hours. She'd even pay overtime.

Get it together, sistah! Why was she acting like she'd never seen a handsome man before? She had three of those in her immediate family. She'd grown up with fine men and dated them, too. Something about this construction worker unnerved her, and she wasn't exactly sure how she felt about it. What she did know for sure was that nothing was going to take her focus off of making Drake Wines the chic, upscale resort she'd envisioned. And speaking of visions, the one just over Taylor's shoulder was exactly what Diamond needed to bring her mind back to the singularly important task at hand—work.

With eyes still on the scene across what would become the resort courtyard, Diamond spoke to Taylor. "I'll be right back." Her long strides quickly ate up the distance between her and the group of men lounging on the ground. One was playing a video game, another two were checking out a sports magazine while a fourth was busy texting away. While still a couple yards away, she demanded, "What's going on here?" The men looked up, but before any of them could speak she looked at her watch and continued. "It's two o'clock in the afternoon, way past lunchtime. And you're reading magazines and playing video games?" She pushed her sunglasses from her face to the top of her head. "Really? Are you serious?"

"Diamond, we—"

"Do I know you?" Diamond asked the man who'd been texting on his cell phone. "Because in the workplace, unless otherwise specifically indicated, I am addressed as Ms. Drake."

Mr. *Sports Illustrated* tried next. "Ms. Drake, we—"

She held up her hand, deflecting further comment. "Never mind with the excuses. Where is your boss?"

Mr. Video Game pointed behind her. "He's right there."

Diamond turned, took one step and ran into a wall—otherwise known as the chest of Jackson Wright.

"Whoa!" Jackson reached out to steady a stumbling Diamond.

"Aw!" Diamond fell into Jackson's arms. *Is it me, or did the earth just quake?*

Later, Diamond would wonder about the tangible jolt of electricity that raced up her spine before coursing through her nether parts. But she gave no thought to that as she quickly put distance between herself and Jackson.

"Is there a problem?" Jackson asked, removing the large hand from around the soft arm he'd just steadied and crossing his arms over a massive chest.

"I'd say that's obvious," Diamond answered, crossing her arms, as well. "Your men are slacking on the job, and that is totally unacceptable."

"My men," Jackson began, his voice low and firm, "are on their lunch hour."

Diamond raised a skeptical brow. "At two in the afternoon?"

"That's right. We knew that Taylor would be conducting a walk-through and wanted to get to a certain point in the work before we stopped. And since these men will also be working past their usual cutoff time, this later lunch will help them get through what for some will be a twelve-hour day." Diamond's chin rose a notch as she continued to look at one of the most amazing examples of mankind she'd ever seen in life.

"They work very hard." Jackson's eyes narrowed as he awaited an answer—correction: an apology.

Diamond offered a different point of view. "How hard they've worked will be determined during the walk-through. And late lunch or not, playing video games and reading magazines on the job is not a good look."

"With all due respect, when on their lunch hour, my men can do whatever they want as long as it's legal."

When it came to the vineyard, it was a rare moment that someone challenged Diamond unless their last name was Drake. And when it came to nerve, Diamond realized that the man standing in front of her had plenty of it. And so did she, which was why he was going to get a serious piece of her mind. But realizing there was an avidly interested audience listening on, she decided now was not the time. Taking a deep, calming breath, she responded, "You may be over these men, but I am over this project. My name is—"

"I know who you are, Ms. Drake. And I also know California labor laws. That's part of my job." He extended his hand. "I'm Jackson Wright. The—"

"I know who you are," Diamond interrupted, paying him back for not letting her finish. She knew it was childish, unprofessional and something she'd probably not even do with her irksome brothers, but she seemed unable to stop this man from pushing her buttons. "You're the supervisor. Listen, I need to walk the site, but I'd like for you to call my assistant and set up a time to meet as soon as possible. There are some things we need to discuss."

Diamond started to walk around Jackson, but he fell into step beside her. "We'll make the appointment, but I'd actually like to handle the first part of the walk-through."

Diamond stopped. "Why?"

"To explain some of the technical aspects of the electrical installations, as well as share some thoughts I have for the restaurant and lounge atriums."

The last thing Diamond wanted was to spend additional time with Jackson Wright. His authoritative audacity intrigued her even as it irritated her. He had her thinking and feeling things she'd locked down deep.

And then fate intervened.

Chapter 4

Taylor walked up to where Jackson and Diamond stood, her face a mask of worry as she talked into her cell. "Hold on," she said into the phone before looking at Diamond. "This is my assistant designer with a crazy emergency. Can you give me ten minutes to deal with this before we begin?"

"No problem," Jackson said, even though he hadn't been the one addressed. "I'll show Ms. Drake around."

Diamond was two seconds from going off on this presumptuous jerk, but her professional persona appeared unruffled. She turned to Taylor. "No worries, Taylor. Join us when you're done."

She really doesn't know who I am. This was Jackson's thought as they walked toward the second largest building in the new architectural scheme. For now, Jackson felt it unimportant to enlighten her. Strange things often happened when women found out he was the owner of Boss Construction: visions of wedding bells and baby booties often began to dance in their heads. Too bad he wasn't the marrying kind, because worse things could happen than having this feisty beauty in bed every night. But having her there for a night, a week, a few months even? It was a possibility, even with her head-strong personality. She was almost worth potentially losing a client over, but his uncle John had taught him nothing if not this one thing about business: don't play where you eat.

And then he went on flirting as if he'd never known Uncle John. "I've been involved in this project from the beginning, pretty lady, and would love to show you around. Let's start at the heart of the construction." Without waiting for an answer, he gently captured Diamond's elbow and steered her toward the large structure that when completed would be Temecula wine country's newest hotel. The restaurant, bar, lounge, gift store and retail offices would make up the ground floor.

Diamond ignored both the flirtatious comment and the shiver that ran down her spine at Jackson's touch. Instead, she lifted her chin and called on the age-old strength that was the Drake resolve: the power that had allowed her great-great-grandfather to not only participate in the Gold Rush but to become wealthy because of it; that had helped her great-grandfather stand his ground and keep hundreds of acres of land when those on both sides of the law tried to steal it from him; that had given her grandfather the foresight to turn many of those acres into top-quality, grape-producing vine-yards; and that had guided her father's vision into what was now the Drake dynasty—an immensely profitable, award-winning vineyard that was the envy of winemakers from Italy to France and Spain to Northern California. *He's just a man, flesh and blood. His presence is affecting me this way only because I'm sex-deprived,* Diamond thought, rationaliz-ing the crazy attraction she was feeling for the man walking beside her. *That reality—not his good looks, bulging muscles or the way his butt fills out a pair of jeans—is why Jackson*

Wright is affecting me so. She shifted the purse that was over her left shoulder, deftly removing her skin from his touch.

Beside her, Jackson's thoughts followed a similar path... the one involving butts and bodies, that is. He marveled at the magnetism between them, thinking of how quickly he could palm the booty that had grabbed his attention as soon as Diamond had turned to speak with the designer. It was her perfectly curved derriere that had caused him to cut off his foreman in midsentence and make a beeline for the attractive woman across the way. Unfortunately, what he'd heard coming out of her mouth as she addressed the workers wasn't nearly as attractive as her round backside. But Jackson wasn't deterred. He could handle a strong woman because he was a strong man. And once he got her in bed, he determined, he'd show her a different kind of power altogether.

"Hold on, let me get you a hard-on, I mean, a hard hat. *Hat,*" he emphasized before quickly walking away. He walked toward a group of men huddled over a floor plan laid out on a truck hood. Diamond pondered how to deal with her uncanny attraction to someone she'd obviously be working with from here on out, even as she noticed how the men seemed to stand at attention as Jackson approached. They listened intently as he spoke with them. Then one of them reached into a crate and pulled out a hard hat. Jackson nodded his thanks and returned to Diamond's side.

"You seem to command a lot of respect," Diamond said as they continued walking toward the tall building. "Are you the supervisor or the foreman?"

"I'm in charge" was Jackson's noncommittal answer. "Put this on," he continued as they stepped inside the massive doorway and into a large, airy foyer.

"Is this really necessary? Most of the foundation and walks look almost complete."

"But they're not. Besides, everybody on-site wears a hard hat. That's the rule."

"You're not wearing one," Diamond responded sarcastically.

Jackson winked, blessing her with a smile. "I'm a rule breaker."

Diamond ignored the squiggle that went directly through her core in no time flat and refused to acknowledge the long, curly lashes that framed the dark brown eye that had winked at her, or the straight white teeth behind thick, cushy lips. She thought of those lips touching hers and used unresolved anger to push desire away. "We need to get something straight," she said, stopping as soon as they were out of sight of the men. "Don't ever question my word in front of your workers. And don't ever speak to me again in a tone of disrespect."

"Respect is earned," Jackson instantly retorted, rising up to his full six feet five inches. "And it's reciprocal. You respect me and my men, and we'll respect you."

"I beg your pardon?" Diamond was incredulous.

"You don't have to beg, Diamond. Just listen." His tone was so authoritative that she stopped talking in spite of herself. "The guys out there are men, not boys. This is work, not school. They were on their lunch hour, not recess. When they tried to explain this, you shut them up with a wave of your hand. Now, I don't know how you do it in the executive offices, but out here that's not how we get down." He stared at her without flinching, his eyes cool, unblinking.

Diamond stared back—and blinked first. "Perhaps I did jump to conclusions. But with the kind of money we're spending, we have the right to expect hard work and get it."

"You are getting what you're paying for," Jackson said, his tone softer as he once again touched Diamond's arm and guided her farther inside the structure. "And more. Come on in, and you'll see what I mean."

They walked through the foyer and into what would become the restaurant. "This is gorgeous," she gushed, shifting her eyes and thoughts from the brawn beside her to the beauty of the building, and once again removed her arm from his touch.

"Yes," Jackson replied, eyeing Diamond. "It is."

Diamond ignored the obvious come-on and stepped inside the main dining area. "The natural light from those large windows makes this space seem even bigger." Her tone was sharp, almost curt, and strictly business. "But they're going to allow in a lot of heat, as well. It gets very hot here in the summer, especially August and September. Even with stellar air-conditioning that might be a problem."

"These are special windows," Jackson explained, relaxing as he settled into his element. "They become tinted in extreme sunlight and temper the heat. Diners will still be able to take in the magnificent view yet not experience discomfort due to extreme heat or cold. The heating and cooling system that we've installed is state-of-the-art and will continually adjust to maintain whatever temperature is programmed into the computer. And these," Jackson continued, running his hands along the smooth, stone walls, "will also serve to both keep out the cold and...bring in the heat." Jackson made no move to hide his desire as his gaze openly raked Diamond's physique.

Diamond spun around, her chin lifting along with her ire. "Are you always this impertinent when speaking to a client? Or have you forgotten that that is who I am, a *client,* not some piece of meat to ogle like a rabid dog!"

Bow wow wow, yippee yo, yippee yay, baby! Her haughty nature turned him on, not off, and stimulated that part of him that liked a good challenge. He raised a brow as he stared back at her, noting how her ample chest heaved with her deep, calming breaths. He wanted to experience this spunkiness in a totally different way. Jackson's resolve to do so strengthened, even as his tactics changed. "I'm sorry. You're right. I'm out of line. But you're a very beautiful, desirable woman. I'd have to be blind not to find you attractive and dead not to react. It was just a little harmless flirtation, but again, I apologize."

"How harmless would it be if I reported you to the owner? I am here in a *professional* capacity, and I expect to be treated in a *professional* manner. Is that understood?"

"Completely," Jackson responded. Still, his eyes smoldered as he answered, and his wide-legged, crossed-arms stance suggested that he wasn't in the least bit afraid of being reprimanded. "Shall we continue, or would you prefer to do the tour with someone less intimidating?"

Diamond was not known for being a neck-rolling, hand-on-hip kind of sistah, but his comment almost provoked both actions. "What did you say?"

Throwing her off guard by changing courses yet again, Jackson reverted to a trait that more than once had saved his life—bravado. "You heard me. You're as attracted to me as I am to you. And that attraction, not my flirtation, is what's upsetting you."

"You have *got* to be kidding," Diamond countered, less angry with his insubordination than the fact that he'd hit the nail on the proverbial head. "Obviously someone has told you that you're God's gift to women...and you believed them."

Jackson's grin was cocky yet genuine. "I've been considered a present a time or two."

"Well, the only thing that's a wrap right now is this conversation. You might want to brush off your résumé because after I have a little chat with the owner you'll probably be unemployed." Diamond turned and headed for the door.

"Wait," Jackson said, reaching out and stopping her. She looked down at the hand squeezing her arm and up into pleading eyes. "Please," he continued, releasing her, while imagining the confusion and laughter that would ensue among his men if she went out there demanding to speak to the owner. "I promise to behave." Now it was Diamond's turn to cross her arms. Her look showed that she didn't believe him. "I need this job," he finished.

"Then you need to climb out of your Neanderthal cave and realize that the days of women's butts being patted in the workplace and sexual innuendo being the standard are long gone."

"Got it."

"I hope you do. Because one more ill-mannered remark and you're history."

"I'll be the perfect gentleman from here on out."

"See that you do." With that, Diamond turned and headed back through what would eventually be the dining room and into the future top-of-the-line kitchen. Jackson answered her questions, professionally and knowledgeably, showing a strong command of the entire project as they moved from the restaurant to the gift shop, then down the hall to the retail offices. Finally, they crossed the lobby and entered the lounge that was situated across from the restaurant. They crossed the Plexiglas-covered dance floor, part of which would house an aquarium, to an expansive DJ booth—one of the few parts of the room that looked completed. Diamond walked up to a large control board. "What's all this?" she asked.

"Magic," Jackson simply replied. "This system allows the controller to create whatever atmosphere that's desired, whether its disco, blue light in the basement, rave, holiday."

Diamond lightly ran her hands over the knobs. "Looks complicated."

"It is." Jackson closed the distance between them. "May I?" he asked, stepping up to the controls and directly beside

Diamond. She nodded and took a step away from him. "I was a DJ back in my college days. And a bit of a geek."

Diamond said nothing, although she thought that "geek" and "Jackson" in the same sentence sounded like bad English.

"This controls the lighting," he began, his voice the epitome of expertise. "See how it goes from bright to dim? And we can also adjust the colors, bounce them off the walls, ceiling, floors or a combination of the three." Diamond watched as Jackson's large, tapered fingers deftly moved from one button to the next. "There are currently eight thousand songs programmed into this computer," he continued, taking a step toward Diamond to punch a button in front of her. "Check this out." Jackson leaned forward and unconsciously placed a hand on her waist. "I'm sorry," he said, quickly removing it. Diamond immediately missed his touch. He turned on a computer, entered a few commands, and within seconds a list of music genres filled the screen. "The sound system is incredible. What type of music do you like?"

"All kinds," Diamond replied. Jackson clicked on a link and began scrolling through songs. "Especially upbeat," she quickly added. The lights were dim, and the last thing Diamond needed was a love song to conjure up images of a certain male body, sans clothing, hard and ready for love.

Jackson flashed a knowing smile. He clicked on an album cover, and soon the sounds of music filled the room. Jackson played with the controls and psychedelic colors bounced off the walls. He flipped another switch, and smoke began swirling down from the ceiling.

"Wow!" Diamond said as she looked at the magic Jackson had spoken of and imagined the room packed with happy dancers. She smiled as Jackson bobbed his head and sang in tune to a popular song. Watching the way he moved his hips to the beat, Diamond could well imagine just how exciting it would be to spend a night with him. *Would be? Girl, what in the heck are you thinking?* There would absolutely, positively be no woulda, shoulda, coulda with this hunkalicious guy standing beside her. Diamond well knew his kind: cocky and arrogant, probably certain that he could get her into his bed. She was certain of that, too, but that was beside the point. Fortunately, she had an iron-clad rule to save her from herself. She never, ever dated anyone in or near the workplace. After a two-month courtship with a former sales manager had ended in a stalker situation with law enforcement involved, she'd vowed to keep her personal and professional lives very separate.

"Now watch how the DJ has the ability to completely change the mood." Once again, Jackson clicked on the song list. The sounds of a sultry saxophone filled the room, the smooth jazz tune evoking images of lovemaking more than words ever could.

Diamond was convinced she was losing it. How else could she explain the fact that she was now undressing Jackson with her eyes? It was a good thing that his back was to her as he continued to fiddle with the knobs—a good thing because it gave her several uninterrupted seconds to take in his broad shoulders, strong back, narrow waist, perfect butt, strong thighs, long legs and big feet. As she continued to stare at his perfect backside encased in jeans, Diamond could barely remember her name.

She looked up in time to see the room darken; tiny lights resembling twinkling stars filled the ceiling. The air in the room shifted along with the lighting. Diamond felt it and believed that Jackson did, too. Attraction crackled like a burning log between them. And what happened to the air in the room? He turned and looked at her, his gaze penetrating, yet unreadable. Diamond forced herself not to look away, tried to maintain the stare, but again…she couldn't. Her eyes dropped to those delectable lips that sat under an aquiline nose, just as

Jackson flicked out his tongue to moisten them. The sax sizzled from the speakers, wrapping them in a sensual cocoon, a world of their own. It was as if time stopped, along with Diamond's rational thinking. Because for the life of her she couldn't think of anything more logical to do than to kiss those lips, to crush the nipples that were even now hardening at the mere thought of being touched against Jackson's hard chest.

She took a step.

Jackson's eyes narrowed as he watched her come closer. He looked at her lips, slightly parted with desire. Wanting him was written all over her face. His message was being proclaimed from an area decidedly lower, by a rapidly increasing bulge in the front of his jeans.

He took a step.

They now stood just inches apart, neither moving, barely breathing. At the risk of having to fire himself for insubordination, Jackson reached out and ran a finger along Diamond's jawline. His touch was more electric than the guitar that now accompanied the sax. She licked her lips and suppressed a shiver. He watched, wondering how they tasted, those lips, wanting to know how she tasted. Her eyes flickered shut and then back open, even as her head tilted seemingly of its own accord. To hell with stalking ex-coworkers and iron-clad declarations. She would be a rule breaker, too. Thoughts of consequences could come later. Right now all she wanted were his lips...on hers...now! He bent his head down. One more step and the kiss would begin. Just one more step...

"There you are!" Taylor said as she entered the room. And right behind her? Donald and Donovan: father and son.

Damn!

Diamond scurried from the intimacy of the DJ booth and Jackson's captivating eyes, looking as professional as she could with her body on fire. She ignored Donald's scowl and

Donovan's smirk and tried to remember how to construct a sentence. *Subject, verb, noun, Diamond. Subject! Verb! Noun!*

Jackson came to her rescue, and in the moment, had he rode in on a white horse, dressed in armor, she couldn't have been any more grateful. "Mr. Drake, always a pleasure to see you, sir. Donovan, good to see you, man." They shook hands.

"Good to see you," Donovan replied, his brow creased in slight confusion.

Jackson knew that further talk with these two men would likely blow his cover. It was time for a quick getaway. "Ms. Drake, it's been a pleasure," he said, his tone courteous, formal, making Diamond immediately wish for the rogue. "But I need to head over to the other building. Gentlemen, if you'll excuse me."

Forcing herself not to watch the firm, hard butt exiting the building, Diamond turned to her dad and brother. "What are you guys doing here?"

"We were on our way to the cellar and saw Taylor outside. When she said you were here, on the first floor of our masterpiece, we thought we'd join you."

"Good, because so far what I've seen is amazing." Jackson's leaving allowed oxygen to once again flow to Diamond's brain. "Taylor, why don't you explain to Dad and Donovan what you shared with me earlier, including the fabrics and colors for the spa?" They continued the tour, and Taylor presented a variety of swatches. But in her mind, the only hue Diamond saw was caramel, and the only face was that of Jackson Wright.

Chapter 5

A half hour later, Diamond wheeled her shiny black BMW into its parking space, threw the car in Park and shut off the engine. She hadn't seen him when they left the site but no matter. Thoughts of Jackson still consumed her. She'd never had her head spun like this, not even when Jamal Pendergrass had kissed her outside the skating rink—her first smooch at the ripe old age of thirteen. What just happened? Diamond didn't understand. As a woman who prided herself on self-control and was known in the dating world as being "hard to get," she was less than enthused that she'd almost made a fool of herself in the workplace. As it was, when she saw her father, in general, and Donovan, in particular, she knew she'd have some 'splainin' to do! Her older brother's knowing smirk hadn't gone unnoticed.

Determined to put Jackson and what had happened behind her, she took a deep breath, reached for her purse and headed into the executive offices. She pasted what she hoped was a

nonchalant look on her face, took another calming breath—
where was the yoga mat when she needed it?—and opened
the door to her office.

Kathleen looked at her always cool, calm and collected
superior and immediately sensed something amiss. "What's
wrong?"

"Does it look like something's wrong with me?" Diamond
snapped. So much for the calm, nonchalant facade.

"You forget how well I know you," Kathleen replied, nonplussed. "Plus, I know a tight mouth when I see one. Come
on, darlin'. Out with it. Did one of those pieces of man candy
get you all hot and bothered?"

Diamond didn't respond.

Kathleen clapped her hands with glee. "That's it! Which
one? No, don't tell me, let me guess. Is it that tall, strapping
man with the tattoo across his chest?"

The "tall, strapping" description definitely fit Jackson, but
Diamond didn't remember a tattoo. "Step into my office," she
said over her shoulder to Kathleen as she left the common
area to enter her more private domain. Maybe talking about
this weird attraction would help her get rid of it.

Kathleen hurried behind her, closing Diamond's office
door once they were both inside. Her green eyes glittered as
she took a seat in one of the tan suede chairs that framed the
large ebony desk. Diamond walked behind it, threw down
her purse and slouched into the large leather executive chair.

"First of all, nothing is wrong. And, for the record, you're
right. There are a lot of attractive men down there."

"Anyone in particular catch your fancy?"

Diamond shrugged. "Not really." *Liar, liar, pants on fire.*
"I was given a partial tour by the supervisor while Taylor
handled a call."

"And…"

"And nothing, Kat. Jeez! He's tall, but then so are several

of the men. Plus, he was wearing a T-shirt." Much to her chagrin. "I don't remember a tattoo."

"The one I'm talking about stands a head and shoulder above the rest. He's a hunk of burning love," Kathleen said dreamily. "I don't see him every day, but the few times I have, he's left quite an impression. Oh, to be young and single again. I bet his legs aren't the only things that are long and strong about him."

"Kathleen!"

"Oh, come now," Kathleen said, her eyes still twinkling. "You don't think I became a mother of five by singing 'Yankee Doodle,' do you?"

"Ha! I guess not. The man who showed me around is really tall."

"Handsome?"

"He looks all right. His name is Jackson."

"Dear, you're trying really hard not to sound impressed, which means he must have knocked your socks off." Kathleen leaned forward. "So when are you guys going out?"

"Out?"

Kathleen clucked. "Out…as in on a date? Really, Diamond, sometimes I wonder if you're twenty-nine or only nine."

"We're not going out," Diamond responded, ignoring the older woman's jab. "I don't date men from the workplace."

"He's hardly that," Kathleen insisted. "He doesn't work for Drake Wines, and he's not in these offices. I think you should go out with him," she went on, despite Diamond's scowl. "If nothing else, it will rid you of the persnickety mood you've had of late. You know I love you, Diamond, but in the past few months, you haven't been your charming, gracious self."

"Careful, Kat," Diamond drily replied, turning on her computer and reaching for the mouse. "You're talking to the woman who signs your paychecks."

"Technically, my paychecks are signed by your father and

the CFO. But you're the boss, so I'll button my lip and head back to my desk." Kathleen reached the door and turned. "But I still think you should go out with him. Who knows what that might lead to?" Her tinkling laughter followed her out of the room.

Diamond couldn't help smiling as she clicked on her task bar and checked out what was left on the day's agenda. Kathleen was Diamond's assistant, but having worked in various capacities at the vineyard for twenty years, she was family, too. *She's right,* Diamond acknowledged, as she scrolled down the page. *I haven't been too charming lately.*

And Diamond knew why. It was the lack of testosterone in her life and, more specifically, in her bed—a problem she didn't see being resolved anytime soon. Even as she shifted from her task bar to her calendar and the evening's obligation—a fundraiser for at-risk youth sponsored by the San Diego Arts Association—she pondered her predicament and Kathleen's earlier comment. How long was she going to let Benjamin Carter, the ex-fiancé who'd strung her along before breaking her heart, ruin her life?

Abruptly cutting off her computer, Diamond reached for her purse and strode toward the door. Kathleen was right. Benjamin's refusal to marry her after their long engagement had affected her more than she dared admit. She had buried herself in work and put her life on hold because of it. She'd gone on only a couple dates in almost a year and was probably setting herself up to be an old maid. *But no more!* "It's time to get back in the game!" she hissed. Maybe she'd meet someone tonight to play with.

Moments later, Diamond had lowered the top of her convertible and was zooming down the tree-lined roads of Drake Vineyard, soon to be known as Drake Wines Resort & Spa. As she neared the construction site, Jackson's handsome face and knowing smile drifted into her mind. She remembered the feel of his hand on her waist, and her body reacted, muscles in certain nether regions clenching at the mere possibility of surrounding someone else's, well, muscle. In spite of her determination not to do so, she eased off the gas, slowing down as her eyes scanned the sweaty bodies still hard at work under the dimming sun. She didn't see him. She told herself that was a good thing and realized that lying to oneself was not cute.

Diamond reached for her phone and called her hair stylist, who was located in San Diego. "Lecia, it's Diamond."

"And let me guess," Lecia said, as she sewed a track of hair into the head of her current client. "You need to see me ASAP, and I'm supposed to fit you in."

Diamond laughed. "Something like that. But it's an emergency. I need a makeover."

"Oh, Lord. Sounds serious. What time can you be here?"

"In about an hour, hour and a half?"

"You'd better be glad I consider you a friend."

"Plus I tip well."

"Ha! That, too. Which I appreciate, since some of these fools hand me an extra dollar and call it a day."

"You hook me up, and I'll make it worth your while. See you soon." Diamond ended the call and was soon speeding down the boulevard to the estate where the entire Drake family still lived. Initially, she'd not been looking forward to a night of gowns and tuxes and rich men trying to impress her with their portfolios. But a certain assistant had suggested change, and a certain well-built construction worker had whetted her appetite. Before the night was over, she decided, she'd find someone to get back in the game with, and try to forget about the man with whom she'd really like to score.

Chapter 6

Jackson pulled up to the valet and exited his latest toy. Next to women, cars were one of his favorite things to collect, and the newly purchased top-of-the-line Maserati GranTurismo fit him to a T. Like him, it was sleek, powerful and stood out in a crowd. He unfolded his tuxedo-clad six-foot-five-inch frame from the sports car, cutting a distinctive swath across the five-star hotel's well-appointed lobby. Envious glances and flirty stares followed him as he walked to the meticulously landscaped garden, where gloved waiters carried trays of bubbly and hors d'oeuvres. Taking a flute from a passing waiter, he surveyed the grounds quickly filling up with the beautiful people: silk, diamonds, cloying perfume and smiles abounding. For a fleeting second the boy he used to be—poor, insecure, troubled—rose up within him. He wondered how these people would react if they knew where he'd grown up, the things he'd done to survive that childhood and where his mother now resided. A beautiful woman coming toward him distracted him from these uncomfortable thoughts. By the time she arrived at his side, the bravado Jackson had often called upon to mask his fears was firmly back in place.

"Jackson, thanks for accepting my invitation." Her sparkling blue eyes drank him in much faster than he sipped his champagne. "You look delicious. I'm so glad you came." She reached up and planted a soft kiss on his chin. "And unaccompanied no less," she whispered seductively. "A virile man such as yourself shouldn't spend the night alone."

Jackson smiled at Erin Bridges, the daughter of a real-estate mogul with whom Jackson had partnered on occasion. No one could deny her classic beauty: shiny blond hair cut into a flattering asymmetrical bob, bright doe eyes framed by ridiculously long lashes and a pouty mouth covered with just the right amount of shimmering gloss. She'd definitely caught his eye when they met five years ago, but after realizing that the business relationship with her father would be an ongoing one with lucrative potential, Jackson had decided that they should not date. Again, his uncle's warning to not use his workplace as a playground helped him put on the brakes. She'd been less than happy with his "let's just be friends" suggestion. But what could she do?

"I see you've pulled off yet another top-notch event," Jackson finally said, waving his hand in acknowledgment of the well-heeled crowd.

"It's easy to do when you have friends in high places," Erin responded. "Besides, this cause really feels good. With the fundraisers planned, we'll be able to send at least twenty-five students to highly accredited colleges and, after graduation, through our partnerships with local businesses such as yours, help some of them get started in their professional careers. Oh, speaking of local businesses, someone has just come in that I want you to meet."

Jackson turned to see to whom Erin referred and saw a

vision that took his breath away. Diamond Drake lived up
to her name, lighting up the courtyard as she waltzed in,
the epitome of grace and beauty. Her dress was a simple
one-shoulder design, the deep-red iridescent fabric perfectly
complementing her sun-kissed sienna skin. Jackson's eyes
continued to travel upward, taking in a long neck and what?
She cut her hair! The short hairdo fit her spunky personality, he immediately decided, noting that it emphasized her
high cheekbones and almond-shaped eyes. Her makeup was
simple, as was her jewelry. *When you are a diamond, you
don't need to overaccessorize.* His gait was strong and purposeful, his thoughts predatory, as he walked toward her.

Later, Diamond would pride herself on not having tripped
in her four-inch heels as shock consumed her. *What is he
doing here?* This was a five-thousand-dollar-per-person
gathering of the county's most elite players. How did a construction worker, even a foreman, wrangle an invite and then
afford such an expensive one? And how did one transform
from looking perfectly at home on a construction site, complete with sweaty T-shirt and dusty jeans, to looking as if he
owned the world in a tux that emphasized his broad shoulders, narrow waist and long legs, and a stark white shirt that
highlighted caramel skin? Diamond's eyes narrowed as they
finally settled on the woman walking beside Jackson, La
Jolla's premiere socialite, Erin Bridges. She felt as if she were
looking at the answer to how Jackson got invited to the event
and didn't try and ignore the stab of jealousy that arose at
the prospect that the construction site might not be the only
place Jackson was making use of his skilled hands.

"Diamond, you look lovely!" Erin reached Diamond with
arms outstretched and gave air kisses to both cheeks. "You
cut your hair. I love it!"

"Decided it was time for a change," Diamond said, running

a hand through the shortened crop she was still getting used to, and feeling suddenly shy under Jackson's intense gaze. With effort, she kept her eyes on Erin. "You look amazing. That dress is stunning."

"Oh, just a little something I picked up last week in Italy. It's a Roberto Cavalli original."

"Roberto…of course." Diamond's statement was to Erin, but she'd lost the fight to keep her eyes off Jackson. Or was his name Magnet? By the way she was drawn to him, she couldn't tell.

"Diamond, I'd like you to meet Jackson Wright, the 'Boss' of Boss Construction and philanthropist to a variety of worthwhile causes."

Diamond's eyes narrowed as realization dawned. Her father and brothers had always referred to the owner of the construction company as Boss, not Jackson. Diamond had assumed they were simply referring to him by his title and had never considered that the name of the company actually referred to a person. It had never mattered to her one way or the other—until now. "So…is your name Jackson or Boss?"

"Jackson, but most of my friends call me Boss."

"Making sure that everyone knows you're the head honcho?"

"That's what my mom called me. She said that even in diapers I was pretty headstrong and was barking orders by the time I was crawling. The nickname stuck." It was one of the few things from his childhood that Jackson had kept.

Diamond felt enough sparks were flying to send a shuttle to the moon. She stared at Jackson and barely noticed when a guest came over to steal Erin away. For a moment, she lost herself in the heat emanating from Jackson's gaze and wondered how hot his kiss would feel. Diamond let the fire in her core rise to her brain. Earlier, Jackson had duped her. He hadn't come clean about who he was at the job.

"Boss Wright?" she murmured, her face fixed in a look of subtle chagrin. "*Owner* of Boss Construction?" She realized that Jackson was still holding her hand and deftly pulled it away from him.

"At your service," Jackson replied, nonplussed, reaching to grab her hand again.

"Stop it!" Diamond spat between clenched teeth, even as she worked to maintain a neutral expression for anyone watching. "You've got a lot of nerve standing here all nonchalant after lying to me this afternoon."

"Lying? How so?"

"By not telling me who you were when showing me around the construction site."

"Oh, you mean back at the vineyard where you were acting like a spoiled BAP, the Black American princess threatening to have me fired because I came on to you? I didn't lie to you. There were simply some things that I didn't reveal."

Diamond cursed her body for reacting to this silkily drawled truth. "I specifically spoke about discussing you with the owner."

"Which you may have known were one and the same had you not interrupted my introduction. Assuming that I was the supervisor is on you."

"I'd say you were being uncooperative at best and deceptive at worst."

"Well, baby," Jackson said, the single glass of bubbly obscuring his common sense, the intense desire for her usurping the lack of confidence left over from his early years and pride developed in his later ones, "you're getting ready to have a cause for rank insubordination because I've got to be honest. Before this night is over, I'd like to get real acquainted with those soft, luscious-looking lips of yours and find out if the rest of your body is as soft as your arm. How's that sound?"

"It sounds like a man who'd like to get slapped," Diamond

retorted, even as the image she'd fought all afternoon—the one that had them skin to skin from head to toe—flashed in her mind. "It sounds like a cocky, arrogant jerk who has obviously gotten women to drop their panties way too easily."

"Well, there is some truth to that."

"I think I've heard enough."

She got ready to walk away, but Jackson's words stopped her. "Ask yourself why I'm so getting on your nerves, why you've been snapping at me since we've met. And don't feed yourself the lame excuse that it's because of not knowing who I was at the site."

"Well, you should know about lame."

"Wow, spoken like a princess reprimanding the help." He continued despite her huff. "Maybe I should have come clean and told you I owned the company, but I'm glad I didn't. My anonymity gave me the opportunity to see firsthand how you treat my men. And like I said this afternoon, you don't have the right to talk down to them or anyone else."

Did this fool just check me on how I handle my business on my property? "I'll admit that your men have always been respectful, an area in which you could learn a thing or two. Like now, telling me how to act and what to say. Just who do you think you are?"

"A man who's not afraid of your last name, that's who," Jackson replied. Mr. Bravado was obviously still riding shotgun. "And one who sees what he wants and goes after it." Diamond got ready to interrupt him, but Jackson held up his hand and continued. "You've got quite the reputation among the men—powerful, no nonsense, untouchable. They say you don't come to the site much, and when you do, you keep your distance. But I detect a fire underneath that cool exterior. We're grown folk, Diamond, and I have no need to beat around the bush. I find you attractive as hell, and I want to get to know you better…a lot better. I think you want to get to know me, too. Am I right?"

Diamond's chin took on its familiar tilt as she tried not to let Jackson's words affect her. The fact of the matter was she was feeling him in more ways than one and not only that but she wanted him to feel her in more ways than one. He was a handsome, intelligent man who she'd bet her paycheck was an awesome lover. But after he'd sexed her real good, then what? And what about her rule of not dating within the workplace, not to mention the one about not having any more casual relationships with noncommittal men? If there was one thing Diamond could spot, it was a man with marital allergies. Her brothers Donovan and Dexter had shown her exactly what that looked like.

As if on cue, said brothers walked into the space and up to where she and Jackson were standing. A part of her was glad to see them as they'd provided an escape of sorts. But the other part knew that her reprieve was over. She'd avoided both her father and Donovan this afternoon, but she was in for a grilling later on tonight. "Hey, bro," she said, reaching up to give Dexter a hug. "I didn't think you were going to make it."

"I just got in," Dexter responded, eyeing Jackson as he gave his sister a hug.

"How was Baltimore?"

"Cool. Rainy." Dexter took a step back. "Why are you so dressed up? And what happened to your hair?"

"Dressing up is normally required at a black-tie event," Diamond sarcastically answered. She fingered her hair. "Do you like it?"

"Yeah, it looks good." Dexter held up his fist to Jackson for a pound. "Hey, Boss."

"Dexter," Jackson responded, before turning to greet Donovan, as well. "Hey, Don. This is why I had to cut our meet-

ing short, man. If I'd known you were coming here, I would
have let you know."

"Looks like there's a few things I might need to know,"
Donovan replied, before turning to Diamond. "I didn't know
you and Diamond were hanging out."

"Just formally met her today, man. And now I see why
y'all have been keeping her under wraps!"

"Yes, just how has that happened?" Diamond asked Donovan. "How is it that you, Dex and Dad have known Jackson
'Boss' Wright for a while now and I'd never met him before
today?"

"No need," Donovan said with a shrug. "You'd never been
a part of the construction projects before, and most of our
initial meetings took place at Boss's office." What Donovan
didn't share was that it was also to protect his baby sis from
getting hurt. He knew that Diamond wanted to get married
and knew that Jackson was a Casanova. Like oil and water—
those two ingredients didn't mix well. "Don't let the smooth
talk fool you, baby sis. This is a great businessman, but he
doesn't let the grass grow under his feet…if you know what
I mean."

"Don't worry, Donovan. Our interaction is strictly business."

Jackson chuckled but instead of responding to Diamond's
comment, still smiling, he addressed Donovan instead.
"You're being a bit hard on a brother, don't you think?"

"Just keeping it real," Donovan replied, his gruff words
tempered by a smile of his own.

"Should Diamond grant me the pleasure of her extended
company, I'll be the perfect gentleman."

Donovan eyed Jackson skeptically, even as he nodded at
Erin, who was motioning for him from across the lawn to
join the group she now entertained. "You do that," he said,

giving the construction owner a fist pound and then leaving the group.

Dexter smiled as a gorgeous Latina sidled up to him. "Hey, Maria," he said, giving her a light kiss on the lips. "I think I'll freshen up my drink and then we'll take our seats. The concert is about to begin."

"Shall we join them?" Jackson asked Diamond.

Diamond thought about sitting next to Jackson while listening to the sultry sounds of smooth jazz, feeling the breeze from the ocean and experiencing the accidental brushes of his fingers across her flaming skin. Not a good idea. "Thanks but I think I'll network a bit more. Oh, and Jackson, I meant what I said to my brother. The interaction between us is to be strictly business. Have I made myself clear?"

Jackson slowly nodded. "Got it." He stood there watching and appreciating her "business" as she walked across the lawn to join her friends.

Chapter 7

Diamond shifted in her seat, hoping that she didn't look as unnerved as she felt. For the past thirty minutes, she could have sworn that she'd felt the heat of Jackson's gaze on the nape of her neck. She'd known the moment he sat down directly behind her not because the woman next to him had immediately introduced herself and her husband but because there was a vibe, an energy, between them that alerted Diamond to whenever he was within touching distance. With every note that oozed from Paul Taylor's saxophone, Diamond felt the heat in her body rise. She watched Paul's nimble fingers as he keyed the melodious notes, but in her mind, Jackson's hands were on her body, playing a song written for her alone.

"Do you want a drink?" Diamond asked her brother, right in the middle of Taylor's solo.

Donovan looked at her questioningly. "You're getting one right now?" he whispered.

Diamond nodded as she composed herself.

"I'll have a beer."

"I'll be right back."

She eased into the aisle and headed to the bar. Taking deep breaths, she willed her heart to stop its erratic pounding and for her body to behave. Before reaching the bar, she decided to take a quick stroll around the gardens, regain her poise, get the drinks and then take her seat once the song ended. The sun had set, and the night sky had come alive with thousands of stars surrounding a bright, full moon. Lamps were strategically placed throughout the garden, highlighting the various shrubs, flowers and other greenery. Diamond took the path nearest the bar and headed toward a fountain near the end of the garden's east side.

Just before she got there, a hand reached out and grabbed her.

Diamond gasped, and in that moment, a tongue on a mission slipped into her open mouth. A strong arm wrapped itself around her waist, and another hand massaged the nape of her neck. The woodsy smell of Jackson's cologne engulfed her, and even though her mind was telling her to pull back, slap his face and curse him out, her traitorous body was pressing against his, even as her tongue engaged in a languid duel. Before she knew what was happening, her arms had reached around to stroke his broad back, and she marveled at the power created by sinew and bone. Somewhere in her mind she felt one of his hands muss up her short do. Jackson moaned and deepened the kiss. His other hand traveled from her shoulder to the small of her back and lower still until it cupped her round, firm booty as if the most natural thing in the world to be doing on a night like this was to be ravished in a moonlit garden while jazz played in the background.

Jackson slowly raised his head and blazed a trail of kisses from her mouth to her neck and back to her temple. "I said

I'd be a gentleman," he whispered, even as he nipped her ear-lobe with tiny love bites, "so I should have asked to kiss you. But an apology at this point would be insincere. You taste way too good for me to feel sorry for what just happened." Jackson ran a firm finger down Diamond's arm. "May I kiss you again?" he asked. His voice was as soft as the kisses he'd rained down on her face. Her nod was almost imperceptible, but her acquiescence was all Jackson needed to raise the stakes. He pulled them deeper into the shadows, backed her against the ivy-covered brick wall and once again plundered her mouth with his tongue. His hips mirrored the movement of his tongue: slow, rhythmic circles as he thrust up against her.

Diamond wasn't even aware that she was joining in the dance of this slow grind until she felt Jackson harden beneath her. Then she felt his hand on the silk of her dress, grasping her hip, easing along her waist and up to her breast. He tweaked her nipple, and Diamond felt as if she would explode. In this love-induced insanity, it didn't matter that she was in a public place, mere yards from where her protective broth-ers sat. All she wanted was this man's arms around her, with his body pressed tight against hers.

And then the audience applauded.

"Stop!" Diamond used the last ounce of her will and pushed against Jackson's massive chest. "We…can't do this."

"I know," Jackson readily agreed. "You're much more than a quick romp in the hay or, in this instance, the garden. Here," he said as he reached inside his jacket pocket and pulled out a card. "My cell number is on the back. Call me. Let's meet up and…finish what we've started." In the next instant, he was gone.

Diamond stayed behind in the shadows, willing her heart-beat to return to normal. She touched a hand to her lips and felt them swollen from the passion of his kisses. She felt that one look at her brothers and the message of what had transpired would be sent faster than a cell phone text. She'd been ravished by Jackson Wright, and she wanted it to happen again and again. Diamond knew it would raise eyebrows and questions, but she had no choice. She couldn't get Donovan's drink, return to her seat, hear the rest of the concert or say thanks to the host. If she was going to save any dignity at all, she had to run out of here as if the devil were chasing her. And that is exactly what she did.

Chapter 8

Diamond stood in her bedroom, ready to greet the day. This had always been one of her favorite rooms in the house, with its separate sitting area and massive bath. On her eighteenth birthday, she'd changed the color scheme from girly pinks and purples to a dramatic black-and-white theme. Just last year she'd changed it again. Now rich tan-colored walls and plush ivory bedding, both of which complemented the dark walnut floors, gave the room a sophisticated yet understated elegance. Splashes of color came courtesy of recently pur-chased Charles Bibbs artwork and freshly cut flowers that always occupied the coffee table and fireplace mantel. At times she thought about venturing out and purchasing a condo or house of her own. But then she'd come to this, her retreat, and forget every thought she had about leaving.

Diamond took one last look in the mirror. She looked calm and refreshed, thanks to a two-hour early-morning workout. This fresh look covered the roiling emotions she felt from her encounter with Jackson two days ago. For this she was thankful, since she was getting ready to walk downstairs and join her family for their traditional Sunday dinner. Everyone would be there, and she was sure all eyes would be on her. Why did she know this? Because she knew how her family operated, and there was very little that happened with one Drake that the others didn't know about sooner or later. Donovan was very close to their father, Donald, so Diamond was sure he'd mentioned her encounter with Jackson and her refusal to discuss it when asked. Dexter was the baby of the family and a mama's boy. Additionally, he couldn't hold water if he carried it in a bucket—an old-time saying that meant he couldn't keep a shred of anybody else's business to himself. Knowing this, Diamond had basically avoided her parents for two days, which—even though she and Dexter still lived at home—wasn't hard to do. The estate included a main house and three fully equipped guest rooms totaling ten thousand square feet. Each child had their own wing, as did their parents. More often than not, Donovan could be found there, too, even though he'd purchased a home near San Diego a few years ago. Diamond's grandparents, David and Mary Drake, lived in one of the guest homes. Their ninety-eight-year-old great-grandfather still lived on the property, as well. These were the people Diamond saw as she rounded the corner and entered the dining room.

"Well, the princess finally decided to grace us with her presence. How are you, baby girl?" Donald Drake came around the table and hugged his daughter. A commanding presence at six foot two and two hundred pounds, Donald had taken the business from a successful company to a dynasty when he'd expanded Drake Wines into most of the fifty states and then internationally. He'd also been on the cutting edge of the health-conscious craze. Their vineyard had gone organic many years ago.

"Good afternoon, Dad." Diamond gave Donald a hug. "Hello, Mom. I love it when you cook for us. Dinner smells great!"

"Ha! It's your grandparents who have the chef, dear. I've cooked dinner almost every Sunday since you were born. But thank you."

After hugging her mom, Genevieve, Diamond greeted everyone else in the room. "Sorry I'm just now coming down. I didn't know y'all were waiting on me."

"Your timing is perfect, dear," Genevieve replied, looking as gracious as ever with her long silver hair swept up in a loose bun. A little dynamo, who at all of five foot five ruled the roost, she was also one of the most loving people on the planet. "Your father's just giving you a hard time."

The family shared small talk as they dished up the succulent feast: roasted duck with fresh vegetables—corn, greens, squash, carrots and onions—from Grandma Mary's large and flourishing garden, juicy heirloom tomatoes, garlic mashed potatoes seasoned with Genevieve's fresh grown herbs, Mary's spicy corn bread and, of course, a fruity pinot noir from the Drake vineyards. After the patriarch, Great-grandfather David Drake Sr.—affectionately referred to as Papa Dee—blessed the food, everyone dug in.

"Dang, Mama," Donovan said after enjoying a mouthful of dark meat and licking his fingers. "You know I don't like fowl."

"What was that?" Genevieve drily replied. "I couldn't hear what you said around all that smacking on that *bird* you don't like!"

Everyone at the table laughed.

"You and Granny are the only ones who can make us eat food we abhor," Diamond commented as she enjoyed a forkful of squash. "Remember how I thought I hated parsnips and I'd been eating them for years?"

"How can I forget?" Mary replied, with a laugh. "I'm the one who kept telling you they were spicy potatoes!"

"Well, I've never met a food I don't like," Dexter piped in, after following a heaping forkful of greens with a bite of corn bread. "That's why no matter how fine my woman is… she's got to be able to cook!"

Diamond raised her eyebrow. "Oh, really? Well, considering the skinny, silicone-injected Barbie dolls you prefer, who don't look like they even eat…good luck with that."

"My women aren't skinny. They're just in shape."

"That chick he was with on Friday had quite a figure," Donovan said. "What was her name, Dex?"

"Maria. Maria Sanchez."

"She's a beautiful woman."

Dexter nodded. "I agree, brother."

Genevieve eyed her son curiously. "Boy, you have a new girlfriend every week. Are we crossing the border this time around?"

"You know me, Ma. I'm an equal-opportunity lover."

"Watch yourself there, boy," Grandfather David warned. "You've got respectable women around this table." After a pause, he continued. "That's a cigar-and-brandy conversation for men alone."

Mary looked at the husband she'd loved for almost sixty years. "Oh, so you're not saying, don't talk like that? You're saying, don't talk like that around the womenfolk? Is that it?"

David's eyes twinkled. "That's it exactly."

"Ooh, no, he didn't," Genevieve said with a laugh. "He's keeping secrets from you, Ma." It was just like her father-in-law to stir things up. There was never a dull moment when a group of Drake men sat around a table.

Mary looked at Genevieve. "Child, I'm not worried. Anything he doesn't share at the table he'll spill in the bedroom."

"Watch yourself, now, Granny," Diamond said, mimicking

her grandfather. "That sounds like a kitchen conversation for women only!"

"It is, baby. And I'll give you the full 411 so you can know how to handle your man."

"Wait!" Dexter's laughter filled the room. "Did my eighty-year-old grandmother just say 411, as in *information?*"

"I'm seventy-eight," Mary responded, eyes twinkling. "Don't push me, now."

Diamond leaned over and hugged Mary. "My granny is in the know!"

"Speaking of in the know," Donovan said cryptically. "Why don't you tell us about your new man?"

Seven sets of eyes looked at Diamond.

Oh, Lord. Here we go. "I do not have a new man," Diamond corrected. "That's what you get for trying to be all up in my business."

"You'd better tell him that," Donovan replied. "Because on Friday night, Jackson was looking at you like a piece of prime real estate that he'd like to own!"

"Please, Donovan," Diamond replied, deadpan. "Stop with the histrionics. First of all, Jackson wasn't looking at me in any particular way, and second, nobody owns me!"

"Hmm," Papa Dee said, speaking up for the first time since picking up his fork and beginning to eat. "Me thinks the lady doth protest too much!"

Diamond got ready to argue and then thought better of it. Who could ever win an argument against someone who'd been on the planet for almost a century?

Donald wiped his mouth with a napkin, then reared back with his glass of wine. "Are we talking about Boss Wright, as in the owner of Boss Construction?"

Donovan nodded. "He was at the benefit Friday night, sniffing behind Diamond like a rottweiler."

"Just make sure his bark is worth his bite," Mary said.

Diamond frowned. *Huh?*

Genevieve explained. "While he talks the talk, make sure he can walk the walk. You could do worse than a successful, wealthy man," she continued. "You're over twenty-nine. It's time you settled down. It's time that all of you get cured of singleitis," she continued, pointedly looking at all three of her children. "Yes, even you," she said to Dexter, when he would have argued. "I had all of you by the time I turned thirty. At the rate you three are going, I'll be Papa's age before I see grandchildren."

Papa Dee chuckled. "Lord, I hope not. You wouldn't be able to bounce them on creaking knees like mine!"

"Do you think this could get serious?" Genevieve asked Diamond.

"There is nothing happening to get serious! Seeing Jackson, Boss, whatever he calls himself, at the benefit was purely coincidental. Donovan is reading way too much into the fact that he and I were conversing. Now can we please change the subject? You guys are starting to get on my nerves."

Donald obliged his daughter and shifted the focus from weddings and babies to wines and spreadsheets. But that didn't stop Donovan from cornering her just before he left the house.

"I've got a question, sis."

Diamond stifled a sigh. When it came to older brothers, sometimes there was a thin line between love and hate. "What?"

"If nothing is happening between you and Jackson, why did you not bring the beer you offered to get, text me about some jive pop-up headache, and then seconds later I watch homeboy return to his seat with a smug look on his face?"

"I don't know, brother. Why don't you ask Jackson?"

"Because I'm asking you."

"I'm a grown woman, Donovan. Which is why you really need to mind your own business."

"You heard what Mama said about wanting us to get married, and I know that's what you want, as well." Donovan stepped closer to his sister and further lowered his voice. "For the record, I don't think your boy Jackson is the marrying kind."

Chapter 9

The next day, Diamond was more than ready to jump into work. Between what little sleep she'd gotten and her mother's interrogation after the brothers had left, it was a miracle that she'd survived the weekend at all—that and the fact that she'd actually dreamed of Jackson. Diamond blushed at the thought.

"Good morning, darlin'!"

"Morning, Kat." Diamond walked up to Kathleen's desk and reached for the typed agenda that sat on her desk. "Looks like somebody had a happy weekend."

"It was amazing. The old codger gave me an early Christmas present. We're going to Ireland!"

"Wow, Kathleen, that *is* amazing. Bernie must have gotten a raise. When are you going?"

"That's why he had to surprise me early. We need to lock in the dates and are hoping to go around the holidays."

Diamond looked up. "As long as it's not Thanksgiving, our new opening weekend, I think we'll be fine."

"You're a diamond, Diamond."

Diamond rolled her eyes. "Whatever."

"Oh, shoot. I was so excited about the Ireland trip that I almost forgot. There was a message on the phone when I arrived. It might be important."

Diamond's stomach flip-flopped. *Jackson?* "Who from?"

"*O Magazine.* The message is in your Microsoft Outlook, along with the others."

"Thanks, Kat." Diamond walked into her office. Before she could sit down, Kat buzzed her on the intercom. "Line one for you, Diamond."

"Who is it?"

"Jackson Wright."

Kathleen hurriedly disconnected the call. Diamond knew why—she would have insisted that Kathleen take a message. Kathleen hanging up was her way of saying, put on your big-girl britches and take the call.

Today, Diamond's "britches" were an ivory-colored Chanel suit, its sleek, formfitting lines subtly accenting her curves. Her ivory pumps and three-strand pearls were classic, while her spiky do lessened the conservativeness of the total look.

Diamond took a breath and put on the last piece of attire needed before answering the phone: a professional demeanor. She punched the speaker button and spoke in a cool, crisp tone. "Diamond Drake."

Jackson laughed, and Diamond was at once irritated. It was the same sound she'd heard Friday night when commenting that their relationship was strictly business. In Diamond's mind, it was the sound of confidence and cockiness, as if Jackson just knew he was the cat's meow. Then she remembered Friday night: music, full moon, smooth jazz, skilled kisses and how her cat had meowed. She clamped her legs together and continued in a huff. "What is so humorous about my name?"

"Not your name, baby," Jackson said, a smile in his voice even though his heart beat at a million miles per hour. "Your attitude. I know you're a consummate professional, baby. You don't have to prove anything to me."

"If you know that, then one, why are you calling me during office hours, and two, why are you calling me *baby* when you should address me as either Diamond or Ms. Drake?"

"Very well," Jackson conceded, his voice taking on a businesslike tone. "Ms. Drake."

Diamond closed her eyes and fought the wave of desire that swept over her. *How is it that he can say my name so professionally yet squeeze sexuality between each consonant and vowel?* With each interaction of the Jackson Wright kind, Diamond was becoming more disconcerted. She'd never before reacted this strongly to a man, never felt such a magnetic pull to another human being. And with all that was presently on her plate, now was not the time! "Yes, Mr. Wright," she said when control once again returned. She stopped short of asking, What can I do for you? But she believed she already knew his answer to that question.

"I just got off the phone with Taylor Stevens. She's requested a meeting tomorrow night, to go over the proposed changes to the restaurant's design that we discussed after the walk-through. I think it would be a good idea for you to join us."

"Thanks, Jackson, but I've already approved those changes. There's no reason for me to be there."

"It may be a time-saver in the long run," Jackson responded. "The change to the roof is extensive. Since I know you're running this project, yours will be valuable input to our meeting."

"Yes, I'm in charge of it now, but Donovan handled the

first phase and Dexter has been kept in the loop, as well. Perhaps one of them is available."

There was a brief pause before Jackson responded. "I understand." He gave Diamond the meeting location information and ended the call.

Diamond immediately dialed Donovan. "Hey, Don."

"Diamond, what's up?"

"Remember the addition Taylor suggested, the one about incorporating a glass ceiling to the lounge area that extends into the garden?"

"Right."

Diamond could hear Donovan shuffling papers in the background, as well as the hurriedness in his voice. She got right to the point. "Taylor and Jackson are having a meeting tomorrow night. They want one of us to be there."

"No can do, sis. I have a meeting with the distributors for the restaurants." As the innovative VP of sales, Donovan had recently secured a lucrative contract with a midlevel restaurant chain. The Drake line would be unveiled there during the holidays.

Diamond hid her disappointment. "No worries. I'll ask Dex."

"He's not here."

"Where is he?"

"In Vegas, mixing business with pleasure. He'll be back the day after tomorrow. Look, sis, I have another call. I've got to go."

Diamond let out a sigh as she hung up the phone. She knew she was being irrational, but there was no way she was ready to face Jackson again. It was too soon after their encounter. She could still feel his hands caressing her buttocks, could still taste his lips. *I'll talk to Taylor. She can handle this.* With the decision made, Diamond reached for the folder containing the advertising company's promo of the second leg of the Drake holiday campaign beginning next month. She'd seen the ads and reviewed the commercial several times but wanted to incorporate the theme into the company's November newsletter. Happy to take her mind off Jackson by letting her creative juices flow, Diamond dove into writing and was just hitting her groove when her intercom buzzed.

"Yes, Kat."

"Line one, Diamond. It's *O Magazine.*"

"Okay, I'll take it. Thanks." Diamond punched the flashing white light. "Diamond Drake." Thirty minutes later, she sat stunned yet excited. *O Magazine* wanted to do a four-page spread on Drake Wines Resort & Spa and not only that but the queen of daytime talk was planning a visit, the filming of which could end up as a special on OWN. She squealed, and after sharing the news with Kat, she walked to her father's office.

"Dad! You'll never guess what just happened."

Donald looked up from the report he was reading, looking very much the part of a successful company COO. "No, but I have a feeling you're going to tell me."

"We're going to be featured in *O Magazine!*" She relayed what the magazine editor had shared with her, including the fact that Oprah Winfrey wanted to visit their vineyard during the holiday season.

"That's great news, honey," Donald said. "When is this supposed to take place?"

"That's the one tiny hitch in the giddyup," Diamond said. "They want to feature us in one of their summer issues, which means the shoot and interviews can happen no later than January or February."

"Well, having been opened a couple months at that point, we should have everything in place."

"I think so, but I'm even more determined to finish the construction on schedule so that we can focus on interior design." Diamond's eyes narrowed with a realization. In order to make sure the renovation was finished and the interior design flawless, she'd have to stay more involved in the renovation than she'd planned. There was no way she'd be able to avoid Jackson—at least for the next four weeks. "I've got a meeting tomorrow night with Jackson and Taylor. Now, along with the last-minute changes we've proposed, I need to let them know that we'll need to implement those changes and complete this project by the third week in November. No excuses, no exceptions."

"That's only four weeks away. Can we do it?"

"We'll have to—even if it means increasing the budget to double the crews."

"Well, baby girl, if anybody can make it happen, it's you."

"Thanks, Dad."

"One more thing, Diamond."

"Yes, Dad."

"Since you're working late tomorrow night, try and take some time off later this week. You're becoming a workaholic, like your old man."

"All right, Dad. I'll think about it." As Diamond left her father's office, she felt confident that everyone would rise to the challenge and make this new deadline. She only wished she were as certain that she could behave herself at the meeting tomorrow night...and keep her hands off Jackson.

Chapter 10

The next evening, Diamond arrived at the restaurant on schedule and quickly found a parking space near the building. She wore her power business suit, and, while she'd convinced herself that this had nothing to do with whom she was meeting, she'd freshened her makeup and sleeked down the short do she was still getting used to.

The waiter led her to the table that Jackson occupied. He stood as she approached. "Ms. Drake."

"All right, Jackson." She sat. "You may call me Diamond."

"As you wish." Jackson sat, as well. "But you very much look like Ms. Drake right now, up to that sleek hairstyle and down to your sexy heels. I really like your hair short like that. It looks good."

The waiter interrupted. "Would you like to place a drink order?"

"We're waiting for another person," Diamond quickly replied, thinking that the last thing she needed was alcohol.

This man's looks alone made her feel tipsy. *I've got to keep my wits about me.*

"While we wait, I think I'll have a glass of cabernet," Jackson said. Mr. Bravado concealed the nervousness he hadn't felt since he'd asked Misty Adams to meet him behind the skating rink: a request that had ended in his loss of virginity. There was something about Diamond Drake that brought out his chivalry and need to protect, along with every insecurity he'd ever known. "Would you like one, Diamond?"

"I'll take a glass of sparkling water with lemon slices." She quickly shifted the focus to business. "Did Taylor forward the ideas we discussed last week?"

Jackson nodded. "I had my architect draw up some diagrams to present. As soon as... Ah, here she is." Jackson stood as Taylor approached the table. Both he and Diamond immediately noticed her demeanor. "Are you okay?"

"No," Taylor said, sitting quickly. "I don't know what it is about this project and disturbing phone calls, but I got another just now as I was parking my car. My dad was en route to meet some friends for dinner. There was an accident."

Jackson's brow creased.

"Taylor," Diamond said, placing a hand on Taylor's arm. "Is he all right?"

"We don't know," Taylor replied, shaking her head. "Yes, I'd like a glass of your top-shelf merlot, please," she said to the waiter who approached their table. And then back to Diamond, she said, "My sister called on her way to the hospital. We're trying to stay optimistic at this point."

"Taylor, we'll totally understand you having to leave this meeting." Jackson's voice was filled with concern. "You must be worried sick."

"Our family's pretty dramatic," Taylor said with a nervous laugh. "It could be a fender bender and an APB would still be sent out to all corners of the globe." The waiter arrived, and Taylor took a healthy gulp from her wineglass. The trio passed on appetizers for the moment and instead tried to focus on work. But it wasn't meant to be. A couple minutes later, Taylor's phone rang. She nodded as she listened to the person on the other end of the phone. "That's good news, but I still want to see him," she said. After hanging up the phone, she began gathering the items she'd placed on the table. "That was my sister. Dad is going to be fine. There were no internal or life-threatening injuries. But there's still no way I can concentrate tonight," she said to Diamond with an apologetic smile. "So sorry to have to run out on you guys, but I'm the consummate daddy's girl."

"I totally understand," Diamond said, knowing that if she'd heard that her father was in an accident, she'd feel the same way. "I'm glad to know that it wasn't more serious."

When Taylor stood, Jackson did, as well. "Sorry to hear about your father, but I, too, am very glad he's okay."

"Thanks, Jackson."

"And when you see your father, give him a hug."

Taylor smiled at Jackson. "I sure will."

Jackson and Diamond watched Taylor rush out of the restaurant. When he sat, Jackson's mood was somber. They ordered appetizers and tried to continue the meeting, but his mind was obviously elsewhere. "Maybe we should continue this discussion another time," Diamond finally said.

"Sorry," Jackson replied. "The news that Taylor received—and the way she received it—hit close to home."

Diamond was used to seeing cockiness and swagger when she looked at Jackson. But now she saw something else—vulnerability. "Do you want to talk about it?"

For a while, it seemed as though Jackson's answer was no. When he began speaking, his voice was low, his eyes downcast. "I lost the people who raised me almost seven years ago," he said, idly fingering the water glass before him. "It was a car wreck."

Jackson looked at Diamond. Her heart clenched at the pain she saw in his eyes. "Oh, Jackson, that must have been terrible."

Jackson nodded, remembering experiences that had been equally as devastating: his mother's drug use, for instance, and his brushes with the law. "A drag-racing teenager killed my aunt Evie and uncle John, who'd built the construction company I own from the ground up. He taught me almost everything I know, especially how to be a man. Had it not been for my uncle's influence, my life would probably look very different from what it does now."

"And someone called you about their accident?"

"I was in a club partying, getting my groove on when I got the call that changed my life." Jackson sat back in the booth, looked beyond Diamond into the worst day of his life. "I'd intended to visit them that day but went on an impromptu date instead." The smile on Jackson's face was fleeting and bittersweet. "I never got a chance for that last hug, you know? Never got to say goodbye."

For the first time since meeting him, Diamond initiated contact. She reached over and placed a comforting hand on Jackson's arm. "I'm sorry."

Jackson shrugged, putting his Teflon veneer firmly back in place. "Death is a part of life."

Diamond was silent, finding it impossible to imagine a life without Donald and Genevieve Drake. The kids often joked with their parents that they had to at least outlive Papa Dee, who was two years shy of one hundred. "Do you have siblings?"

"No."

The dark look crossed Jackson's face so quickly that Diamond thought she'd imagined it. It occurred to her how little she knew about Jackson Wright. But now felt like an inappropriate time for questions. She looked at her watch. "I should be going. Is there any way we can continue this meeting Thursday, at the site?"

"Can I confirm that morning? I don't know what's going on until Marissa tells me."

"Marissa?"

"My assistant."

"Oh, okay."

Jackson smiled for the first time in several minutes. "You thought I was talking about my woman or wife?"

"No, I—"

"Ha! Yes, you did."

There it was…that irritating chuckle. Here was the Jackson that Diamond had come to know, the one who helped her remember that she didn't like him, wasn't attracted to him and wasn't interested in anything more than business when it came to him. "Look, I don't care who Melissa—"

"*Marissa,* Marissa Hayes. She's been my assistant since I took over the business six years ago."

Is that a smile or a smirk on his face? Diamond took a surreptitious breath to calm her ire. No man had ever gotten her this hot, in anger or desire. *I'm not going to give him the satisfaction of thinking he's upset me. I'm not jealous! I couldn't care less about Marissa!* "Thanks for the company history," Diamond nonchalantly replied in a tone that her mother, the queen of dry, would be proud of. "If you're free, around one o'clock Thursday will work for me. If I'm not available, you can leave a message with my assistant, Kathleen Fitzpatrick. She's been with the company for twenty years."

With that, Diamond walked out of the restaurant with her head held high. But it was not fast enough to escape the sound of Jackson's low, soft chuckle that tickled her back the way his fingers had three days before.

Chapter 11

"My, don't we look lovely," Kathleen said as soon as Diamond entered the office.

"I look the same as always, Kat."

"It's understandable," Kathleen continued, her fingers flying across the keyboard and eyes glued to the screen, "since that handsome construction fellow is meeting you for lunch."

This news stopped Diamond in her tracks. "Jackson called?" Of course, she'd hoped he would. That's why she'd taken special care with her wardrobe and added an extra spray of perfume to the day's preparations, her "same as always" comment notwithstanding. She'd hoped that these extra touches would come off casual and nonchalant. She wore a tan-colored pencil skirt with a billowy floral top that cinched at the waist. The neckline was tasteful yet hinted at treasures. She returned her short hair to its spiky form. It was just another day at the office—no big deal. But Kathleen had noticed. "We mentioned meeting today at one o'clock," Diamond continued, "but we didn't discuss lunch."

"I assumed it would be a lunch meeting since that's how you generally handle clients who meet between noon and two."

"Did you mention that to him?"

"No."

"Good. We'll meet at the site and then, if necessary, come back to the office."

"So I shouldn't set up a spread in the conference room?"

"No, Kat, but thank you for asking." *Jeez, what is with this woman? Doesn't she know that just seeing Jackson stirs up an entirely different kind of appetite?*

Diamond went into her office. Four hours passed in which Diamond had no idea what she did. Floating on autopilot was an understatement. All she could think about was the dichotomy that was Jackson Wright: the superassured macho man she'd first met juxtaposed with the caring, vulnerable human being she'd glimpsed Tuesday night, after hearing the news about Taylor's dad. Wafting through these thoughts were the memories that had rarely left her since the concert: his kiss. By the time Kathleen buzzed to let her know that Jackson had arrived, Diamond was a composed, organized, calm-looking mess.

When Jackson entered her office, Diamond came around her desk. "Hello, Jackson."

"Ms. Drake," Jackson replied, looking absolutely decadent in black jeans, red shirt and cowboy boots.

Cowboy boots? When it comes to Mr. Wright, will the surprises ever end?

In the most utmost act of professionalism, he reached out for a handshake. "It's good to see you again."

"You just saw me Tuesday night," Diamond answered, hoping that she sounded appropriately relaxed. "Let's set up here, at the conference table. Once I'm sure we're on the same page, we can go to the site." She missed Kathleen's confused expression, having totally forgotten that mere moments ago she'd informed Kathleen that the exact opposite would occur.

Jackson followed Diamond to the area of her large L-shaped office that housed an oval conference table. While he'd vowed that unlike during other encounters he would be the "strictly business" brother Diamond said she wanted, he couldn't help but notice how the skirt she wore cupped her luscious booty the way his hands longed to, couldn't stop remembering how his hands felt buried in her hair. He thought of other things he'd like to bury in other places before forcing away the train of thought and the inevitable evidence of desire that would embarrass them both.

"Nice office," he said, eating up the distance to the table with long, sure strides and placing his briefcase on the table. "Did Taylor design it?"

"No. We didn't meet her until this renovation. Her credentials are impeccable and awards impressive. But then again, seeing as you're in the building profession, I might be telling you something that you already know."

"Taylor Stevens isn't famous yet, but in the architectural community, she's a household name." Jackson spread the drawings on the table as he talked. "We've worked together in the past, and I can tell you that these are some of the most ambitious plans I've seen from her."

"Even so, we need to kick things up another notch."

Jackson raised his brow in question.

Diamond told him about the call from *O Magazine*. "I'm totally in love with what we've planned so far. If you have any further ideas that would add to this site's uniqueness, I'm open."

Jackson's eyes darkened at thoughts of the woman before him being open and in love. "Come here," he commanded, changing the subject along with his demeanor—still professional, but with just enough sexy thrown into his voice to make Diamond's heart skip a beat. "I want to show you how I'm going to make all of your dreams come true."

Diamond's breath caught in her throat. What she was dreaming about in this moment had absolutely nothing to do with Drake Wines Resort & Spa and everything to do with the man standing next to her. He evoked in her images best left forgotten, like diamond rings and wedding bells, silk dresses with shoes dyed to match. In her mind's eye, Diamond saw Jackson sauntering down the aisle, his bow askew, that lovable, cocky smile on his face. She almost moaned aloud. *Strictly professional. That's how I roll. No colleagues or playboys.* Ignoring the sudden wetness between her legs, she walked closer to where Jackson was standing.

"I propose that we install a glass ceiling, from the fireplace and front sitting area—" Jackson's long, tapered finger slid across the paper "—all the way to here, the second sitting area where the piano bar and Stage B will be erected."

Jackson continued with his explanation, but Diamond didn't hear it. All she could do was feel the heat emanating from his body and imagine how it would feel on top of her. His hand rested on the paper, and she imagined it massaging her body, imagined sucking his fingers into her mouth, one by one and imagined setting him as on fire as she was right now. Even with her three-inch heels, Jackson was still taller, with a virility that oozed out of his pores. There had been other moments of celibacy in her life, and never before had she been so flustered; never before had she wanted a man as much as she wanted this one. Now all she had to do was make sure that Jackson never found this out.

"Diamond? Are you listening?"

"Of course. I agree that an expanded glass ceiling is a wonderful idea. What's the added cost?" Jackson looked at her and smiled. A smile like that should come with a warning label and sirens or something to give a sister a chance to brace herself. "Did I say something funny?"

"Your question would have made sense two sentences ago—when I threw out a proposed figure for the upgrade, along with the fact that I'd already brought additional proposals for your dad and the finance department."

There was no comment for that one; Diamond buried her embarrassment under the pretense of studying the drawings on the table. And what was it about being near this man that made her lose her hearing?

"The accelerated schedule shouldn't be a problem, especially since you're willing to approve additional manpower. And with the holidays approaching, the guys will relish the work."

Diamond's office phone rang. "Hey, Dad," she said. "We were just talking about you."

"Who's we?"

"Jackson is here going over the additions we discussed. He's worked up some figures, and if you have a moment, we'd like to stop by your office."

"Ginny and I have a date tonight. So you'd best stop by now."

Diamond smiled at her father's words. Her parents had been dating for thirty-five years.

Moments later, Jackson and Diamond stepped into the massive corner office of Donald Drake. Masculinity oozed from every pore of this tycoon's body and every fiber of his office, from the dark mahogany and black leather furniture to the framed 1930 Winchester Model 12 shotgun that had been given to Papa Dee when he was sixteen. Jackson felt right at home. "Mr. Drake," he said, walking in with hand outstretched, "good to see you again."

The men exchanged a firm handshake.

"Likewise, Boss," Donald said, with a scrutinizing gaze. "And how many times have I said you can call me Donald?"

Jackson smiled. "More than once, sir."

"All right, then. I toured the site again yesterday, and I must tell you that I've never seen finer workmanship."

"Thank you, sir."

"I wasn't too crazy about your idea of the stone-rock setting for the Jacuzzis, but it works. Makes it look as though those pools spring right from the ground."

"I'm glad you're satisfied."

"More than pleased, son."

Son. And again, visions of wedding bells danced in her head. Diamond gave it a subtle shake. She was more than a little troubled at the effect Jackson had on her. She wasn't thinking about relationships right now, let alone marriage. And when she did, it would be to someone logical and practical, not to this stallion standing tall beside her, the one who made her lose her mind. And losing it she was. Why else would she be standing here with thoughts that were delusional?

"Dad, we have the drawings for the glass ceiling I discussed with you." Diamond walked toward Donald's large desk as she spoke. They viewed the drawings, discussed the upgrades and then, as Jackson and Diamond prepared to leave his office, Donald made a suggestion that suggested to Diamond that she wasn't the only crazy in the room.

"Jackson, I know you've tasted our wine, but have you perused our vineyard?"

"No, Donald, I haven't."

Donald looked at his daughter. "Diamond, why don't you give Jackson the grand tour?"

Chapter 12

Jackson and Diamond left Donald's office and, after stopping by Diamond's office for the key to the golf cart used to tour the grounds, headed for the parking lot. "I thought Dexter had shown you the grounds," Diamond said, trying to still her rapidly beating heart. The thought of her and Jackson alone between large, shielding grapevines away from the hubbub of the business had all kinds of thoughts ping-ponging inside her head. "This is such an inspiring piece of property that it's sure to further enhance the skills you and your team are bringing to the renovation."

"Oh, so you're interested in my skills, huh?" Jackson teased.

"Are you always so cocky?" Diamond cut Jackson a look. "Behave."

They reached the golf cart as Jackson replied, "I make no such promises, sweetheart. Beautiful day spent in a beautiful vineyard with a beautiful woman?" He turned sultry eyes on Diamond's lips as he licked his own. "Anything can happen."

Diamond started the cart. "Anything" couldn't happen fast enough. In this moment, it was decided. She was going to sleep with this man. It was either that or lose her mind, and there was no way she could do that with a building project that needed to be completed in thirty days and Oprah's people arriving two months after that. She knew just where the seduction would take place. *Now. Today. Rules be damned!* Of course, these thoughts were fleeting. There was positively no way she could be with this man. No way!

"Ideally I'd start the tour at the eastern edge of the vineyard," she said as she came to a stop in front of a large farmlike structure just down the lane from the executive offices. "But since we're so close, let's start here, our shipping headquarters. The wines are stored in the cellar below it." She hopped out of the cart, and without waiting to see if Jackson followed her, she walked to the ornately decorated double doors.

She and Jackson stepped inside and it was if they'd entered a large showroom housing row after row and case after case of wines that were ready for shipment. "Wow," Jackson said, whistling softly. "This is impressive."

Diamond smiled, her chest swelling with pride. "This is the heartbeat of Drake Wines, where the wines are housed once they're bottled." They began walking down a long, wide aisle. "The wines are shelved by type and year, beginning with the whites, reds, burgundies and then moving on to the sparkling varieties."

They reached the last aisle, and Jackson noticed a stairway. "Where do those steps lead?"

Diamond looked at Jackson. "The cellar," she said, a bit breathlessly. "That's where the wines are aged. Now, on to the vineyards."

"Aged in those large oak barrels, like we see in the movies?"

"Yes," Diamond said, over her shoulder, taking into account the fact that Jackson hadn't moved. "They are sixty-gallon containers made from premium oak."

"I want to see them."

"We don't have much time." She was halfway to the door. "Unless you're scared."

Screech.

This is how she'd ended up climbing trees, eating bugs and lying facedown in a shallow creek bed, covered with mud—because her brothers had dared her. She should have learned her lesson. But "should" was on vacation and "would" turned around and marched back to where Jackson stood.

Determined to wipe the smirk off of his face, she squared her shoulders and sounded as businesslike as she could with wet panties. "Follow me."

She started down the stairs. Jackson's eyes darkened as he watched her from behind. Actually, as he watched her behind...the way the pencil skirt caressed each cheek that clenched—first left, then right—with each step she took. He felt himself harden and did nothing to control his ardor. He wanted Diamond, pure and simple. And he wanted her now.

They reached the bottom step, where there was a small landing with heavy metal doors on three sides. "Different rooms are used to house the different wines," she explained matter-of-factly. "The temperatures vary depending on which grape is being used but for the most part hover around fifty-eight degrees." Even as she said this, she realized that her thermometer had been stuck on one setting since first laying eyes on Jackson Wright...hot. *I will not give this man the satisfaction of seducing me,* she vowed, after unlocking and then opening one of the doors. *That's probably what he's used to, what he expects.* Determined to control her uncontrollable passion for him, she took a calming breath and turned around. "These barrels—"

Jackson swallowed Diamond's gasp as the lips he'd claimed the moment she turned parted and welcomed his tongue. The kiss was forceful, demanding—his hands searching, finding, massaging soft flesh. He wrapped strong arms around her before burying one hand in her soft, spiky hair and using his other one to press her against his burgeoning manhood. His tongue mimicked the hips that were grinding against her, leaving no doubt as to what he desired. He ran his hand up her back and around to the soft breasts crushed against his chest. Brushing a finger against the soft material that hid part of her treasure, he smiled when a hardened nipple was his instant reward. But there was a problem: too much fabric between them. Thrusting his tongue deeper, Jackson reached for the belt that cinched Diamond's blouse at her waist. One would have thought he'd designed it—so quickly was he able to undo the clasp. *Butter.* That's what Diamond's skin felt like. It was silky smooth and on fire. He placed his hand on her lacy bra, rubbed her areola through the fabric and then he tweaked it.

Diamond came undone.

She reached for the hem of her blouse and broke the kiss just long enough to pull the silky fabric over her head. She noticed that Jackson's chocolate-brown orbs were black with desire. What she didn't know was that they mirrored her own. Resuming the kiss, she wrapped her arms around Jackson's neck, crushing her breasts against his chest. But there was just one problem. There were still too many clothes. She reached for Jackson's T-shirt, pulling it out of his jeans. Taking the hint, Jackson quickly shed it, tossing it in the direction Diamond's blouse had gone.

"I want to make love to you," he murmured, sending a trail of kisses from her mouth to her neck and back. "Now."

It was time to wave the white flag, throw in the towel and join the one she couldn't beat. "Me, too." She reached behind her and unzipped her skirt. Shimmying out of it and enjoying the freedom, she reached behind her and unsnapped her bra. Her breasts seemed to cheer, swaying their silent invitation.

Jackson was quick to RSVP. He rubbed one nipple and licked the other, lapping as if it oozed Drake Wines' pinot noir 2002, one of the vineyard's most popular winners. His fingers found the edge of her thong, and one of them slid inside, running along the folds of her pleasure then slipping inside for a more thorough greeting. Diamond's head dropped back, her legs spread of their own volition. Another finger slipped inside, and he began playing her box like she was a piano and he was Duke Ellington. Taking the "A" train would have been too fast. So Jackson tapped her like a satin doll, and her slippery folds mimicked that material. She moaned, grinding herself against Jackson's hand. He felt her hand slide up his leg and rest on his massive package. She squeezed him through the thick jean fabric.

And Jackson came undone.

Picking up Diamond as if she were a feather, he walked them to a row of barrels, placed Diamond on top of one and dropped to his knees. He spread her legs and placed soft kisses on alternating thighs. He felt Diamond's hands rubbing the soft black curls on his head. It spurred him on and up her leg, where, after spreading her wider, he licked her through the lacy thong that matched the bra that was now who knew where. She hissed. Jackson chuckled that cocky, knowing laugh. *Yeah, I'm on to something, baby girl. And I'm just getting started.* With the precision of a fencer's sword, his tongue tickled her nub. After a love bite on the same sweetness, he moved aside the lace and got down to business, reaching, it seemed, for Diamond's core.

And found it.

Diamond's legs began to quiver as an orgasm uncoiled from the pit of her paradise and spread throughout her entire body. She'd never experienced such an intense sensation, never witnessed such mastery of the oral organ in her life. She heard mewling, whimpers, and then realized that these sounds were coming from her own mouth. Feeling as limp as an abandoned double-Dutch rope, she slumped against Jackson's shoulder.

Jackson uttered three words, "I'm not finished." And Diamond's vajayjay began tingling all over again.

Chapter 13

He stood and kissed her leisurely, thoroughly, the taste of Diamond's essence on his tongue. He stepped back, and she felt bereft and abandoned, her thoughts scattered like ashes in the wind. Then Jackson's jeans and boxers fell to the cement floor and brought Diamond's attention into laser focus. Was that for real, and if so…was that all for her?

Jackson's hardened, engorged shaft stood proudly before him, swaying from its own weightiness. Diamond's mouth watered, and her swallow was audible.

A small smile scampered across his face as, like a panther on the prowl, he walked back to her. "Do you want this?"

Diamond's eyes never left his as she nodded. She couldn't get any words past the constriction in her chest. And really, what was there to say? She'd thank Santa later for Christmas in October. This man was a gift, and right now she didn't even care if he knew that she knew it. She let the longing show openly on her face as she watched him open the condom foil and wrap his package. Diamond swallowed again and licked her lips. In one fell swoop, Jackson picked her off the barrel, which was a good thing since her legs still resembled the abandoned double-Dutch rope. She wrapped her legs just above his perfectly round derriere, noting its hardness and making a mental note to take a closer examination at a later date. He walked them to the wall, penned her against it, and then the dance began in earnest.

He stroked her slowly, inch by excruciatingly beautiful inch, allowing her body time to adjust to his sizable girth. Diamond's fingernails dug into his shoulders as she absorbed a myriad of sensations, including the realization that nothing in her romantic life had prepared her for this moment.

It took a while before he was fully inside her, but at the moment he settled flush against her, Jackson thought that he'd died and gone to heaven. And if that were so, this brother never wanted his feet to touch earth again. He sighed with contentment, turning his head to capture Diamond's mouth in a scorching kiss. His tongue made leisurely circles inside her hot mouth, and soon his hips were moving in a circular motion.

Not to be outdone, Diamond's hips duplicated his motion, and her core ignited. Jackson pulled out, teased her with the tip of his penis and then plunged back in again—seemingly even deeper than before. Was it possible for a man to grow two additional inches on the spot? If not, this was the day for miracles, because Diamond swore that was what happened. He tickled her core with his determination; over and again he touched her there…slow and purposeful, fast and sure. His body tingled all over as he felt her kissing every part of his face. Emotions he swore were beneath him came rushing to the surface—emotions that spoke of commitment and loyalty and forever.

Once again, Diamond's legs began to shake from the

strength of his desire and her conviction. It was as if her very breath was being taken away but she still managed to cry out as he pumped harder. Faster. Deeper. *Damn!* Her climax was meteorological, complete with stars and flashes of lightning. She had never been a screamer, but now short bursts of sound bounced off the cement walls as wave after wave after wave of ecstasy washed over her. Tears came to her eyes at the beauty of it all. After a series of staccato thrusts, Jackson joined her in the afternoon cataclysmic paradise they'd created. Had there been an audience, they would have stomped their feet in standing ovation and demanded an encore. Jackson wanted an encore his damn self!

"What's that sound?" Diamond asked, once she'd summoned enough strength to open her mouth.

"My phone," Jackson replied. He'd heard the vibration several times during the course of their lovemaking but had tuned out all but the feel of being inside Diamond's delectable body. Yet now he admitted that since it was the middle of a business day and he was the owner of a multimillion-dollar company, he just might want to answer. It could be important.

He eased out of Diamond and set her on the ground as if she were a delicate, priceless piece of blown glass. He kissed her lightly on the mouth and then walked away.

Diamond watched Jackson stride across the room in all of his naked glory and retrieve the phone from the holder on his jeans. Indeed, his ass was all that and a case of Drake's finest grape, but she quelled the urge to join him where he stood and give it the massaging it seemed to be calling for. He was trying to handle business, after all. So instead, she walked on still-shaky legs in search of the thong that had been carelessly tossed aside. Her stomach rumbled, and she realized that the calories from her light lunch had been more than expended. She thought that if Jackson's schedule allowed it, she'd suggest they share an early dinner and then, maybe, go somewhere clandestine and have each other for dessert. She found her thong, and while daydreaming of Jackson and Diamond, Part II, she donned it and her bra, skirt and blouse. So deep was she in this daydream that she didn't notice that Jackson had dressed quickly as well and that the face that just moments before shone with the afterglow of serious lovemaking was now etched with unease.

"Is everything all right?"

"No," Jackson said, already heading toward the stairs. "Everything is not all right. I've got to go."

"Jackson!" Diamond called to his rapidly retreating back. But without a backward glance he was up the steps and through the door. Diamond marched up the stairs in her bare feet ready to demand an answer and, considering what they'd both just experienced, a more proper goodbye. No matter what the person on the phone had just told him, how could he just up and leave like she was already yesterday's news? "Jackson!" she called out again as she entered the large warehouse. She hurried down the aisle toward the double doors, but as she neared the front of the building, her eyes told her what her heart already knew...he was gone.

Chapter 14

Jackson reached the Boss Construction parking lot and swerved into his reserved space. The thirty minutes that it had taken him to reach the office—when under the legal speed limit it would have taken at least forty-five—had done nothing to cool his ire. He'd mentally kicked himself for not answering the phone earlier and potentially putting both his valued assistant and his business in even more danger. It wasn't like he was an eighteen-year-old teenager with raging hormones. Why hadn't he answered his phone when he'd heard it vibrating through his jeans on the cement floor? He knew the reason. Because his head had been between Diamond's delicious legs, and his singular focus after that had been to place his dick there.

The elevator couldn't come soon enough, and once it reached the Boss offices on the thirty-story building's top floor, Jackson's long strides quickly ate up the distance between the lobby and the spacious corner offices with spectacular views of the Pacific Ocean on one side and downtown San Diego on the other. Once Jackson entered, however, he didn't see the illustrious tableau that painters would envy. The first thing he saw was a still-shaken Marissa sitting on the couch and his attorney, Abe Swartz, occupying one of the wingbacked chairs opposite her. Both stood when Jackson entered, and Marissa raced to his side.

"Where were you?" she asked, while in an uncharacteristic show of emotion she flung her arms around Jackson's waist. "I was so afraid." In this moment, Jackson knew that whatever had happened in his office was more serious than a threatening letter. "I hope you don't mind that I called Mr. Swartz," Marissa continued, nervously twisting the ring on her right hand. "But I didn't want to involve the police before speaking with you. I didn't know what else to do."

Jackson took a step and placed a hand on Marissa's shoulder. "I'm sorry I didn't get your calls from the beginning. I was…in a meeting, and my phone was on vibrate. You did the right thing in waiting until I got here." Jackson reached over and shook Abe's hand. "Guys, come into my office." Once there and seated, he looked back at Marissa. "Now, tell me again exactly what happened."

Marissa took a deep breath as she prepared to repeat what she'd shared via telephone as Jackson raced down the I-15. "I went to lunch around twelve-thirty, and when I got back, I noticed that Gia wasn't at the receptionist desk. This was strange only because we'd talked before I left and she'd said that she was working through lunch so that she could take off at four for her daughter's dentist appointment. I didn't think too much about it until I came back here, inserted my key and found the door already unlocked."

Jackson sat forward. "You're sure the door was unlocked."

"Positive."

"Was it open?"

"No, the door was closed, but it was definitely unlocked. That dead bolt has a distinctive click, plus if I don't put my key in just the right way, it sometimes sticks. I'd barely put my key in when I turned the knob and the door opened."

Jackson looked around the office. Everything seemed to be in its rightful place. "Were any of the file cabinets opened?"

Marissa shook her head.

"Anything missing that you can see?"

"No."

Jackson took a breath and eyed Marissa with a serious expression. "Are you sure you locked the door?"

Marissa shot out of her chair and began to pace the room. "Of course I'm sure, Boss! How many times have you told me to be sure to lock up? You've reiterated how costly it could be if some of the information on upcoming projects got into the wrong hands. I locked the door and then double-checked it, as always. It. Was. Locked!"

"All right, Marissa. I know this is alarming, but you've got to calm down. We have a situation, but since it looks like nothing was taken, I don't get why you're so upset."

"It's because of the information she didn't share with you," Abe interrupted. "I told her to wait until you got here so you could see for yourself."

The hairs on the back of Jackson's neck stood up. "See what?"

"This," Marissa said, motioning him out of his office and over to her cubicle, which was just outside his door.

Jackson rounded the corner of the wood-and-glass enclosure that afforded Marissa a modicum of privacy and saw the shattered glass that was once her computer screen, along with the bullet holes that riddled the area around it.

While still trying to take in the shock of someone firing a weapon in his office, Abe walked up and silently handed him a slip of paper. "This was placed on Marissa's chair."

Jackson glanced at Abe and took the piece of paper. His heart caught as he read the words that had been written with one of his assistant's markers: *The next bullet has your name on it. And as you can see, there will be no stopping me when I'm ready to 187 your no good snitch ass.*

Snitch? This definitely sounded like a word from his former life. But who from those years so long ago would want to threaten him now? And why? Jackson looked up in time to see Marissa's eyes flutter close. He didn't have to ask whether or not she'd read the note. "I'm sorry you had to find all of this," he said to her softly, his voice filled with compassion. "But I'm glad you weren't here when…whoever did this came by." He now totally understood her earlier outburst and felt like a heel for having been enjoying a little bit of heaven while his assistant was going through hell. Very few knew just how much turmoil his assistant had endured, why he'd hired her as his assistant with virtually no secretarial experience and why, after a painful incident she went through a few months ago, he was even more protective. Even fewer people in the present circles he traveled knew about Jackson's past. At first he'd hidden it to fit in with the private-school kids, and now he hid it because he felt it was no one's business. It was a part of his life that he wasn't proud of but also the part that caused the insecurity: having to fend for himself from the age of seven, not having a father or mother to guide these early, formative years and falling into a crowd whose machismo was often judged by how many pounds of crack you'd sold, places you'd robbed or people you'd killed. He'd left his old life more than a decade ago but at times still felt like he didn't belong to the life he'd fully embraced once he turned sixteen. "I'm sorry," he said again, knowing these words were not enough. But for now, they would have to do. "Let's go back into my office."

The three of them returned to Jackson's office, where he shut the door. "No one heard gunshots?" he asked Marissa.

She shook her head.

"I'm sure a silencer was used," Abe said.

Jackson nodded, his mind whirling with thoughts of who was behind the increasingly ominous threats.

"I know you want to keep this quiet," Abe said. "But a crime has been committed. It's time for the police to get involved. The place needs to be dusted for fingerprints, and the employees need to be questioned."

"No!"

Abe's eyes narrowed. His voice remained calm. "Someone came into this building, broke into your office and damaged your property...with a gun! I'd say these threats are now too close for comfort, Jackson."

"If news leaks out about any of this, especially the part that involves weapons, the press will have a field day. They'll turn finding a bullet hole into some kind of gang activity. You know how small this industry is, how easily a bid can be swayed from one company to the next. I don't want to have that kind of negative publicity." What he said was true, but that wasn't all of it. Though it was irrational, a part of Jackson was ashamed of his old life: the things he'd done and the plight of his mother. There was a slight yet undeniable fear that if all of the truth ever came out, his empire could disappear just as rapidly as it had come to him. He and Marissa shared a look, one that Abe Swartz observed. "We have to keep a lid on this."

Abe leaned more comfortably into the large leather chair that sat opposite Jackson's desk. He steepled his fingers and gazed at Jackson intently. "I knew your uncle a long time," he said at last. "And I'll honor his memory by keeping this quiet, for now, and helping you as much as I can. But I'm going to need two things from you. One, I need to know what it is you're hiding and, two, who you've pissed off enough to want to see you dead."

Chapter 15

Back at Drake Wines, Diamond stewed. Her fingers itched to dial Jackson's number. But she would not. She'd rather dive headfirst into a vat of smushed grapes—fully clothed… in designer originals. She'd chided herself a thousand times for giving in to her desires, let alone the fact that she had enjoyed herself immensely while doing so. Her nether muscles clenched at the memory, and as much as she hated it, her body wanted more of Jackson "Boss" Wright. Even now she could hear him laugh, that irritatingly smug sound that hours earlier she'd deemed one of the sexiest noises she'd ever heard. Of course, at the time a certain body part was being tickled by his tongue. *Enough!* Diamond snatched up the revisions of the latest newsletter she'd printed out and forced herself to concentrate. *Yeah, right. Good luck with that.*

A light tap sounded on Diamond's door. "I'm outta here," Kathleen said, as she entered. "Do you need anything before I go?"

"Nope." Diamond spoke without looking up. "Close the door on your way out." She knew Kathleen still stood there, could envision the look of motherly concern on her face. Her frustration caused her to speak more sharply than she intended. "I'm fine, Kat. See you tomorrow."

There was silence for a moment and then she said, "Bye, Diamond." A soft click of the door punctuated Kathleen's departure.

Diamond sighed, even as Jackson's voice invaded her conscience: *Black American princess.* She knew that right now her actions were those of exactly that, a spoiled diva. Kathleen was the last person who deserved such treatment. But she was still too much in sulk mode to dismiss her assistant getting all up in her business—sanely translated— showing genuine concern. *At least she's gone and I can mope in private.* But, no; Kathleen was obviously a glutton for punishment because less than a minute later the click of the doorknob signaled her return.

Okay, I've had it. Steaming, Diamond whirled around. "What is it now? Oh, hey, Dex."

A slight smirk accompanied Dexter into the room. "Hey, sis." He walked over and sat in the chair across from Diamond's desk.

Diamond never looked up. "I'm busy, so whatever it is, make it quick."

Dexter leaned over, snatched what she was reading out of her hands and laughed at her glowering countenance like he was twelve.

"I mean it, Dexter." Oh, she was really serious now, full name used and all. "I'm trying to get out of here."

Dexter placed the paper back down. "Hot date tonight?"

Diamond huffed, glared at Dexter and returned to her reading, hoping he'd get the don't-mess-with-me-'cause-I'm-not-in-the-mood message. "Bye, brother."

He didn't. Rather, he kept sitting there, staring, a stupid I've-got-a-secret look on his face. Diamond didn't even care what that was about. But she was getting ready to find out.

"Or was that date this afternoon?"

Had everybody on the premises been drinking nosy water? Not four hours away from her first dalliance in a year and suddenly everyone was interested in her dating schedule and mental status. That "everyone" at this point included only Kathleen and Dexter was beside the point. Two people in her business were two people too many. Diamond stopped looking at the report she'd been holding but not reading the past ten minutes and tried to keep her cool by adopting a nonchalant attitude. "Ha-ha. My brother's got jokes. You must have seen Jackson by my offices earlier. He owns the construction company that is doing our renovation, or have you forgotten that minor detail?" She waited. The smirk remained on Dexter's face. "It was business."

Dexter's eyes stayed locked on hers. The smirk stayed, too. "Uh-huh."

"Whatever." Diamond was proud of how apparently bored she must look. The disguise took effort.

"You're going to sit there and tell me that nothing happened between you and Jackson when you took him on a tour of the vineyard?"

So he's talked to Daddy. Either that or he saw Jackson leaving the warehouse. "That got interrupted. Jackson received a phone call from his assistant. Emergency. Had to dash back to his office."

"That may be true, but he didn't leave too quickly."

Diamond shrugged. "I don't know how he left. I stayed behind to check out the inventory."

Dexter laughed. "You checked out more than wine." He reached into his pocket. "I admit to my share of dallying, but—" flicking his wrist, he tossed something on Diamond's desk "—this ain't mine."

The reflection of the gold foil on Diamond's varnished desktop shone like a thousand suns.

"What's that?" she asked, her casual attitude slipping a notch.

"If we were in court, I'd call it admissible evidence," Dexter said, stretching his legs out in front of him.

"And I'd argue reasonable doubt." Diamond willed herself not to blush as she flicked the "evidence" off her desk. "Not to mention that you're nasty…picking up an anonymous condom wrapper. A dozen people are in and out of that cellar. It could belong to any of them."

"Uh-huh." Dexter continued to eye his sister. "But the way you're over there squirming, I'd say I'm closer to the truth."

"What you're closer to is getting kicked out of my office. Shouldn't you be focused on your own love life, hanging out with your Latin flavor and whatnot?"

"Besides," Dexter continued, ignoring Diamond's attempt to shift the focus, "I was down at the site earlier and talked to some of the men. One of them saw you showing Jackson around. The rumor mill is hopping, sister."

"Just make sure you don't add to it, brother. My interest in Jackson ends at the construction site."

"Maybe," Dexter said, rising from the chair and heading to the door. "But is that all that Jackson wants?"

Diamond waited until her brother had closed the door and then leaned back heavily against the chair. The truth of the matter was Diamond had no idea what Jackson wanted. And from the hurried way he left after they'd made love, she deduced that when it came to anything outside of the workplace, maybe the cocky, arrogant love machine that still had her throbbing had already gotten what he came for.

Chapter 16

Jackson placed his hands on either side of the marble shower and let the six powerful shower jets hit him from all sides. Abe's interrogation—because to call it a discussion would be putting it too mildly—had been grueling but necessary. It had been years since Jackson had opened up about his less than humble beginnings, the start in life that he swore to put behind him the moment he left South Central and landed in San Diego's tony suburb of La Jolla. He'd hoped—prayed even—that the severing from his childhood could be clean and complete. A part of him, however, knew that there was no total escape from the ties that bound him. Family was family, and blood was thicker than concrete.

Moving his head from side to side, he let the water run over his close-cropped curls and tried to work out the kinks in his neck. Mental pictures from another meeting, the one that had happened before Abe's pointed questioning, came to mind. He instantly hardened and was reminded that the

break-in and letter weren't the only things that had Jackson
tight. After Abe left, he'd tried to reach Diamond. Her assistant had told him that she was unavailable. He could just
about guess what that meant. She was pissed and didn't want
to talk. He'd be the first to admit that his exit was whack.
But she needed to know that the extenuating circumstances
made his quick getaway necessary.

Cutting off the water, he stepped from the shower and,
after wrapping a towel around his waist, he reached for his
phone. There was one text: from Marissa. She'd been able
to locate Diamond's personal number. He opened it up and
smiled for the first time since he and Diamond made love.
Seconds later, he tapped the number that Marissa had sent
him, and seconds after that, he heard the voice that made
things beat faster and get harder. "Hello, Diamond. It's Jackson."

The intake of breath on the other end of the phone was audible. "Jackson! How did you get my cell number?"

"That's one thing you need to learn about me, baby girl. I
always get what I want."

The next evening, Jackson and Diamond sat at a restaurant
located midway between Temecula and San Diego. It was a
Friday night, and as such, the place was fairly crowded. But
Jackson had finagled a corner booth for them and then sat
down beside Diamond instead of opposite her.

"Thanks for coming," he said after they'd placed drink
orders.

"You left me little choice," Diamond replied, trying without success to keep the pout out of her voice.

"Spoiled brat," Jackson mumbled.

"What did you say?"

"I said sorry about that." And he managed to keep a
straight face while doing so. "But I knew that you'd come

kicking and screaming, even with the threat of telling your dad about our little tryst."

"Yeah, well, it may be too late to keep a lid on it anyway." Diamond told Jackson about Dexter's find. "I came because we need to talk. What happened was a one-time lapse in judgment. It won't happen again."

Jackson shrugged. The sooner the world knew that he and Diamond had a thing going, the better. As for what they had being over, he figured that for now he'd let her hang on to that illusion. "Here." He held out a box.

"What's this?"

"A peace offering. Open it."

She did and couldn't help laughing at what was inside. "A diamond-covered rooster brooch, Jackson. Really?"

"A rooster is one word for it. But others call it a cock."

Diamond laughed in spite of herself. "How romantic," she drily finished.

"Just wanted to give you something to remember me by."

She looked at this arrogant, cocky guy, caught the hint of vulnerability and longing for acceptance shining in those dark eyes. He put up a good front, but Diamond knew this gift was a bigger deal than Jackson was making of it. "Okay, it's gawdy but kinda cute." She began pinning it to her designer tee.

"Here, let me."

Okay, pinning a rooster on someone's shirt should not be romantic, but it was. Diamond breathed in Jackson's fresh, woodsy scent, felt the heat from his fingers as they brushed against her skin. If she turned her face to the right, just a bit, their lips would be in dangerously close proximity to each other, and if she placed her right hand just above the thigh just inches away, then, well, she could squeeze his rooster.

Their drinks arrived. Diamond quickly reached for hers and, after a sip, stirred around the amber-colored liquid with the maraschino cherry that perched on top. "Why'd you have to leave?" she said, in a Herculean effort to force her thoughts away from farm animals.

"Problems at the office." *And that's putting it mildly.*

Sounded like the perfect answer…for one hiding a female. "Are you going to give me details, or is this classified information?"

"It's classified."

Never long on patience, Diamond quickly found herself bored with Jackson's word games. But his vagueness was welcomed; it was what she needed to stay clear on what was happening here—a big, fat nothing. "Well, since I seem to be the only one with new information, here it is. From this day forward, ours will be a business-only relationship. You are to conduct yourself accordingly. We have to work together for the next few weeks, after which it will be perfectly okay if I never see you again. Now, since we've cleared the air, I'll be leaving. I've better things to do on a Friday night—"

"Like what?"

"Like none of your business." Diamond would swallow her tongue before she'd release the fact that a night of novel reading was the exciting item on her agenda. She took another sip of her drink, piercing Jackson with her gaze.

"You're right, Diamond, you deserve an explanation on why I had to leave so quickly. But that's only one of the reasons I asked you here. The other reason is this—what happened yesterday was amazing. I've had my share of lovers, but I've never felt the way I did yesterday afternoon."

"And how was that?" Diamond queried, chiding herself for doing so while hiding her surprise—and her feelings—behind sarcasm.

Jackson leaned forward, took Diamond's small hands into his much larger ones. "It felt like magic. When I was inside you, baby, it was like coming home. I know you said what happened was a one-time fling, but for the record, I want to hang out with you for a minute."

"How long is a minute?" Diamond asked.

Jackson shrugged. "Until we're both satisfied or…whatever."

Diamond sat back and gazed at the man in front of her. Yet again, she was seeing a side of Jackson that she hadn't seen before. This one was honest and tender and looked finer than anyone had a right to in just a simple, pale yellow buttondown shirt. The familiar heat in her core began uncoiling. Diamond looked away. "I felt the same way about what happened. It was different." She looked at him. "Special. But no matter how good the sex, Jackson, and it was amazing, I'm looking for more in my life—permanence, commitment. And that's not you."

Inwardly, Jackson flinched. She'd mentioned commitment, but that's not what he heard. His translation? That a man like him—former wannabe gangbanger and drug dealer and all-around ghetto child—wasn't good enough for a princess. But on the outside? Cool as the proverbial green summer vegetable. In spite of this, he pressed her. "You don't even know me."

"Yes, but I've heard about you, and the story is that you're a ladies' man."

"I've never led a woman on. Everything that has gone down in my love life has been by mutual consent."

"Perhaps, but mutual consent doesn't always cancel out a broken heart." Now, Diamond deduced, it was her turn to be honest. "I don't know if I could keep my feelings casual where you're concerned, but one thing I know for sure is I'm not willing to spend my time with a Casanova and spin my wheels in a going-nowhere affair."

Jackson slowly nodded. "Fair enough."

Diamond realized there was much more to this man than

met the eye or made the paper. For all the news about Jackson Wright she'd gleaned from her brothers, there was little known beyond his professional acumen and carefree, playboy ways. An uncomfortable feeling came over her as she acknowledged this truth: she wanted to know more, and she wanted to "fling" at least one more time.

Chapter 17

Diamond sat back and looked around, for the first time noticing the candle-holding hollowed pumpkins that graced the tables and announced Halloween. "What happened at your company yesterday?"

"I thought you had to leave."

She made a show of looking at her watch. "I have some time."

Jackson leaned toward her. "Can you keep a confidence?" His voice was low, his breath wet against her earlobe.

Diamond nodded, swallowed.

"Promise?"

"Yes."

"There was a break-in at my office."

Diamond's brow knitted in confusion and concern. "What would someone want so badly from you that they'd steal to get it?"

Jackson shifted in his seat and took a drink. This wasn't

going to be as easy as he thought. There was no way he could tell her that the person broke into his office to *leave* something. "I've got some people looking into it. What can I say?" Jackson said with a shrug, his voice as casual as if he were discussing basketball scores. "Everyone isn't happy with my success."

"You have enemies?"

"No doubt."

Diamond smiled. "What successful person doesn't have a hater or two?"

Jackson's mind went to who he believed was his number-one nemesis: Solomon Dent. Solomon had been John Wright's right-hand man, the man who thought himself a shoo-in for the position that Jackson now occupied. John had included Solomon in his will, had stipulated that he be president for a period of five years before turning over the reins to his nephew, but for Solomon, a little piece of the pie wasn't enough. He'd wanted it all. After a vicious court battle, Jackson prevailed. Solomon was awarded a substantial financial settlement. But the job hadn't been just about money but also prestige. A man with his ego could still be smarting over the early, forced departure. The fact that it was self-inflicted seemed to have been lost in translation.

And there were others rivals: both from his professional and private life, including a man who blamed Jackson for his ex-fiancée's alienated affections. The truth was the junior architect had fallen in love with Jackson. But he hadn't returned her affections. Even when she'd shown up buck naked on his doorstep, save for a sarong, he'd turned her down. But to hear old boy tell it, Jackson had pulled her kicking and screaming from the brother's arms. More than one person had overheard the threats of what this man wanted to do if he ever caught Jackson late at night in a dark alley. And after today's note he'd acknowledged another possibility, one that seemed far-reaching at best: that someone from his childhood thought he'd talked out of school and, now, more than a decade since he'd moved from the hood, was attempting retribution.

The waitress came and took their orders. Once she'd left the table, Jackson asked, "Have you eaten here before?"

Diamond nodded, working hard to keep a neutral expression on her face.

She was only partly successful. Jackson couldn't tell what lay under the flash of darkness that appeared in her eyes. Hurt? Anger? Disappointment? "Bad memories?"

"Something like that" was her vague response. "But the food is good."

"It's nothing compared to the dessert I have in mind."

The dark look of desire in Jackson's eyes was unmistakable. Diamond placed a hand on her stomach to try and still the butterflies that gathered there. Fat chance. She wanted this man with a vengeance, which was the very reason why, as much as she wanted to, she really shouldn't be intimate again. If she was this turned out after one good sexing, what would she be like after a second round? A candidate for Dr. Drew is what, she decided, working with the good doctor to cure an addiction of the Jackson kind.

"Diamond Drake," Jackson murmured. "Where'd you get that name?"

Diamond smiled. "My father. Unlike most men who want sons, Dad always wanted a little girl. When I arrived, he deemed me his jewel and named me after one that was beautiful yet resilient."

"And humble, too."

"Those are my dad's words, not mine." Diamond arched a brow. "Do you disagree with my father?" The look on Jackson's face brought instant moisture between her legs.

"Do I look like I disagree with him? Baby, you're as fine as Drake wine in the summertime."

"Ha! That sounds like a line my dad would use!"

"I don't doubt it, especially since it came from the arsenal of sayings Uncle John used on Aunt Evie."

For the first time since meeting, the two experienced a casual camaraderie, and Diamond's smile was genuine as she looked across the table at a man she already adored. "Tell me about your—"

A couple entering the dining room stopped Diamond mid-speak.

"Who is it?" Jackson asked without turning around.

Of all the restaurants and of all the nights, what are the chances? Diamond wasn't able to keep the frown off her face as she answered, "You're getting ready to come face-to-face with my bad memory." She looked up as the couple approached their table. Benjamin Carter was as handsome as she remembered: a bald-headed chocolate drop who made up in length what he lacked in height. Until this afternoon, she'd thought his was the appendages of appendages. But now she knew better. *Thank, God.* The woman beside him could have been Diamond's cousin, so much did they look alike. Similar height, weight, complexion and, had Diamond not recently cut hers, shoulder-length hair. Yep, definitely could have been the Bobbsey Twins.

"Hello, Diamond."

Diamond nodded. "Benjamin."

You could cut the tension with a Q-tip.

"I just wanted to say a quick hello. How's the family?"

"Fine," Diamond answered Benjamin but eyed her twin.

"Hello," the woman said—smile sincere, hand outstretched. "I'm Pat, Benjamin's wife."

Hold on. Back up. Did she say "wife"? Diamond summoned up an act that was Oscar-worthy. Her expression remained so blank you would have sworn she'd shot Botox. She shook Pat's hand. "Diamond Drake."

A flash of recognition appeared, but Pat was going for an Emmy herself. "It's a pleasure to meet you."

"And this," Diamond said while casually placing a hand on his thigh as if it were the most natural thing to do, "is Jackson Wright." She leaned into him as she added, "Baby, this is my ex I told you about. The one I dumped…remember?"

Oh, snap. Those words shot out so fast that even sprinter Usain Bolt couldn't have caught them. Grandma Mary would not have been pleased, but a residual of hurt that Diamond thought dead and buried had resurrected and pushed class and decorum right out of the way. She clamped her mouth shut, but the horse was not only out of the barn…it could run straight into Pat's mouth, which hung wide open. "I'm sorry," she said. "That wasn't nice."

"No, it wasn't, but that's your nature," Benjamin retorted. "Which is why I dumped *you.* Come on, Pat," he said, reaching for his wife's hand. "Let's join our more civilized company." A slightly bewildered-looking Pat followed her husband, Diamond's snort her only goodbye. The departing couple almost bumped into the waitress, who was delivering salads to Jackson and Diamond's table.

Jackson waited until the waitress had left. "So," he murmured, running a finger up Diamond's arm. Her shiver of a response brought a smile. "Do you want to tell your *baby* what that was all about?"

Her desire for Jackson had pierced through the anger, but Diamond still reached for her purse. "I'm leaving." Benjamin and Pat had been seated a distance away, but right now Yankee Stadium would have been too small a common room for her and her ex.

Jackson placed a staying hand on Diamond's arm. "Baby, wait. We've not yet eaten."

"I've lost my appetite."

Chapter 18

After tossing several bills on the table, Jackson rushed after the ball of fire that was his date. "Diamond, wait!"

She increased her stride, not wanting Jackson to see how badly Benjamin's unexpected news had upset her. When had he gotten married? And how had he done so without her finding out? She reached her car, but when it came to long strides, five foot nine was no match for six foot five. Jackson had gotten there one step ahead of her and now placed his hand on the door.

"Give me your keys," he demanded.

"Why?" Diamond angrily brushed what she swore was the last tear she'd cry over men from her cheek.

"Because I don't want you driving upset." Jackson held out his hand, with a don't-you-dare-try-me look in his eyes.

"I'm not upset," she said, cursing another tear that dared to fall. Jackson crossed his arms and leaned against Diamond's car. After a brief glare down, she gave him the keys. "So now you're going to drive two cars," she said with all the dryness of the Mojave Desert. "This I've got to see."

Jackson reached for her hand. "I'll bring you back to your car later, but right now, you're coming with me."

"Where are we going?"

"My place."

"Uh, I don't think so."

"I didn't ask what you thought. That was a statement, not a question. Now, I can either pick you up or you can walk on your own, but either way you're not going to be alone right now. You're coming with me."

Diamond took Jackson's hand, and together they walked to his Maserati. She immediately recognized the white BMW beside it. She'd been with Benjamin when he purchased it— two months before she'd pressed him to set a wedding date and he'd flat out refused. And now he was married? Again, the tears threatened, and Diamond realized that Jackson had been right. This was no time for her to be alone.

Jackson's sports car ate up the distance between the restaurant and his home. After keying in the code, a large wrought-iron gate opened, and Diamond felt as though she'd been transported to the Mediterranean. Strategically placed lights emphasized the large home's majesty, its pale-salmon coating a stark contrast to the black night sky. Its various levels and angles were architecturally sophisticated, and the turret at the back of the building added to the mansion's overall charm.

Diamond, who'd grown up in the lap of luxury and whose ten-thousand-square-foot estate was no small potatoes, was impressed. From what she could see, the grounds were as stunning as the building, but there was more—something indefinable—about Jackson's surroundings. The place felt like a fortress, no, a sanctuary. That was it. As soon as they'd entered the gates, Diamond felt protected beyond the ordinary. Her shoulders lowered as she visibly relaxed and whispered, "This is amazing." It seemed as if to speak louder would break some type of magical spell.

Jackson smiled, appreciative of Diamond's obvious good taste. "Thank you, baby. It's called *Cielo*...my little slice of heaven."

"Heaven...that's what *cielo* means?"

Jackson nodded. Following his uncle's and aunt's deaths, Jackson had thought of moving into their place, but the memories were too great and painful. So he'd sold their home and all its contents and built the oceanfront dwelling of his dreams from the ground up. It was also during this time that he changed the company name: from Wright Works to Boss Construction.

"It's beautiful, Jackson."

Bypassing the five-car garage, Jackson navigated the circular drive until they reached the home's front door. He turned off the engine, then leaned over and placed a gentle kiss on Diamond's cheek. "Wait here."

Diamond watched as he exited the car, curious as to his intentions. She soon found out. Jackson bounded around to her side of the car and opened her door. "M'lady," he said with a bow.

Diamond smiled, suddenly feeling like a teenybopper on her first date. She held out her hand. "M'lord."

Jackson kissed her hand before tucking it in the crook of his arm. "Welcome to my home. *Mi casa es su casa.*"

They went inside. In a glance, Diamond took in the two-story ceiling, generous foyer, sparkling crystal chandelier and a double winding staircase that seemed straight out of a fairy tale. Her heels clicked against the smooth marble flooring as she followed Jackson into a formal living room. Luxury with a capital *L* oozed from every nook and cranny, and while the trappings were undoubtedly expensive, a homeyness somehow exuded, the kind that made you want to take off your shoes and stay awhile.

Jackson gave Diamond's hand a final squeeze. "Make yourself at home." Diamond observed his long, sure strides as he crossed the floor to the fireplace. After placing a few pieces of kindling on top of the larger logs already arranged, he pushed a button and within seconds a fire blazed in the hearth.

"Real wood," Diamond said, as she continued to walk around and admire the room. "I like that."

Jackson's eyes narrowed as purposeful strides ate up the distance between them. "And I like this."

Diamond closed her eyes for the kiss but instead felt strong, protective arms wrap themselves around her. For a moment, they simply stood there, feeling each others' rapid heartbeat, breathing in a combination of woodsy and floral scents. Diamond could feel heat, but she wasn't sure whether it emanated from his body or hers. The wetness? It was definitely her. She brought her arms to Jackson's back, reveling in the broad expanse of manliness she felt there. His hands traveled, too, and soon they were kneading her shoulders.

"You're so tight."

Diamond rested her head against his shoulder and enjoyed his ministrations. "That feels good."

He kissed her temple.

So does that.

And the top of her head.

And that. Just a kiss, she reminded herself. *That's all. Nothing more can happen.*

Then he nipped her ear before sucking the lobe into his mouth, and Diamond got the distinct feeling that she'd be picking her car up in the morning.

Chapter 19

Diamond tightened her grip around Jackson's waist—and just in time. Because Jackson lifted her head and claimed her mouth in a kiss so hot that she needed something to hold on to lest she keel straight over. His long, thick tongue sought and found territory unclaimed in the previous meeting. He massaged her head, neck and shoulders, his tongue massaging the inside of her mouth. Intending to take full advantage of the one-kiss-that's-all-and-nothing-else-can-happen moment, Diamond shifted her head for better access, skimming her fingers along the small of his back before resting her hand on his firm, round butt. Her nipples hardened, begged for attention; her kitty throbbed intensely. If possible, she knew it would have audibly meowed. She broke the kiss, looked deep into Jackson's eyes and was sure she conveyed this message: *sorry, I can't be with you again.* Her telepathic signals must have been off because he promptly took her hand and headed to those beautiful double wrought-iron fixtures that Diamond would later dub the stairway to heaven.

Also later, Diamond would take her time and admire the ample landing, loft-style sitting room and bedrooms located on both sides of the hallway. Now she fixed her eyes on their obvious destination: a set of double doors at the end of the hall. *Time to put on the breaks, Diamond. Speak now or forever hold your peace!* Jackson opened the door. Diamond stifled a gasp. At any moment, she expected to see a choir of angels because this sure looked like paradise. Diamond eyed the custom-made king-size bed that rested on a large platform of cherry wood. It beckoned, but Jackson kept walking past the walk-in closet to another door that opened into the en suite bathroom. But really, that was too tame a word. This room was a virtual spa, complete with sauna, bidet and vessel sinks amid sparkling glass, hand-carved stone and a plant-filled water feature. A massive skylight revealed a scenic expanse of twinkling stars.

"Take off your clothes," Jackson commanded, his voice low and husky. "I want to see you naked."

Was she a dim-witted robot acting on command? Why was she reaching for the hem of her sleeveless tee and pulling it over her head when she should be saying, Thank you very much but could you please take me home? Jackson deftly unbuttoned and unzipped her jeans, kissing her stomach and thighs as he helped rid her of them. *Oh, that's why.* He watched as she unfastened her bra. It hit the ground. Her thong joined it.

"Better?" Diamond asked, her grin devilish and saucy.

"Indeed." Jackson's eyes never left Diamond's as he quickly unbuttoned his shirt, pulled off his T-shirt and removed his slacks.

Mr. Happy swayed from side to side like a massive pendulum. Two more seconds of staring and Diamond may have been hypnotized. But she had better ideas for that work of art. All afternoon she'd thought of how it would taste in her mouth. This was right after the thoughts that they'd never be together again. She took a step, wrapped her fingers around his magic shaft and noted that her fingers could not touch. *Day-um!* Had it grown some more? She licked her lips and bent her head…

"No, not yet," Jackson whispered. He moved away, and Diamond felt as bereft as Tom Hanks in *Castaway,* as if she were floating on a single plank in the midst of an ocean and her volleyball had suddenly floated away.

"Come here."

She walked to the tub. She looked down into a mass of tiny bubbles, surprised because she hadn't seen him pour bubble bath.

"Get in."

The silkiness of Jackson's voice made further questions unnecessary. At this point, Jackson could have told her to paddle a blow-up raft to Catalina Island, and if he was the promise on the other side, she would have been a rowing sister. She sat down in the midst of the bubbles, and right away it was as if a thousand tiny fingers were massaging her skin; from head to toe, she felt the sensations. She closed her eyes and let out an audible sigh. Now there was no doubt. This was heaven.

After a moment, she felt a touch on her arm. Jackson directed her forward and then slipped in behind her. He pulled her back against his chest, wrapped his arms around her and, for a moment, they simply enjoyed the bliss of design's next level from the Jacuzzi…the bubble massage. His hands began to roam her body. Diamond's legs immediately parted in silent invitation. He chuckled, and she would have felt chagrin had it not been for the fact that instead of her nana it was her nipples he wanted. He tweaked one and then the other as he placed feathery kisses along her neck. While still rolling a springy nub between his fingers, he took the other hand and found Diamond's treasure. He slid a finger along her silky folds, and Diamond almost exploded right then. She spread her legs, but he continued to tease—barely rubbing her nub with the tip of his finger, while increasing the pressure on her achy breast. The feeling of his hands on her skin and the stimulating bubbles was ecstasy enough, but then, without warning, he buried his tongue in her ear and his finger inside her. Diamond cried out in surprise at the spasm that signaled the first of several orgasms she would have this night.

Before she could stop trembling, Jackson stepped out of the tub, lifted her into his arms and strode into the bedroom. Without thought of value, he laid her still-wet body on top of the raw silk comforter and climbed onto the bed. He stared at her, and Diamond's body reacted to his fervent gaze. Incredibly, though she'd just experienced release, her nipples hardened and her muscles tightened. Would she ever get enough of this guy?

Obviously Jackson didn't think so. Because after a few seconds of lightly running his fingers all over her body, he whispered a simple command: "Spread your legs."

Diamond obeyed.

"Wider."

Diamond swallowed, closed her eyes and followed instructions. There was an excruciating moment where nothing happened, and she imagined Jackson staring down at her. This turned her on even more. Then she felt a burst of air on her exposed flesh, followed by quick, short licks of tongue. She moaned and blindly reached for his head, wanting—no, *needing*—to feel the pressure of him flush against her, inside her, everywhere. He complied, lapping, nibbling, tasting her over and again. Diamond relished the assault, but figuring what was good for the goose was equally so for the gander, she rolled over, got on her knees and issued a command of her own. "Lie back."

Jackson's obedience was accompanied by a slow, easy smile. He put his hands behind his head, watching Diamond's every move. She clasped his ample manhood, massaged it from base to tip. She ran a thumbnail along his sac. He hissed. Now it was Diamond's turn for the knowing chuckle. *Ah, yes.* Wetting her lips, she leaned down and kissed the tip before taking in as much of him as possible. She used her tongue to worship at his sizable shrine, following the path of his vein like a GPS, caressing his shaft as if it were a Smithsonian contender. She took him into her mouth and sucked. Hard. Jackson's intake of breath was immediate, followed by a deep moan.

Oh, oh. Playtime was over, and Jackson was now in command. He reached for a condom and shielded himself. He lifted her to her knees, got behind her and, after using his tongue in ways that Diamond could only have imagined, poised himself for entry. He made them one with a single body-tingling, mind-boggling powerful stroke. Up. Down. In. Out. Oh…so…slowly. His thrusts were powerful, purposeful, as if to brand her very soul. Diamond grabbed fistfuls of comforter, matching him thrust for vigorous thrust. They loved, then slept and loved some more. And as streaks of orange and purple announced the dawn, Jackson was loving her still.

Chapter 20

Monday morning arrived, and Diamond was as chipper as the birds that trilled outside her bedroom window. She'd spent the weekend with Jackson, not picking up her car from the restaurant until last night, after Jackson begrudgingly drove her away from their lair of love. Unable to keep her mind on work—or anything else but Jackson for the past seventy-two hours—she rose from her desk and walked to the window. Yes, indeed, today was a beautiful day.

A light tap and then Kathleen stepped into Diamond's office. "Good morning, Diamond. You're here early." Diamond turned, Kathleen took in the glow on her face, and the mother of five immediately knew how it had gotten there. Heck, the late, great Ray Charles could have seen the glow. The astronauts parked at the moon's space station could have seen that glow. "Enjoy your weekend?"

"It was okay," Diamond said, trying for a tone of major disinterest.

She was trying so hard that Kathleen almost suggested adding a yawn for effect.

Diamond returned to her desk. "How was yours?"

"Oh, the usual. Sex all weekend—swinging from chandeliers, hitting high notes, just another forty-eight in the Fitzgerald household." Diamond smirked. "Okay, since you want the PG version, I went with Carol and the grands to Old Town—costumes, haunted houses, too much candy, the works."

"You didn't dress up."

Kathleen looked genuinely chagrined. "Why, of course I did, me lady. Dressed up as an Irish maid, I did," she announced in a respectable brogue. "Then went home and showed Bernie my lucky charms."

"Ha!"

"But we were both too tired to do much more than look."

Both ladies laughed and then got down to Drake Wines business. "Oh, one more thing," Diamond said, wrapping up. "I have a meeting with Jackson Wright at two."

"Another one?" Kathleen asked innocently. "He was just here on Thursday."

Diamond knew Kathleen was fishing, but she didn't take the bait. "Yes, and with the expedited schedule, we'll probably be joined at the hip for the next two weeks." Diamond thought of ways they'd been joined last weekend and felt herself grow warm. "That's it, Kat. Please hold my calls for the next hour."

A crush of meetings and an hour-long phone call with the writer doing the *O Magazine* story helped time fly by. Before she knew it, two o'clock arrived. It had been less than twenty-four hours since his scorching kiss in the restaurant parking lot, but her stomach flip-flopped at the thought of seeing Jackson. He made her feel all gooey and girly inside, and today she'd swapped her more businesslike attire for a decidedly feminine look. When Kathleen announced his arrival, Diamond made one final adjustment to her apparel, quickly checked herself in the mirror and was out the door.

"You look good enough to eat," Jackson said once they were buckled in the cart and heading toward the grapevines. *And you bless a pair of jeans like nobody's business.* "I'm at work, and the trees have eyes. Behave."

Jackson admired her openly. "You smell good. And I like the dress. What color would you call that…pink? Rose?"

"It contains both," Diamond answered, warmed by the flattery. Flattery would indeed get Jackson everywhere he'd already been.

"I like it."

"Thanks."

There was a companionable silence and then he said, "Did your parents mention anything about us?"

"No, but Mom called to tell me what time dinner was being served and to make sure I'd be there."

"Dex talked?"

"I don't know. But even if he didn't, my mom could make money on a psychic hotline. 'Staying with friends,'" Diamond said, making air quotes, "doesn't exactly qualify as an explanation for a weekend away from the Drake Estate."

"But you're a grown woman. She keeps tabs on you like that?"

"Not exactly. But my staying out all weekend is unusual behavior." Actually, *unheard of* would have been a better description. The two other dates she'd had since being dumped by Benjamin had been most forgettable, a fact that she hadn't withheld from the household. So the fact that she'd spent the weekend out and on news of such was as quiet as a church mouse…well…that was something that wouldn't get by Mrs. Genevieve Drake—not on any day of the week.

They reached the easternmost tip of the vine field, and

away from work and prying eyes, Diamond removed the short-waist white jacket, revealing her halter dress beneath. Jackson immediately took advantage and placed a soft, wet kiss on her bare shoulder.

"Do I have to wear this jacket and bake in the heat? Or will you act right?"

"Baby," he said, eyeing her behind and licking his lips, "I *am* acting right."

Diamond ignored him. "In the journey of wine from grape to glass," she said as if narrating a PBS special, "this—" making a sweeping motion across the mass acreage "—is where it all begins. The plots are sectioned off by type of grape—barbera, cabernet franc, cabernet sauvignon, sauvignon blanc, chardonnay, chenin blanc and merlot." Jackson ran a finger down her arm. She swatted it away. "We also grow a few lesser known or less popular varieties such as pinot noir and its clone, pinot gris, Grenache, Shiraz, Viognier and Zinfandel."

They walked down a row where plump, dark grape clusters swung from the vine. Jackson stopped. "Which grape is this?"

"That's the Nebbiolo," Diamond said. "Like you, a bad boy." Jackson's brow cocked in question. "Notoriously hard to grow and tame. Along with tannic and tarry qualities, it has a chocolaty taste."

"Hum, like me indeed." Diamond swatted his shoulder. "So now you think I'm vain, huh?"

"I prefer *cocky*." Too late Diamond realized the double entendre.

"I know you do," Jackson said, his smile rivaling the sun that shone overhead. "You *preferred* it all weekend long."

"Whatever." Though the sudden reddened hue of Diamond's skin showed that she knew exactly of what he spoke.

Jackson rubbed his finger across the grape's firm skin. "Can I eat one?"

"Sure." Diamond reached into her pocket and pulled out a type of Swiss knife. "Here, let me." She snipped off a small cluster. "I have water in the cart."

"What do you have to do…wash off the insecticides and pesticides you spray on this crop?"

"Our wines are organic, thank you very much. We use only natural pesticides to keep the bugs away. This is just to remove the dirt."

Jackson popped a grape into his mouth. "God made dirt, so dirt don't hurt."

Diamond laughed. She hadn't heard that saying since grade school. "You're silly."

"Or there's another one…what's a little dirt among friends. Baby, these are sweet. Here, taste one." Diamond reached for the grape, but Jackson pulled back. "Open that sweet mouth of yours." She did, and when taking the grape, Diamond's lips brushed against Jackson's fingers. Just like that, the smoldering sparks became flames.

"I'm hot, too," Jackson said, pulling the shirt he wore over his head to reveal hard, rippling muscles.

Diamond could stare at his chest all day and never get enough. She could do many things with Jackson all day and never get enough. Even his tattoo wasn't a deterrent. Normally, Diamond didn't like them, but on him it was one of the sexiest things she'd ever seen, especially when outlining it with her tongue.

"Here, have another one."

Jackson placed the grape between his teeth and leaned forward. It was probably a futile battle to resist him, not to mention a day late and a dollar short; nonetheless, she played hard to get. She pulled a grape from the cluster in his hand and plopped it into her mouth. "Delicious."

"Really? Let me taste it."

And before she could protest further, there was chest against breast and tongue in mouth. The taste of grapes mixed with desire was a potent combination, and as crazy as the notion was, Diamond wanted to be taken there, on the spot, between two rows of "bad boy" grapes. Fortunately, there were one or two vestiges of sanity left, and she used them to form her next five words: "Let's go to Papa Dee's."

Chapter 21

Diamond walked to the cart with Jackson right on her heels. "Papa who?"

"Dee," she replied over her shoulder. "Short for David." She jumped into the cart, started it and was off milliseconds after Jackson's heel left the dirt.

"Dang, girl. Slow down!"

Diamond went on as if she were having tea in the garden instead of driving a cart forty miles an hour over gravel. "David Drake Sr. is my great-grandfather. He was born in that house on the hill. I'll show you the room. My great-great-grandfather Nicodemus built this place...well, him and his worker friends, with their bare hands." Diamond hit a rut. The cart rose a foot off the ground and came down with a thud. "Whoa! Sorry."

Jackson was busy leaving finger imprints on the dash through a Jaws of Life-style clutch. He shot a fierce scowl at Diamond. "Slow down!"

"Ha!" Diamond pressed her foot on the gas and went from grass to gravel on two wheels. "Spoken by the person who drives a Maserati. Cute."

They reached the house on the hill, a two-story, square-shaped number with a red hipped roof. Compared to the Drake Estate, one would describe it as humble; yet there was a majestic quality to it, an unmistakable air of importance that emanated from the worn planks of wood. Jackson and Diamond exited the cart, their conversation muted by the energy around them.

Jackson walked up to the side of the house that was facing them and looked into the window. He ran his hand along the pane and noted the pristine workmanship still evident a hundred years after completion. It was as if he could sense the worth of the men who'd built it, imagined their camaraderie while working together, mixed with determination and pride. "Good work," he said.

Diamond joined him at the window. "The entrance is around here," she said, her voice low, reverent. "It's locked, but there's a secret hiding place for the key. You have to promise not to tell anyone where it is."

Jackson looked chagrined. "Who would I tell?"

Diamond's smile was soft, unreadable. "Come on."

They walked around to the side of the house where a porch that spanned the length of the house had seen better days. There were three short steps to the door. Jackson bypassed those and stepped directly onto the porch's wooden planks. They creaked under his weight. Diamond walked to the edge of the porch, lifted one of the planks and retrieved a large, old heavy key. The lock protested, but eventually the knob turned and the couple went inside. Jackson's eyes filled with wonder as he noted the excellent craftsmanship of the wooden floors, beveled windows and pressed brick fireplace. Built-in bookcases framed the fireplace, and the dining room was beamed and Dutch-paneled, with a heavy plate rail and buffet spanning the back wall. Faded floral wallpaper suggested a woman's touch. The whole place reeked with the Obama mantra: Yes, we can.

Jackson asked, "How'd your family get this land?"

"My great-great-grandfather Nicodemus was part Creole, from New Orleans, and came here with his owner in the late 1800s. He and Pierre Drake, his owner, had grown up together and were more like brothers than master and slave. When they made the trip west to expand the Drake family fortunes, Pierre almost died. But Nicodemus's mother, Henriette, was trained in the healing arts. She passed her knowledge of herbs and other natural ingredients as remedies on to her children. Aside from having a magical way with animals, Nicodemus was what was called back then a root doctor. He saved Pierre's life. The family was so grateful that they promised to will part of the land to him, and when Pierre died, that's exactly what happened."

"That's an amazing story, Diamond. And such a rarity— people of color owning so much land."

"That hasn't come without its struggles," Diamond admitted. "More than once, various entities have tried to steal this rich property. But the Drakes were smart people, and their will was ironclad. It also hasn't hurt that we've remained in contact with our White counterparts and attend their family reunion every year."

"Your ancestor's former owners?"

Diamond nodded. "When the last lawsuit came, trying to take the land from Papa Dee, it was Pierre's great-great-grandson, now a lawyer, who successfully argued the case... and won."

Diamond shared more stories as they toured the rest of the house including the bath, pantry and upstairs bedrooms, and Jackson began to see the pride and strength behind the woman he'd secretly viewed as a spoiled rich girl. While walking through the home that Nicodemus had built, he felt their lust was replaced with something deeper, stronger… something that lasted longer than an orgasm's spasms, and unknowingly, the two became intoxicated with something else of which the house reeked—love. And they hadn't physically touched.

After leaving the house on the hill, Diamond made quick work of the rest of the tour, which included the hopper, presses and fermenting tanks. On the ride back, they discussed an idea that had resulted from Jackson's offhanded comment, "Y'all should do something with that house." A short time later, Diamond wheeled the cart back into the executive-offices parking lot.

"I've got it!" she said when they reached her office. "We could turn it into a standalone honeymoon suite!"

Jackson rubbed his jaw in thought. "Undergird the foundation, restore it back to its original luster with furnishings to match the era…"

"It would be so charming." Diamond reached her computer and began typing furiously, her mind abuzz. "We could even offer it as a themed wedding site, which, considering the history of this area, would go over huge!" When Jackson didn't comment, she turned and saw him reading a text with that delectable mouth set in a firm, strained line. "What is it?"

"Business," Jackson said, rising.

"Not again," Diamond responded, her voice sounding as firm as that of a military-school teacher. She stood, adding more softly, "Not like this. I care about you, Jackson, and whatever's going on with you appears more serious than a break-in. What is it?"

Jackson looked at Diamond a long moment and realized that it was the first time he'd ever heard any woman other than Aunt Evie speak to him with such raw concern. "I'm getting threats," he said evenly, his voice devoid of emotion. "Someone is vowing to kill me."

Chapter 22

Diamond stared at Jackson a full five seconds before responding, "Kill you as in...dead?"

Jackson took a page from Genevieve Drake's book of dry wit. "What other kind of killing is there?"

"Of course, you're right. I'm just...taken aback."

Jackson walked over to a leather love seat and sat down. "It started several weeks ago, anonymous letters with no return address, and has escalated from there. Last week's break-in wasn't to steal anything. It was to leave a warning."

"What kind of warning?"

Jackson looked at Diamond, took in her genuinely disturbed expression and decided to be truthful. "Someone came in with a silencer and shot up my assistant's computer. They left a note saying the next bullet has my name on it."

"What are the police saying?"

"Nothing. We didn't go to the police."

"Why not?"

"I don't want this getting leaked to the press. My attorney hired a private investigator. He's flown into town and wants to meet with me. But his schedule is tight. He flies out tomorrow. So after a quick chat with the foreman to make sure all construction is on schedule, that's where I'm headed."

Diamond walked over to the love seat. She reached out and touched Jackson's arm. The thought of someone wanting to hurt him sent chills down her spine. She swallowed fear and summoned up courage. "You'll be fine, Jackson." She looked him dead in the eye and spoke with the confidence of God's right-hand man. "Whoever is behind this will be caught. The danger will pass."

A smile scampered across Jackson's face. "You sound pretty sure of yourself."

Diamond had to sound sure to feel sure. If something happened to Jackson, she didn't know what she'd do. "I am."

"How so? Are you going to be my protector?"

An idea instantly formed in her head. "We have people on the payroll. My father can make a call—"

Jackson spoke sternly. "No! I can handle my business." And then more softly, he said, "I gotta run, baby girl. Don't worry your pretty little head about me. Because like you said, I'll be fine."

Forty-five minutes later, Jackson sat in a living room suite at Tower 23 near downtown San Diego. Abe Swartz sat at the other end of the couch, and across from him sat one of the country's preeminent private eyes: Frank Stanton.

"I was surprised to learn that you already have news," Jackson said to the well-dressed man in the wingback chair. "You work quickly."

Frank nodded, the slightest trace of Georgian roots coming through in his accent. "Time is money. I try and spend my client's wisely."

"He's the best," Abe interjected, glad he was able to get Frank on such short notice. It hadn't hurt that he had connections with a Georgia judge who just happened to be good friends with the investigator.

"I appreciate your time." Jackson sat back and poured a glass of lemon water from the pitcher beside him. "What do you have so far?"

"For now, I'm focusing my investigation on your uncle's former colleague, Solomon Dent. He has a nephew with a criminal past. Lately, it turns out, they've been spending quite a bit of time together. This nephew, Brandon Dent, has also been spending quite a bit of time with a guy he met behind bars, a guy who just got out of prison. Now my hunch is that maybe, just maybe, some of this has to do with you."

Jackson's eyes narrowed. "Why do you think that?"

"The timing. Brandon was released from jail in August, and this cohort of his was released a few weeks ago."

When it came to Jackson's old neighborhood, more guys had gone to prison than to college. He could name a dozen people who'd experienced this fate from his block alone. "What's the dude's name?"

"Right now, all I've got is Slim Shady."

Jackson all but snorted. "That's a nickname for a rapper, Eminem."

"Okay." Frank studied Jackson a moment. "Other than the names you gave Abe, is there anyone from your past you can think of who'd want to try and hurt you?"

Jackson slowly shook his head. "I left Inglewood when I was thirteen, went back for about a month when I was sixteen and after that my focus changed." Jackson was quiet a moment, remembering how he'd gone back to the hood for his sixteenth birthday. Visiting a popular teen hangout in San Diego one day, he'd run into the cousin of one of his childhood friends. They'd talked about the neighborhood and life "back in the day." It made Jackson nostalgic to go home and reconnect. But two years away from the inner-city lifestyle had changed him. When what he'd thought was an innocent ride to the gas station turned out to be something totally different—something that ended in murder—his life forever changed. That incident spawned a determination to seek a more positive and successful path in life. "I had a long talk with my uncle, who brought me into the company as his protégé shortly after returning from this last trip to the hood," he finally continued. "I made new friends out here."

"And what about your old friends. No further contact?"

Jackson shook his head. "A lot of my old friends are either dead or in prison. But I can't think of any of them who would have a beef with me. Not one that's this deep, wanting to catch a case for murder and whatnot."

Frank reached into his inside jacket pocket and pulled out a pen and pad. "I want you to write down the names of the friends you grew up with, those guys on the block who you know went to prison."

Jackson hesitated, his street mentality kicking in. Naming names, for any reason, usually led to bad things for those involved. And then there was the note: *Your no good snitch ass.* "I don't think it's necessary, man. Like I said, I didn't have any beef with any of them."

"But one of them might have had a beef with you."

"I don't think so."

Frank shrugged. "Suit yourself. But you've obviously gotten on someone's bad side, and until we figure out who that is, I think everyone should be guilty until proven innocent. *Capiche?*"

A rash of images from Jackson's past rushed into his mind: red lights flashing while sirens blared; random, illegal car and house searches; running from police and not knowing why they chased you; being handcuffed first and asked questions later; getting pulled over for DWB: driving while Black. Yeah, he *capiche'd* all too well.

He stood. "I think you should keep the focus on Solomon Dent. I can't see anyone from the block coming for me after all these years."

Frank also stood. "Maybe not. Like I said, I'm just going on a hunch here. We'll keep Solomon in our crosshairs and a finger on his nephew, Brandon, as well. I'll be in touch."

Jackson walked over to Frank, a looming presence for a guy who was at least seven inches shorter. "You do that," he said as he shook Frank's hand. "Abe, thanks."

He left the meeting. His mind whirled. Memories he'd suppressed for decades came back full force—his past, the old life, the secrets he'd buried under the opulence of a La Jolla mansion, a booming business and the love of an uncle and aunt who'd treated him like a son. The hurt of losing them returned, along with the fear that had accompanied life in the streets with no one to guide you. Then, into the pain crept the feeling he'd experienced earlier...when he'd stared at an old brick hearth still bearing burn marks from fires long burned out. And later, he'd been struck with an assurance not felt since his parents died: *You'll be fine, Jackson. Whoever is behind this will be caught. We've got people on the payroll.* It was from his spoiled diva princess protector who'd come from generations of stock that never backed down. Jackson almost laughed out loud. A very special lady had his back. He could get used to this.

Chapter 23

"Hi, Mom." Diamond entered the kitchen and kissed Genevieve on the cheek. Many had wondered why the wife of a wine mogul with this kind of empire would still be in the kitchen, when chefs had been hired by those with far less. The truth of the matter was that Genevieve Drake had learned the love of cooking at her mother's elbow. The act brought her joy and peace. After what she'd heard this afternoon, it was peace she needed.

"Hey, baby." Genevieve turned, then resumed stirring.

"What's for dinner? Smells delish."

"Braised short ribs served with this special pomegranate sauce."

"Yum. Grandpa's going to be happy."

"Believe it or not, he and Mama are going to a doo-wop concert at the casino. Papa Dee is a bit under the weather. It's just us tonight. Want to make the salad?"

"Mom! You know when they passed out cooking genes I was out to lunch."

"Ha! If you think making a salad is cooking, then I'd have to agree. And if it weren't for the fact that I personally taught you a few dishes, you might get away with that claim."

"I'd have to get up early to get one over on you, huh?"

"You'd better know it!"

"Okay, let me rephrase. Your daughter knows *how* to cook. She just never learned to *like* it." With that, Diamond reached for a carrot stick, dodged Genevieve's swatting spoon and left the kitchen. She reached the great room and almost ran into Dexter.

Dexter jumped back. "Slow down, fool!"

"I love you, too, brother." Diamond blew him a kiss, walked over to the wet bar and picked up an unlabeled bottle of wine. "The new pinot noir?" she questioned. "What clone is this?"

"That's old school, from the mother, baby girl. It's the real deal."

"From Papa Dee's secret arsenal?"

Dexter nodded. While all of the children had been shown the process of winemaking, Dexter was the one who'd embraced it like a second skin. He'd gotten his undergrad degree in viticulture with a minor in enology and his grad degree in business. Papa Dee's stamp of approval had come years later when after taking a sip of Dexter's creation he said, "I think this is the best wine that I've ever had." A few years later, Dexter, who also worked in business development, officially became the company's winemaker.

Diamond continued to admire the bottle. "Wow," she said, her tone almost reverent. "Can I open it?"

"Sure."

Dexter was proud of the clones he'd hoisted from vines his great-grandfather had planted more than twenty-five years ago. Using cuttings and buds from Papa Dee's original, they'd created a nice blend of fine red wines. The years 2002 and 2007 were especially good, but there was a very limited selection bottled in 1989. PNDO, Pinot Noir Drake Original, was sold for one week once a year and was available by invitation only. Those on a budget need not seek admittance to this club as the cost of one bottle equaled that of a high-end computer.

Diamond poured the wine through an aerator, filled their glasses and gave one to Dexter. There was no talking. This was serious business right here. Both of them held the glass up to the light, noting the opaqueness, the deep garnet—almost burgundy—color tinged with orange. They stuck their noses into the glass and inhaled deeply. A hint of cherry was recognized along with the blackberry fragrance. *Stellar!* After swirling their glasses for several seconds, they inhaled again. "Is that huckleberry?"

Dexter nodded. "And the slightest hint of oak."

Diamond closed her eyes and inhaled deeply. Wispy scents of cinnamon, clove and nutmeg spices ticked her nose. "The spice aromas cut through so nicely," Diamond gushed, with unabashed admiration. "But still very fruit forward. This vintage absolutely gets better with age."

Each took a quick, audible sip, letting the liquid rest on their tongues before swallowing. Dexter nodded his approval at the continued improvement of his self-proclaimed masterpiece. "Very little R.S."

Diamond nodded her agreement about residual sugar. "With just the right amount of acidity. And the low tannin level is why I prefer this to merlot."

Dexter heard voices in the foyer and looked at his watch. "Hey, sis. I need to warn you—"

"Wine tasting is over," Genevieve interrupted, sweeping

into the room with all the majesty and none of the weariness of someone who'd just whipped up a four-course meal.

Diamond hoisted her glass "It's PNDO, Mom!" she exclaimed.

"Great. Bring a couple bottles to the table. Dinner is served." She started for the door but turned to see Diamond and Dexter rooted to the spot. "Well?"

Diamond glanced at Dexter. "In a minute, Mom," he said.

"All right, son," Genevieve replied and left the room.

"What do you have to tell me?" Diamond whispered, anxiously glancing toward the hall where yet more footsteps approached. *It's just us tonight:* the statement sounded innocuous enough when her mother had said it, but now...

"Daddy knows about—"

"Diamond, Dexter," Donald interrupted, as he stepped through the entrance. As great as this space was, Donald's presence filled the room; and this had little to do with his sizable height and bulk. No, this room was filled with the authority and power afforded only to those who were not only successful and wealthy but also still in possession of common sense. "We need you now. Family meeting."

It was obvious that he wasn't leaving without them. Diamond knocked back the wine in the glass she was holding and, cutting a look at the brother she already blamed for whatever, followed her father to the room that, she had a sneaking feeling, would resemble the Inquisition before long.

Chapter 24

The table was set exquisitely with Waterford crystal and bone china that had been in the family for two generations. Small talk was made as Genevieve ladled up bowls of creamy mushroom soup. Donald and Donovan dug into their servings with gusto, while Genevieve took small, ladylike sips. Dexter continued to make a meal out of the warm bread fresh from the oven, slathered with butter and homemade jam, while Diamond felt small drops of soup collide with the knot in her stomach.

Finally, she'd had enough of the tension. She placed her napkin on her lap and spoke to the room at large. "Out with it already, jeez! What is going on?"

Genevieve looked at Donald.

Donovan looked at Genevieve.

Diamond glanced at Dexter, who'd suddenly become transfixed by something at the bottom of his wineglass.

Donald eyed the jewel of the family, his only daughter,

whom he'd protect with his life. He finished his bite and put down his napkin. "I received some disturbing news today, honey. About Jackson Wright."

Diamond turned to Dexter. If looks could kill, she'd be up on murder charges right about now.

"We know you're seeing him, and no, Dexter did not tell us."

"Who did?" Belatedly, Diamond realized that this hastily blurted question may not have been the proper rebuttal. How many times had this *Law & Order* fan heard the buzz word: deny, deny, *deny!*

"He heard it through the grapevine, literally," Donovan said, with an unceremonious scraping of his silver spoon against the now empty soup bowl.

"After Roberto saw y'all *in* the grapevine," Genevieve clarified.

Where had the head grower been hiding? And aside from the fact that she'd enjoyed his kisses…hadn't she told Jackson to behave? This was all his fault! "What is with the interrogation?" she asked saucily, figuring that the best offense might be a good defense. "I was over twenty-one, last time I checked."

"And the last time *I* checked, your workday started around nine and ended around six," Donald easily countered. "When I suggested you give Jackson a tour, necking in the fields isn't what I had in mind."

"Now, Donald," Genevieve intervened, memories of parts of the land she and Donald had christened rising up as fresh as the bread that sat on the table. "Let's keep the focus on what's important here."

Diamond crossed her arms. "And what's that?"

The way Donald took his time and placed a healthy rib on his plate, you'd think what was important was his dinner. The conversation lulled as everyone but Diamond helped themselves to braised ribs and warm potato salad. After taking a bite, he continued, "I had Jackson checked out."

"Dad, you background everyone who does business with us. And?"

"And when I hired his construction company for our renovation, our check was limited primarily to his business background. After I discovered your interest in him, I determined that a little more digging was in order."

"And I'm determining that you need to mind your own business." Donald shot Diamond a stern look. "Sorry, Dad. I don't mean to be disrespectful. I'm just…frustrated that you felt the need for a full-out investigation."

Diamond was angry but not overly surprised. Theirs was a close-knit family, who knew the goings-on in each other's lives. As the only daughter, Diamond's personal life seemed especially prone to the microscopic interest of both her parents and brothers, and seeing her walk down the aisle was one of Genevieve's utmost desires—one that had intensified after Diamond turned twenty-nine.

"Daughter—" Donald waited until Diamond looked at him "—in the words of Richard Nixon, let me make one thing perfectly clear." Donald methodically wiped barbeque sauce off his fingers. "I don't care if you live to be a hundred and marry five times…you are first and foremost a Drake, whose safety and welfare will always be my business." Diamond stared at her father, waiting for him to continue. "Now, normally I wouldn't have found this out so quickly, but it just so happens that a guy in the L.A. Sheriff's office was a classmate of mine."

"Lucky you."

Knowing she was upset, Donald gave his daughter a pass. "That luck as you call it continued, because when I mentioned his name it turns out that his sister knows Jackson Wright's mother."

"You sure you don't want to take your chances in Vegas?" Diamond mumbled. "'Cause you're on a roll."

"That's enough, Diamond." Genevieve's voice was soft yet firm—that iron-fist-in-velvet-glove trick that she'd perfected.

"Jackson Wright was born Jackson Burnett. He grew up in the streets of L.A., and while no criminal record was found, word has it that he dabbled in gang activity. His mother, Sharon Burnett, became strung out on drugs, eventually driving under the influence and committing vehicular manslaughter. The victims were a mother and her two children. She received twenty-five to life and is currently incarcerated at a prison in central California."

No one ate. Movement was slight. Donald continued.

"When Jackson was thirteen, he went to live with his uncle, John Wright, Sharon's half brother. John adopted him, took him under his wing and produced the man we see today. I believe he's a good man, Diamond, but I also believe you have a right to know what he once was."

Diamond looked at her father. "The past is the past, Dad. If you think he's a good man, then why tell me all of this?"

"Has Jackson told you?" The look on Diamond's face told everyone that he had not.

"You need to know the type of man you're dealing with, Diamond," Genevieve said softly, her eyes full of compassion. "Someone who has been abandoned, betrayed and lived through some very tough situations. There may be emotional scars there that make commitment difficult. Honey, we've seen the hurt that Benjamin caused and want you to be very clear as you move forward before you become more involved. That's all."

"Don't sweat it, big sis," Dexter said, to lighten the mood. When it came to serious, heavy scenes…he'd rather not, thank you very much. "You know my frat conference is coming up soon. Some big ballers will be there for sure. I'll keep an eye out."

"Myles keeps asking about you," Donovan offered, referring to one of his golfing buddies.

"Myles has children my age," Diamond shot back.

Donovan laughed. "Not quite. He's forty-eight and in great shape. Besides, his two twenty-something children live with their mother in Phoenix."

Diamond placed her napkin on the table. "I'm not interested." She stood. "Please excuse me."

Diamond reached her living quarters in the east wing and paced the length of it. Thoughts from the dinner conversation crowded her mind like the Times Square crowd on New Year's Eve. What her father had shared was bad enough but worse was how this information was potentially connected to what Jackson had told her this afternoon: that someone was trying to kill him.

Faster and faster the thoughts came. *Jackson. Adopted. Commitment issues. Born Jackson Burnett. Mom in prison. Gang activity. Abandoned. Betrayed. Emotional scars. Adopted. Not Jackson Wright, Jackson Burnett. Betrayed. Abandoned. Prison. Difficult. Commitment. Difficult. Commitment. Difficult. Somebody's trying to kill me!* Diamond's hands went to her ears.

Beep. Beep. The call tone was a welcomed intrusion on her thoughts. She snatched up the phone, looked at the caller ID and her heart dropped. Having no idea how the conversation would play out, she answered, "Hello, Jackson."

"Hey, baby." His voice was low, sexy and oozing with desire.

"Hello, Jackson." Diamond closed her eyes, all too aware that she sounded like the proverbial broken record and that her voice held all the warmth of an ice cube.

"You said that already." Pause. "What's wrong?"

Diamond gripped her iPhone and again paced the room. "Just left a family meeting. There's a lot going on."

"Care to share?"

Do you care to share? A beat and then, "I'd rather talk about you. How did the meeting with the investigator go?"

"It went all right. He had a few leads. They're working on it."

"What about you? Have you thought more about who could be behind the notes, break-in and gunshots?"

"Not really. That's what I'm paying Frank to do."

"Frank?"

"Yeah, the private eye."

"Have you ever considered, I mean, I don't know much about your background—" *only, like, everything* "—but do you think it could be someone from your past, your childhood?" Silence. Not good. She knew she was treading on dangerous ground, but she needed to know that Jackson trusted her and that he would confide in her. She wanted him to tell her what she now knew. "Jackson? Did you hear me?"

"I heard you."

There was an even longer hesitation and then this: "What difference does it make? You're still going to have my back, right, no matter who it is?"

"Of course."

"All right, then."

"Tell me about your childhood, Jackson."

"Why?" Diamond knew he was angry, could imagine him standing, pacing. "What does my childhood have to do with you?"

"You have to do with me, baby. Where you come from is a part of that. It helps me know you better, the way you knew me better once I told you about Papa Dee and Nicodemus."

"Yeah, well, my history ain't nothing like that."

"I'd still like to know it."

"No. You wouldn't. Look, I don't want to talk about this anymore."

"Well, I do!" *Okay, playing the demanding princess card is probably not the best tactic.* Diamond softened her voice. "Baby, do you think it matters to me where you come from or how you grew up?"

"Looks like it. You're questioning me like you're Johnny Cochran. I'm halfway expecting you to bring out a glove."

"I just want to know, that's all. Maybe this is a conversation best had in person. Can I come over?"

There was a pause long enough you could drive a train through it and then, "Hell, no."

Click.

"I know this man did not just hang up on me." Diamond stared at the phone as if it had the answer. She couldn't snatch up her purse fast enough, and even though she knew that it was irrational—that hot nights and sticky thighs had not only blurred the professional boundary but obliterated it and, with it, her employer clout—she reverted back to the familiar: being the boss. And a man who reported to her, okay...kinda, sorta...had overstepped his bounds. Before the night was over, she determined, he would know that that was sooo not okay.

Chapter 25

Jackson sat in the darkness—brooding. The only thing rarer than the vintage cognac he nursed from a tumbler was the fact that the drink was in his hand. He was an occasional one-glass wino, a "have a beer with the fellas" kind of man—one more keen to have a six-pack on his body than one in the fridge. Sure, he'd smoked a little weed in his day, much like others in the neighborhood where he grew up, but for the most part, Jackson liked to have his wits about him. But he'd been searching for those wits ever since getting off the phone with Diamond. *Tell me about your childhood, Jackson.* This curiosity with his roots had seemingly come out of nowhere. Her request, the break-in and Frank's questioning about friends from his past had forced his mind back to a time he'd felt best left forgotten: his other life, his mother. He thought of their last meeting, and tears welled up in his eyes. *No!* Jackson had spent too much time lamenting things he couldn't change. Determined to stay focused on the future and not the past, he tossed back the drink, snatched up his keys and bounded from the house. The names of several women crossed his mind: any one of which could help him push back those things he'd rather not think about. Bypassing the Maserati, he jumped into his least expensive but most treasured vehicle: the Jeep his aunt and uncle had bought him. He whizzed down the drive, opened the gate…and came headlight to headlight with Diamond Drake.

It was lights, camera, action all right, but this drama was all too real. Jackson jumped out of his Jeep and strode to the driver's side of Diamond's BMW. "What are you doing here?"

It was not quite the welcome she expected, but since she'd had time to do some thinking on the drive over, it was one that she understood. "I need to talk to you."

"What about? My *childhood?*"

"About a lot of things."

"Well, you should have called first. As you can see, I'm on my way out."

"This shouldn't take long, Jackson. I've come all this way."

"Then you'll know how to get back to where you came from, won't you? Move your car." Jackson turned and headed back to his vehicle.

Diamond jumped out of hers. "I'm not going anywhere!"

Jackson stopped and spun around.

"You heard me," Diamond hissed, arms crossed, legs spread, balancing herself on three-inch spikes as if doing so on cobblestone was an everyday occurrence. "I'm not leaving until we talk."

The look on Jackson's face as he approached her caused Diamond's breath to catch in her throat. While his expression was unreadable, his eyes flashed with intense anger, and his body was taut with restraint. Diamond wanted to gobble him up and run for cover at the same time.

He walked up to her, almost nipple to nipple, so close that their breaths mingled. "What did you say?"

In light of his skulking presence it was difficult, but the little girl who'd held her own with two rambunctious brothers held her ground here. She channeled Nicodemus and Papa Dee.

Several tense seconds passed between them.

"All right, princess." Jackson slowly backed away from her. "Enter at your own risk."

Diamond watched Jackson get into his car. He backed up and waited. So did she. Suddenly, she didn't feel so confident. *Enter at your own risk? What does that mean?* Her mother's words sounded in her left ear: *You need to know the type of man you're dealing with...* Genevieve was right. She really didn't know Jackson—clarification: she knew Jackson *Wright,* not Jackson *Burnett.* Her father's words filtered through her right ear: *I believe that Jackson is a good man.* Decision made, Diamond walked to her car and soon followed Jackson into his estate. Through her rearview mirror, she watched the gates close behind her. Her heart pounded. But she was inside and the gates were closed. There was no turning back.

Once parked, Jackson took a couple steps, then turned and looked at her. "Well?" When she said nothing, he shook his head and walked inside. She followed him. He walked into a well-appointed living room: warm earth tones with splashes of red, the understated elegance of a designer's touch. He walked over to a chair and sat. There were no offers for her to do so, no invitations to water, wine or a turn in the turret.

What the hell am I doing here?

Outside the gates, she'd been too filled with the items on her own agenda to pay much attention to his appearance. But now she took in the black button-down shirt that was tucked into equally black slacks. His copper-toned skin looked creamy smooth against the fabric, and she could tell that the understated platinum jewelry he wore had not been purchased at a discount store. She looked into his eyes, and along with anger and impatience, she saw something else— sadness. In her mind, she could imagine the little boy with a druggie mother, no father and seemingly no way out of a bad situation. Her feelings were as jumbled as uncooked ramen noodles, but in this moment, she decided to speak simply, directly and from the heart.

"Earlier I asked about your childhood, but the fact of the matter is…I already know."

Jackson crossed his arms. "Know what?"

"About…your past." She looked at him, and in that moment if given a choice would rather have stared down a Category 5 hurricane. "It's standard procedure for our company to check out anyone connected to the vineyard." She hadn't asked but felt sure God would forgive her this small white lie.

"I'm not connected to Drake Wines."

"But you're intimately involved with a major expansion, for millions of dollars."

Once adopted, Jackson's uncle had gone to great lengths to "protect" him. Files had been purchased, records erased. His eyes narrowed. "Just what is it that you think you know?"

Diamond knew that if there was ever any chance of gaining his trust she had to tell him the truth. "I know that you were born Jackson Burnett, were adopted by your uncle and that your mother is in prison."

His reaction was immediate—and explosive. "My past is none of your damn business," he said, shooting out of the chair. "And that ain't some background-check information. You had to know somebody, pay money for that!"

Diamond took a step toward him. "My dad found out we were…involved—"

"Oh, and let me guess—he made a phone call. Like the

one you were going to make for me earlier? When I trusted you and told you what was going on at my company? How long have you known this, huh? Since you met me? Was that the appeal? Thought you'd come down from your castle and hang out with somebody who used to live in the hood? Am I the closest you could get to a gangster?" Even though he'd been cleared of any involvement, Jackson always felt ashamed about what had happened at the gas station. Call it guilt by association, but Jackson felt as responsible as those behind bars for what had gone down.

"Jackson, that's not fair."

"And what you did is?" Jackson wondered just how much Diamond's father had been able to uncover and whether his money had been as effective as Uncle John's. "You know I was adopted. You know my mom is in prison. What else do you know?"

My God, is there more? "That's it. My father received this news today and told me tonight, right before I called you."

"And instead of telling me what you knew straight out, you decided to play games. *Tell me about your childhood, Jackson,*" he mimicked. "This is ridiculous."

"Okay, maybe you're right. Maybe that wasn't the best approach. I was in shock. I was confused. But I'm here. Doesn't that say something?" Silence. "He only did it because he knows that I have feelings for you. *Deep* feelings, Jackson. Some would call him overprotective—"

"Overprotective, hell. He's stepped way out-of-bounds, Diamond. And so have you!"

"It's only because he loves me so much." Diamond saw the flash of hurt in Jackson's eyes and realized how her words may have made him feel. He'd had an aunt who'd adored him and an uncle who'd raised him with love and respect, but he didn't know his biological father…had never felt his love. She took a step toward him. "I'm sorry for what happened to you, Jackson."

"Uh-huh, cool. Get out."

She took another step. "I don't care about your past. I believe that you're a good man."

"You had no right to delve into my background. If I'd wanted you to know about it, I would have told you."

Realization dawned. *He's ashamed. Even though the circumstances weren't his fault, he's ashamed about not knowing his father and about what his mother did.* "It was an intrusion, and for that, I'm sorry. But I don't apologize for caring about you."

"I mean it, Diamond. I want you to leave." Jackson's entire body was tense.

But where Jackson felt anger, Diamond saw only fear. She took another step. "I don't apologize for loving you."

His chest rose and fell with the intensity of his breathing as he fought to keep the pain from the past at bay and maintain control of his emotions.

Diamond took one last step and came face-to-face with her heartbeat. She tentatively reached up and caressed his face. A single tear slid down her cheek. "I love you, Jackson Wright."

One second passed...two...five. He grabbed her, crushed her to his chest. She could feel the rapidity of his heartbeat. She put her arms around him, wishing she could love his hurt away. She knew that might not be possible, but at the very least, she could ease it for awhile.

"You said to enter at my own risk, right?"

"Yes," Jackson mumbled, barely above a whisper.

"Well, mister, you're the one who's in trouble."

"How?"

"Because I want to assault your body. I want to feel you

inside me, long and deep." She stepped back, looked into his eyes. "Will you make love to me, Jackson?"

His eyes immediately darkened with desire. In answer, he swept her up and headed for the stairs.

Chapter 26

Jackson reached the double staircase, but instead of taking the one that led to his master suite, he went in the other direction. After setting Diamond down as if she were a fragile treasure, he took her hand and walked down a short hall with a door at the end. He opened it, revealing yet another stairway. Wordlessly, they mounted the steps, and when Jackson opened the door at the top of the climb, Diamond's eyes widened. They were outside, in the turret she'd seen earlier, with a 360-degree view of San Diego County. Her eyes took in the magnificence of the night: twinkling city lights in one direction, the ocean before them and stars above. Jackson's eyes were for her alone.

He reached for her and placed a kiss on her forehead. It was soft, almost reverent, and Diamond teared up at its sincerity. He kissed one temple and then the other, all the while reaching for the zipper on the front of her dress and pulling it down...farther and farther...exposing her warm skin to the cool of the night. Her nipples pebbled as the wind caressed them—barely concealed in a sheer mesh bra—and as Jackson's mouth found hers, he forced his tongue inside.

He kissed her, tenderly, fervently, whirling his tongue inside her mouth as his finger swirled around her nipple. Diamond shuddered as his hands roamed her upper body, and he buried his hand in her hair, pulling her even closer and deepening the exchange. The assault was so intense that Diamond's knees almost buckled. But there was no need to worry. Jackson was ahead of her, and even now, he was leading her to a low-sitting platform covered with colorful pillows of various sizes and textures that occupied one wall of the circular outdoor room. She eased down on the pillows, and after hurriedly taking off his clothes, he joined her there, massaging her skin, licking her nipples through the soft mesh, fingering her paradise, driving her wild. Diamond gasped as his tongue trailed down her body, lingering at her stomach and navel before he went down farther and kissed her thighs.

"You're so soft," he whispered, kissing the insides of her thighs and then blowing on the wetness. Closer and closer he came to her heat, only to place a trail of kisses back down her legs all the way to her toes, where he sucked them one by one. Diamond was out of her mind with desire. Her body thrashed with impatience and the knowledge of what was to come.

Jackson wouldn't be hurried. He kissed a path back up her legs, hips, stomach and breasts and seared her with another hot, wet kiss.

"Jackson, please."

He chuckled and made his way back down, spreading her wide and parting her folds with his sharp, talented tongue. Over and again he licked her, flicking her nub while placing a finger inside, heightening her pleasure, taking her over the edge. At the height of her orgasm, and with no thoughts of condoms by either of them, he slowly eased himself inside of her, her heat pulsating around inch after delicious inch. He filled her to the core, pulled out and then filled her again. Over and over, deeper and deeper, slowly, oh…so…slowly he loved her, twisting his hips from side to side, setting up a rhythm that would be known to them alone. She grabbed his ass and pulled him closer still, her legs in the air as she spread them to accommodate his expanding girth, tears of ecstasy now on a free flow. He got up and pulled her with him, walked them over to a part of the turret that jutted out over his well-landscaped yard. The infinity pool glistened against the darkened sky; the lights of San Diego continued to beckon in the distance.

But Diamond couldn't see; she could only feel as Jackson came up behind her, held her hips and entered her again. That they were naked and standing outside added to the friction and her delight. He kneaded her backside, running his hands over her flesh as he pounded her over and again. The wind blew, and goose bumps broke out on Diamond's flesh. It began to rain, but their dance continued. There was something about making love outside that felt naughty and decadent, even as it felt organic and pure. He lifted her onto him, placed her back to the wall and entered her again. The intensity of his thrusts intensified, his tongue mimicking his hip movements as he kissed her senseless. He pounded her relentlessly, as if he could go on forever. She wished he would. The rain outside, her lover inside her, Diamond felt herself explode again. This time, Jackson joined her. They both saw stars, and neither was looking at the sky.

Chapter 27

"Come on, baby." Jackson wrapped Diamond in a throw he retrieved from a chest. They went inside and were soon enjoying the warm water pulsating from the multiple jets in Jackson's master bath. Diamond admired his body as she rubbed a fresh, lemony-scented soap all over it, kneading the tension from his neck and shoulder muscles much as he'd done to her not long ago. They rubbed their soapy bodies against each other, bringing themselves once again to arousal. Neither could get enough. With all of the lovemaking that had occurred one might not have thought it possible, but when Diamond's hand went around his limp shaft, it immediately sprang to life and along with it, Diamond's desire. She wanted to satisfy Jackson as much as he'd satisfied her and soon found herself kissing him all over. Her tongue was akin to molten lava, scorching his shoulders and broad expanse of chest. She tongued his navel and discovered a secret. He was ticklish. Then she dipped her head lower and his laughter turned into a satisfied moan. She wrapped her mouth around him, licking him like a lollipop with a prize inside. Again water served as the backdrop as these two lovers explored and enjoyed each other. Diamond loved Jackson so tenderly, so completely that it was almost his undoing. He grabbed the hand that rested at his waist, pulled her up and took the lead. Wordlessly, he walked them over to the bench on the shower's far wall. He sat down and so did Diamond—on him. And just like that, once again, he was in her—filling her full, loving her deeply, leaving no room for anything else, especially doubt. Diamond leaned forward. Blood rushed to her head the way love was rushing to her heart. She was overcome with passion and emotion, marveling at the fact that there was this much ardency in the world. He reached around for her nipples, grabbing and squeezing as she continued to jump for joy on his joystick, increasing the pace and their pleasure with each rise and rotation. If their cries had been a song, it would have been in perfect harmony. Her high-pitched whimpers matched his low, deep grunts. Their worlds exploded. When it was over, they sat gasping for breath, grasping for an explanation to this insatiable hunger.

"Baby," Jackson said when his breathing returned to normal, "it's time to shower again."

A short time later, they lay in Jackson's custom-made bed. Diamond's sated body spooned against his; a high-thread-count sheet rested over their bodies. She knew she could stay here forever, in his arms. His parentage didn't matter. His past was of no consequence. Her heart just might get broken again, but she wasn't going anywhere far from this man— not if she could help it. Theirs was a companionable silence. Diamond thought Jackson had fallen asleep, but he hadn't.

"My first memory is when I was three or four years old," he said, his voice soft, his breath hot and wet against her earlobe. "A fair came to the neighborhood. You know, one of those traveling kinds where they set up a Ferris wheel, Tilt-A-Whirl, Spider and whatnot? They set up in a grocery store parking lot right down the street from where we lived. I don't remember what I rode, probably a merry-go-round at that age, but I remember all the lights and the people. Oh, and the cotton candy. It's crazy how your mind recalls things, but I remember pulling that confection off the stick and stuffing it into my mouth. It was blue, and I thought the way it disappeared in my mouth was magic. I must have eaten three or four of those things.

"My next really strong memory is a few years later, when I was around seven. I came home from school and noticed that Mom was acting strange. She was talking fast, and her eyes were glazed. She was high, of course, but my young mind didn't grasp that right away. She left, came back with a hamburger and fries and told me to watch TV until she got back. I didn't see her for a week."

Diamond turned to face Jackson, who was now lying on his back, staring at the ceiling. She couldn't believe what she was hearing. *What kind of mother would leave her child like that?* She placed a hand on his chest and whispered, "You must have been so scared."

"The first day I wasn't. Thought it was kind of nice to stay up late, watching TV, eating almost a whole box of Cap'n Crunch. But the next day, when I came home from school and she still wasn't there…that's when I began to worry."

"She was out getting high?"

Jackson nodded. "And doing whatever it took to support her habit. The day after she came back, I came home from school to a houseful of people—my mom's boyfriend at the time and some of his friends. He was from New York and had brought back this new drug, one sweeping across the five boroughs faster than a plane streaks across the sky—crack cocaine. Alvin Johnson. That was the name of the man who ruined my mother's life and mine in the process. I hate him to this day."

To this point, Diamond had considered hate a draining, nonproductive emotion. But in this instance, it was the only one that made sense. "That's who your mom was picking up when she had the accident?"

"Yes, but that was years later, when I was thirteen. By then, I was pretty hard myself, had taken to petty crimes and being the lookout for a fairly high-ranking drug dealer. I was just getting ready to move into the big leagues—dealing— when she got arrested. That's when my uncle stepped in and saved my life."

"Had you known him before?"

"Vaguely. I remember him coming around a few times, him and my mom arguing. He told her to go into treatment, and she told him to go to hell." Jackson laughed, but his voice held no humor. "I was only in the system two days before he came and got me. I don't know what he did or said to her, but my mom terminated her rights almost immediately afterward. John and Evie Wright adopted me the following year, and became the parents I'd never had. That's when my life changed for the better. I've not looked back." Jackson shifted uncomfortably, turned to look at Diamond.

She looked back, eyes filled with love…and nonjudgment. He continued staring at her, and she would have sworn that a tear was forming in his eye when he looked away. "Jackson… what is it?" Her voice was soft, quizzical.

Again, she wondered if he would say anything. But finally he did. "I went back one time."

Diamond said nothing, just turned, laid her head on his chest and lazily ran her hand up and down his arm.

"The end of July, the weekend of my sixteenth birthday, I ran into the cousin of a dude I grew up with. It felt good seeing somebody from the old neighborhood. Until that point, I didn't even realize that I'd missed them. I told him that it was my birthday, and he said I should celebrate with the boys. I told him it sounded like a plan.

"My birthday was on a Friday that year. I told Uncle John and Aunt Evie I wanted to celebrate in my old neighborhood. They weren't crazy about the idea but finally gave their consent to my leaving. I hit the block, and it was like I never left. I meant to stay three days and stayed almost a month—partying, drinking, getting high, having fun. My boys almost had me convinced that I needed to move back there, that I could stay with one of them. I asked about school, but they waved that comment away. 'We're making more paper than the teachers,' they told me. And it was true."

"How were they doing that?"

"Selling drugs. And other illegal activities."

Diamond paused, her mind filled with what "illegal activities" could entail. "What made you come back home—to La Jolla?"

"I got a wake-up call."

Jackson became silent then. Diamond thought he'd gone to sleep, but when she looked at him she saw that his eyes were gazing at the ceiling. She wondered about the wake-up call, but clearly it was something he did not want to talk about. "When was the last time you saw your mom?"

Jackson was silent for another long moment. He swallowed once, again tamping down a dam of emotions that threatened to spill over into the bed and this new life. "About five years ago." His voice was low, reflective, laced with heaviness. "Went to see her at the prison. Asked her about my father, my biological. She told me it was Alvin. I called her a liar. It was an ugly scene. She cursed me out, told me never to come back there. All these years later and she's still choosing him over me. I vowed to never see her again."

"But Jackson," she said, her heart aching with the pain of these revelations. "She's your mother."

"Evie Wright was my mother," Jackson hissed. "And she's dead. And as far as I'm concerned, Sharon Burnett is dead, too. I've cut her out of my life."

"But what about your heart?"

"There, too." That's what he said. But the lone, almost imperceptible tear that fell from his eye suggested otherwise.

"I'm sorry about what happened to you, baby. Those experiences would have crushed a lesser man."

"Yeah, well, they almost did me in."

"But they didn't. You survived and thrived, and for that I'm so grateful. I love you, Jackson."

Five seconds passed. Ten. Fifteen.

Jackson's arms tightened around her. "I love you, too."

Chapter 28

Jackson and Diamond talked into the night. Dawn was streaking across the sky when she left his mansion, her heart full of love and dreams of a life with him. And more than what she'd ever hoped for had happened. He'd told her he loved her! This single declaration energized her, replaced the sleep she'd exchanged for a night of lovemaking. When she entered the great room for the meeting that had been arranged before the Wright/Burnett revelation, she was awake, aware and ready for action.

"Good morning, everybody," she fairly sang into the room.

Genevieve's brow rose oh-so-slightly. "Sounds like you've had a very good morning."

"Morning, sis," Dexter mumbled around a freshly baked croissant, sent to the main house by David and Mary's chef.

Various greetings continued along with small talk as Donovan and Grandpa David entered the room. Papa Dee was the last to arrive, his steps precise and unhurried. He sat, accepted a cup of coffee and waited for the meeting to begin.

Diamond took a last sip of her green tea and began, her tone as businesslike as her tailored navy suit. "Has everyone reviewed the proposal I emailed yesterday?"

Nods and affirmatives resounded.

"As I stated in the outline, I believe that restoring Papa Dee's house to its original luster, while updating it with a pristine, top-of-the-line kitchen and spa bath, will create the buzz to make this a destination wedding location—especially after we install the Jacuzzi behind it and build a gazebo at the crest of the hill, for actual weddings, anniversaries and other such ceremonies to take place."

"Nice work, daughter," Donald said, pride evident in his voice. "We've been wondering what to do with Grandpa's house for some time. I think this is a brilliant idea."

"It's all right," Dexter drawled, all too ready to lessen the chance of any serious head swelling. "But if we're going to have all different types of ceremonies there, we can't call it a honeymoon suite."

Diamond typed away on her iPad.

"This is good stuff," Donovan chimed in. "But I think we should limit gatherings to those on the smaller scale, say a hundred guests or less. That way, we can focus on the quality and take into account parking, accommodations, et cetera."

"But the suite would be available to whomever, correct?" Genevieve asked. "Not just to those who get married on our property."

"Yes," Diamond answered. "The suite would be booked on a first come, first serve basis."

"I especially like the idea of a chef and butler attending to the honeymooners or whomever stays there," Genevieve continued. "Perhaps Mom Mary will even do the honors of preparing a signature dessert, based on one of Papa Dee's favorites."

"Well, that would be pralines, hands down," Papa Dee said, his voice raspy, eyes bright. "My mama used to make batches of 'em every Christmas and hand them out to the folk in the neighborhood."

"We could include them in the welcome basket along with a couple bottles of our sparkling wines, gourmet cheese, nuts, crackers, fruits." Diamond typed these suggestions as well, her excitement growing with every keystroke. "Perhaps I'll do a simple brochure detailing the history of the house and include a picture of Papa."

"You're getting ready to be famous, old man," Dexter teased, leaning over to pat Papa Dee on the back. "People coming from all over just to see your birthplace."

"Aw, you go on now," Papa replied. But his eyes twinkled.

Ever the businessman, Donald shifted gears from nostalgia to numbers. "What's the cost of this addition?"

"That ground will be covered in the meeting I've scheduled for this afternoon, where Jackson and Taylor will be in attendance." She made sure to sound as businesslike as possible, but at the mention of his name a soft flush crept from her neck to her hairline. "I know it's short notice, but hopefully we can all make it. I want the restored home to be unveiled along with the rest of Drake Wines Resort & Spa, and I definitely want it included in the *O Magazine* shoot happening in late January."

Genevieve watched as her daughter tried to maintain a businesslike veneer. But she'd seen the flush and knew the look. She'd *worn* that look many times after Donald had thoroughly and completely satisfied her. "Sweetheart, how did you come up with this wonderful idea?"

Diamond took a calming breath and answered, "It was inspired by a comment Jackson made as we were touring the grounds. He was quite impressed with the quality of work-manship and thought, as we do, that it should not only be preserved but enjoyed."

"Is the house all he's enjoying?" Donald asked.

"No, Dad. It isn't. You'll all bug me until I tell you anyway, so I'll say it outright. Jackson and I are officially dating. And I'm officially in love with him."

Donald and Genevieve exchanged glances. Donovan sat back in his chair and sighed. Dexter chuckled.

"I know what you all might be thinking about Jackson's past. But I'm not dating the boy who left Inglewood when he was thirteen. I'm dating a caring, thoughtful, amazing man who now runs a multimillion-dollar company. This is my life and my decision. When it comes to me and Jackson, please respect my wishes...and back off."

Later, the family met again. This time, it was in the confer-ence room in the center of the building that housed the Drake Vineyard executive offices. David, Mary, Donald, Genevieve, Donovan, Dexter and Diamond had been joined by Jackson and Taylor. For ninety-eight-year-old Papa Dee, it was nap time. He was not present. Normally the elder Drakes would not be present either, but since this was a family heirloom of sorts, Diamond wanted their contributions. The meeting went smoothly, and after a drive out to the house on the hill, and a walk-through with all parties coming together on the plans for Papa Dee's birthplace—whose official name would become the Papa Dee Suite—the plans were approved.

"I'm very excited about these plans," Taylor said as she, Diamond and Jackson headed to the cart that Diamond had driven. "I already have some ideas that I believe would be perfect to both capture the turn-of-the-century feel when this home was built and give it the luxuriousness that a honey-moon haven and the like demands."

Diamond smiled at Taylor. "I can't wait. How soon can we meet?"

"The rest of my week is jam-packed, and my parents' anniversary party is this weekend, but I can get my staff started on creating three proposed looks. I can also have them gather fabric swatches, search for furniture… Would Tuesday or Wednesday of next week work?"

"How long have your parents been married?"

"Thirty years," Taylor proudly answered.

"I'm so glad the accident with your father wasn't more serious."

"He's zipping around on the golf course as if it never happened."

"That's wonderful, Taylor. It's important that we take time out and celebrate what's really important. Tuesday or Wednesday sounds fine to me," Diamond continued, back to business. "But that only gives us two weeks for construction. Jackson, how do you feel about that?"

Jackson shrugged. "It's doable. But we're going to have to get cranking and work around the clock. I'll also have to subcontract some of the work with a couple other construction companies. They're quite reputable and ones I've often worked with, so this won't be a problem. With the expanded plans we've already added to the hotel's dining and lounge areas, and now this… Let me speak to my foreman and let you know by end of business day today."

He was just getting ready to jump into the back of Diamond's cart when Donald drove up in his. "Boss, why don't you come along with me? I want to run a couple things past you."

"Sure, Donald." He gave Diamond's shoulder a quick squeeze and then walked past the cart that carried Donovan and Dexter to the one where Donald sat waiting. He hopped in and Donald began the hundred-plus-yard trek from the house on the hill to the office. "I have to tell you, sir...it's a wonderful opportunity for me to restore that house up there. With all of the history it holds and what it means to your family, not to mention those who'll begin their lives together under its roof, well, it's an honor."

"We feel really good about it—especially my grandfather. He'll be thrilled about the slab you've suggested, honoring our forefather, Nicodemus. And speaking of honor—" Donald continued, reaching the executive offices and shutting off the engine while turning to look Jackson in the eye "—I'd like to know your intentions where my daughter is concerned."

Chapter 29

The air fairly crackled between these two strong, powerful men as Donald awaited his answer. Just then, Donovan and Dexter pulled up beside them and exited their cart. They saw Donald and Jackson eyeing each other and paused. The look told the brothers that they'd been on one accord: that Donald was now asking Jackson the question they'd pondered on their way down. They walked to Jackson's cart without hesitation. Three pairs of chocolate-brown Drake eyes stared at Jackson, who looked up and saw Diamond and Taylor approaching. "Let's take this powwow into your office," he suggested to Donald, jumping out of the cart as he did so. "And then I can share exactly what is on my mind."

The men entered Donald's office. He closed the door. The four men painted a formidable picture: all tall, dark, handsome, exuding testosterone and confidence to the nth power. Jackson looked just as capable of kicking butt and taking names as a Drake on any day. His air of authority gave one the indication that he believed this about himself, as well.

"I care about your daughter," he said to Donald. "Your sister," he said to Donovan and Dexter. "I have no intention of hurting her." The Drake men relaxed their shoulders somewhat, but their stances remained firm. "I respect the Drake name but am not intimidated by it, which is why I want to make myself clear on any issue regarding myself, my company and/or my family. If you want to know something…ask me." He looked at Donald. "With all due respect, sir, your conducting an investigation into my life was way out of line."

"When it comes to my daughter, there are no rules of conduct," Donald replied. "I'd do it again in a heartbeat."

"We're a close-knit family who protects our own and have each other's backs at all times." Dexter took a step in Jackson's direction. "Do you have a problem with that?"

"No problem," Jackson casually answered. "As long as it doesn't happen again."

"As long as Diamond is happy, we're cool," Donovan countered. "Don't start none, won't be none."

The merest smile scampered across Jackson's face. "That's probably something you should discuss with Diamond. But my guess is…she's very satisfied. Now, gentlemen, if you'll excuse me I have a five-star hotel to finish building and a homestead to renovate." He reached out and shook each man's hand, then walked out of the office with back straight and head held high.

The men watched him leave. "What do you think?" Donald asked, after a moment.

"Good man," Donovan answered.

"No doubt," Dexter agreed.

"We could do worse than a successful construction company owner in the family," Donald said.

"Absolutely." Dexter rubbed his chin thoughtfully. "In fact, it might be time for me to build my dream home. Get the family discount, you feel me?"

The men laughed. "Let's just hope his dating Diamond has a better ending than she and Benjamin did," Donovan said, concern for his sister showing in his eyes.

"Yes, let's hope," Donald agreed. "Because if he hurts my daughter, he'll answer to me. And I mean that."

Down the hall, Diamond paced. She called Kathleen. "Are they out yet? Have you seen anyone?"

"No, dear, and I've been looking." Kathleen hadn't felt this type of drama since *As The World Turns* had left the air. "I'll buzz you as soon as I know."

"Okay." Diamond remained tense. She'd seen the men talking when she drove up with Taylor and watched them walk into the building. Had Taylor not wanted to get clear on a few decor points, she would have marched down the hall and into the room right behind them. As it was, she was beside herself with curiosity. Her dad and brothers were a formidable bunch. But then…so was Jackson.

Diamond's cell phone rang. "Hi, Mom."

"Hello, darling. Do you have a moment?"

"Yes."

"Good. Can you come by the house? I'd like to have a little chat."

Diamond was torn. She wanted to talk to her mom but equally wanted to stand by should a referee be needed. The desire to confide in Genevieve won out. She trusted Jackson to hold his own.

"Kat, I'm going to see Mom for a moment."

"You're not going to wait—"

"Until the dust settles? Not now. But if you hear a rumble, give me a call."

Genevieve greeted Diamond at the door. Her eyes glistened with excitement. For a moment, Diamond could imagine her mother at her age: young, beautiful, vibrant, full of passion. This closeness with her mother warmed her heart.

They hugged, then Genevieve pulled Diamond into the living room. "My goodness, girl. I had no idea that Jackson Wright was such a handsome man!"

"Isn't he?"

"You know, in some ways he reminds me of how your father was when I met him—confident, borderline arrogant, self-assured, intelligent as all get-out and handsome. Baby, couldn't nobody bless a suit the way your father could!"

"And I remember the story. You said you knew right away that Dad was the one."

"As soon as I laid eyes on that lanky joker, yes, sir." Genevieve's eyes sparkled with memories.

"Mom, I've never felt about anyone the way I do Jackson. I thought I knew love with Benjamin but—" Diamond shook her head "—now I know that there are levels to loving, and what I feel now...I've never felt before."

"I felt the same way about your father," Genevieve said as she poured tea. She handed a cup to Diamond. "At just the thought of Donald Drake, at the mention of his name, my heart would beat faster. Still does." Genevieve put a hand on Diamond's arm. "When the information regarding Jackson's past came to your father, I was quite concerned. But after meeting him and seeing the way he looks at you...Diamond, I think he just might be the one."

"Really, Mom, you think so?"

Genevieve nodded.

These words made Diamond's heart soar. "So you were watching him, right? How does he look at me?"

"Diamond, baby, he looks at you like your father looks at me...with eyes full of love."

Chapter 30

The next three weeks passed by in a whirlwind of love, work and bottles of Drake premier wine. Both were busy, but Diamond and Jackson still managed to spend quality time together. They carved it out where they could find it, like now, the day before the resort's grand opening. Earlier, the family and Drake Wine employees had toured the new facility. Their wide eyes and gape-mouthed expressions told Jackson of the bang-up job he and Boss Construction had done better than words ever could. Donald Drake couldn't have been more impressed at what Jackson had pulled off in so little time. The only other time he'd seen quality work performed this fast was when Ty Pennington was screaming into his bullhorn and telling another family "Welcome home!" The thirty-room hotel was fully booked for the holiday weekend, and largely due to a lineup of R & B classic artists and smooth jazz favorites, their Sunday "Brunch & Beats" was sold out through Valentine's Day.

Diamond looked at her watch. She couldn't believe it was ten o'clock and she was still working. Kathleen had left just moments before. Everyone was tired. *This time tomorrow, it'll be done. Drake Wines Resort & Spa will be officially opened for business.* The day after that, Thanksgiving, her family had planned a private celebration. Diamond couldn't wait.

Placing her keys in her hand, she reached for the door and gasped as a tall, hulking figure blocked the path in front of her. "Jackson! Baby! You scared me half to death!"

Jackson pulled her into his embrace. "What are you still doing here, baby? Where's security? I don't like the idea of you being out here alone." While not sharing everything with Donald and her brothers, he had mentioned that there were people who'd like nothing better than to cause him problems, and with their relationship becoming public, Diamond may be targeted, as well.

"Phillip is probably making his rounds," she said, pulling out her cell phone. "But I'm going to call Donovan nonetheless, make sure that the extra security are on the premises."

After placing the call, she turned to Jackson. "Now, Mr. Wright, let me ask you the same question. What are you doing here this late? I'm sure you're exhausted. Your men have been working around the clock. And the hard work has paid off. I've said it a thousand times and I'll say it again—the place looks amazing."

"Thank you, love." He took her hand and walked them to the side of the building where the carts were parked. "Get in," he told her, reaching beneath the seat to where he now knew they kept the keys.

"Where are we going?" Diamond asked, even as a wave of excitement surged through her.

"This will be our last night with the place all to ourselves. We're going to go and christen the Papa Dee Suite."

"Wait. I'll be right back." Diamond went into the office. "Let's stop by the rack," she said. They did, and shortly after entering the warehouse, Diamond returned with a chilled bottle of sparkling wine, a vintage bottle from another great year. The two were silent as Jackson expertly navigated the cart up the winding road that led to the old house. The night was cool, the moon was full and the stars twinkled like so many diamonds in the sky. Jackson turned the cart onto the pine-tree-lined entrance that now welcomed guests. Small lights twinkled from the boughs, creating a magical ambience around the freshly painted white house that beckoned in the distance. The house had been expertly lifted and now sat on a large expanse of smooth stone. The original porch had been refortified and expanded to the length of the front of the house. As a nod to its history, a lone plank remained loose, with a key inside.

Diamond smiled as she retrieved the key to the newly installed mahogany door outfitted with beveled glass, a single rose etched into the design. They entered and were immediately enveloped with the energy of the remodeled home, now with gleaming hardwood floors, floral silk-covered walls and a fireplace where wood sat stacked ready for use. The downstairs had stayed true to the original design, but upstairs the transformation had been more striking. A wall had been removed to turn the entire upstairs into a master suite, add a walk-in closet and an en suite bath with every amenity. A gas fireplace now anchored the upstairs area. Jackson walked over and turned it on, while Diamond tried out the stereo system, prestocked with thousands of tunes in every genre. The mood set, Jackson walked to the table where Diamond had placed the bubbly, popped the cork and filled their flutes.

"To an amazing woman," he said, his eyes shining with

love for her, "who knows who I am, where I've been, and accepts every part of me. I love you, Diamond."

"I love you, too."

They drank as the nostalgic sounds of John Coltrane's "Naima" set the mood—sultry and soulful, melodic and hot. Dancing around the room, they drank not only the sparkling vintage but the love that was pouring from each other's eyes. "I want to ask you something," Jackson said, grinding his already hardening manhood into Diamond's soft flesh.

"Yes?" Her whisper was filled with notes that suggested that at any moment he could have asked her to run down the I-15 buck naked and she would have obliged.

"Are you seeing anyone else?"

Diamond stopped moving. "Where did that come from?"

"From my wanting to know. Is there anyone else in your life right now?"

Diamond laid her head back on Jackson's shoulder and resumed their slow groove. "No. What about you?"

"No one." Silky notes dribbled from Coltrane's sax into the room, making them giddy, like the bubbly, like each other. "I was tested six months ago and always practice safe sex. But I believe what I have with you is special, Diamond. We did it the other night by accident, but from now on out, when we make love, I don't want anything between us."

The thought of her and Jackson in the raw, flesh to flesh, made Diamond tingle all over. It brought back memories of the lone other night where it had been so, when she'd poured out her love and he'd emptied his heart by sharing his past. She closed her eyes as he kissed her temple, sure that he could detect the rapidity of her heartbeat. "I'm on the Pill," she said at last, having started back on them six months ago to help lessen her cramps and regulate her periods. "I want to feel you, too."

As Coltrane's sax slid into Thelonious Monk's piano—

and in between hot and sticky kisses—Jackson and Diamond
undressed. They walked to the glass, steel and mosaic stone
shower. Diamond smiled as she reached for the cellophane-
wrapped sponge, remembering Jackson's response when she
commented on their proliferation for shower-taking. "I like
tasting you all over, baby. And I don't like to fake the funk…
or lick it." They'd showered, and then Jackson had shown her
exactly what he'd meant.

Jackson took it from her. "Here, let me."

He opened the liquid soap, poured a generous amount on
the sponge and took special pains as he tended to Diamond's
neck, shoulders, back and butt with kisses on the same.
"Spread your legs, baby." He washed her tenderly, lovingly
before his tongue replaced the sponge. He dipped his tongue
in her feminine flower, lapped her juices like the sweet-
est nectar until the musky odor of their abiding affection
filled the room, along with Diamond's mewling and traces
of "'Round Midnight." He finished washing her down to her
toes, and then she returned the favor. When she came to the
massive weapon that would soon be inside her, she stroked
it lovingly, circling the perfectly shaped mushroom tip with
her finger and following it with her tongue. Grabbing Jackson's hard, round buttocks, she took him in, licking, sucking,
setting up a rhythm that almost took her man over the edge.
He took her hand, but instead of the bed, he picked her up
and walked them to the wall. Her legs instinctively circled
his waist, and when they did, she was an open target and his
sword was poised for the sweet attack. With one long thrust,
he joined them together, squeezing her cheeks, stroking her
sensitive entrance, branding her body with his dick. Balancing her against the wall, he took hold of her hips and took
their dance to yet another level. Every time Diamond thought
it couldn't get any better, he surprised her. By rotating his
hips to a groove of his own, he touched every part of Dia-

mond's essence and every fiber of her soul. Just before her release, he stopped, led her to the edge of the bed and guided her to her knees. There, once again, he took a loving hold of her hips, teasing her with his tip, kissing her shoulders, back, buttocks, thighs, kissing her as if she were ambrosia. "I love you, Diamond," he whispered, as with quick, sure strokes he guided himself inside her. "I love the feel of you, my love." He settled in deep and leaned over. "Do you like this, baby? Do you like the feel of me inside you?" Diamond nodded, but when she didn't answer audibly he pulled out and slowly pushed in again. "Do you like this?"

"Yes," Diamond stuttered, grinding herself against him, taking him deeper still.

"What about this?" he asked, moving in and out and side to side, then becoming still again. He reached around, tweaked her nipples and then, without warning, drove himself deeply inside her with such an intensity, such ferocity, that Diamond felt as intense of a release as she'd ever felt start at her core that straightened her hair and curled her toes. She'd never been a screamer and was therefore surprised to learn the high C bouncing off the walls was not the stereo but her own voice.

"Jackson!"

Her shout sent him over the edge, and then he joined her on the bed. He cuddled her close, feeling a contentment he hadn't thought possible, no longer able to imagine life without this jewel he'd found. "You make me happy, baby," he whispered in her ear.

"And you make me work," she replied.

He chuckled. "What?"

"That's right. Because of you, I have to call housekeeping for a late-night cleanup."

"Oh! What just happened is my fault then, huh?"

"Absolutely." She turned to face him. "And I enjoyed every

delicious minute of it. I think Nicodemus would have liked you and would be glad to know that the home has once again been christened by a Drake."

Chapter 31

Jackson walked into the office carrying flowers and a blue box. Marissa looked up in wonder, not so much that her boss had bought flowers. He often surprised her with such thoughtful treats. No, it was the fact that he was humming that caught her off guard.

"What happened to you?" she asked, her dimple twinkling as she spoke. "Are those gifts for me or the woman who put that smile on your face and that pep in your step?"

"These flowers are for the best assistant in the world," he said. "I appreciate you postponing your trip home to help with these last-minute details of the Drake opening. This," he said, placing the Tiffany box on the desk, "is for you to wear to the opening tonight."

"Me? Boss, you know I don't do those fancy-smancy gatherings."

"You'll like this one. The place is really beautiful, the

Drakes are good people and Diamond has two brothers. Both are handsome and available."

"Diamond Drake? That's who has you smiling like you're auditioning for a toothpaste commercial? I know what you're trying to do, Jackson. And I appreciate it. But my flight leaves first thing in the morning. And Thanksgiving is the busiest travel holiday of the year. I still need to pack and—"

"I'm sorry. Did I form that as a question? I meant to say that part of your job requirement is that you attend the grand opening of Drake Wines Resort & Spa."

Marissa huffed, but in actuality she was only mildly annoyed. In the past year, a so-called friend and a betrayed trust had sent her reeling. Jackson and this job had been a lifeline. If not for this anchor, she would have drowned. "Why would they open the day before Thanksgiving anyway?" she said, reaching for the famous blue box. "I'm sure their workers would rather be with their families."

"Their rationale is that oftentimes those without families are forgotten. Not everyone has a home to go to, and not everyone has a family that they're dying to see. The fact that both the restaurant and hotel are sold out is proof enough that their choice was a good one."

Marissa opened the box and pulled out a beautiful watch: functional yet elegant at the same time. "This is beautiful, Jackson. But really…it's too much."

"Does that mean I can skip your raise this year?"

Marissa hurriedly put the watch back in the box and pushed it toward Jackson. "Don't get it twisted, Boss. I'd rather put my money in the bank than wear it on my arm."

"Ha!"

"Thank you, Jackson. We have a lot to be thankful for."

"No more letters?"

Marissa shook her head. "Not for almost three weeks. A couple hang-ups but that could be anyone. I think the beefed-up security since the break-in and the very obvious cameras around the place have scared off whoever this was."

"I hope you're right. In the meantime, we have an opening to attend. Why don't you ride with me? You can take off now, and I'll pick you up in a couple hours."

Marissa reached for her purse. "When it comes to getting off early, you don't have to ask me twice. I'll see you soon!"

Jackson left her area and walked around the office. It mostly resembled a ghost town, but he saw one lone light shining at the back of the office. He walked in. It was his newest employee, a junior architect he'd recently recruited from the East Coast.

"Carlton? Are you kidding me?" Jackson stepped into his office. "What are you doing here? I thought you'd be chilling with your folks in D.C. by now."

"Hey, Boss. Getting it in, I guess. You know how we do."

"I appreciate the dedication and all but working through Thanksgiving? That's not required, bro."

"I guess it's my Type A personality. I'm almost done with this set of sketches. They're for the Chicago job. Another hour and then I'm out. Catching a nine o'clock red-eye."

"That's what's up. You have a good one, man."

"You, too."

Jackson continued down the hall to his office. As soon as he made sure everything was locked up tight, he left the Boss Construction offices and headed for the elevator. Just as he reached it, his phone rang. "Jackson."

"Sorry to bother you, Jackson. This is Frank."

"Happy holidays, man."

Frank continued in his no-nonsense style. "I've got news."

Normalcy continued around him, but Jackson's body went on high alert. "Today?"

"Evil doesn't pause for the holidays."

"Talk."

"A childhood friend of yours has been snooping around, asking questions. We finally got one of the neighborhood know-it-alls to talk."

"I thought I told you that I didn't want you digging into my childhood."

"Yeah, well, call me hardheaded. My wife sure does. I had a hunch, Jackson, and it wouldn't go away. When all the investigative roads kept leading back to Brandon Dent, I homed in on his prison connections. I learned the identity of Slim Shady."

"It's not Marshall Mathers?" Jackson asked, his mind once again going to the only Slim Shady he knew of…hip-hop's well-known White rap artist.

"No, Marshall isn't the name I came up with."

Obviously Frank didn't get the joke. "Who is it, then?"

"Shay Thomas." Complete silence as Jackson processed this news. "Name ring a bell?"

"Yes," Jackson said after slowly releasing a breath. "He was one of my best friends from back in the day."

"Did you know he went to prison?"

Jackson closed his eyes against the memories. "Yes."

"Word on the street is he blames you for the bid he did." He was silent as he imagined a myriad of emotions playing across Jackson's face. "Do you have any idea what he's talking about? What crime he committed that you know about and why he'd want to do you harm?"

"Yes."

"And it never crossed your mind that telling me about this might be a good idea?"

"I didn't think it was necessary. Shay and I were best friends. He knows I had nothing to do with why he's in prison. That he might be the person behind the threats never crossed my mind."

Frank then said, "Shay was released from prison a couple

months ago. Went back to the neighborhood and started asking about you. Says you broke a confidence and it's time for payback. He saw an article on you in a magazine, Jackson. So he knows where you work and maybe even where you live. You need to watch your back, be careful of your surroundings until we get to the bottom of this."

They ended the call, and Jackson proceeded to his car. While driving home to change for the opening, his mind whirled, his entire body was tense. *My boy Shay is free? And saying I broke a confidence? What the hell is he talking about?* Jackson recalled the last time he saw his former best friend, whom they used to call Toe-2-Toe for the way he liked to fistfight. It was the return back to the neighborhood for his sixteenth birthday. He hadn't seen his childhood friends for two years, and by the time he returned, hoping to reestablish a connection, Shay and Jackson's other best friend, Wesley "Glock" Adams, were deep into gang activity. Shay, one year older than Jackson, was already a major dealer. One particular night, amid the haze of alcohol and weed, Shay had confided to his friends that he'd been threatened by a rival gang member who wanted his clientele. Shay vowed to do whatever it took to protect his gravy train. They rode around most of the night, drinking and smoking. Jackson, who hadn't ever consumed this level of alcohol and weed in one sitting, fell asleep in the backseat. That's why he didn't hear Shay and Wesley plan a robbery at a gas station in the rival gang's territory, believing that the gang member who'd threatened him would get pinned with the crime. Nor was he aware when they pulled up to a convenience store and pulled a gun on the lone Middle Eastern man behind the counter. The man resisted by pulling a weapon from under the counter, but his thirty-eight-caliber handgun was no match for the 10mm Glock that Shay carried. The convenience store owner was killed; the three boys were arrested. But thanks to an outstanding lawyer who convinced the judge and prosecuting attorneys that Jackson had no knowledge of or involvement in the crime, he was released without standing trial. And thanks to his uncle John's influence, his court records were eventually expunged. Shay and Wesley were found guilty of murder in the first degree, and a year after that, Wesley was killed in a prison fight. This news, along with learning that Uncle John wanted to someday turn the construction company over to him, was the catalyst to changing the direction of Jackson's life. He got in with a new crowd in suburban San Diego, young men who wanted legitimate success. With his former best friends gone and his mother in prison, his old neighborhood no longer held any type of attraction. He never returned.

But one thing was certain, Jackson thought as he pulled out his phone and dialed a number. It was time to go back now.

Chapter 32

When Jackson and Marissa arrived at Drake Wines Resort & Spa, the party was already in full swing. He left the car with the valet, and admired the thoughtful landscaping, which included palm trees, colorful rows of bird-of-paradise, red amaranth and other colorful flowers. Inside they were greeted by sleek slate flooring, floor-to-ceiling windows and glistening chandeliers. Jackson noted Taylor's final touches to the canvas he'd created as they walked through the packed dining room and over to where the Drake siblings were standing. He did not, however, pick up on the pair of eyes that were watching him.

"Hello, everyone," Jackson said, after giving Diamond a quick hug and squeeze. "I'd like to introduce my assistant, Marissa Hayes. Marissa, this is Dexter Drake."

"Um, pleased to meet you," the ever-flirtatious Dexter drawled.

"The eldest in the clan, Donovan."

"A pleasure," Donovan said, shaking her hand and placing the other one lightly on her arm. They touched, and a bolt as powerful as an electrical current passed between them. Marissa quickly pulled back her hand and diverted her eyes. Donovan's eyes narrowed as he noted her unease. An unexplainable urge arose within him—the desire to see a smile on that beautifully chocolate, dimpled face.

"And this is Diamond."

Diamond leaned forward for a light hug.

"I've heard so much about you," Marissa said, still feeling the tingles from Donovan's handshake. "You're even more beautiful than Jackson described."

"That's more than I can say. Jackson," Diamond teased, "why didn't you tell me you had *America's Next Top Model* working in your office?"

"My bad," Jackson replied, with hand over heart. "And the thing is, she's as beautiful on the inside as she is on the outside."

"Well, welcome to Drake Wines Resort & Spa," Diamond concluded. "Take the tour, taste the food and enjoy the wine. I'm going to steal your boss for a minute. Enjoy." Diamond reached for Jackson's hand and led them away from the crowd. "Okay, out with it," she said when they were alone.

"Out with what?"

"Don't even try it, Jackson. Something's wrong. I see it in your eyes."

It took effort, but Jackson summoned a smile. Maybe nothing would come of the phone call he made earlier; maybe Shay's return to their old neighborhood was a one-time thing. "Nothing for you to worry your pretty little head about, princess."

"Oh, quit it already with the 'princess' routine. Contrary to your misguided belief, I'm not a China doll who will run fleeing at the first sign of trouble. You ought to know that by now." Diamond continued to stare at Jackson. "This has to do with what happened at your office, doesn't it? Do you know who did it? Did they catch the guy?" She rose to her full height—which in her three-inch heels was almost six feet—full of spunk and attitude. Jackson had no doubt that if the culprit walked into the room she'd kick butt now and ask questions later!

Jackson didn't have to try and smile this time. "Dang, baby. When they do catch him, he'd better stay out of your way!"

"That's right," she said, relaxing her stance. "Don't even try and mess with my man."

Jackson's smile widened. "Hum...I like the sound of that."

Donald and Genevieve approached them, looking like royalty in black tux and sparkling forest-green gown.

The two men shook hands. "All of wine country has turned out to view your handiwork," Donald said to Jackson. "I think your business in this area is getting ready to pick up considerably."

"Thank you, sir. We're already booked solid for the next six months. The new customers will have to get in line."

"That's a good problem to have."

Jackson turned to Genevieve and placed a kiss on her cheek. "Mrs. Drake, you look lovely."

Genevieve smiled appreciatively as her gaze swept six feet five inches of perfection. "You clean up pretty well yourself," she said. "You look almost as good as your handiwork." She swept her hand up to the ceiling where the sun shone brightly through the glass ceiling. "This ceiling is one of my favorite features. It's absolutely stunning."

"Almost as stunning as you," Jackson replied, with a twinkle in his eye.

"Careful, Jackson," Donald said. "That's a married woman you're flirting around with."

Diamond laughed. "Dad!"

The four continued to share small talk until Jackson felt his phone vibrate against his waist. He pulled it out and looked at the caller ID. "Excuse me." After walking a short distance away, he answered the call. "Blade! Happy Thanksgiving, man."

"Happy Thanksgiving, stranger!" Sonny "Blade" Wilkins was one of the best barbers on the West Coast and the Mayor of Crenshaw Boulevard. His nickname came from the way he could carve hair into letters, pictures and more using a single-edged razor blade. He'd been around as long as Jackson had been alive. Very little happened in or around the neighborhood that Blade didn't know about. "When I got your message I just about keeled over dead!" A rumbling laughter followed this comment.

Jackson didn't realize until then how long it had been since he'd heard the sound and how much he'd missed it. "It has been a long time. I wasn't even sure your number would work."

"I don't know why you'd think that," Blade replied in mock indignation. "I been on the block for almost forty years. Ain't going nowhere."

"It's good to talk to you, Blade. What's shakin', man?"

"Nothing much except the leaves in the trees. What's up with you, Boss? Living so high on the hog that you can't come and visit the chittlins every once in a while?"

"Ha! I apologize, man, been busy."

"Trust me, I know how it is when you become one of those corporate executives…forget about the little people."

"Man, you need to stop."

"You know I'm just messin' with you, son. How you livin…besides large?"

"I'm blessed, man, no complaints."

"How's your mama?"

Jackson immediately ridged. "How am I supposed to know?"

Blade's pause conveyed his displeasure. But his tone was calm, almost fatherly, when he continued. "She may not have been the best mother, but boy, she's the only one you've got. You have been to see her, haven't you?"

Jackson sighed. "Not for a while."

"Why not?"

Jackson gave Blade the condensed version of his last prison visit with Sharon Burnett. "It hurts me more to be around her than to be away," he finished, vulnerability coating every word he spoke. "I don't need to be reminded of my life back then, or that she loves others more than me."

There was a long pause before Blade answered. "Now, lookie here, son. I need you to listen to me. As bad as it was, your mother did the best she could in raising you. I knew her mother, your grandmother, and I can tell you something. Life for neither one of those women was easy." Blade was unaware of the sheen of tears that covered Jackson's eyes before being rapidly blinked away. "You have nothing to be ashamed of, not about your mother or your past. In fact, where you've been and where you are now should fill you with pride. Don't you see it, Boss? Your story reads like the American dream. You can use what happened to you as an example to other young men out here in the street. You hear me?"

It came slowly, but finally Jackson answered. "Thanks for saying that, Blade." It wasn't the first time he'd heard such words. He and Uncle John had had a similar conversation shortly after Jackson had moved in. But hearing them from another father-figure whom he deeply respected gave the words new meaning. Now, in adulthood, they made sense. In that simple yet profound moment something shifted, and for the first time Jackson considered not hiding his past, but using it to help others. And he also thought about once again visiting his mom.

"All right, enough of me playing Dr. Phil," Blade said to lighten the mood. Jackson could hear something being poured in the background. "What can I do for you?"

"I'm looking for some information, and I'd like to keep the fact that I'm asking around confidential."

"I can do that."

"I heard that Shay is out of prison."

"I heard that, too. Haven't seen him though."

Jackson rubbed his chin as he pondered this info. Back in the day, Shay, Wesley and Jackson practically lived at Blade's Barbershop. For them, Blade was almost like the father none of them had had. If back in the neighborhood, Jackson would have thought that one of Shay's first stops out of the joint. "Will you do me a favor and let me know if you see him?"

"Why do I get the feeling that this isn't about sharing a beer and talking about old times?"

Jackson barely hesitated before coming clean with Blade. He figured the more the old man knew, the better his chances of getting the info he needed. He shared the short version of the story. "Someone broke into our offices and, uh, damaged some equipment…among other things," Jackson finished.

"Ah, so that's why you thought of Shay." Both men knew that Shay could pick a lock faster than most folk could use a key.

"To tell the truth, Shay never crossed my mind. I'd been focused on a past employee, somebody mad because they were out of a job. It wasn't him, but turns out his nephew had lived life on the other side of the law and knew Shay. The investigator on this case started snooping around and found out that Shay, who has gone from Toe-2-Toe to Slim Shady by the way, was released a little before the first letter arrived. It's a long shot because I don't know what kind of beef Shay would have with me." Again, Jackson's mind went to the crime that had sent Shay and Wesley to prison. But Shay knew why Jackson hadn't gotten prison time. He was innocent of any wrongdoing!

"If I see him, do you want me to try and find out for you?"

"I'd appreciate it."

"If he asks, should I give him your number?"

Keep your friends close and your enemies closer. "Yes."

Jackson ended the call and rejoined the party. He joked with Diamond's brothers and mingled with guests. The wine flowed and the evening passed and Jackson almost forgot that he had a problem. Until around ten o'clock, when he received a text from Blade:

Walked the neighborhood and ran into Shay. He asked about where you were. Wouldn't tell me why he wanted to see you. Didn't feel good, Jackson. I think ur right to keep an eye on ur boy.

Chapter 33

Thanksgiving with the Drakes was a splendid affair. They'd spent it holed up in their estate and, except for one call from the hotel's general manager, had been able to enjoy the holiday much like the rest of America—work free. Jackson had joined them, as had Dexter's latest love interest. But now, at the end of the evening, it was just the family.

"What happened to Jackson?" Dexter asked, as he reached for a handful of nuts before taking a seat. The family had retired to the great room—ties loose, shoes off, nightcaps in hand.

"Something came up," Diamond replied, a slight scowl on her face. He'd acted strangely all evening. To say she was concerned was an understatement.

"He is a very handsome man," Genevieve commented.

"With a very attractive bank account," the ever money-conscious Donovan added. "That never hurts to help a man look good."

"Much better than that Benjamin joker," Donald said, casually swirling a tumbler of vintage cognac. "That man was a leech if ever I saw one. Sorry, baby, but you know I never totally trusted your ex. And that's the truth."

"What counts is a man's character, heart and integrity. Those are the reasons I'm dating Jackson."

"Sounds like wedding bells to me," Dexter said. "When's the date, sister?"

"Both of y'all need to get out of my business and focus on your own. Donovan, you're the oldest. You should be married with children by now. And you," Diamond said, as she pointed a manicured finger at Dexter, "need to quit playing the field like you're Michael Vick at the Superbowl and choose a wifey."

"Whoa! Not so fast, sister. I'm the baby boy with more wild oats to sow."

"Dexter," Genevieve chided.

"Sorry, Mom, but you know what I mean. I probably won't get married until I'm forty years old."

"At which time your mom and I will be pushing, what, seventy?" Donald queried. "Thanks a lot."

Genevieve's back straightened as she looked around the room. "Listen, you three. I'm all for being selective when it comes to choosing one's mate, but it is time we expanded this family and ensured the legacy. I believe that I've been more than patient when it comes to my desire of being a grandmother. But my patience is running thin. Y'all better get on it!"

"Did Miss Proper English just say 'y'all'? Mama, you'd better make that your last glass of wine!"

Genevieve laughed. "I guess I am a little tipsy."

"And I'm a little tired," Donald said, standing. "Wife, let's go to bed."

"What time does your plane leave tomorrow?"

"At 9:00 a.m." Donald and Genevieve were joining two other couples for a mini-vacation in Cabo San Lucas. "Good night, all."

The three siblings hugged their parents and then settled back onto the couch and chair, watching their parents hold hands as they left the room.

"I hope I can have a love like that," Diamond said with a sigh.

"If that's going to happen," Dexter said, "you need to find out what's going on with your boy."

"Why, what did you notice?" *I thought I was the only one who detected his jumpy mood.*

"I don't know, but when he and that fine assistant—"

"That fine, *aloof* assistant," Donovan interjected with a scowl.

"Her name is Marissa," Diamond offered.

"When he and that fine, aloof Marissa were waiting for the valet they were in conversation and it looked pretty intense."

Diamond's interest was immediately piqued. "Did you hear anything?"

Dexter shook his head. "Wasn't close enough to hear what they were saying but from the look on your boy's face, he wasn't too happy."

Jackson exited the 10 Freeway onto Crenshaw Boulevard. How long had it been since he'd seen these streets? Ten years? Fifteen? He couldn't remember. After leaving the party, he'd traded his tailored suit for jeans and a T-shirt, and stopped the Maserati for his old faithful Jeep to blend in with the Crenshaw cruisers. Memories assailed him as he passed restaurants and wig shops, the Angeles Funeral Home and the West Angeles Church of God In Christ that he'd attended once or twice as a child. He reached Leimert Park, passed Blade's Barbershop and continued on a few blocks before pulling up in front of the well-kept lawn of a small residence. He parked the Jeep and looked around as he bounded the steps. The street was quiet, but there was a chill in the air.

"Hey, Jackson. Good to see you, son."

"You, too, Blade," Jackson said, as he hugged the older gentleman, who seemed not to age. The barber's slight body was still as wiry as Jackson remembered, his bald head perfectly round, his face free of wrinkles. "The neighborhood hasn't changed much."

"The more things change, the more they stay the same." Blade eyed Jackson a long moment. "I don't know if it was a good idea for you to come down here. I told you that when Shay asked about you, it didn't seem like good was on his mind."

"Good was rarely on Shay's mind," Jackson responded. "Sounds like what you said is right. The more things change, the more they stay the same."

Both men were quiet a moment, lost in their thoughts. Then Blade looked at Jackson with narrowed eyes. "Do you think this has something to do with the botched robbery, with why Shay went to jail?"

"That's what I've thought," Jackson responded as he paced the room. "But why would he have a beef against me for something that was his own damn fault? I was passed out in the backseat and didn't even hear them planning the crime. Didn't wake up until I heard gunshots, followed by Shay and Wesley racing to the car and us spending the next fifteen minutes trying to outrun the police." Jackson stopped pacing, placed his hands on his hips. "So Shay came into the shop specifically to ask about me?"

"No, I ran into him, standing on over there by Eso Won Books. All buff and whatnot, you know how they pump iron behind bars. Looks good, though, for someone who's just spent the last fifteen years in prison."

"Where is he?" Jackson asked, heading to the door.

"Hold up now, son," Blade said, walking to and standing in front of the door. "You've got too much going for you to tangle with Shay. If he wants to hurt you, he has much less to lose."

"I'm not going to spend the rest of my life looking behind my back or over my shoulder, Blade. I no longer live in the hood but I've never backed down from somebody wanting to bring it. And I'm sure as hell not going to start now."

Chapter 34

"**I** don't like the sound of this, Jackson," Diamond said, pacing her office much as Jackson had done in Blade's house last night. She shifted the phone to her other ear, sat and immediately stood back up to pace again.

"Don't worry about it, baby girl. I can take care of myself."

"No doubt, but why did you feel the need to go back to your old neighborhood and stir things up? What if this Shay character comes after you?"

"Baby, there's a different code of ethics in the streets. You can't have people thinking you're afraid of them. All I did was go to a couple spots and spread the word that I'm not hiding and I'm not running."

Diamond snorted. "Men! You and your pissing contests."

"Shay has always been a lot of talk and little action. I'll be okay."

Diamond's tone turned sultry. "I want to see you. You ran away from me last night."

"I want to see you, too, baby. But I forgot something at the office. Came back to get it and am now going over some plans one of my architects left for me."

"But it's the holiday weekend, baby! We're supposed to be eating leftover turkey and watching classic DVDs."

"I'll be leaving here around four, five o'clock. I'll call you then."

"Sounds like a plan. I love you."

"I love you, too, Diamond."

Diamond spent the day with her grandparents and Papa Dee. At three o'clock, she took a shower, packed a bag for the weekend and headed downstairs.

"Going somewhere, little sister?" Dexter asked as he made himself a turkey salad sandwich.

Diamond picked a chip off of his plate. "He doesn't know it yet but I'm taking advantage of the fact that my watchdogs, otherwise known as Donald and Genevieve, are out of town. I'm spending the weekend with Jackson. He works too hard and I want to remind him that there are more important things in life than running a business."

Dexter laughed. "You're one to talk. I think you're more driven than me or Donovan."

"Hey, I've got to hold my own!"

"Oh, you're holding your own all right. And then some! So you're headed to that fancy estate you told me about?"

"He's at work. I'm going to surprise him there. What are you doing?"

"I'm headed to San Diego myself, to Donovan's house."

"He's actually going to spend some time there?"

"Yep, got a poker game all set up. Time for some male bonding."

Diamond hugged her brother. "You guys have fun. I love you."

Dexter hugged her back. "I love you, too."

About an hour later, Diamond pulled up in front of a tall office building in downtown San Diego. After a quick check of her makeup she exited the car and entered the empty lobby, looking for her phone where she'd stored the elevator access code that would take her to the Boss Construction offices located on the top two floors. She scrolled through her memos. *Ah, here it is.* She keyed in the code, and with it being the Friday after a holiday and the place empty, the elevator door opened almost immediately. She stepped in, turned around—and looked into a pair of the coldest eyes she'd ever seen.

"Oh," she exclaimed, as her hand went to her throat. "I didn't hear you behind me."

"I know." The stranger smiled. His teeth were straight and white and set in a handsome face. The smile didn't reach his eyes.

A chill went down her back. *Danger, Will Robinson! Danger, Will Robinson!* If theirs had been a public company, she would have bet her shares of Drake Wine stock that she was staring into the reason that Jackson was jumpy last night.

Instinct took over. "Darn it, I forgot my phone." She stepped toward the door just as it was about to close. And felt a strong hand wrap itself around her arm.

"Not so fast, pretty lady. I think you need to take this ride with me."

"Oh, thank you," Diamond said, offering as big a smile as you can muster when about to pee your pants. "But I'm seeing someone."

"Let me guess. Jackson *Boss* Wright?" He sneered as if something profane had just been said.

Charm hadn't worked, so she tried bravado. Attitude replaced the smile. The stranger's grip felt like steel. "You really need to let go of my arm."

"Okay." He shoved her back against the elevator wall. "Go ahead and key in the code that will take us to the penthouse. I know that's where you're headed. I've been follow-ing your boy for days, was even at y'all's bougie-ass hotel the day it opened." Diamond's eyes widened. "That's right," the stranger proudly continued. "I've been biding my time, waiting for just the right moment, and since seeing old boy's ride in the garage, I've been waiting almost three hours for somebody to come help me get up in this bitch. So, with all this waiting I've been doing, you might not want to try my patience."

Call her crazy, but Diamond didn't think this guy wanted to go to Jackson's office to sing "Kumbaya." Again she lunged toward the door. An arm wrapped around her waist, slammed her against an equally hard chest. She squirmed, kicked, tried to bite. It would take the Jaws of Life to free her.

"Go ahead. Try and get away. I like my women feisty."

Diamond froze. She didn't want to appeal to any part of this man. *Be calm. Think! Don't let him know you're scared. Shitless.* "I hope you like them stubborn, too. Because if you're waiting for me to start this elevator, we'll be here all night."

Diamond blinked, and there was a gun in her face.

"You've obviously got me confused with your punk-ass boyfriend upstairs. I'm tired of playing with you. Start the el-evator." He pressed the muzzle of the gun against her temple. "Now!"

"I don't have it, the code, I don't have it." The man grabbed her hair. "Really! I swear. I've only been here once and I called Jackson to get in. The phone is there." A shaky finger pointed to a box on the wall.

The stranger's eyes narrowed. "Pick it up," he finally said, with a slight lift of his head. "Call your man. I'll be listening, so don't try anything foolish. Or else there'll be two people dying tonight."

Diamond swallowed, willed her nerves to stop jumping.

She squeezed the receiver against her ear. Jackson answered, and her heartbeat went into overdrive.

"Hey, baby."

"Diamond?"

"Who else, fool? And don't even think about not buzzing me up there. I don't care how pissed off you are about the note I left turning your ass down last night."

Long pause. Diamond imagined Jackson looking at the phone as if it had sprouted horns. *Note, note, the threatening note.* Diamond thought with all of her might, trying to send a telepathic warning. *I've never written you a note in my life. Think, Jackson. Who's been sending you notes!*

He didn't get the memo.

The elevator began its rise to the top floor. Diamond's heart dropped to her feet. A myriad of thoughts and escape scenarios raced across her brain. Would Jackson meet her at the elevator door or be in his office? Should she try and run in the other direction...divert the attention away from him? Then she thought of the gun—the sneer on the face of the man who held it, the hatred she saw in his eyes. No, this wasn't the day to take a bullet. Unfortunately for her she'd forgone a bulletproof vest for the more everyday Baby Phat top with skinny jeans.

She looked at the numbers: 20, 21, 22... *Think, Diamond! You have got to do something!* She took a step away from the stranger. And the gun.

He stepped right with her. "Try anything and I'll drop you like a bad habit," he said, his tone deceptively soft. "Think I'm playing? Just try me."

"Can I at least put my keys away? I locked myself out of the car once. Jackson knows it's the first thing I do now, put my keys in my purse."

The stranger adopted a wide-legged stance, trained the gun directly at Diamond's chest. "Like a bad habit," he drawled.

Diamond placed the keys inside her purse, pushing a button on her phone in the process. *Thank God my hands-free is still plugged into the phone. We won't hear whoever answers.* Thankful, too, that she watched the occasional crime show. She forced herself to look at the stranger, took in smooth brown skin, the mole on the right side of his face, just above his mustache, and a tattoo partially visible at the neckline of his tee. If they needed an artist sketch later, she was their girl.

"Who are you?" she asked, careful to talk loud enough to be heard through the leather of her purse.

The stranger gave her the once-over. "You'll find out soon enough. And who knows. Once I've handled my business with Boss I just might—" he licked his lips "—handle my business with you."

Diamond knew that she'd use every ounce of fight inside her to not be assaulted by this man. Her mind went into overdrive. *Who did I call last? Whoever it was...please pick up!*

Chapter 35

Several men sat in Donovan's luxuriously appointed, state-of-the-art game room. Six of them were around a mahogany game table playing poker. Dexter had just given up his hand to take a call from his flavor of the month, who'd joined the family at yesterday's dinner. "Hold on, baby. This is my sister on the other line. Hello?"

"Does handling your business with Jackson involve using that gun?"

Dexter's brow furrowed as he looked at his phone. "Diamond?"

"Don't worry about my business with your boy. Just chill and you might not get hurt."

Diamond raised her voice. "Do I look stupid to you? Do *you* think that *I* think you're going to commit a crime and leave a witness? Murdering the owner of San Diego's top construction company, in his swanky penthouse offices no less? This is going to be all over the news. You'll never get away."

Dexter stepped back into the game room. "Don. Come check this out, man."

One look at his brother's face and Donovan knew whatever was happening was serious. "Excuse me, fellas." He walked over to Dexter, who quickly led them out of the room, down the hall and into a bedroom where he closed the door.

"What's up?"

"Shh." Dexter pushed the speaker button. "Listen."

They reached the top floor. The stranger placed Diamond in front of him and put the gun to her head. "I'm warning you. Don't try nothin'," he growled, pushing the hard steel against her head for emphasis. "I'll shoot your fine ass in a heartbeat."

The door opened. Diamond tensed. Closed her eyes.

No Jackson.

They stepped into the darkened office area. Diamond drew short, erratic breaths. Her hands were clammy. Her heart beat a rhythm almost out of her chest. "Don't do this," she hissed.

"Shut up" was the whispered reply.

"Baby?" Jackson's footsteps sounded as he stepped off of a carpeted area onto the marbled hallways. "What are you—"

Jackson rounded the corner, took in the scene and found out that a man could still live when his heart stopped beating.

He stopped in his tracks, his face hard and unsmiling. Touching his woman alone was worth taking this fool's life. "Shay."

Diamond tried to move forward but Shay pulled her back. "Damn, dog. No smile, no hug? What kind of greeting is that for a brothah you haven't seen in a nickel and a dime?"

"Let her go, man. Whatever beef you have is with me, not her."

Shay tightened his grip, removed the gun from Diamond's

head and pointed it at Jackson. "You may think you're the boss, but I'm running this show. Now put your hands up and back into your office, nice and slow like."

"Shay…"

"Shut up and do what I tell you!"

Jackson looked at Diamond. Eyes filled with fear stared back at him and belied the calm demeanor she was trying so hard to convey. Shay placed the gun against Diamond's temple. "Back up!"

Jackson raised his hands and backed into his office. In his mind, his hands were around Shay's throat squeezing the life out of his former best friend's now worthless body. "Okay," he said, once they'd entered. "Now what?"

"At first, I was just going to kill you, but in the time it took me to get into this fortress you call an office, I've come up with another idea…call it a farewell gift from one friend to another. Here's how it's going to go down. You're going to sit down at that computer and conduct a little transfer. You're going to deposit a cool mil into this account." With the gun again in Diamond's back, and his eyes darting between her and Jackson, he reached into his pocket and pulled out a card. Jackson clenched his fists. "Don't move!" He prodded Diamond with the gun butt, over to Jackson's desk, where he laid down the card.

Then he jerked Diamond up against him, ran a hand over her body. Jackson clenched his jaw, took a step. Shay raised the gun to Diamond's head. Jackson froze. "And you, sexy, are going to do everything I tell you unless you want Boss to watch while I splatter your pretty brains all over the floor." The shiver was involuntary and Diamond cursed herself for her nervousness. Shay laughed, sinister and dark. "Damn, man. She's shaking and everything, like she loves you or something. What do you think, Boss," Shay taunted. "I'd say taking your woman and making her my sex slave, screwing her brains out and then passing her on to my friends just might make up for one or two of the almost twenty years you made me do."

Diamond struggled to break away. Shay laughed, rubbed the gun along her cheek.

He knew it was pointless to reason, but Jackson tried anyway. "Shay, we grew up together. You know me, man—"

"I thought I did."

"And you know I'd never rat you out. I've never been a snitch, man."

"Mighty funny then, that while me and Wesley both end up in prison, you don't even do a day in jail. If you didn't sing for the reward money or cooperate with the prosecutors, then how did that happen?"

"It happened because I didn't do anything, man. You know this!" Jackson took Shay's silence as a sign that he just might be listening. "Think about it, Shay. My uncle had hella paper. Why would I want ten lousy g's?"

"Oh, so you do remember that *lousy* amount offered as reward money." He took a quick look around. "Guess that's chump change to you now."

"Maybe Wesley tried to cut a deal, maybe that's how the prosecutor found the gun in the side panel."

"Well, now, wouldn't that be convenient considering the fact that he's dead!"

Donovan and Dexter pulled into the Boss Construction parking lot. One sentence was all Donovan needed to hear before they'd called the police and jumped into Dexter's Mercedes. Had there been any doubts that the car could indeed do 155 miles per hour, they'd definitely been put to rest on the drive over. Dexter killed the engine. As one, the brothers exited and walked across the lot, their steps steady and sure.

Donovan opened the door to the building. "The police said to wait for them."

Dexter shot his brother a look. "Yeah, right."

They stepped inside and rushed to the bank of elevators. Dexter pushed the button. The elevator dinged. Entering, he hurriedly pushed the button to the thirtieth floor. The light indicator blinked. "Damn!" He slammed his hand against the code panel, then looked at Donovan. "What are we going to do?"

Donovan was already heading out the elevator. "Stairs! Come on!"

Dexter was right behind him. "Won't the doors to the floors be locked?"

They reached the stairs and started to climb. "With our sister in danger on the other side of that door, it will take more than a lock to stop us."

"Man, I'm tired of talking. You've got five minutes to make the transfer."

"Shay, listen. I can't transfer this kind of money by computer. They have checks and balances on any transactions over ten thousand dollars. This transfer can only happen in person or over the phone."

Jackson watched Shay's finger slide to the trigger. He was surprised to find that the cool, calm, collected voice being heard in the room was his own. "Listen, Toe-2-Toe," Jackson continued, seeing a slight reaction at the use of his ex-friend's childhood name. "You don't want to do this, man. You just got out of prison. And you especially don't want to hurt somebody you've just met, who's never done anything to you. Let her go, man. Let this be between you and me."

Shay glanced at his watch. "Four minutes."

Jackson's mind spun with ways to thwart Shay's plan, for both him and Diamond to make it out of this mess alive.

"Look, I can transfer ten grand right now and set up the rest on Monday. It's the holidays, Shay, the banks are closed! Any more than ten thousand dollars won't go through! I can give you ten, you let her go, and then I'll lay low with you wherever you want until I can give you the rest." Belatedly, Jackson remembered the safe in his office. "Look, man. I've also got some cash here. In the safe behind that picture. Probably another ten g's or so. I'll give that to you, too."

Shay snorted. "Like you have a choice."

"This is your game, player." Jackson held up his hands in a sign of surrender.

"No! Get the cash out of the safe first."

Jackson watched Shay trail him over to where the safe was. "Just open it. Reach inside and your girl becomes a pleasant memory."

Jackson opened the safe and then stepped away, as Shay had commanded. "Get that money, sexy," Shay ordered Diamond, his voice becoming higher as his thrill increased. "Get me something to put this money in. No, Boss, you stay still. I'm talking to your bitch."

A curtain of fury came over Jackson. In spite of the gun, he began to walk toward Shay. "Disrespect my woman again," he said, his tone low and deadly, "and there won't be a gun big enough to keep me off your ass."

"We'll see about that," Shay responded, with a touch less bravado than before. He took the bag of money that Diamond handed him and then ordered Jackson over to the computer for the bank transaction.

Jackson sat down at the computer and picked up the card that Shay had laid on the desk. "This is too many numbers." He looked up. "This must not be a California account."

"Don't worry about where the money is going. Just know that I'll be meeting up with it soon and living the good life the way you've been doing for all these years."

Jackson began typing.

"Wait!" Shay moved himself and Diamond a bit closer to Jackson. "Turn that screen around so that I can see it. I need to make sure that you're depositing my money, not sending an email to the police." Shay laughed. It held no humor.

Jackson adjusted the computer and pulled up one of his smaller bank accounts. The balance showed just a little over one hundred thousand. He clicked a couple keys, put in the number Shay had given him, and within minutes, the screen showed that the transaction had been completed.

"There you go, man," Jackson said, leaning back as if relaxing but actually gauging the distance between him and the gun. Could he make a lunge before Shay fired? "Ten thousand in your bank account with more where that came from on Monday. In fact, by doing the transfer in person I can get you two million. Because even though I had nothing to do with you going to prison, you're my friend from back in the—"

Thud. Thud. Thud.

Shay's head snapped around toward the sound.

Mere seconds of distraction. Just what the construction owner ordered. He pushed Diamond away from Shay while simultaneously reaching for the gun. His forward momentum caused the men to fall to the floor. Jackson tried to grab the weapon. Shay tried to fire it. They rolled and Jackson was on top. Diamond stood frozen, her eyes glued to Jackson's hand wrapped around Shay's hand, both gripping the gun. *Call the police!* But she couldn't move. Jackson almost had the gun away from Shay. *You've almost got it. Come on, baby!*

They rolled again. Now Shay was on top.

Oh, no!

The battle was for the aim of the gun—Shay pushing it down toward Jackson's head, Jackson forcing Shay's arm to the sky.

Finally, Diamond remembered how to move her legs. She

ran to the phone. But wait. *Is that a set of golf clubs over in the corner?* Acting on pure instinct, Diamond grabbed an iron and ran over to the fighting men. Jackson snatched the gun. A millisecond later Diamond channeled Tiger Woods and swung like she was trying to drop a hole in one from three hundred yards. Shay went down. Jackson jumped up and trained the gun on Shay. Even if his former homeboy had some fight left in him, he'd have to come to first.

Jackson rushed over to Diamond. "Baby." He hugged her tight against him even as he kept one eye trained on the non-moving hump lying on the floor. "I thought I was going to lose you."

Diamond couldn't talk past the lump in her throat. She buried her head into Jackson's chest, relishing the feel of him, the smell of him, the sound of his heartbeat.

Footsteps filled the silence. Dexter burst into the room. "Diamond!"

Donovan was right behind him. He took in the scene, most notably, Jackson and Diamond alive and well. The man on the floor, not so much. Shay moaned and Jackson immediately put Diamond behind him. He trained the gun on Shay's head. "Don't move."

More footsteps. The police. "Hands up! Get down on the ground. Down on the ground!"

A second officer spoke up. "That's Jackson Wright. He owns this place."

The other officers looked around, confused.

"Him." Jackson nodded toward Shay as he placed down the gun and leaned against his desk. The weight of what almost happened bore down on him, body and soul. "His name is Shay Thomas and he just tried to kill us. He's the one you want."

The police officers surrounded Shay and escorted him

out of the building to the tune of his Miranda rights. Neither Jackson nor Diamond saw him leave. They only had eyes for each other.

Chapter 36

It was a little after midnight when the limousine carrying Jackson, Diamond, Dexter and Donovan turned into the grand entrance of the Drake Estate. In just twenty-four short hours the grounds had gone from a Thanksgiving haven to a winter wonderland. After four hours in a cramped police station, no one noticed. Rudolph with his red nose and his posse could have sideswiped them with Santa drinking Drake's finest, and they wouldn't have noticed. It had been one hell of a night.

"Baby," Diamond said, in yet another attempt to shift away from Jackson. "I'm getting a crick in my neck."

Jackson loosened his grip yet kept an arm around her shoulder. He'd barely been a hair's breadth away from her since Shay was taken away in cuffs. As if she were a mirage, a puff of smoke that would disappear if he let her go.

"Parents are here," Donovan said matter-of-factly when the front of their mansion came into view.

Dexter sighed. "Damn."

"I told them not to end their vacation!" Diamond said, pounding her fist on the car's soft leather.

"You know good and well Daddy wasn't going to hear what he heard, and see what he probably saw on TV, and keep chilling in Cabo."

They were bum-rushed as soon as they walked through the door.

"Diamond!" Genevieve rushed over to hug her daughter. Good luck while said jewel was glued to Jackson's side.

"Baby girl," Donald said, his voice gruff with emotion. He joined his wife and hugged his daughter, or tried to, anyway. But he actually hugged part of Diamond and all of Jackson's arm. "Do you mind?"

Jackson released her. Reluctantly. He stepped away a full six inches, saw an opening and placed a hand on top of Diamond's head. Yes, he did.

"Baby, we were so worried about you. The news said that the man was armed!" While Jackson's clout had managed to keep Diamond's name out of the story, all of the other details had somehow found their way onto "breaking news."

Donald gave a final squeeze and stepped back. "The only thing that matters is that you're okay."

"I'm fine, Daddy."

Warm and fuzzy left the room when Donald turned to Jackson. "You put my daughter in harm's way. She could have lost her life tonight because of whatever you're involved in."

"Dad, no—"

"Baby, it's all right," Jackson said, pulling up to his full six foot five while looking Donald dead in the eye. "I want to talk to your father."

"Good," Donald said. Clearly, this wasn't his first time at the rodeo. "We need to discuss this man-to-man."

"I agree." Jackson and Donald turned to leave the room.

Two strong men. Diamond envisioned another rumble. "Dad, wait."

"Let them go," Genevieve whispered. "They'll be all right."

Forty-five agonizing minutes later, Jackson rejoined Diamond, who was now alone in the great room. She rushed him as soon as he entered the room. "What happened? What did you say to my father?"

"I told him what happened." He reached for her hand.

Diamond held back. "Where are we going?"

Jackson sighed, the weight of what had almost happened, what he'd almost lost, still pressing him down. "I also told him that we'd see everyone in the morning. I'm tired, love. But I need you with me. Let's go home."

The average person wouldn't have noticed, but Jackson was still alert enough to discern the additions to security detail around his home: the camera attached to a phone pole a mile away and above his gate, a small red beam indicating a motion detector so sensitive that it would know when Molly Mosquito went to visit Nicholas Gnat. Once inside his estate, security was visible. Two guards were posted just inside the gate. Jackson knew that four more cased the perimeter of the ten-acre estate.

Diamond looked at the guards, and then at Jackson. "Is this necessary?"

Jackson shrugged. "Maybe, maybe not. But I'm not going to take a chance of you being endangered again. Got it?"

Diamond nodded.

They entered the sanctuary of Jackson's home and immediately felt more peaceful. As beautiful as the Drake Estate was, there was something about being near the water, hearing the waves crash against the shore, that soothed and comforted like no other sound. Diamond took off her shoes and stifled a yawn.

"Tired, baby?"

"After subduing a killer, being grilled by the police and then, even worse, Genevieve, and now seeing that it is 3:00 a.m.?" Diamond channeled the dry sarcasm her mother was known for to perfection. "Yeah, a little bit."

Jackson laughed, a sound that earlier in the evening he would have doubted he'd hear again. "I deserved that. I'm tired, too. But do you think you could take a shower with me?"

They entered the master suite, shed their clothes and were soon sitting on the marble bench in Jackson's massive shower. Water poured over them as they sat hugging each other, thankful to do so, thankful to be alive. As exhausted as she was, Diamond would have thought herself incapable of getting excited for physical pleasure, but Jackson's roaming hands were like a caffeine shot and within minutes he had her body humming like a bird.

He kissed her, softly, lovingly, on her temple—his favorite place besides his *other* favorite place—ear and cheek. One hand kneaded the back of her neck while the other sought and found an already taut nipple. He tweaked it, and at the same time he slanted his mouth over Diamond's and demanded entry with his tongue. Soon the twirling and sucking began—hot, wet—as if tasting each other for the first time. Strong arms enveloped Diamond as Jackson, spurred on by the knowledge that he'd almost lost this piece of paradise, deepened the kiss. His tongue plunged to the depths of her mouth, seemingly to the depths of her soul. He hardened immediately and completely, his engorged shaft now tickling Diamond's thighs.

She opened them, wanting him as much as he wanted her. Wanting to fill his width and length inside her, wanting him to stroke away the fear the day had brought and memories of what she'd almost lost. She wanted to be owned by him, claimed by him, branded by him. She circled her hand around his dick. "This," she whispered into his mouth. "I want this."

On the way over, Jackson had planned a tender scene of seduction. Those plans flew out the window as his body, hot and shaking with wanting, took over his mind. He needed to be inside of this woman, now. Needed to be connected. Needed to belong. Obviously Diamond was thinking the same thing because she stood, positioned herself over his happy stick and slowly, oh…so…slowly, sank down on his heat. She groaned at how fully he filled her, even as her hips welcomed this awesome intrusion by swirling around and around as she rose up and down, over and again. She bent over, placed her hands on the floor, giving Jackson a bird's-eye view of her backside. The position heightened both of their pleasures, and Jackson squeezed her sweet cheeks as he intensified the ride. It was a beautiful symphony—the water, the rhythm, the delicious friction. It was too much, it wasn't enough. Jackson wanted, no, *needed* to be closer, deeper. With one final swat of her butt, he lifted her off him, stood and picked her up. Diamond's legs immediately went around his waist, giving him unobstructed access to his destination. He placed her against the wall and, looking deep into her eyes with more love than Diamond thought possible from one being, sank into her yet again. His hips and tongue were a concerto as they matched rhythms: swirling, grinding, searching for the innermost of places, that place untouched by anyone else. That place that neither had ever felt before. He licked her neck, long, wet strokes, and the combination of that and the relentless pounding happening below was a decadent combination that made Diamond cry out with joy. Jackson moaned, burying himself to the hilt and leaning them both against the wall to catch their breaths.

But he wasn't finished. He was just getting started.

Chapter 37

Still joined, he walked them over to one of the immense showerheads. "Hang on, baby," he said, when they stood directly beneath it. She grabbed ahold of the showerhead, he placed her legs over his shoulder, and there, totally exposed and at his mercy, Diamond began the ride of her life. Grabbing her hips, Jackson took over, became the maestro of their lovemaking as yet again he yielded thrust after powerful thrust, rotating her hips in time to his rhythm. Mewling sounds came to Diamond's ears. Belatedly, she realized it was she who was making them. She wrapped her arms around his broad shoulders and let Jackson own her, brand her, love her with an intensity she'd never thought possible. They climaxed together.

"Jackson!"

"Diamond!"

He eased her down, sat her on the bench. Washed her. Kissed her. Hugged her.

And still, he hadn't had enough of Diamond Drake.

After making quick work of his own shower, they walked into his suite. "Are you hungry?" he asked.

She realized she was starving.

"Come on. Let's see if Chef left anything tasty downstairs."

They raided the kitchen and soon returned to the master suite with Kobe roast beef sandwiches and a bottle of wine. When Diamond looked at the label she chided Jackson. "You'd better be glad you have mad lovemaking skills, otherwise you'd be in trouble for patronizing the competition!" Her words were only mildly serious; for the most part the neighboring vineyards were friendly and their wine up to snuff.

Jackson uncorked the bottle of 2010 Thornton Tempranillo and filled their glasses. They ate and recalled the evening.

"I don't think I've ever been as frightened as when I rounded the corner and saw that gun to your head."

"I don't think I've ever been as frightened as when I *felt* it at my head."

"I'm so sorry, baby."

"It wasn't your fault, Jackson. I think that Shay Thomas has had it out for you a long time, maybe even when you thought he was your friend. The look of hate that I saw in his eyes..." Diamond shuddered. "I've never been that close to pure evil."

Jackson smiled. "You held your own, though. I've been calling you a BAP but I had that shit twisted. Underneath those designer duds and painted nails was a ride-or-die chick." Diamond swatted him playfully. Jackson laughed and took her in his arms. "My ride-or-die chick," he whispered, as he placed kisses all over her face. "I love you, girl."

Soon their hunger for each other replaced their need of food. They finished their glasses of wine. Jackson lit a fire in the marble fireplace that anchored the suite. Diamond lay down on the faux fur in front of it. She sighed in contentment as she watched Jackson walk around the room in all his naked glory. Michelangelo could not have sculpted a finer work of art. He lit candles, set his iPod to a selection of love songs and, once he felt he'd set a proper mood, joined Diamond in front of the roaring fire.

This time, their lovemaking was slow, deliberate, the way Jackson had originally intended. He turned his body so that his head was at her toes and then he lovingly sucked one into his mouth. Who knew that making love to one's feet could be so stimulating? Diamond found out, and soon she'd scooted her body down to where her mouth was in line with one of her favorite parts of Jackson's body. She wet her lips and took in as much of his burgeoning erection as possible. Jackson's groan was low and deep as she licked and sucked, nibbled and tasted. Not one to be outdone, Jackson spread her legs and dove headfirst into her wetness. He tickled her nub with his tongue, flicked it into life until it was a pebbled hardness between her legs. He licked her thoroughly, everywhere, in every way. They used their bodies to communicate the love that words alone could not convey. As the vestiges of dawn streaked across the sky in orange, pink and purple hues, Jackson once again plunged deep inside her, stroking her into yet another frenzy. He was insatiable. He was a beast! Diamond matched him stroke for stroke, loving every minute. She felt him wholly inside her, as if touching her very soul. She felt his love not only in body, but in spirit. This time, as she cried out, tears of happiness rolled down her face.

"You all right, baby?" He reached for a couple nearby pillows and, still lying on the fur, cuddled Diamond spoon-style in his arms.

"I'm perfect," Diamond answered. "I never thought I could

feel this way." She turned to look at him, her eyes wide and searching. "Is this real, baby? Or is this a dream?"

"I don't know," he replied, playfully flicking her nose with his finger. "But if it is, then please don't wake me up."

And that's how Diamond went to sleep: sated, naked, and in Jackson's arms. As soon as he was sure she slept soundly, Jackson got up and went online, searching for the perfect thank-you gift for Diamond saving his life. An hour later he'd found what he was looking for and, after a series of phone calls, was ensured that a delivery would be made the following morning at the place of his instruction.

The next day, Jackson and Diamond arrived at the Drake Estate in time for Saturday brunch. On a self-prescribed vacation from cooking for the holidays, Genevieve had called upon David and Mary's chef to prepare for the festivities. The table was laden with brunch favorites: pecan waffles, eggs Benedict, home-style potatoes and breakfast meats. Pitchers of mimosas completed the menu, made with fresh-squeezed orange juice and a Drake sparkling chardonnay. The only thing more plentiful than the food was the laughter. At their bequest, Jackson and Diamond had shared the details of their hazardous adventure as Papa Dee, David Jr., Mary, Donald, Genevieve, Donovan and Dexter looked on.

"Your daughter is gangster," Jackson said to Donald, as he reached for another strip of crispy bacon. "She handled that nine-iron like a pro!"

"Glad to see those golf lessons counted for something," Donald grumbled.

"Y'all don't know nothing 'bout gangster," Papa Dee said, his ninety-eight-year-old eyes twinkling with laughter and life. "Did I tell you about the time when I was twenty and I outran Al Capone and his gang?"

"No, Dad," David Jr. said, "but I think we're getting ready to hear the tale."

Just then, Jackson received a phone call. "I'm sorry, but this is business," he said upon rising. "I'll make it as brief as possible."

It was almost fifteen minutes before Jackson returned. Diamond's eyes asked the obvious—*where have you been?*

"Later" was the one-word response Jackson whispered in her ear.

As brunch neared its end, Donald stood. "I'd like to propose a toast. I'd like to once again thank God that Jackson and Diamond are safe. And I'd like to say cheers to the new Drake posse!"

Laughter abounded amid the cheers.

Jackson stood. "I'd like to propose a toast, also, if I may." The room quieted. "Yesterday when I saw the gun against Diamond's head, *my* life flashed before my eyes. Because in that moment I realized just how much she meant to me and how much I didn't want to lose her. In the short time I've known all of you, and for the first time since my adoptive parents died, I've felt the bond of family. I want to thank you for welcoming me into your home and your lives, and if Diamond will have me, I'd like to become a part of this family forever." Jackson got down on one knee. "This is the business I was handling just now, baby. Dealing with the contact who dropped off this package."

Diamond's eyes widened in disbelief as her hand slowly lifted to cover her open mouth. *No, this isn't happening. This man is not proposing to me!*

But he was.

"Diamond, I love you. You are more precious than your namesake, more valuable than any jewel. I didn't know true love until you walked into my life and I'll never know true love again without you. You saved my life, baby, in more ways than one. Will you do me the immense honor of becoming my wife? Will you marry me?"

He reached into his pocket, pulled out a blue box, opened it and, amid gasps and sounds of impressed approval, placed a perfectly designed five-carat, princess-cut Tiffany diamond on her finger.

The room held its breath.

Diamond smirked. "What? No rooster?"

"Rooster?" Papa Dee exclaimed. "What is that child talking about?"

"It's a private joke," Jackson replied, his smile slight as he continued to gaze intently at Diamond, waiting for her answer.

"Well, go on, girl," Dexter prodded. "Don't keep the man hanging all day!"

Diamond could barely speak for the tears. "Yes!" she finally whispered. "A thousand times, yes!" she continued with increased volume. She leaned over and hugged the love of her life.

He stood, picked her up and twirled them around. "I love you, Diamond Drake."

Diamond placed a soft kiss on his mouth. "I love you, Boss."

And as her family applauded, Diamond recognized two things—with big risks came big rewards, and dreams? They really could come true.

* * * * *

THE PRICE OF SUCCESS

MAYA BLAKE

First and foremost for my dear sister, Barbara, who gave me the book that started this wonderful journey. For my husband, Tony, for his unwavering support and firm belief that this dream would become reality. For my HEART sisters—your incredible support kept me going right from the beginning—thank you! And finally for my darling MINXES! You are the best cheerleaders a girl can have and I'd be totally lost without you.

CHAPTER ONE

THE moments before the crash played out almost in slow motion. Time paused, then stretched lethargically in the Sunday sun. And even though the cars were travelling at over two hundred and twenty kilometers an hour, there seemed an almost hypnotic, ballet-like symmetry in their movement.

Sasha Fleming stared, frozen, her heart suspended mid-beat, terrified to complete its task as Rafael's front wing clipped the rear tyre of the slower back marker. Hundreds of thousands of pounds' worth of carbon fibre bent backwards, twisted in on itself. Ripped metal tore through the left tyre, wrenching the car into a ninety-degree turn.

The world-renowned racing car launched itself into the air. For several brief seconds it looked more like a futuristic aircraft than an asphalt-hugging machine.

Inevitably, gravity won out. The explosion was deafening as sound erupted all around her. The screech of contorting metal rang through her head, amplified by the super-sized loudspeakers all around her. In the next instant the white concrete wall just after the Turn One hairpin bend was streaked with the iconic racing green paint of Rafael's car.

'He's crashed! He's crashed! The pole sitter and current world champion, Rafael de Cervantes, has crashed his Espiritu DSII. Only this morning the papers said this car was uncrashable. How wrong were they?'

Sasha ripped off her headphones, unable to stomach the frenzied glee in the commentator's voice or the huge roar that rose around the Hungaroring circuit.

Her heart, now making up for its sluggishness, was beating so hard and so fast it threatened to break through her ribcage. Her eyes remained glued to the bank of screens on the pit wall, and she and two dozen pit crew members watched the horrific events unfold.

'Turn up the sound,' someone yelled.

Curbing a wild need to negate that command, she clamped her lips together, arms folded tight around her middle. Memories of another time, another crash, played alongside the carnage unfolding on the screen. Unable to stem it, she let the memories of the event that had changed her for ever filter through to play alongside this appalling spectacle.

'Sometimes the only way to get through pain is to immerse yourself in it. Let it eat you alive. It'll spit you out eventually.'

How many times had her father told her that? When she'd broken her ankle learning to ride her bike. When she'd fractured her arm falling out of a tree. When she'd lost her mum when she was ten. When she'd suffered the desperate consequences of falling for the wrong guy.

She'd got through them all. Well…almost.

The secret loss she'd buried deep in her heart would always be with her. As would the loss of her father.

The commentator's voice scythed through her thoughts. *'There's no movement from the car. The race has been red-flagged and the safety car is on its way. So is the ambulance. But so far we haven't seen Rafael move. His engineer will be frantically trying to speak to him, no doubt. I must say, though, it's not looking good…'*

Sasha forced in a breath, her fingers moving convulsively to loosen the Velcro securing her constricting race suit. A shudder raked her frame, followed closely by another. She tried to swallow but she couldn't get her throat to work.

Alongside the thoughts zipping through her head, her last conversation with Rafael filtered through.

He'd been so angry with her. And the accusations he'd flung at her when she'd only been trying to help…

Ice clutched her soul. Was this *her* fault? Had *she* played a part in this carnage?

'The ambulance is there now. And there's Rafael's brother, Marco, the owner of Team Espiritu. He's on his way to the crash site…hopefully we'll get a progress report soon.'

Marco. Another fist of shock punched through her flailing senses. She hadn't even been aware he'd finally arrived in Hungary. In her two years as reserve driver for Team Espiritu, Marco de Cervantes hadn't missed a single race—until this weekend.

The whole paddock had been abuzz with his absence, the celebrities and royalty who jetted in from all over the world specifically to experience the de Cervantes lifestyle, visibly disappointed. From Rafael's terse response when she'd asked of his brother's whereabouts, Sasha had concluded the brothers had fallen out.

Her heart twisted tighter in her chest at the thought that Marco had finally arrived only to witness his brother's crash.

A daring cameraman broke through the flanking bodyguards and caught up with Marco. Tight-jawed, his olive skin showing only the barest hint of paleness, he kept his gaze fixed ahead, his set expression not revealing the slightest hint of his emotional state as he strode towards the courtesy car waiting a few feet away.

Just before he got into the car he turned his head. Deep hazel eyes stared straight into the camera.

Sasha's breath stilled. Icy dread flooded her veins at the banked fury in their depths. His features were pinched, his mouth a taut line, the lines bracketing his mouth deep and austere. Everything about him indicated he was reining in tight emotion. Not surprising, given the circumstances.

But, eerily, Sasha knew his emotion extended beyond the events unfolding now. Whatever emotion Marco was holding in, it went far beyond his reaction to his brother's horrific accident.

Another shiver raked through her. She turned away from the

screen, searching blindly for an escape. The back of the garage where the tyres were stacked offered a temporary sanctuary.

She'd taken one single step towards the opening when her heart sank. Tom Brooks, her personal press officer, broke away from the crew and made a beeline for her.

'We need to prep for an interview,' he clipped out, fingers flying over his iPad.

Nausea rose to join all the other sensations percolating inside her. 'Already? We don't even know how Rafael is.' Or even if he was still alive.

'Exactly. The eyes of the world will be on this team. Now's not the time to bungle our way through another disastrous sound-bite,' he said unsympathetically.

Sasha bit her lip. Her heated denial of a relationship with Rafael only a week ago had fuelled media speculation, and brought unwanted focus on the team.

'Surely it's better to be well informed before the interview than to go on air half-cocked?'

His face darkened. 'Do you want to be a reserve driver for ever?'

Sasha frowned. 'Of course not—'

'Good, because I don't want to play press officer to a reserve driver for the rest of my career. You want to be one of the boys? Here's your chance to prove it.'

A wave of anger rose inside her. 'I don't need to be heartless to prove myself, Tom.'

'Oh, but you do. Do you think any of the other drivers would hesitate at the chance that's been presented?'

'What chance? We don't even know how Rafael is doing yet!'

'Well, you can sit on your hands until the moment's snatched from you. The handful of female X1 Premier Racing drivers who've gone before you barely made an impact. You can choose to become a meaningless statistic, or you can put yourself in the driver's seat—literally—and lay the paddock rumours to rest.'

She didn't need to ask what he meant. A wave of pain rolled through her. Pushing it back, she straightened her shoulders. 'I don't care about rumours. I'm a good driver—'

'You're also Jack Fleming's daughter and Derek Mahoney's ex. If you want to be taken seriously you need to step out of their shadows. Do the interview. Stake your claim.'

As his fingers resumed their busy course over his iPad, unease rose inside Sasha. As much as she disliked Tom's acerbic attitude, a part of her knew he was right. The move from reserve to full-time driver for Team Espiritu was a once-in-a-lifetime opportunity she couldn't afford to squander—not if she wanted to achieve her goals.

'I have a reporter ready to meet—'

'No.' Her gaze flicked to the screen and her resolve strengthened. 'I won't give an interview until I hear how Rafael is.'

Two ambulances and three fire engines now surrounded the mangled car. Sparks flew as the fire crew cut away the chassis.

Marco de Cervantes stood scant feet away, ignoring everyone, his impressive physique firmly planted, hands balled into fists, his unwavering gaze fixed on his brother's still form. Sasha's heart squeezed tighter.

Please be alive, Rafael. Don't you dare die on me...

Tom's stern look mellowed slightly as he followed her gaze. 'I'll prepare something while we wait. Find a quiet place. Get yourself together.' He glanced around, made sure he wasn't overheard and leaned in closer. 'This is the chance you've been waiting for, Sasha. *Don't blow it.*'

Marco de Cervantes stepped into the private hospital room in Budapest, sick dread churning through his stomach. He clenched his fists to stop the shaking in his hands and forced himself to walk to his brother's bedside. With each step the accident replayed in his mind's eye, a vivid, gruesome nightmare that wouldn't stop. There'd been so much blood at the crash site... *so much blood...*

His chest tightened as he saw the white sheet pulled over his brother's chest.

Absently, he made a note to have the staff replace the sheets with another colour—green, perhaps, Rafael's favourite colour. White hospital sheets looked...smelled...too much like death.

Rafael wasn't dead. And if Marco had anything to do with it this would be his last senseless brush with death. Enough was enough.

He drew level with the bed and stared down into his brother's pale, still face. At the tube inserted into his mouth to help him breathe.

Enough was enough.

Marco's throat closed up. He'd chosen to give Rafael time to come to his senses instead of forcing him to listen to reason. And by doing so he'd allowed his brother to take the wheel behind the world's most powerful car while still reeling from emotional rejection.

Unlike him, his brother had never been able to compartmentalise his life, to suppress superfluous emotions that led to unnecessarily clouded judgement. Rafael coalesced happiness, sadness, triumph and loss into one hot, sticky mess. Add the lethal mix of a seven hundred and fifty horsepower racing car, and once again *he* was left picking up the pieces.

His breath shuddered. Reaching out, he took Rafael's unmoving hand, leaned down until his lips hovered an inch from his brother's ear.

'You live—you hear me? I swear on all things holy, if you die on me I'll track you to hell and kick your ass,' he grated out, then swallowed the thickness in his throat. 'And I know you'll be in hell, because you sure as heck won't get into heaven with *those* looks.'

His voice caught and he forced back his tears.

Rafael's hand remained immobile, barely warm. Marco held on tighter, desperately infusing his brother with his own life force, desperately trying to block out the doctor's words...*his brain is swelling...there's internal bleeding...nothing to do but wait...*

With a stifled curse, he whirled away from the bed. The window of the ultra-private, ultra-exclusive, state-of-the-art hospital looked out onto a serene courtyard, with discreet fountains and carefully clipped flowers meant to soothe the troubled patient. Beyond the grounds, forests stretched as far as the eye could see.

Marco found no solace in the picturesque view. He found even less to smile about when his eyes lit on the paparazzi waiting beyond the hospital's boundaries, powerful lenses trained, ready to pounce.

Shoving a hand through his hair, he turned back to the bed.

A flash of green caught the corner of his eye. He focused on the flat-screen TV mounted on the wall and watched Rafael's accident replayed again in slow motion.

Bile rose to his throat. Reaching blindly for the remote, he aimed it at the screen—only to stop when another picture shifted into focus.

Anger escalated through him. Five minutes later he stabbed the 'off' button and calmly replaced the control.

Returning to Rafael's bedside, his sank onto the side of the bed. 'I know you'd probably argue with me, *mi hermano*, but you've had a lucky escape. In more ways than one.'

Jaw clenching, he thanked heaven his brother hadn't heard the interview just played on TV. Marco had first-hand knowledge of what people would sacrifice in their quest for fame and power, and the look of naked ambition in Sasha Fleming's eyes made his chest burn with fury and his skin crawl.

His fist tightened on the bed next to his brother's unmoving body.

If she wanted a taste of power he would give it to her. Let her acquire a taste for it the way she'd given Rafael a taste of herself.

Then, just as she'd callously shoved Rafael aside, Marco would take utter satisfaction in wrenching away everything she'd ever dreamed of.

'Excuse me, can you tell me which room Rafael de Cervantes is in?' Sasha infused her voice with as much authority as possible, despite the glaring knowledge that she wasn't supposed to be here.

The nurse dressed in a crisp white uniform looked up. The crease already forming on her brow caused Sasha's heart to sink.

'Are you a member of the family?'

'No, but I wanted to see how he was. He was...*is* my team

mate.' The moment the words left her lips she winced. *Way to go, Sasha.*

True to form, the nurse's frown dissolved as realisation dawned. 'His team mate...? You're Sasha Fleming!'

Sasha summoned her practised camera smile—the one that held the right amount of interest without screaming *look at me*, and lifted the oversized sunglasses. 'Yes,' she murmured.

'My nephew *loves* you!' The nurse gushed. 'He pretends not to, but I know he thinks you rock. Every time he sees you during Friday Practice his face lights up. He'll be thrilled when I tell him I met you.'

The tension clamping Sasha's nape eased a little. 'Thanks. So can I see Rafael?' she asked again. When the frown threatened to make a comeback, Sasha rushed on. 'I'll only be a moment, I promise.'

'I'm sorry, Miss Fleming. You're not on my list of approved visitors.'

Steeling herself against the nerves dragging through her, Sasha cleared her throat. 'Is Marco de Cervantes here? Maybe I can ask him?'

She pushed the mental picture of Marco's cold, unforgiving features to the back of her mind. She was here for Rafael. Surely, as his team mate, his brother wouldn't bar her from seeing him?

'No, he left half an hour ago.'

Shock slammed into her. 'He *left*?'

The nurse nodded. 'He didn't seem too happy, but considering the circumstances I guess it's to be expected.'

For a moment Sasha debated asking if the nurse would make an exception. Break the rules for her. But she dismissed it. Breaking her own rules, getting friendly with Rafael, was probably the reason he'd ended up in this situation. She refused to exacerbate it.

Plucking her sunglasses off her head, she slid them down to cover her eyes. In her jeans and long-sleeved cotton top, with a multi-coloured cheesecloth satchel slung across her body, she looked like every other summer tourist in the city. Her disguise had helped her evade the paparazzi on her way in. She prayed it would hold up on her way out.

With a heavy heart she turned towards the elevator doors, which stood open as if to usher her away from here as fast as possible.

'Wait.' The nurse beckoned with a quick hand movement and leaned forward as Sasha approached the desk. 'Maybe I can sneak you in for a few minutes,' she whispered.

Relief washed over Sasha. 'Oh, thank you so much!'

'If you don't mind signing an autograph for my nephew?'

A tinge of guilt arrowed through her, but the need to see Rafael overcame the feeling. With a grateful smile, Sasha took the proffered pen.

'What the hell are you doing in here?'

Sasha spun round at the harsh voice, and gasped at the dark figure framed in the doorway. A few minutes, the nurse had said. A quick glance at her watch confirmed her sickening suspicion. She'd been here almost an hour!

'I asked you a question.'

'I came to see Rafael. There was no one here—'

'So you thought you'd just sneak in?'

'Hardly! The nurse—' Sasha gulped back her words, realising she could be putting the nurse's job in jeopardy.

'The nurse what?'

Marco advanced into the room, his formidable presence shrinking the space. She scrambled to her feet, but she still had to tilt her head to see his face.

His cold-as-steel expression dried her mouth further.

She shook her head. 'I just wanted to see how he was.' She stopped speaking as he drew level with her, his hard eyes boring into her.

'How long have you been here?'

She risked another glance at her watch and cringed inwardly. Dared she tell him the truth or blag her way through? 'Does it really matter?'

'How long?' he gritted, his gaze sliding over his brother as if assessing any further damage.

'Why are you checking him over like that? Do you think I've harmed him in some way?' she challenged.

Hazel eyes slammed back to her. His contempt was evident as his gaze raked her face. 'I don't *think*! I *know* you've already harmed my brother.'

His tone was so scathing Sasha was surprised her flesh wasn't falling from her skin.

'Rafael told you about our fight?'

'Yes, he did. I can only conclude that your presence here is another media stunt, not out of concern for my brother?'

'Of course it isn't!'

'Is that why the media presence at the hospital gates has doubled in the last hour?'

Her gaze drifted to the window. The blinds were drawn against the late-afternoon sun, but not closed completely. She'd taken a step to look for herself when steely fingers closed on her wrist. Heat shot up her arm, the reaction so unfamiliar she froze.

'If you think I'm going to let you use my brother to further your own ends, you're sorely mistaken.'

Alarmed, she stared up at him. 'Why would you think I'd do that?'

A mirthless smile bared his teeth, displaying a look so frightening she shivered.

'That press conference you gave? About how much you cared for him? How your thoughts were with him and his family? *About how you're willing to step into his shoes as soon as possible so you don't let the team down?* What were your exact words? *"I've earned the chance at a full-time seat. I've proven that I have what it takes."*'

Sasha swallowed, unable to look away from the chilling but oddly hypnotic pull of his gaze. 'I...I shouldn't have....' The echo of unease she'd felt before and during the interview returned. 'I didn't mean it like that—'

'How *did* you mean it, then? How exactly have *you*, a mere reserve driver, earned your place on the team? Why do *you* deserve Rafael's seat and not one of the other dozen top drivers out there?'

'Because it's my time! I deserve the chance.' She wrenched at her captured arm. His hand tightened, sending another bolt of heat through her body.

Straight black brows clamped together. His arresting features were seriously eroding her thought processes. Even livid to the point where she could imagine heat striations coming off his body he oozed enough sex appeal to make her finally understand why his bodyguards were forever turning away paddock groupies from his luxury hospitality suite. Rumour had it that one particularly eager groupie had scaled the mobile suite and slipped into his bedroom via the skylight.

'*Your time?* Why?' he challenged again, stepping closer, invading her body space and her ability to breathe. 'What's so special about *you*, Sasha Fleming?'

'I didn't say I was special.'

'That's not what I got from the press junket. In fact I deduced something along the lines that the team would be making a huge mistake if you weren't given Rafael's seat. Was there even the veiled threat of a lawsuit thrown in there?'

The thought that this might be her only chance to find a decent seat had resonated in the back of her mind even as she'd felt sickened at the thought of how wrong the timing was.

'Nothing to say?' came the soft taunt.

She finally managed to wrench her wrist from his grasp and stepped back. 'Mr de Cervantes, this is neither the time nor the place to discuss this.'

Her glance slid to Rafael, her throat closing in distress at the tubes and the horrid beeping of the machines keeping him alive.

Marco followed her gaze and froze, as if just realising where he was. When his gaze sliced back to hers she glimpsed a well of anguish within the hazel depths and felt something soften inside her. Marco de Cervantes, despite his chilling words and seriously imposing presence, was hurting. The fear of the unknown, of wondering if the precious life of someone you held dear would pull through was one she was agonisingly familiar with.

Any thought of her job flew out of her head as she watched him wrestle with his pain. The urge to comfort, one human being to another, momentarily overcame her instinct for self-preservation.

'Rafael is strong. He's a fighter. He'll pull through,' she murmured softly.

Slowly he pulled in a breath, and any hint of pain disappeared. His upper lip curled in a mocking sneer. 'Your concern is touching, Miss Fleming. But cut the crap. There are no cameras here. No microphones to lap up your false platitudes. Unless you've got one hidden on your person?' His eyes slid down her body, narrowing as they searched. 'Will I go on the internet tomorrow and see footage of my brother in his sick bed all over it?'

'That's a tasteless and disgusting thing to say!' Spinning away, she rushed to the leather sofa in the suite and picked up her satchel. Clearly it was time to make herself scarce.

Careful not to come within touching distance of Marco de Cervantes, she edged towards the door.

'Any more tasteless than you vying for his seat even before you knew for certain whether he was alive or dead?' came the biting query.

Sasha winced. 'I agree. It wasn't the perfect time to do an interview.'

A hint of surprise lightened his eyes, but his lips firmed a second later. 'But you did it anyway.'

Blaming Tom would have been easy. And the coward's way out. The truth was, she *wanted* to be lead driver.

'I thought I was acting in the best interests of the team. And, yes, I was also putting myself forward as the most viable option. But the timing was wrong. For that, I apologise.'

That grim smile made another appearance. Her body shuddered with alarm. Even before he spoke Sasha had the strongest premonition that she wasn't going to like the words that spilled from his lips.

'You should've taken more time to think, Miss Fleming. Because, as team owner, *I* ultimately decide what's in the best interests of Team Espiritu. Not you.'

He sauntered to his brother's bedside and stood looking down at him.

Sasha glanced between the two men. This close, the resemblance between them was striking. Yet they couldn't have been more different. Where Rafael was wild and gregarious, his brother smouldered and rumbled like the deepest, darkest underbelly of a dormant volcano. The fear that he could erupt at any moment was a very real and credible threat. One that made her throat dry and her heart race.

Finally he turned to face her. Trepidation iced its way to her toes.

'My decision and mine alone carries. Your timing wasn't just wrong. It was detestable.' His voice could have frozen water in the Sahara. 'It also makes my decision incredibly easy.'

Her heart stopped. 'Wh—what decision?'

'Relieving you of your job, of course.' The smile widened. 'Congratulations. You're fired.'

CHAPTER TWO

'*What?*'

'Get out.'

Sasha remained frozen, unable to heed Marco de Cervantes's command. Finally she forced out a breath.

'No. You—you can't do that. You can't fire me.' Somewhere at the back of her mind she knew this to be true—something about contracts…clauses—but her brain couldn't seem to track after the blow it had been dealt.

'I can do anything I want. I *own* the team. Which means I own you.'

'Yes, but…' She sucked in a breath and forced herself to focus. 'Yes, you own the team, but you don't *own* me. And you can't fire me. I haven't done anything wrong. Sure, the press interview was a little mistimed. But that isn't grounds to sack me.'

'Maybe those aren't the only grounds I have.'

Cold dread eased up her spine. 'What are you talking about?'

Marco regarded her for several seconds. Then his gaze slid to his brother. Reaching out, he carefully smoothed back a lock of hair from Rafael's face. The poignancy of the gesture and the momentary softening of his features made Sasha's heart ache for him, despite his anger at her. No one deserved to watch a loved one suffer. Not even Marco de Cervantes.

When his gaze locked onto her again Sasha wasn't prepared for the mercurial shift from familial concern to dark fury.

'You're right. My brother's bedside isn't the place to discuss this.' He came towards her, his long-legged stride purposeful and arrestingly graceful. His broad shoulders, the strength in his lean, muscled body demanded an audience. Sasha stared, unable to look away from the perfect body packed full of angry Spanish male.

In whose path she directly stood.

At the last second her legs unfroze long enough for her to step out of his way. 'It's okay. I'll leave.'

'Running away? Scared your past is catching up with you, Miss Fleming?'

She swallowed carefully, striving to maintain a neutral expression. Marco de Cervantes didn't know. He *couldn't.*

'I don't know what you're talking about. My past has nothing to do with my contract with your team.'

He stared into her face for so long Sasha wanted to slam on the shades dangling uselessly from her fingers.

'Extraordinary,' he finally murmured.

'What?' she croaked.

'You lie so flawlessly. Not even an eyelash betrays you. It's no wonder Rafael was completely taken with you. What I don't understand is why. He offered you what you wanted—money, prestige, a privileged lifestyle millions dream about but only few achieve. Isn't that what women like you ultimately want? The chance to live in unimaginable luxury playing mistress of a *castillo*?'

'Um, I don't know what sort of women *you've* been cavorting with, but you know nothing about me.'

Impossibly, his features grew colder. 'I know everything I need to know. So why didn't you just take it? What's your angle?' His intense gaze bored into her, as if trying to burrow beneath her skin.

It took every control-gathering technique she'd learned not to step back from him.

'I have no *angle*—'

'Enough of your lies. Get out.' He wrenched the door open, fully expecting her to comply.

Her eyes flicked to Rafael's still form. Sasha doubted she'd see him again before the team's month-long August break. 'Will you tell him I came to see him when he wakes up—please?' she asked.

Marco exhaled in disbelief. 'With any luck, by the time my brother wakes up any memory he has of you will be wiped clean from his mind.'

She gasped, the chill from his voice washing over her. 'I'm not sure exactly what Rafael told you, but you've really got this wrong.'

Marco shrugged. 'And you're still fired. Goodbye, Miss Fleming.'

'On what grounds?' she challenged, hoping this time her voice would emerge with more conviction.

'I'm sure my lawyers can find something. Inappropriate enthusiasm?'

'That's a reason you should be keeping me on—not a reason to fire me.'

'You've just proved my point. Most people know where to draw the line. It seems you don't.'

'I *do*,' she stressed, her voice rising right along with the tight knot in her chest.

'This conversation is over.' He glanced pointedly at the door.

She stepped into the corridor, reeling from the impact of his words. Her contract was airtight. She was sure of it. But she'd seen too many teams discard perfectly fit and able drivers for reasons far flimsier than the one Marco had just given her. X1 Premier Racing was notorious for its court battles between team owners and drivers.

The thought that she could lose everything she'd fought for made her mouth dry. She'd battled hard to hold onto her seat in the most successful team in the history of the sport, when every punter with a blog or a social media account had taken potshots at her talent. One particularly harsh critic had even gone as far as to debate her sexual preferences.

She'd sacrificed too much for too long. Somehow she had to convince Marco de Cervantes to keep her on.

She turned to confront him—only to find a short man wearing a suit and a fawning expression hurrying towards them. He handed Marco a small wooden box and launched into a rapid volley of French. Whatever the man—whose discreet badge announced him as Administrator—was saying, it wasn't having any effect on Marco.

Marco's response was clipped. When the administrator started in surprise and glanced towards the reception area, Sasha followed his gaze. The nurse who had let her in stood behind the counter.

The administrator launched into another obsequious torrent. Marco cut him off with an incisive slash of his hand and headed for the lifts.

Sasha hurried after him. As she passed the reception area, she glimpsed the naked distress in the nurse's eyes. Another wave of icy dread slammed into her, lending her more impetus as she rushed after Marco.

'Wait!'

He pressed the button for the lift as she screeched to a halt beside him.

Away from the low lights of the hospital room Sasha saw him—really saw him—for the first time. Up close and personal, Marco de Cervantes was stunning. If you liked your men tall, imposing and bristling with tons of masculinity. Through the gap in his grey cotton shirt she caught a glimpse of dark hair and a strong, golden chest that had her glancing away in a hurry.

Focus!

'Can we talk—please?' she injected into the silence.

He ignored her, his stern, closed face forbidding any conversation. The lift arrived and he stepped in. Sasha rushed in after him. As the doors closed she saw the nurse burst into tears.

Outraged, she rounded on him. 'My God. You got that nurse sacked, didn't you?'

Anger dissolved the last of her instinctive self-preservation and washed away the strangely compelling sensation she refused to acknowledge was attraction.

'I lodged a complaint.'

'Which, coming from you, was as good as ordering that administrator to sack her!'

Guilt attacked her insides.

'She must live with the consequences of her actions.'

'So there's no in-between? No showing mercy? Just straight to the gallows?'

Deep hazel eyes pinned her where she stood. 'You weren't on the list of approved visitors. She knew this and disregarded it. You could've been a tabloid hack. Anybody.'

His eyes narrowed and Sasha forced her expression to remain neutral.

'Or maybe she knew *exactly* who you were?'

She lowered her lids as a wave of guilty heat washed over her face.

'Of course,' he taunted softly. 'What did you offer her? Free tickets to the next race?'

Deciding silence was the best policy, she clamped her lips together.

'A personal tour of the paddock and a photo op with you once you became lead driver, perhaps?'

His scathing tone grated on her nerves.

Raising her head she met his gaze, anger at his high-handedness loosening her tongue. 'You know, just because your brother is gravely ill, it doesn't give you the right to destroy other people's lives.'

'I beg your pardon?' he bit out.

'Right now you're in pain and lashing out, wanting anyone and everyone to pay for what you're going through. It's understandable, but it's not fair. That poor woman is now jobless just because *you're* angry.'

'*That poor woman* abused her position and broke the hospital's policy for personal gain. She deserves everything she gets.'

'It wasn't for personal gain. She did it for her nephew. He's a fan. She wanted to do something nice for him.'

'My heart bleeds.'

'You do the same, and more, for thousands of race fans every year. What's so different about this?'

Dark brows clamped together, and his jaw tightened in that barely civilised way that sent another wave of apprehension through her. Again she glimpsed the dark fury riding just below his outward control.

'The difference, Miss Fleming, is that I don't compromise my integrity to do so. And I don't put those I care about in harm's way just to get what I want.'

'What about compassion?'

His brows cleared, but the volatile tinge in the air remained. 'I'm fresh out.'

'You know, you'll wake up one morning not long from now and regret your actions today.'

The lift doors glided open to reveal the underground car park. A few feet away was a gleaming black chrome-trimmed Bentley Continental. Beside it, a driver and a heavily muscled man whose presence shrieked *bodyguard* waited. The driver held the back door open, but Marco made no move towards it. Instead he glanced down at her, his expression hauntingly bleak.

'I regret a lot that's happened in the past twenty-four hours—not least watching my brother mangle himself and his car on the race track because he believed himself to be heartbroken. One more thing doesn't make a difference.'

'Your emotions are overwhelming you right now. All I'm saying is don't let them overrule your better judgement.'

A cold smile lifted one corner of his mouth. 'My *emotions*? I didn't know you practised on the side as the team's psychologist. I thought you'd ridden down with me to beg for your job back, not to practise the elevator pitch version of pop psychology. You had me as your captive audience for a full thirty seconds. Shame you chose to waste it.'

'Mock me all you want. It doesn't change the fact that you're acting like—' She bit her lip, common sense momentarily overriding her anger.

'Go on,' he encouraged softly. Tauntingly. 'Acting like what?'

She shrugged. 'Like...well, like an ass.'

His eyes narrowed until they were mere icy slits. 'Excuse me?'

'Sorry. You asked.'

Anger flared in his eyes, radiated off his body. Sasha held

her breath, readying herself for the explosion about to rain on her head. Instead he gave a grim smile.

'I've been called worse.' He nodded to his bodyguard, who took a step towards them. 'Romano will escort you off the premises. Be warned—my very generous donation to this hospital is contingent on you being arrested if you set foot anywhere near my brother again. I'm sure the administrator would relish that challenge.'

Despair rose to mingle with her anger. 'You can't do this. If you don't listen to me I'll…I'll talk to the press again. I'll spill everything!'

'Ah, I'm glad to finally meet the *real* you, Miss Fleming.'

'Ten minutes. That's all I want. Let me convince you to keep me on.'

'Trust me—blackmail isn't a great place to start.'

She bit her lip. 'That was just a bluff. I won't talk to the press. But I do want to drive for you. And I'm the best mid-season replacement you'll find for Rafael.'

'You *do* place a high premium on yourself, don't you?'

Unflinching, she nodded. 'Yes, I do. And I can back it up. Just let me prove it.'

His gaze narrowed on her face, then conducted a lazy sweep over her body. Suddenly the clothes that had served as perfect camouflage against the intrusive press felt inadequate, exposing. Beneath the thin material of her T-shirt her heart hammered, her skin tingling with an alien awareness that made her muscles tense.

As a female driver in a predominantly male sport, she was used to being the cynosure of male eyes. There were those who searched for signs of failure as a driver, ready to use any shortcomings against her. Then there were the predators who searched for weaknesses simply because she was a woman, and therefore deemed incapable. The most vicious lot were those who bided their time, ready to rip her apart because she was Jack Fleming's daughter. Those were the ones she feared the most. And the ones she'd sworn to prove wrong.

Marco de Cervantes's gaze held an intensity that combined

all of those qualities multiplied by a thousand. And then there was something else.

Something that made her breath grow shallow in her lungs. Made her palms clammy and the hairs bristle on her nape.

Recalling the sheer intensity of the look he'd directed into the camera earlier, she felt her heartbeat accelerate.

'Get in the car,' he bit out, his tone bone-chilling.

Sasha glanced into the dark, luxurious interior of the limo and hesitated. The feelings this man engendered in her weren't those of fear. Rather, she sensed an emotional risk—as if, given half a chance, he would burrow under her skin, discover her worst fears and use them against her. She couldn't let that happen.

'If you want me to hear you out you'll get in the car. Now,' he said, his tone uncompromising.

She hesitated. 'I can't.'

'*Can't* isn't a word I enjoy hearing,' he growled, his patience clearly ebbing fast.

'My bike.' He quirked one brow at her. 'I'd *rather* not leave it here.'

His glance towards the battered green and white scooter leaning precariously against the car park wall held disbelief. 'You came here on *that*?'

'Yes. Why?'

'You're wearing the most revolting pair of jeans I've ever seen and a scarf that's seen better days. Add that to the oversized sunglasses and I don't need to be a genius to guess you were trying some misguided attempt to escape the paparazzi. I am right?' At her nod, he continued. 'And yet you travelled on the slowest mode of motorised transport known to man.'

She raised her chin. 'But there's the beauty—don't you see? I managed to ride straight past the paparazzi without one single camera lens focusing on me. You, on the other hand... Tell me— how did they react when you rocked up in your huge, tinted-windowed monstrosity of a car?'

His jaw tightened and he glared at her.

'Exactly. I'm not leaving my bike.'

'Security here is—'

'Inadequate, according to you. After all, *I* managed to get through, didn't I?' She threw his words back at him.

One hand gripped the door of the car. 'Get in the car or don't. I refuse to argue with you over a pile of junk.'

'It's my junk and I won't leave it.'

With a stifled curse, Marco held out his hands. 'Keys?'

'Why?'

'Romano will return the scooter to your hotel.'

Sasha's eyes widened. Romano weighed at least two hundred and fifty pounds of pure muscle. The thought of what he'd put her poor scooter through made her wince.

'And before you comment on Romano's size I'd urge you to stop and think about his *feelings*,' Marco added mockingly.

Touché, she conceded silently.

Digging into her satchel, she reluctantly handed over her keys. Marco lobbed them to his bodyguard, then raised an imperious eyebrow at her.

With a resigned sigh, Sasha slid past his imposing body and entered the limo.

The door shut on them, enclosing them in a silent cocoon that threatened to send her already taut nerves into a frenzied tailspin.

As the car glided out of the car park it occurred to her that she had no idea where Marco was taking her. She opened her mouth to ask, then immediately shut it when she saw his gaze fixed on the small box.

Despite his bleak expression, his profile was stunningly arresting. The sculpted contours of his face held enough shadow and intrigue to capture the attention of any red-blooded female with a pulse—a fact attested to by the regular parade of stunning women he was photographed with.

His strong jaw bore the beginnings of a five o'clock shadow, and an even stronger, taut neck slanted onto impossibly broad shoulders. Under the discreetly expensive cotton shirt those shoulders moved restlessly. She followed the movement, her gaze sliding down over his chest, past the flat stomach that showed no hint of flab. Her eyes rested in his lap. The bulge beneath his zipper made heat swirl in her belly.

'Have you seen enough? Or would you like me to perform a slow striptease for you?'

Her cheeks burned. Her neck burned. In fact for several seconds Sasha was sure her whole body was on fire. Mortified, she hastily plucked her sunglasses from atop her head and jammed them onto her face.

'I… You didn't say where we were going.'

'I've called a meeting with Russell and the chief engineer. I'm handing over the reins temporarily so I can concentrate on making arrangements for Rafael to be evacuated home to Spain.'

'You're moving him?'

'Not yet, but the medical team is on standby. He'll be moved the moment it's deemed safe.'

'I see.'

Sharp eyes bored into her. 'Do you? You've talked your way into a last-chance meeting and yet you're wasting time exhibiting false concern for my brother.'

She sucked in a breath. 'My concern isn't false. I'd give anything for Rafael not to be in that place.'

Sasha watched, fascinated, as his hand tightened around the box. 'In my experience *anything* tends to arrive with a very heavy price tag and a carefully calculated catch. So be very careful with your choice of words.'

Sasha licked her lips, suddenly unable to breathe at the expression in his eyes. 'I'm sure I don't know what you mean.'

The look in his eyes hardened. 'You really should try a different profession. Your acting skills are highly commendable.'

'Driving suits me just fine, thanks. Where are we going, exactly?'

Keeping his gaze on her, he relaxed back in his seat. 'My hotel.'

'Your hotel?' she repeated dully. Her senses, still reeling after she'd been caught staring at Marco de Cervantes's man package, threatened to go into freefall. The thought of being alone with him—truly alone—made anxiety skitter over her skin. 'I don't think that's a good idea.'

'You don't have a choice. You wanted this meeting.'

Desperation lent her voice strength. 'The rest of the team will be wondering where I am. Maybe I should let them know.' Tom had asked where she was going after the press conference, but she'd been deliberately evasive.

'The team will be out doing what they do after every Sunday race. Bar hopping and trying it on with the local girls.'

'I don't think they'll be doing that tonight. Not with Rafael…' She bit her lip, unable to continue as she glimpsed the flash of pain in those hazel eyes.

But he merely shrugged. 'Call them if you want. Tell them where you're going. And why.'

Not expecting her bluff to be called, Sasha floundered. The circumstances of her past made it impossible to make friends with anyone on her team. The constant whispers behind her back, the conversations that stopped when she walked into a room, made it hard to trust anyone.

Tom only cared as far as her actions impacted upon his career. The only one who had cared—really cared—had been Rafael. A wave of pain and regret rushed through her. Until their row last night she'd foolishly let herself believe she could finally trust another human being.

Feigning nonchalance, she shrugged. 'I'll tell them later.'

Unable to stomach the mockery in Marco's eyes, she turned away.

Absently she stroked the armrest, silently apologising for calling the Bentley Continental a monstrosity. Amongst the luxury, sometimes vacuous, creations car manufacturers produced, the Bentley was one of the more ingenious styles. It had been her father's favourite non-racing car—his pride and joy until he'd been forced to sell it to defend himself.

'We're here.'

They were parked beneath the pillared portico of the Four Seasons. A liveried doorman stepped forward and opened the door on Marco's side, his bow of deference deep to the point of being obsequious.

Casting her gaze past him, Sasha felt her mouth drop open at the sheer opulence of the marbled foyer of the stunning hotel. The whole atmosphere glittered and sparkled beneath a super-sized revolving chandelier, which was throwing its adoring light on sleekly dressed patrons.

Sasha remained in her seat, super-conscious of how inappropriate her old hipster jeans and worn top were for the gold-leaf and five-star luxury spread before her. She was pretty sure she would be directed to the tradesman's entrance the moment the doorman saw her scuffed boots.

'Come out. And lose the glasses and the scarf. No one cares who you are here.'

She hesitated. 'Can't we just talk in the car?' she ventured.

He held out a commanding hand. 'No, we can't. We both know you're not shy, so stop wasting my time.'

She could argue, defend her personal reputation against the label Marco had decided to pin on her, but Sasha doubted it would make a difference. He, like the rest of the world, believed she was soiled goods because of her past and because she was a Fleming.

What good would protesting do?

The only weapon she had to fight with was her talent behind the steering wheel.

Her father's time had been cruelly cut short, stamped out by vicious lies that had destroyed him and robbed her of the one person who had truly loved and believed in her.

Sasha was damned if she would let history repeat itself. Damned if she would give up her only chance to prove everyone wrong.

Gritting her teeth, she ignored his hand and stepped out of the car.

Marco strode across the marble foyer, the box clutched firmly in his grip. Its contents were a vivid reminder, stamped onto his brain.

Behind him he heard the hurried click of booted heels as Sasha Fleming struggled to keep up with him.

He didn't slow down. In fact he sped up. He wanted this meeting over with so he could return to the hospital.

For a single moment Marco thanked God his mother wasn't alive. She couldn't have borne to see her darling son, the miracle child she'd thought she'd never have, lying battered and bruised in a coma.

It was bad enough that she'd had to live through the pain and suffering Marco had brought her ten years ago. Bad enough that those horrendous three weeks before and after his own crash had caused a rift he'd never quite managed to heal, despite his mother's reassurances that all was well.

Marco knew all hadn't been well because *he* had never been the same since that time.

Deep shame and regret raked through him at how utterly he'd let his mother down. At how utterly he'd lost his grip on reality back then. Foolishly and selfishly he'd thought himself in love. The practised smile of a skilful manipulator had blinded him into throwing all caution to the wind and he'd damaged his family in the process.

His mother was gone, her death yet another heavy weight on his conscience, but Rafael was alive—and Marco intended to make sure lightning didn't strike twice. For that to happen he had to keep it together. He *would* keep it together.

'Um, the sign for the bar points the other way.'

Sasha Fleming's husky voice broke into his unwelcome thoughts.

He stopped so suddenly she bumped into him. Marco frowned at the momentary sensation of her breasts against his back and the unsuspecting heat that surged into his groin. His whole body tightened in furious rejection and he rounded on her.

'I don't conduct my business in bars. And I seriously doubt you want our conversation to be overheard by anyone else.'

Turning on his heel, he stalked to the lift. His personal porter pushed the button and waited for Marco to enter the express lift that serviced the presidential suite.

Sasha shot him a wary look and he bit back the urge to let a feral smile loose. Ever since Rafael's crash he'd been pushing back the blackness, fighting memories that had no place here within this chaos.

Really, Sasha Fleming had chosen the worst possible time to make herself his enemy. His hands tightened around the box and his gaze rested on her.

Run, he silently warned her. *While you have the chance.*

Her eyes searched every corner of the mirrored lift as if danger lurked within the gold-filigree-trimmed interior. Finally she rolled her shoulders. The subtle movement was almost the equivalent of cracking one's knuckles before a fight, and it intrigued him far more than he wanted to admit.

'We're going to your suite? Okay...'

She stepped into the lift. Behind her, Marco saw the porter's gaze drop to linger on her backside. Irritation rose to mingle with the already toxic cauldron of emotions swirling through him. With an impatient finger he stabbed at the button.

'I see the thought of it doesn't disturb you too much.' He didn't bother to conceal the slur in his comment. The urge to attack, to wound, ran rampage within him.

Silently he conceded she was right. As long as Rafael was fighting for his life he couldn't think straight. The impulse to make someone pay seethed just beneath the surface of his calm.

And Sasha Fleming had placed herself front and centre in his sights.

He expected her to flinch. To show that his words had hit a mark.

He wasn't prepared for her careless shrug. 'You're right. I don't really want our conversation to feed tomorrow's headlines. I'm pretty sure by now most of the media know you're staying here.'

'So you're not afraid to enter a strange man's suite?'

'Are you strange? I thought you were merely the engineering genius who designed the Espiritu DSII and the Cervantes Conquistador.'

'I'm immune to flattery, Miss Fleming, and any other form of coercion running through your pretty little head.'

'Shame. I was about to spout some seriously nerd-tastic info *guaranteed* to make you like me.'

'You'd be wasting your time. I have a team specially selected to deal with sycophants.'

His barb finally struck home. She inhaled sharply and lowered her gaze.

Marco caught himself examining the determined angle of her chin, the sensual line of her full lips. At the base of her neck her pulse fluttered under satin-smooth skin. Against his will, another wave of heat surged through him. He threw a mental bucket of cold water over it.

This woman belonged to his brother.

The lift opened directly onto the living room—a white and silver design that flowed outside onto the balcony overlooking the Danube. Marco bypassed the sweeping floor-to-ceiling windows, strode to the antique desk set against the velvet wall and put the box down.

Recalling its contents, he felt anger coalesce once more within him.

He turned to find Sasha Fleming at the window, a look of total awe on her face as she gazed at the stunning views of the Buda Hills and the Chain Bridge. He took a moment to study her.

Hers wasn't a classical beauty. In fact there was more of the rangy tomboy about her than a woman who was aware of her body. Yet her face held an arresting quality. Her lips were wide and undeniably sensual, and her limbs contained an innate grace when she moved that drew the eye. Her silky black hair, pulled into a loose ponytail at the back of her head, gleamed like a jet pool in the soft lighting. His gaze travelled over her neck, past shoulders that held a hint of delicacy and down to her chest.

The memory of her breasts against his back intruded. Against him she'd felt decidedly soft, although her body was lithe, holding a whipcord strength that didn't hide her subtle femininity. When he'd held her wrist in Rafael's hospital room her skin had felt supple, smooth like silk...

Sexual awareness hummed within him, unwelcome and unacceptable. Ruthlessly he cauterised it. Even if he'd been remotely interested in a woman such as this, flawed as she was, and without a moral bone in her body, *she* was the reason his brother had crashed.

Besides, poaching had never been his style.

'So, what would it take to convince you to keep me on?' She addressed him without taking her eyes from the view.

Annoyance fizzled through him.

'You're known for having relationships with your team mates.'

Her breath caught and she turned sharply from the window. Satisfaction oozed through him at having snagged her attention.

Satisfaction turned to surprise when once again she didn't evade the question. 'One team mate. A very long time ago.'

'He also crashed under extreme circumstances and lost his drive, I believe?'

A simple careful nod. 'He retired from motor racing, yes.'

'And his seat was then given to you?'

Her eyes narrowed. 'Your extrapolation is way off base if you think it has any bearing on what has happened with Rafael.'

'Isn't it curious that you bring chaos to every team you join? Are you an unlucky charm, Miss Fleming?'

'As a former racer yourself, I'm sure you're familiar with the facts—drivers crash on a regular basis. It's a reality of the sport. In fact, wasn't a crash what ended *your* racing career?'

For the second time in a very short while the reminder of events of ten years ago cut through him like the sharpest knife. Forcing the memories away, he folded his arms. 'It's *your* circumstances that interest me, not statistics. You dumped this other guy just before a race. This seems to be your *modus operandi*.'

Her chest lifted with her affronted breath. He struggled not to let his gaze drop. 'I resent that. I thought you ran your team on merit and integrity, not rumour and hypothesis.'

'Here's your chance to dispel the rumours. How many other team mates have you slept with?'

'I had a *relationship* with one. Derek and I went out for a while. Then it ended.'

'But this...relationship grew quite turbulent, I believe? So much so that it eventually destroyed his career while yours flourished?'

She snorted. 'I wouldn't say flourished, exactly. More like sweated and blooded.'

'But you did start out being a reserve driver on his team. And you did dump him when his seat became available to you?'

Marco watched her lips tighten, her chin angling in a way that drew his eyes to her smooth throat.

'It's obvious you've done your homework. But I didn't come here to discuss my personal life with you—which, as it happens, is really none of your business.'

'When it relates to *my* brother and *my* team it becomes my business. And your actions in the past three months have directly involved Rafael.' He reached for the box on the table. 'Do you know what's in this box?' he asked abruptly.

A wary frown touched her forehead. 'No. How would I?'

'Let me enlighten you. It contains the personal effects that were found on Rafael's person when he was pulled out of the car.' He opened the box. The inside was smeared with blood. Rafael's blood.

Blood he'd spilled because of this woman.

He lifted a gold chain with a tiny crucifix at the end of it. 'My mother gave this to him on the day of his confirmation, when he was thirteen years old. He always wears it during a race. For good luck.'

A look passed over her face. Sadness and a hint of guilt, perhaps? He dropped the chain back into the container, closed it and set it down. Reaching into his pocket, he produced another box—square, velvet.

She tensed, her eyes flaring with alarm. 'Mr de Cervantes—'

His lips twisted. 'You're not quite the talented actress I took you for, after all. Because your expression tells me everything I need to know. Rafael asked the question he'd been burning to ask, didn't he?' he demanded.

'I—'

He cut across her words, not at all surprised when the colour fled her face. 'My brother asked you to marry him. And you callously rejected him, knowing he would have to race directly afterwards. *Didn't you?*'

CHAPTER THREE

SASHA clenched her fists behind her back, desperately trying to hold it together. Even from across the room she could feel Marco's anger. It vibrated off his skin, slammed around the room like a living thing.

Her heart thudded madly in her chest. She opened her mouth but no words emerged.

'Here's your chance to speak up, Miss Fleming,' Marco incised, one long finger flipping open the box to reveal a large, stunning pink diamond set within a circle of smaller white diamonds.

She'd never been one to run from a fight, and Lord knew she'd had many fights in her life. But, watching Marco advance towards her, Sasha yearned to take a step back. Several steps, in fact…right out through the door. Unfortunately she chose that moment to look into his eyes.

The sheer force of his gaze trapped her. It held her immobile, darkly fascinating even as her panic flared higher. She'd dealt with disrespect, with disdain, even with open slurs against her.

Seething, pain-racked Spanish males like Marco de Cervantes were a different box of frogs.

'Did you refuse my brother or not?' he demanded, and his low, dangerous voice scoured her skin.

Suppressing a shiver, she said, 'You've got it wrong. Rafael didn't ask me—'

'Liar.' He snapped the box shut. 'He sent me a text last night. You said no.'

'Of course I said no. He didn't mean—'

He continued as if she hadn't spoken. 'He thought you were just playing hard to get. He was going to try again this morning.'

Sasha knew the brothers were close, but Rafael hadn't given her any indication he was *this* close to his brother. In fact the reason she'd grown close to him, despite his irreverent antics with the team and his wildly flirtatious behaviour with every female he came into contact with, was because she'd glimpsed the loneliness Rafael desperately tried to hide. Loneliness she'd identified with.

She watched Marco's nostrils flare with ever deepening anger as he waited for her answer. She licked her lips, carefully choosing her words, because it was clear that Rafael, for his own reasons, hadn't given Marco all the facts.

'Rafael and I are just friends.'

'Do you take me for a fool, Miss Fleming? You really expect me to believe that you viewed the romantic dinners for two in London or the spontaneous trip to Paris last month as innocent gestures of a mere friend?'

Another stab of surprise went through her at the depth of Marco's knowledge. 'I went to dinner with him because Rav... his date stood him up.'

'And Paris?'

'He was appearing at some function and I was at a loose end. I tagged along for laughs.'

'For laughs? And you then proceeded to dance the night away in his arms? What about the other half a dozen times you've been snapped together by the paparazzi?' he demanded.

She frowned. 'I know you two are close, but don't you think you're taking an alarmingly unhealthy interest in your brother's private life?'

His head jerked as if she'd slapped him. His hazel eyes darkened and his shoulders stiffened as if he held some dark emotion inside. Again she wanted to step back. To flee from a fight for the first time in her life.

'It's my duty to protect my brother,' he stated, with a finality that sharpened her interest.

'Rafael's a grown man. He doesn't need protecting.'

His raised a hand and slowly unfurled his fingers from around the velvet box. 'Then what do you call this? Why did my brother, the reigning world champion, who rarely ever makes mistakes, deliberately drive into the back of a slower car?'

Her gasp scoured her throat. 'The accident wasn't deliberate.' She refused to believe Rafael would have acted so recklessly. 'Rafael wouldn't put himself or another driver in such danger.'

'I've watched my brother race since he was six years old. His skill is legendary. He would never have put himself into the slipstream of a slower car so close to a blind corner. Not if he'd been thinking straight.'

Sasha couldn't refute the allegation because she'd wondered herself why Rafael had made such a dangerous move. 'Maybe he thought he could make the move stick,' she pursued half-heartedly.

Long bronze hands curled around the box. Features tight, Marco breathed deeply. 'Or maybe he didn't care. Maybe it was already too late for him when he stepped into the cockpit?'

Horror raked through her. 'Of course it wasn't. Why would you say that?'

'He sent me a text an hour before the race to tell me he intended to have what he wanted. *At all costs.*'

Sasha's blood ran cold. 'I…no, he couldn't have said that! Besides, he didn't mean—' She bit her lip to stop the rest of her words. Although they'd rowed, she wasn't about to betray Rafael's trust. 'We're just friends.'

'You're poison.' His hand slashed through the denial she'd been about to utter. 'Whatever thrall you hold over your fellow team mates, it ends right now.'

Sliding the box containing the engagement ring into his pocket, he returned to the desk. Several papers were spread across it. He searched through until he found what he was looking for.

'Your contract is a rolling one, due to end next season.'

Still reeling from the force of his words, Sasha stared at him. 'My lawyers will hammer out the finer details of a pay-off in the next few days. But as of right now your services are no longer needed by Team Espiritu.'

With the force of a bucket of cold water, she was wrenched from her numbness.

'You're firing me because I befriended your brother?'

The hysterical edge to her voice registered on the outer fringes of her mind, but Sasha ignored it. She'd worked too hard, fought too long for this chance to let mere hysteria stand in her way. If she had to scream like a banshee she would do so to make Marco de Cervantes listen to her. After years of withstanding vicious whispers and callous undermining, she would not be dismissed so easily. Not when her chance to see her father's reputation restored, the chance to prove her own worth, was so close.

'Do you want to stop for a moment and think how absurd that is? Do you really want to carry on down that road?' she demanded, raising her chin when he turned from the desk.

'What road?' he asked without looking up.

'The sexist, discriminatory road. Or are you going to fire Rafael too when he wakes up? Just to even things up?'

His gaze hardened. 'I've been running this team for almost a decade and no one has ever been allowed to cause this much disruption unchecked before.'

'What do you mean, unchecked?'

'I warned Rafael about you three months ago,' he delivered without an ounce of remorse. 'I told him you were trouble. That he should stay away from you.'

Her anger blazed into an inferno. 'How dare you?'

He merely shrugged. 'Unfortunately, with Rafael, you only have to suggest there's something he can't have to make him hunger desperately for it.'

'You're unbelievable—you know that? You think you can play with people's lives!'

His face darkened. 'Believe me, I'm not playing. Five million.'

Confused, she frowned. 'Five million...for what?'

'To walk away. Dollars, pounds or euros. It doesn't really matter.'

Fire crackled inside her. 'You want to pay me to give up my seat? To disappear like some sleazy secret simply because I became friends with your brother? Even to a wild nut-job like me that seems very drastic. What exactly are you afraid of, Mr de Cervantes?'

Strong, corded arms folded over his chest. His body was held so tense she feared he would snap a muscle at any second. 'Let's just say I have experience with women like you.'

'Damn, I thought I was one of a kind. Would you care to elaborate on that stunning assertion?'

One brow winged upward. 'And have you selling the story to the first tabloid hack you find? I'll pass. Five million. To resign and to stay away from the sport.'

'Go to hell.' She added a smile just for the hell of it, because she yearned for him to feel a fraction of the anger and humiliation coursing through her. The same emotions her father had felt when he'd been thrown out of the profession that had been his life.

'Is that your final answer?' he asked.

'Yes. I don't need to phone a friend and I don't need to ask any audience. My final answer—*go to hell*!'

Sasha braced herself for more of the backlash he'd been doling out solidly for the last hour. But all he did was stare at her, his gaze once again leaving her feeling exposed, as if he'd stripped back a layer of her skin.

He nodded once. Then he paced the room, seemingly lost for words. Finally he raked both hands through his hair, ruffling it until the silky strands looked unkempt in a sexy, just-got-out-of-bed look that she couldn't help but stare at.

Puzzled by his attitude, she forced her gaze away and tried to hang on to her anger. She didn't deserve this. All she'd tried to be was a friend to Rafael, a team mate who'd seemed to be battling demons of his own.

After her experience with Derek, and the devastating pain of losing the baby she hadn't known she was carrying until it was too late, she'd vowed never to mix business with pleasure. Derek's jealousy as she'd risen through the ranks of the racing world had eroded any feelings she'd had for him until there'd been nothing left.

As if sensing her withdrawal, he'd tried to hang on to her with a last-ditch proposal. When she'd turned him down he'd labelled her a bitch and started a whispering campaign against her that had undermined all her years of hard work.

Thankfully Derek had never found out the one thing he could have used against her. The one thing that could have shattered her very existence. The secret memory of her lost baby was buried deep inside, where no one could touch it or use it as a weapon against her.

Even her father hadn't known, and after living through his pain and humiliation she'd vowed never to let her personal life interfere with her work ever again.

Rafael's easy smile and wildly charming ways had got under her guard, making her reveal a few careful details about her past to him. His friendship had been a balm to the lonely existence she'd lived as Jack Fleming's daughter.

The thought that Marco had poisoned him against her filled her with sadness.

'You know, I thought it was Rafael who told *you* about my past. But it was the other way round, wasn't it?' she asked.

She waited for his answer, but his gaze was fixed on the view outside, on the picturesque towers of the Royal Castle. A stillness surrounded him that caught and held her attention.

'For as long as I can remember I've been bailing Rafael out of one scrape or another.'

The words—low, intense and unexpected—jolted aside her anger.

'He's insanely passionate about every single aspect of his life, be it food, driving or volcano-boarding down the side of some godforsaken peak in Nicaragua,' he continued. 'Unfortunately the perils of this world seem to dog him. When he was eleven, he discovered mushrooms growing in a field at our vineyard in León and decided to eat them. His stomach had to be pumped or he'd have died. Two years later, he slipped away from his boarding school to run with the bulls at Pamplona. He was gored in the arm. Save for a very substantial donation to the school, and my personal guarantee of his reformation, he would've been thrown out immediately.'

His gaze focused on her. 'I can list another dozen episodes that would raise your hair.'

'He's a risk-taker,' Sasha murmured, wondering where the conversation was headed but deciding to go with it. 'He has to be as a racing driver; surely you understand that?' she argued. 'Didn't you scale Everest on your own five years ago, after everyone in your team turned back because of a blizzard? In my book that's Class A recklessness.'

'I knew what I was doing.'

'Oh, okay. How about continuing over half the London-Dakar rally with a broken arm?'

His clear surprise made her lips twist. 'How—?'

'Told you I had nerd-tastic info on you. You own the most successful motor racing team in the history of the sport. I want to drive for you. I've done my homework.'

'Very impressive, but risk-taking on the track is expected— within reason. But even before Rafael ever got behind the wheel of a race car he was…highly strung.'

'If he's so highly strung that you have to manage him, then why do you let him race? Why own the team that places him in the very sport likely to jeopardise his well-being?'

His eyes darkened and he seemed to shut off. Watching him, Sasha was fascinated by the impenetrable mask that descended over his face.

'Because racing is in our blood. It's what we do. My father never got the chance to become a racer. I raced for him, but because I had the talent. So does Rafael. There was never any question that racing was our future. But it's also my job to take care of my brother. To save him from himself. To make him see beyond his immediate desires.'

'Have you thought that perhaps if you let him make his own mistakes instead of trying to manage his life he'll wise up eventually?'

'So far, no.'

'He's a grown man. When are you going to cut the apron strings?'

'When he's proved to me that he won't kill himself without them.'

'And are you so certain you can save him every single time?'

'I can put safety measures in place.'

She laughed at his sheer arrogance. 'You're not omnipotent. You can't control what happens in life. Even if you could, Rafael will eventually resent you for controlling his life.'

Marco's lips firmed, his eyelids descending to veil his eyes.

She gave another laugh. 'He already does, doesn't he? Did you two fight? Was that why you weren't at the track this weekend?'

He ignored her questions. 'What I do, I do for his own good. And you're not good for him. My offer still stands.'

Just like that they were back to his sleazy offer of a buy-off. Distaste filled her.

She looked around the sleekly opulent room at the highly polished surfaces, the velvet walls, the bespoke furniture and elegant, sweeping staircases that belonged more in a stately home than in a hotel. Luxurious decadence only people like Marco de Cervantes could afford. The stamp of power and authority told her she wouldn't find even the smallest chink in the de Cervantes armour.

The man was as impenetrable as his wealth was immeasurable.

In the end, all she could rely on was her firm belief in right and wrong.

'You can't fire me simply to keep me out of Rafael's way. It's unethical. I think somewhere deep down you know it too.'

'I don't need moral guidance from someone like you.'

'I disagree. I think you need a big-ass, humongous compass. Because you're making a big mistake if you think I'm going to go quietly.'

His smile didn't quite reach his eyes. 'Rafael told me you were feisty.'

What else had Rafael told him? Decidedly uncomfortable at the thought of being the subject of discussion, she shrugged.

'I haven't reached where I am today without a fight or three. I won't go quietly,' she stressed again.

Several minutes of silence stretched. Her nerves stretched along with them. Just when she thought she'd break, that she'd have to resort to plain, old-fashioned, humiliating begging, he hitched one taut-muscled thigh over the side of the desk and indicated the chair in front of it.

'Sit down. I think a discussion is in order.'

Marco watched relief wash over her face and hid a triumphant smile.

He'd never had any intention of firing Sasha Fleming. Not immediately, anyway. He'd wanted her rattled, on a knife-edge at the possibility of losing what was evidently so precious to her.

The bloodthirsty, vengeance-seeking beast inside him felt a little appeased at seeing her shaken. He also wanted to test her, to see how far she would go to fight for what she wanted. After all, the higher the value she placed on her career, the sweeter it would be to snatch it away from her. Just as he'd had everything wrenched from *him* ten years ago.

He ruthlessly brushed aside the reminder of Angelique's betrayal and focused on Sasha as she walked towards him.

Again his senses reacted to her in ways that made his jaw clench. The attraction—and, yes, he was man enough to admit to it—was unwelcome as much as it was abhorrent. Rafael was in a coma, fighting for his life. The last thing Marco wanted was to acknowledge a chemical reaction to the woman in the middle of all this chaos. To acknowledge how the flare of her hips made his palms itch to shape them. How the soft lushness of her lower lip made him want to caress his finger over it.

'Regardless of the state of the team, I have a responsibility towards the sponsors.'

His office had already received several calls, ostensibly expressing concern for his brother's welfare. In truth the sponsors were sniffing around, desperate to find out what Marco's next move would be—specifically, who he would put in Rafael's place and how it would affect their bottom line.

She nodded. 'Rafael was scheduled to appear at several sponsored engagements during the August hiatus. They'll want to know what's happening.'

Once again Marco was struck by the calm calculation in her voice. This wasn't the tone of a concerned lover or a distraught team mate. Her mind was firmly focused on Team Espiritu. In other circumstances, her single-mindedness would have been admirable. But he knew first-hand the devastation ambition like hers could wreak.

Before he could answer a knock sounded on his door. One of his two butlers materialised from wherever he'd been stationed and opened the door.

Russell Latchford, his second-in-command, and Luke Green, the team's chief engineer, entered.

Russell approached. 'I've just been to see Rafael—' He stopped when he saw Sasha. 'Sasha. I didn't know you were here.' His tone echoed the question in his eyes.

Sasha returned his gaze calmly. Nothing ruffled her. Nothing except the threatened loss of her job. The urge to see her lose that cool once again attacked Marco's senses.

'Miss Fleming's here to discuss future possibilities in light of Rafael's accident.'

As team principal, it was Russell's job to source the best drivers for the team, with Marco giving final approval. Marco saw his disgruntlement, but to his credit Russell said nothing.

'Have you brought the shortlist I asked for?' Marco asked Russell.

Sasha inhaled sharply, and he saw her hands clench in her lap as Russell handed over a piece of paper.

'I've already been discreetly approached by the top five, but every driver in the sport wants to drive for us. It'll cost you to buy out their contracts, of course. If you go for someone from the lower ranking teams it'll still cost you, but the fallout won't be as damaging as poaching someone from the top teams.'

Marco shook his head. 'Our sponsors signed up for the package—Rafael and the car. I don't want a second-class driver.

I need someone equally talented and charismatic or the sponsors will throw hissy fits.'

Luke spoke up. 'There's also the problem of limited in-season testing. We can't just throw in a brand-new driver mid-season and expect him to handle the car anywhere near the way Rafael did.'

Marco glanced down at the list. 'No. Rafael is irreplaceable. I accept that the Drivers' Championship is no longer an option, but I want to win the Constructors' Championship. The team deserves it. All of these drivers would ditch their contract to drive for me, but I'd rather not deal with a messy court battle. Where do we stand on the former champion who retired last year? Have you contacted him?'

Russell shook his head. 'Even with the August break he won't be in good enough shape when the season resumes in September.'

'So my only option is to take on a driver from another team?'

'No, it isn't.' Sasha's voice was low, but intensely powerful, and husky enough to command attention.

Marco's eyes slid to her. Her stance remained relaxed, one leg crossed over the other, but in her eyes he saw ferocious purpose.

'You have something to add?'

Fierce blue eyes snapped at him as she rolled her shoulders. As last time, he couldn't help but follow the movement. Then his eyes travelled lower, to the breasts covered by her nondescript T-shirt. Again the pull of desire was strong and sharp, unlike anything he'd experienced before. Again he pushed it away and forced his gaze back to her face.

A faint flush covered her cheeks. 'You know I do. I know the car inside out. I've driven it at every Friday Practice since last season. The way I see it, I'm the only way you can win the Constructors' Championship. Plus you'd save a lot of money and the unnecessary litigation of trying to tempt away a driver mid-season from another team. In the last few practices my run-times have nearly equalled Rafael's.'

Marco silently admitted the truth of her words. He might not sit on the pit wall for every single minute of a race—the engineer and aerodynamicist in him preferred the hard facts of the telemetry reports—but he knew Sasha's race times to the last fraction.

He also knew racing was more than just the right car in the right hands. 'Yes, but you're yet to perform under the pressure of a Saturday practice, a pole position shoot-out and a race on Sunday. I'd rather have a driver with actual race experience.'

Russell fidgeted and cleared his throat. 'I agree, Marco. I think Alan might be a better option—'

'I've consistently surpassed Alan's track times,' she said of the team's second driver. 'Luke will confirm it.'

Luke's half-hearted shrug made Marco frown.

'Is there a problem?'

The other man cleared his throat. 'Not a problem, exactly, but I'm not sure how the team will react to…you know…'

'No, I don't know. If you have something to say, then say it.'

'He means how the team will react to a woman lead driver,' Sasha stated baldly.

Recalling her accusation of sexism, he felt a flash of anger swell through him. He knew the views of others when it came to employing women as drivers. The pathetically few women racers attested to the fact that it was a predominantly male sport, but he believed talent was talent, regardless of the gender that wielded it.

The thought that key members in his team didn't share his belief riled him.

He rose. 'That will be all, gentlemen.'

Russell's surprise was clear. 'Do you need some time to make the decision?'

His gaze stayed on Sasha. Her chest had risen in a sharp intake of breath. Again he had to force himself not to glance down at her breasts. The effort it took not to look displeased him immensely.

'I've requested figures from my lawyers by morning. I'll let you know my decision.'

His butler led them out.

'Mr de Cervantes—' Sasha started.

He held up a hand. 'Let me make one thing clear. I didn't

refuse you a drive because of your gender. Merely because of your disruptive influence within my team.'

Her eyes widened, then she nodded. 'Okay. But I want to—'

'I need to return to my brother's bedside. You'll also find out my decision tomorrow.' He turned to leave.

'Please. I…need this.'

The raw, fervent emotion in her voice stopped him from leaving the room. Returning to her side, he stared down at her bent head. Her hands were clenched tighter. A swathe of pure black hair had slipped its knot and half covered her face. His fingers itched to catch it back, smooth it behind her ear so he could see her expression.

Most of all, he wanted her to look at him.

'Why? Why is this so important to you?' he asked.

'I…I made a promise.' Her voice was barely above a whisper.

Marco frowned. 'A promise? To whom?'

She inhaled, and before his eyes she gathered herself in. Her spine straightened, and her shoulders snapped back until her whole body became poised, almost regal. Then her eyes slowly rose to his.

The steely determination in their depths compelled his attention. His blood heated, rushing through his veins in a way that made his body clench in denial. Yet he couldn't look away.

Her gaze dropped. Marco bit back the urge to order her to look at him.

'It doesn't matter. All you need to know is if you give me a chance I'll hand you the Constructors' Championship.'

Sasha heard the low buzzing and cursed into her pillow. How the blazes had a wasp got into her room?

And since when did wasps make such a racket?

Groaning, she rolled over and tried to burrow into a better position. Sleep had been an elusive beast. She'd spent the night alternately pacing the floor and running through various arguments in her head about how she would convince Marco to keep her on the team. In the end exhaustion had won out.

Now she'd been woken by—

Her phone! With a yelp, she shoved off the covers and stumbled blindly for the satchel she'd discarded on the floor.

'Huhn?'

'Do I take it by that unladylike grunt that I've disturbed your sleep?' Marco de Cervantes's voice rumbled down the line.

'Not at all,' she lied. 'What time is it?' She furiously rubbed her eyes. She'd never been a morning person.

Taut silence, then, 'It's nine-thirty.'

'What? *Damn.*' She'd slept through her alarm. Again.

Could anyone blame her, though? Being part of Team Espiritu meant staying in excellent accommodation, but this time management had excelled itself—the two thousand thread-count cotton sheets, handmade robes, the hot tub, lotions and potions, the finest technology and her personal maid on tap were just the beginnings of the absurd luxury that made the crew of Marco's team the envy of the circuit. But her four-poster bed and its mattress—dear Lord, the made-by-angels mattress—was the reason—

'Do you have somewhere else to be, Miss Fleming?'

'Yes. I have a plane to catch back to London at eleven.' Thankfully she didn't have a lot of things to pack, having put her restless energy to good use last night. And the airport was only ten minutes away. Still, she was cutting it fine.

'You might wish to revise that plan.'

She froze, refusing to acknowledge the thin vein of hope taking root deep within her. 'And why would I need to do that?'

'I have a proposition for you. Open your door.'

'What?'

'Open your door. I need to look into your eyes when I outline my plan so there can be no doubt on either part.'

'You're *here*?' Her eyes darted to her door, as if she could see his impressive body outlined through the solid wood.

'I'm here. But I'll soon be a figment of your imagination if you don't open your door.'

Sasha glanced down at herself. No way was she opening the door to Marco de Cervantes wearing a vampire T-shirt that declared *'Bite Me'* in blood-red. And she didn't even want to think of the state of her hair.

'I… Can you give me two minutes?' If she could get in and out of a race suit in ninety seconds, she sure as hell could make herself presentable in a fraction of that time.

'You have five seconds. Then I move on to my next call.'

'No. Wait!' Keeping the phone glued to her ear, she rushed to the door. Pulling it open, she stuck her head out, trying her best to shield the rest of her body from full view.

And there he stood. Unlike the casual clothes of yesterday, Marco was dressed in a bespoke suit, his impressive shoulders even more imposing underneath the slate-grey jacket, blue shirt and pinstriped tie, his long legs planted in battle stance. His hair was combed neatly, unlike the unruly, sexy mess it'd been yesterday. The strong desire to see it messy again had her pulling back a fraction.

Eyes locked on hers, he lowered his phone. 'Invite me in.'

'Why? Are you a vampire?' she shot back, then swallowed a groan.

Frown lines creased his brow. *'Excuse me?* Are you high?'

Sasha silently cursed her morning brain. 'Hah—I wish. Oh, never mind. I'm…I'm not really dressed to receive guests, but I didn't want you to leave, so unless you want to extend that five-second ultimatum this will have to do.'

His frown deepened. 'Are you in the habit of answering your hotel door naked?'

Heat crawled up her neck and stung her face. 'Of course not. I'm not naked.'

'Prove it' came the soft challenge.

'Fine. See?' Belatedly she wondered at her sanity as she stepped into his view and felt the dark, intense force of Marco's gaze as it travelled over her.

When his eyes returned to hers, the breath snagged in her lungs. His hazel eyes had darkened to burnt gold with dark green flecks; the clench of his jaw was even more pronounced. He seemed to be straining against an emotion that was more than a little bit frightening.

She stepped back. He followed her in and shut the door. The luxury hotel suite that had seemed so vast, so over the top, closed in on her. She took another step back. He followed, eyes locked on her.

Her phone fell from her fingers, thankfully cushioned by the shag-pile carpet. Mouth dry, she kept backing up. He kept following.

'I make it a point not to credit rumours, but it seems in this instance the rumours are true, Sasha Fleming.'

The way he said her name—slowly, with a hint of Latin intonation—made goosebumps rise on her flesh. Her nipples peaked and a sensation she recognised to her horror as desire raked through her abdomen, sending delicious darts of liquid heat to the apex of her thighs.

'What exactly do you think is true about me?'

'Sex is your weapon of choice,' he breathed, his eyes lingering on the telltale nubs beneath her T-shirt. 'The only trouble is you wield it so unsubtly.'

'I beg your pardon?' she squeaked as the backs of her legs touched the side of the bed. 'Did you just say—?'

'You need to learn to finesse your art.'

'What in heaven's name are you blathering about? Are you sure *you're* not the one who's high?' she flung back.

'No man likes to be bludgeoned over the head with sex. No matter how…enticing the package.'

'You're either loopy or you've got me confused with someone else. I don't bludgeon and I don't entice.'

He kept coming.

She leaned back on the bed and felt the hem of her shirt riding up her thighs. 'For goodness' sake, stop!'

He stopped, but his gaze didn't. It continued its destructive course over her, leaving no part of her untouched, until Sasha felt sure she was about to combust from the heat of it.

Desperate, she let her tongue dart out to lick her lips. 'Look… Derek—I presume that's where you got your little morsel from— said a lot of unsavoury things about me when we broke up. But I'm not who…whatever you think I am.'

'Even though I can see the evidence for myself?' he rasped in a low voice.

She scrambled over the side of the bed and grabbed the robe she'd dropped on the floor last night. With shaking fingers, and a mind scrambling to keep pace with the bizarre turn of the conversation, she pulled the lapels over her traitorous body.

Having pursued her profession in fast cars financed by billionaires with unlimited funds, Sasha knew there was a brand of women who found the whole X1 Premier Racing world a huge turn-on: women who used their sexuality to pursue racers with a single-mindedness that bordered on the obsessive.

She'd never considered for a second that she would ever be bracketed with them—especially by the wealthiest, most sought-after billionaire of them all. The idea would have been laughable if the sting of Derek's betrayal still didn't have the ability to hurt.

'Well, whatever it is you *think* you see, there's no truth to the rumour. Now, can we please get back to the reason you came here in the first place?'

Her words seemed to rouse him from whatever dark, edgy place he'd been in. He looked up from her thighs, slowly exhaled, and looked around the room, taking in the rumpled bed and the contents of her satchel strewn on the floor.

When he paced to the window and drew back the curtain she took the opportunity to tie the robe tighter around her, hoping it would dispel the electricity zinging around her body.

He turned after a minute, his face devoid of expression. 'I've decided not to recruit a new driver. Doing so mid-season is not financially viable. Besides, they all have contracts and sponsorship commitments to fulfil.'

Hope grew so powerful it weakened her legs. Sinking down onto the side of the bed, she swallowed. 'So, does that mean I have the seat for the rest of the season?'

He shoved his hands into his pockets, his gaze fixed squarely on her. 'You'll sign an agreement promising to honour every commitment the team holds you to. Half of the sponsors have agreed to let you fulfil Rafael's commitments.'

He hadn't given a definite *yes*, but Sasha's heartbeat thundered nonetheless. 'And the other half?'

'With nowhere to go, they'll come round. My people are working on them.'

Unable to stem the flood of emotion rising inside, she pried her gaze from his and stared down at her trembling hands. She struggled to breathe.

Finally. The chance to wipe the slate clean. To earn the respect that had been ruthlessly denied her and so callously wrenched from her father. Finally the Fleming name would be spoken of with esteem and not disdain. Jack Fleming would be allowed to rest in peace, his legacy nothing to be ashamed of any more.

'I…thank you,' she murmured.

'You haven't heard the conditions attached to your drive.'

She shook her head, careless of the hair flying about her face as euphoria frothed inside her. 'I agree. Whatever it is, I agree.' She wouldn't let this opportunity slip her by. She intended to grab it with both hands. To prove to anyone who'd dared to naysay that they'd been wrong.

His eyes narrowed. 'Yesterday you promised to give *anything* not to have Rafael in hospital. Today you're agreeing to conditions you haven't even heard. Are you always this carefree with your consent? Perhaps I need to rethink making you lead driver. I shudder to think what such rashness could cost me on the race track.'

'I… Fine—name your conditions.'

He quirked a mocking brow. '*Gracias*. Aside from the other commitments, there are two that I'm particularly interested in. Team Espiritu *must* win the Constructors' Championship. We're eighty points ahead of the next championship challenger. I expect those points only to go up. Understood?'

A smile lit up her face. 'Absolutely. I intend to wipe the floor with them.'

'The second condition—'

'Wait. I have a condition of my own.'

His lips twisted. '*Déjà vu* overwhelms me. I suppose I shouldn't be surprised.'

Sasha ignored him, the need to voice a wish so long denied making her words trip from her lips with a life of their own. 'If...*when* I secure you the Constructors' Championship, I want my contract with Team Espiritu to be extended for another year.'

When his eyes narrowed further, she rushed to speak again.

'You can write it into my contract that I'll be judged based on my performance during the next three months. If we win the Constructors' you'll hire me for another year.'

'Winning a Drivers' Championship means that much to you?'

His curiously flat tone drew her gaze, but his expression remained inscrutable. Her heart hammered with the force of her deepest yearning. 'Yes, it does.'

His eyelids descended, veiling his gaze. The tension in the room increased until she could cut the atmosphere with a butter knife. But when he looked back up there was nothing but cool, impersonal regard.

'Very well. Win the Constructors' Championship and I'll extend your contract for another year.'

She couldn't believe he'd agreed so readily. 'Wow, that was easy.'

'Perhaps it's because I don't believe in talking every subject to death. My time is precious.'

'Yes, of course...'

'As I was saying, before you interrupted, my second condition is more important, Miss Fleming, so listen carefully. You'll have no personal contact with any male member of the team; you will go nowhere near my brother. Any hint of a non-professional relationship with another driver or anyone within the sport, for that matter, will mean instant dismissal. And I'll personally make it my mission to ensure you never drive another racing car. Do we understand each other?'

CHAPTER FOUR

'IF YOU'VE finished your breakfast, I'll take you on the tour of the race track.'

Sasha looked up from her almost empty plate of scrambled eggs and ham to find Marco lounging in the doorway that connected the vast living room to the sun-drenched terrace of *Casa de Leon*.

She'd been here three days, and she still couldn't get her head round the sheer vastness of the de Cervantes estate. Navigating her way around the huge, rambling two-storey villa without getting lost had taken two full days.

With its white stucco walls, dark red slate roofs and large cathedral-like windows, *Casa de Leon* was an architect's dream. The high exposed beams, sweeping staircases and intricately designed marble floors wouldn't have been out of place in a palace. Every piece of furniture, painting and drape looked as if it cost a fortune. Even the air inside the villa smelled different, tinged with a special rarefied, luxurious quality that made her breath catch.

Outside, an endless green vista, broken only by perfectly manicured gardens, stretched as far as the eye could see... It was no wonder the countless villa staff travelled around in golf buggies.

Realising Marco was waiting for an answer, she nodded, drawing her gaze from the long, muscular legs encased in dark grey trousers. 'Sure. I'll just finish my coffee. Aren't you having anything?' She indicated the mouth-watering spread of seasonal fruit, pastries and ham slices on the table.

Disengaging himself from the doorway, he came towards her, powerfully sleek and oozing arrogant masculinity. 'I'll have a coffee, too.'

When he sat and made no move to pour it himself, she raised an eyebrow. 'Yes, boss. Three bags full, boss?'

His hazel eyes gleamed and Sasha had the distinct feeling he was amused, although not a smile cracked his lips. In fact he looked decidedly strained. Which wasn't surprising under the circumstances, she reminded herself.

Feeling the mutiny give way, she poured him a cup. 'Black?'

'*Sí*. Two sugars.'

She looked up, surprised. 'Funny, I wouldn't have pegged you for the two-sugars type.'

'And how *would* you have pegged me?'

'Black, straight up, drunk boiling hot without a wince.'

'Because my insides are made of tar and my soul is black as night?' he mocked.

She shrugged. 'Hey, you said it.' She added sugar and passed it over.

'*Gracias.*' He picked up a silver spoon and stirred his drink, the tiny utensil looking very delicate in his hand.

Sasha found herself following the movement, her gaze tracing the short dark hairs on the back of his hand. Suddenly her mouth dried, and her stomach performed that stupid flip again. Wrenching her gaze from the hypnotic motion, she picked up her cup with a decidedly unsteady hand.

'How are you settling in?' he asked.

'Do you really want to know?'

The speed with which Marco had whisked her from Budapest to Spain after she'd signed the contract had made her head spin. Of course his luxury private jet—which he'd piloted himself—had negated the tedium of long airport waits and might have had something to do with it. They'd flown to Barcelona, then transferred by helicopter to his estate in Leon.

He took another sip. 'I wouldn't have asked otherwise. You should know by now that I never say anything I don't mean.'

Now she felt surly. Her suite was the last word in luxury, complete with four-poster bed, half a dozen fluffy pillows and a deep-sunken marble bath to die for. Just across from where she sat, past the giant-sized terracotta potted plants and a bar-becue area, an Olympic-sized swimming pool sparkled azure in the dappling morning light. She'd already sampled its soothing comfort, along with the sports gym equipped with everything she needed to keep her exercise regime on track. In reality, she wanted for nothing.

And yet…

'It's fine. I have everything I need. Thank you,' she tagged on waspishly. Then, wisely moving on before she ventured into full-blown snark, she asked, 'How is Rafael?'

Marco's gaze cooled.

Sasha sighed. 'I agreed to stay away from him. I didn't agree to stop caring about him.'

'The move from Budapest went fine. He's now in the care of the best Spanish doctors in Barcelona.'

'Since you'll probably bite my head off if I ask you to send him my best, I'll move on. How far away is the race track?'

'Three miles south.' Lifting his cup, he drained it.

'Exactly how big is this place?'

When Marco had announced he was bringing a skeleton team to Spain to help her train for her debut at the end of August, she'd mistakenly thought she would be spending most of her time in a race simulator. The half an hour it'd taken to travel from Marco's landing strip to his villa had given her an inkling of how immense his estate was.

His gaze pinned on her, he picked up an orange and skilfully peeled it. 'All around? About twenty-five square miles.'

'And you and Rafael own all of it?'

'Sí.' He popped a segment into his mouth.

Sasha carefully set her cup down, her senses tingling with warning. That soft *sí* had held a slight edge to it that made her wary. His next words confirmed her wariness.

'Just think, if only you'd said yes all this would've been yours.'

She didn't need to ask what he meant. Affecting a light tone, she toyed with the delicate handle of her expensive bone china cup. 'Gee, I don't know. The race track would've been handy, but what the hell would I do with the rest of the... What else is there, anyway?'

His gaze was deceptively lazy—deceptive because she could feel the charged animosity rising from him.

'There's a fully functioning vineyard and winery. And the stables house some of the best Andalucian thoroughbreds in Spain. There's also an exclusive by-invitation-only resort and spa on the other side of the estate.'

'Well, there you have it, then. My palate is atrociously common—not to mention that if I drink more than one glass of wine I get a raging headache. As for thoroughbreds—I couldn't tell you which end of the horse to climb if you put me next to one. So, really, you're way better off without me in your family. The spa sounds nice, though. A girl could always do with a foot rub after a hard day's work—although I have a feeling the amount of grease I tend to get under my nails would frighten your resort staff.'

A tiny tic appeared at his temple. 'Are you always this facetious, or do you practice?'

'Normally I keep it well hidden. I only show off when asked really, really nicely,' she flung back. Then she stood. 'From the unfortunate downturn of this conversation, I take it the offer of a tour is now off the table?' She tilted her chin, determined not to reveal how deep his barbs had stung.

'As much as I'm tempted to reward your petulance with time on the naughty step, that will only prove counterproductive.' Wiping his hands on a napkin, he rose to tower over her. 'You're here to train. Familiarising yourself with the race track is part of that training. I'll leave the naughty step for another time.'

Wisely deciding to leave the mention of the naughty step alone, Sasha relaxed her grip on the back of the chair. 'Thank you.'

Sasha followed him into the villa, staunchly maintaining her silence. But not talking didn't equate to not looking, and, damn it, she couldn't help but be intensely aware of the man beside her. His smell assailed her nostrils—that sharp tang of citrus coupled with the subtle undertones of musk that shifted as it flowed over his warmth.

Against the strong musculature of his torso his white polo shirt lovingly followed the superb lines of a deep chest and powerful shoulders. All that magnificence tapered down to a trim waist that knew not an ounce of fat.

Judging by his top-notch physicality, she wasn't surprised Marco had been the perfect championship-winning driver ten years ago.

'Why did you give up racing? You resigned so abruptly, and yet it's obvious you recovered fully after your crash.'

She saw his shoulders tense before he rounded on her. The icy, forbidding look in his eyes made her bite her lip.

Nice one, Sasha.

'That is not a subject up for discussion, Miss Fleming. And before you take it into your head to go prying I caution you against it. Understood?'

He barely waited for her nod before he wrenched open the front door.

Outside, two golf buggies sat side by side at the bottom of the steps. She headed towards the nearest one.

'Where are you going?' he bit out.

She stopped. 'Oh, I thought we were going by road.'

He nodded to the helipad, where a black and red chopper sat gleaming in the morning sun. 'We're touring by helicopter.'

It was a spectacularly beautiful machine—the latest in a long line of beautiful aircraft.

'Any chance you'll let me fly it?'

He flashed a mirthless grin at her. 'I don't see any pigs flying, do you?'

'Wow, this is incredible! How long have you had this race track?'

Marco glanced up from the helicopter controls, then immediately wished he hadn't. It was bad enough hearing her excitement piped directly into his headphones. The visual effects were even more disturbing.

When he'd offered her an aerial tour of the race track he hadn't taken into account how she was dressed. In most respects, her white shorts could be described as sensible—almost boyish. He'd been out with women who wore far less on a regular basis. Her light green shirt was also plain to the point of being utilitarian.

All the same, Marco found the combination of her excitement and her proximity...*aggravating.* Even more aggravating were the flashbacks he kept having of her leaning back on the bed in her hotel room, her T-shirt riding up to reveal skin so tempting it had knocked his breath clean out of his lungs...

Her naked ambition and her sheer drive to succeed were living things that charged the air around her. Marco knew only too well the high cost of blind ambition, and yet knowing the depths of Sasha Fleming's ambition and what she would do to achieve her goals didn't stop him from imagining how it would have felt to lift her T-shirt higher...just a fraction...

He was also more than a little puzzled that she'd made no attempt to gain his attention since that episode in her room. Women flaunted themselves at him at every opportunity—used every excuse in the book to garner his interest. Some even resorted to...*unconventional* means. Most of the time he was happy to direct them Rafael's way. He'd long outgrown the paddock bunny phase; had outgrown it even before Angelique, the most calculating of them all, had stepped into his orbit and turned his world upside down.

Marco sobered, seething at himself for the memories he suddenly couldn't seem to dispel so easily. Focusing on the controls, he banked the chopper and followed the straights and curves of the race track hundreds of metres below.

'I built it ten years ago,' he clipped out in answer to her question.

'After you retired?' she asked, surprised.

'No. Just before.' His harsh response had the desired effect of shutting her up, but when he glanced at her again, he noted the spark of speculation in her eyes. Before he could think about why he was doing so, he found himself elaborating. 'I thought I'd be spending more time here.' He'd woven foolish dreams about what his life would be like, how perfect everything had seemed. He'd had the perfect car; the perfect woman.

'What happened?'

The crushing pain of remembrance tightened around his chest. 'I crashed.'

She gave a sad little understanding nod that made him want to growl at her. What did she know? She was as conniving as they came.

Forcing his anger under control, he flew over the track towards the mid-point hill.

Sasha pointed to six golf buggies carrying mechanics who hopped out at various points of the track. 'What are they doing?'

'The track hasn't been used for a while. They're conducting last-minute checks on the moveable parts to make sure they're secure.'

'I can't believe this track can be reshaped to simulate other tracks around the circuit. I can't wait to have a go!'

Excitement tinged her voice and Marco couldn't help glancing over at her. Her eyes were alight with a smile that seemed to glow from within. His hands tightened around the controls.

'The track was built before simulators became truly effective. One concrete track would've served only to make a driver expert at a particular track, so I designed an interchangeable track. The other advantage is experience gained in driving on tarmac, or as close to tarmac—as you can get. Wet or dry conditions can make or break a race. This way the driver gets to practise on both with the right tyres. Electronic simulators and wind tunnels have their places, but so does this track.'

The helicopter crested another small hill and cold sweat broke out over his skin. Several feet to the side of the track a mound of whitewashed stones had been piled high in a makeshift monument. Marco's hand tightened on the lever and deftly swerved the aircraft away from the landmark he had no wish to see up close.

'Trust me, I'm not complaining. It's a great idea. I'm just surprised other teams haven't copied the idea. Or sold their first-born sons to use your track.'

'Offers have been made in the past.'

'And?'

He shrugged. 'I occasionally allow them to use the track I designed. But for the whole package to come together they also need the car I designed.'

A small laugh burst from her lips. The sound was so unexpectedly pleasing he momentarily lost his train of thought, and missed her reply.

'What did you say?'

'I said that's a clever strategy—considering you own the team you design for, and the only other way anyone can get their hands on a Marco de Cervantes design is by shelling out…how much does the *Cervantes Conquistador* cost? Two million?'

'Three.'

She whistled—another unexpected sound that charged through his bloodstream, making him even more on edge than he'd been a handful of seconds ago.

She leaned forward into his eyeline. He'd been wrong about the shirt being functional. Her pert breasts pressed against the cotton material, her hands on her thighs as she peered down.

Marco swallowed, the hot stirrings in his abdomen increasing to uncomfortable proportions. Ruthlessly he pushed them away.

Sasha Fleming was bad news, he reminded himself.

Rafael had got involved with her to his severe detriment. Marco had no intention of following down the same road. His only interest in her was to make sure she delivered the Constructors' Championship. Now he knew what she really wanted—the Drivers' Championship—he had her completely at his mercy.

Control re-established, he brought the helicopter in to land, and yanked off his headphones. Sasha jumped down without his help and Marco caught the puzzled look she flashed him. Ignoring it, he strode towards Luke Green. His chief engineer had travelled ahead to supervise the initial training arrangements.

Sasha drew closer and her scent reached his nostrils. Marco's insides clenched in rejection even as he breathed her in. His awareness of her was becoming intolerable. Even her voice as she greeted Luke bit into his psyche.

'Is everything in order?' he asked.

Luke nodded. 'We're just about to offload the engine. The mechanics will check it over and make sure it hasn't been damaged during the flight.'

'It takes three hours max to assemble the car, so it should be ready for me to test this afternoon, shouldn't it?' Sasha asked, her attention so intent on the tarpaulin-covered engine Marco almost enquired if she yearned to caress it.

'No. You'll begin training tomorrow morning,' he all but growled.

Her head snapped towards him, her expression crestfallen. 'Oh, but if the car's here...'

'The mechanics have been working on getting things ready since dawn. This engine hasn't been used since last December. It'll have to go through rigorous testing before it's race-ready. That'll take most of the day—at least until sundown.'

He turned back to Luke. 'I want to see hourly engine readouts and a final telemetry report when you're done testing.'

'Sure thing, boss.'

Grabbing Sasha's arm, he steered her away from the garage. Several eyes followed them, but he didn't care. He was nothing like his brother. He had no intention of ever making a fool of himself over a woman again.

Opening the passenger door to his Conquistador, he thrust her into the bucket seat. Rounding the hood, he slid behind the wheel.

'Why do I get the feeling you're angry with me?' she directed at him.

Marco slammed his door. 'It's not a feeling.'

The breath she blew up disturbed the thick swathe of hair slanting over her forehead. 'What did I do?' she demanded.

He faced her and found her stunning eyes snapping fire at him. The blue of her gaze was so intense, so vivid, he wanted to keep staring at her for ever. The uncomfortable erotic heat he'd felt in her Budapest hotel room, when she'd strutted into view wearing that damned T-shirt that boldly announced *'Bite Me'*, rose again.

For days he'd been fighting that stupid recurring memory that strayed into his thoughts at the most inconvenient times.

Even here in Leon, where much more disturbing memories impinged everywhere he looked, he couldn't erase from his mind the sight of those long, coltish legs and the thought of how they would feel around his waist.

Nor could he ignore the evidence of Sasha's hard work and dedication to her career. Every night since her arrival in Spain he'd found her poring over telemetry reports or watching footage of past races, fully immersed in pursuing the only thing she cared about.

The only thing she cared about...

Grabbing the steering wheel, he forced himself to calm down. 'Marco?'

When had he given her permission to use his first name? Come to think of it, when had he started thinking of her as Sasha instead of Miss Fleming?

Dios, he was losing it.

With a wrench of his wrist the engine sprang to life, its throaty roar surprisingly soothing. Designing the Espiritu race cars had been an engineering challenge he'd relished. The *Cervantes Conquistador* had been a pure labour of love.

Momentarily he lost himself in the sounds of the engine, his mind picking up minute clicks and torsion controls. If he closed his eyes he would be able to imagine the aerodynamic flow of air over the chassis, visualise where each spark plug, each piston, nut and bolt was located.

But he didn't close his eyes. He kept his gaze fixed firmly ahead. His grip tightened around the wheel.

Her gaze stayed on him as he accelerated the green and black sports car out of the parking lot. The screech of tyres drew startled glances from the mechanics heading for the hangar. Marco didn't give a damn.

After a few minutes, when he felt sufficiently calm, he slowed down. 'It's not you.'

She didn't answer.

Shrugging, he indicated the rich forest surrounding them. 'It's this place.'

'This place? The race track or *Casa de Leon*?'

His jaw clenched as he tried in vain to stem the memories flooding him. 'This is where my mother died eight years ago.'

Her gasp echoed in the car. 'Oh, my God, I'm so sorry. I didn't know. You should've said something.'

He slowed down long enough to give her a hard look. 'It isn't common knowledge outside my family. I'd prefer it to remain that way.' He wasn't even sure why he'd told her. Whatever was causing him to act so out of character he needed to cauterise it.

She gave a swift nod. 'Of course. You can trust me.' Her colour rose slightly at her last words.

The irony wasn't lost on him. He only had himself to blame if she decided to spill her guts at the first opportunity. Flooring the accelerator, he sent the car surging forward as his *other* reason for wanting to escape the memories of this place rose.

Sasha remained silent until he pulled up in front of the villa. Then, lifting a hand, she tucked a strand of hair behind her ear. 'How did it happen?' she asked softly.

Releasing his clammy grip on the steering wheel, Marco flicked a glance at the villa door. He knew he'd find no respite within. If anything, the memories were more vivid inside. He didn't need to close his eyes to see his mother laughing at Rafael's shameless cajoling, her soft hazel eyes sparkling as she wiped her hands on a kitchen towel moments before rushing out of the villa.

'For his twenty-first birthday my father bought Rafael a Lamborghini. We celebrated at a nightclub in Barcelona. Afterwards I flew down here in the helicopter with my parents. Rafael chose to drive from Barcelona—five hours straight. He arrived just after breakfast, completely wired from partying. I tried to convince him to get some sleep, but he wanted to take my parents for a spin in the car.'

The familiar icy grip of pain tightened around his chest.

'Rafael was my mother's golden boy. He could do no wrong. So of course she agreed.' Marco felt some of the pain seep out and tried to contain it. 'My father insisted later it was the sun that got in Rafael's eyes as he turned the curve, but one eyewitness confirmed he took the corner too fast. I heard the crash from the garage.' Every excruciating second had felt like a lifetime as he sped towards the scene. 'By the time the air ambulance came my mother was gone.'

'Oh, Marco, *no!*'

Sasha's voice was a soft, soothing sound. The ache inside abated, but it didn't disappear. It never would. He'd lost his mother before he'd ever had the chance to make up for what he'd put her through.

'I should've stopped him—should've insisted he get some sleep before taking the car out again.'

'You couldn't have known.'

He shook his head. 'But I should have. Except when it comes to Rafael everyone seems to develop a blind spot. Including me.'

Vaguely, Marco wondered why he was spilling his guts. To Sasha Fleming, of all people. With a forceful wrench on the door, he stepped out of the car.

She scrambled out too. 'And your father? What happened to him?'

His fist tightened around the computerised car key. 'The accident severed his spine. He lost the use of his body from the neck down. He's confined to a wheelchair and will remain like that for the rest of his life.'

Sasha looked after Marco's disappearing figure, shocked by the astonishing revelation.

Now Marco's motives became clear. His overprotective attitude towards Rafael, his reaction to the crash, suddenly made sense. Watching his mother die on the race track *he'd* built had to be right up there with enduring a living hell every time he stepped foot on it.

So why did he do it?

Marco de Cervantes was an extraordinary engineer and aerodynamicist, who excelled in building astonishingly fast race cars, but he could easily have walked away and concentrated his design efforts on the equally successful range of exclusive sport cars favoured by Arab sheikhs and Russian oligarchs.

So what drove him to have anything to do with a world that surely held heart-wrenching memories?

She slowly climbed the stairs and entered the house, her mind whirling as she went into her suite to wash off the heat and sweat of the race track.

After showering, she put on dark jeans and a striped blue shirt. Pulling her hair into a neat twist, she secured it with a band and shoved her feet into pair of flat sandals.

She met Marco as she came down the stairs. The now familiar raking gaze sent another shiver of awareness scything through her. He stopped directly in front of her, his arresting face and piercing regard rendering her speechless for several seconds.

'Lunch won't be ready for a while, but if you want something light before then, Rosario can fix you something.'

The matronly housekeeper appeared in the sun-dappled hallway as if by magic, wiping her hands on a white apron.

'No, thanks. I'm not hungry.'

With a glance, he dismissed the housekeeper. His gaze returned to her, slowly tracing her face. When it rested on her mouth she struggled not to run her tongue over it, remembering how his eyes had darkened the last time she'd done that.

'I have a video call with Tom Brooks, my press liaison, in five minutes. Can I use your study?'

His eyes locked on hers. 'Why's he calling?'

'He wants to go over next month's sponsorship schedule. I can give you a final printout, if you like.'

She deliberately kept her voice light, non-combative. Something told her Marco de Cervantes was spoiling for a fight, and after his revelations she wasn't sure it was wise to engage him in one. Pain had a habit of eroding rational thought.

Being calmly informed by the doctor that she'd lost the baby she hadn't even been aware she was carrying had made her want to scream—loudly, endlessly until her throat gave out. She'd wanted to reach inside herself and rip her body apart for letting her down. In the end the only thing that had helped was getting back to the familiar—to her racing car. The pain had never left her, but the adrenaline of racing had eased her aching soul the way nothing else had been able to.

Looking into Marco's dark eyes, she caught a glimpse of his pain, but wisely withheld the offer of comfort on the tip of her tongue. After all, who was *she* to offer comfort when she hadn't quite come to terms with losing her baby herself?

Silently, she held his gaze.

For several seconds he stared back. Then he indicated his study. 'I'll set it up for you.'

She followed him into the room and drew to a stunned halt. The space was so irreverently, unmistakably male that her eyes widened. An old-style burgundy leather studded chair and footrest stood before the largest fireplace she'd ever seen, above which two centuries-old swords hung. The rest of the room was oak-panelled, with dusty books stretching from floor to ceiling. The scent of stale tobacco pipe smoke hung in the air. It wouldn't have been strange to see a shaggy-haired professor seated behind the massive desk that stood under the only window in the room. Compared to the contemporary, exceedingly luxurious comfort of the rest of the villa, this was a throwback to another century—save for the sleek computer on the desk.

Marco caught the look on her face and raised an eyebrow as he activated the large flat screen computer on the immense mahogany desk.

'Did your designer fall into a time warp when he got to this room?'

'This was my father's study—his personal space. He never allowed my mother to redesign it, no matter how much she tried.

He hasn't been in here since she died, and I...I feel no need to change things.'

A well of sympathy rose inside Sasha for his pain. Casting a look around, she stopped, barely suppressing a gasp. 'Is that a stag's head on the wall?' she asked, eyeing the large animal head, complete with gnarled, menacing antlers.

'A bull stag, yes.'

She turned from the gruesome spectacle. 'There's a difference?'

The semblance of a smile whispered over his lips. Sasha found she couldn't tear her gaze away. In that split second she felt a wild, unfettered yearning to see that smile widen, to see his face light up in genuine amusement.

'The bull stag is the alpha of its herd. He calls the shots. And he gets his pick of the females.'

'Ah, I see. If you're going to display such a monstrosity on your wall, only the best will do?'

He slanted her a wry glance. 'That's the general thinking, yes.'

'Ugh.'

He caught her shudder and his smile widened.

Warmth exploded in her chest, encompassed her whole body and made her breathless. Sasha found she didn't care. The need to bask in the stunning warmth of his smile trumped the need for oxygen. Even when another voice intruded she couldn't look away.

When Tom's voice came again she roused herself with difficulty from the drugging race of her pulse, carefully skirted a coffee table festooned with piles of books, and approached the desk as the screen came to life.

'Hello? Can you hear me, Sasha?' Tom's voice held its usual touch of impatience, and his features were pinched.

Marco's smile disappeared.

Sasha mourned the loss of it and moved closer to the screen. 'I'm here, Tom.'

He huffed in response, then his eyes swung over her shoulder and widened.

'Sit down,' Marco said from behind her, pushing the massive chair towards her.

She sat. He reached over her shoulder and adjusted the screen. Then he remained behind her—a heavy, dominating presence.

Tom cleared his throat. 'Uh, I didn't know you'd be joining us, Mr de Cervantes.'

'A last-minute decision. Carry on,' Marco instructed.

'Um…okay…'

She'd never seen Tom flounder, and she bit the inside of her mouth to keep from smiling.

'Sasha, you have a Q&A on the team's website next Friday. I've e-mailed the questions to you. I'll need it back by Wednesday, to proofread and get it approved by the lawyers. On Friday night you have the Children of Bravery awards in London. Tuesday is the Strut footwear shoot, followed by the Linear Watches shoot in Barcelona. On Sun— Is there a problem?' he asked testily when she shook her head.

'That's not going to work. I can't take all that time off just for sponsorship events.'

'This is the schedule I've planned. You'll have to deal with it.'

'Seriously, I think it makes more sense to group everything together and get it done in the shortest possible time—'

'*I'm* in charge of your schedule. Let *me* work out what makes sense.'

'Miss Fleming is right.' Marco's deep voice sounded from behind her shoulder. 'You have several events spaced out over the period of a week. That's a lot of time wasted travelling. Do you not agree?'

'But the sponsors—'

'The sponsors need to work around her schedule, not the other way round. They can have Thursday to Saturday next week. Otherwise they'll have to wait until the end of the month. Miss Fleming gets Sundays off. Your job is to manage her time properly. Make it happen.'

Marco reached past Sasha and disconnected the link. Although it was a rare treat to see Tom get his comeuppance, a large part of her tightened with irritation.

'I'm perfectly capable of arranging my own schedule, thank you very much.'

'It didn't seem that way.'

'Only because you didn't give me half a chance.' She craned her neck to gaze up at him, feeling at a severe disadvantage.

His head went back as he glared down his arrogant nose at her. 'I didn't like the way he spoke to you,' he declared.

Her heart lurched, then swung into a dive as a wave of warmth oozed through her. Sasha berated herself for the foolish feeling, but as much as she tried to push it away it grew stronger.

Despite the alien feeling zinging through her, she tried for a casual shrug. 'I don't think he likes me very much.'

A frown creased his forehead. 'Why not?'

Her bitter laugh escaped before she could curb it. Rising, she padded several steps away, breathing easier. 'Probably for the same reasons you don't. He doesn't think I have any business being a racing driver. He believes I've made him a laughing stock by association.'

'Because of your gender or because of your past indiscretions?'

'According to you they're one and the same, aren't they?' she retorted.

The hands gripping the back of the chair tightened. 'I told you in Budapest your gender had nothing to do with my decision to fire you. Your talent as a full-time racing driver is yet to be seen. Prove yourself as the talented racing driver you claim to be and you'll earn your seat. Until then I reserve my judgement.'

'You reserve your judgement professionally, but you're judge, jury and executioner when it comes to my personal life?'

A cold gleam had entered his eyes, but even that didn't stop her from staring into those hypnotising depths.

'We agreed that you will have *no* personal life until your contract ends, did we not? You wouldn't be thinking of reneging on that agreement so soon, would you?'

Sasha just stopped herself from telling him she already had no personal life. That she hadn't had one since Derek's lies and the loss of her baby had put her through the wringer. Rafael had been her one and only friend until that had headed south.

'Sasha.'

The warning in the way he said her name sent a shiver dancing down her spine. She glanced up at him and bit back a gasp.

When had he drawn so close? Within his eyes she could see the flecks of green that spiked from his irises. And the lashes that framed them were long, silky. Beautiful. He had beautiful eyes. Eyes that drew her in, wove spells around her. Tugged at emotions buried deep within her...

Eyes that were steadily narrowing, demanding an answer.

She sucked in a breath, her brain turning fuzzy again when his scent—lemony, with a large dose of man—hit her nostrils. 'No, Marco. No personal life. Not even a Labradoodle to cuddle when I'm lonely.'

A frown deepened. 'A what?'

'It's a dog. A cross between a Labrador and a poodle. I used to have one when I was little. But it died.'

'Pets have no place on the racing circuit.'

She glared at him. 'I wasn't planning on bringing one to work. Anyway, it's a moot point, since my schedule isn't conducive to having one. I detest part-time pet owners.'

Her phone buzzed in her back pocket. She pulled it out and activated it. Seeing the promised e-mail from Tom, she turned to leave.

'Where are you going?' he demanded.

She faked a smile to hide the disturbing emotions roiling through her body. 'Oh, I thought the inquisition was over. Only Tom has sent the Q&A and I want to get it done so I don't take up valuable race testing time.'

Her snarky tone didn't go unmissed. His jaw clenched as he sauntered over to her. She held her breath, forcing herself not to move back.

'The inquisition is over for now. But I reserve the right to pursue it at a later date.'

'And *I* reserve the right not to participate in your little witch hunt. I read the small print and signed on the dotted line. I know exactly what's expected of me and I intend to honour our agreement. You can either let me get on with it, or you can impede me and cause us both a lot of grief. Your choice.'

She sailed out of the room, head held high. Just before the door swung shut Sasha suspected she heard a very low, very frustrated growl emitted by a very different bull stag from the one hanging on the wall.

Her smile widened as she punched the air.

Marco didn't come back for dinner. Even after Rosario told her he'd gone to his office in Barcelona Sasha caught herself looking towards the door, half expecting him to stride through it at any second.

Luke had dropped off the engine testing results, which she'd pored over half a dozen times in between listening out for the sound of the helicopter.

Catching herself doing so for the umpteenth time, she shoved away from the table, ran upstairs to her suite and changed into her gym clothes.

Letting herself out of the side entrance, she skirted the pool and jogged along the lamplit path bordering the extensive gardens. Fragrant bougainvillaea and amaranth scented the evening air. She breathed in deeply and increased her pace until she spotted the floodlights of the race track in the distance. Excitement fizzed through her veins.

A few hours from now she'd start her journey to clear her father's name. To prove to the world that the Fleming name was not dirt, as so many people claimed.

Fresh waves of sadness and anger buffeted her as she thought of her father. How his brilliant career had crumbled to dust in just a few short weeks, his hard work and sterling dedication to his team wiped away by vicious lies.

The pain of watching him spiral into depression had been excruciating. In the end even his pride in her hadn't been enough...

Whirling away from her thoughts, and literally from the path, she jogged the rest of the way to the sports facility half a mile

away and spent the next hour punishing herself through a stren-
uous routine that would have made Charlie, her physio, proud.

Leaving the gym, Sasha wandered aimlessly, deliberately
emptying her mind of sad memories. It wasn't until she nearly
stumbled into a wall that she realised she stood in front of a
single-storey building. Shrouded in darkness, it sat about half
a mile away from the house, at the far end of the driveway that
led past the villa.

About to enter, she jumped as the trill of her phone rang
through the silent night.

Hurriedly, she fished it out, but it went silent before she could
answer it. Frowning, she returned it to her pocket, then rubbed
her hands down her arms when the cooling breeze whispered
over her skin.

Casting another glance at the dark building, she retraced her
steps back to the villa. Her footsteps echoed on the marble floors.

'Where the hell have you been?'

Marco's voice was amplified in the semi-darkness, drawing
her to a startled halt. He stood half hidden behind one of the
numerous pillars in the vast hallway.

'I went to the gym, then went for a walk.'

His huge frame loomed larger as he came towards her. 'The
next time you decide to leave the house for a long stretch have
the courtesy to inform the staff of your whereabouts. That way
I won't have people combing the grounds for you.'

There was an odd inflection in his voice that made the hairs
on her neck stand up.

'Has something happened?' She stepped towards him, her
heart taking a dizzying dive when he didn't answer immediately. 'Marco?'

'*Sì*, something's happened,' he delivered in an odd, flat tone.

He stepped into the light and Sasha bit back a gasp at the
gaunt, tormented look on his face.

'Rafael… It's Rafael.'

CHAPTER FIVE

FEAR pierced through her heart but she refused to believe the worst. 'Is he...?' She swallowed and rephrased. 'How bad is it?'

Marco shoved his phone into his pocket and stalked down the hall towards the large formal sitting room. Set between two curved cast-iron balconies that overlooked the living room from the first-floor hallway, a beautifully carved, centuries-old drinks cabinet stood. Marco picked up a crystal decanter and raised an eyebrow. When she shook her head, he poured a healthy splash of cognac into a glass and threw it back in one quick swallow.

A fire had been lit in the two giant fireplaces in the room. Marco stood before one and raked a hand through his hair, throwing the dark locks into disarray. 'He's suffered another brain haemorrhage. They had to perform a minor operation to release the pressure. The doctors...' He shook his head, tightly suppressed emotion making his movements jerky. 'They can't do any more.'

'But the operation worked, didn't it?' She didn't know where the instinct to keep talking came from. All she knew was that Marco had come looking for her.

He sucked in a deep, shuddering breath. 'The bleeding has stopped, yes. And he's been put into an induced coma until the swelling goes down.'

She moved closer, her heart aching at the pain he tried to hide. 'That's good. It'll give him time to heal.'

His eyes grew bleaker. He looked around, as if searching for a distraction. 'I should be there,' he bit out. 'But the doctors think

I'm in their way.' He huffed. 'One even accused me of unreasonable behaviour, simply because I asked for a third opinion.'

The muttered imprecation that followed made Sasha bite her lip, feeling sorry for the unknown hapless doctor who'd dared clash with Marco.

She sucked in a breath as his gaze sharpened on her.

'Nothing to say?'

'He's your brother. You love him and want the best for him. That's why you've hired the best doctors to care for him. Maybe you need to leave them alone to do their jobs?' He looked set to bite her head off. 'And if he's in intensive care they probably need to keep his environment as sterile as possible. Surely you don't want anything to jeopardise his recovery?'

His scowl deepened and he looked away. 'I see you not only wear a psychologist's hat, you also dabble in diplomacy and being the voice of reason.'

Although Sasha did not enjoy his cynicism, she felt relieved that his voice was no longer racked with raw anguish. 'Yeah, that's me. Miss All-Things-To-All-People,' she joked.

Eyes that had moments ago held pain and anguish froze into solid, implacable ice. '*Sí*. Unfortunately that aspect of your nature hasn't worked out well for my brother, has it? Rafael needed you to be *one* thing to him. And you failed. *Miserably.*'

'I tried to talk some sense into him…'

Rafael hadn't taken it well when she'd pointed out the absurdity of his out-of-the-blue proposal. He'd stormed out of her hotel in Budapest the night before the race, and she'd never got the chance to talk to him before his accident.

Marco turned from the mantel and faced her. 'Don't tell me… You were *conveniently* unsuccessful?' he mocked.

'Because he didn't mean it.'

He pounced. 'Why would any man propose to a woman if he didn't mean it?'

When she didn't answer immediately, his scowl deepened. In the end, she said, 'Because of…other things he'd said.'

'What *other* things?' came the harsh rejoinder.

'*Private* things.' She wasn't about to deliver a blow-by-blow account. It wasn't her style. 'I thought he was reacting to his last break-up.'

He dismissed it with a wave of his hand. 'Rafael and Nadia broke up two months ago. Are you suggesting this was a re-bound?' Marco asked derisively. 'My brother's bounce-back rate is normally two *weeks*.'

Sasha frowned. 'Rafael's changed, Marco. To you he may have seemed like his normal wild, irreverent self. But—'

'Are you saying I don't know my own brother?' he demanded.

Slowly, Sasha shook her head. 'I'm just saying he may not have told you everything that was going on with him.'

Her breath caught at the derisive gleam that entered Marco's eyes.

'His text told me everything I needed to know. By refusing him, you gave him no choice but to come after you.'

'Of course I didn't!'

'Liar!'

'That's the second time you've called me a liar, Marco. For your own sake I hope there isn't a third. Or I'll take great plea-sure in slapping your face. Contract or no bloody contract. Whatever Rafael led you to believe, I *didn't* set out to ensnare him, or encourage him to fall for me—which I don't think he did, by the way. And I certainly didn't get him riled up enough to cause his accident. Whatever demons Rafael's been battling, they finally caught up with him. I'm tired of defending myself. I was just being his friend. Nothing else.'

Heart hammering, she took a seat on one of the extremely delicate-looking twin cream and gold striped sofas and pulled in a deep breath to steady the turbulent emotions coursing through her. Emotions she'd thought buckled down tight, but which Marco had seemed to spark to life so very easily.

'I find it hard to believe your actions have taken you down the same path twice in your life.'

'An unfortunate coincidence, but that's all it is. I have to live with it. However, I refuse to let you or anyone else label me some sort of *femme fatale*. All I want is to do my job.'

He sat down opposite her. When his gaze drifted down her

body, she struggled to fight the pinpricks of awareness he ignited along the way.

'You're a fighter. I admire that in you. There's also something about you…'

His pure Latin shrug held a wealth of expression that made her silently shake her head in awe.

'An unknown quality I find difficult to pinpoint. You're hardly a *femme fatale*, as you say. The uncaring way you dress, your brashness, all point to a lack of femininity—'

Pure feminine affront sparked a flame inside her. 'Thanks very much.'

'And normally I wouldn't even class you as Rafael's type. Yet on the night before his accident he was fiercely adamant that *you* were the one. Don't get me wrong, he's said that a few times in the past, but this time I knew something wasn't quite right.'

Despite his accusation, sympathy welled inside her. 'Did you two fight? Was that why you didn't come to Friday's practice?'

His nod held regret. 'I lost it when he asked for the ring.'

'You had it?'

He pinched the bridge of his nose and exhaled sharply. 'Yes. It belonged to our mother. She didn't leave it specifically to either of us; she just wanted the first one of us to get married to give it to his bride.' He shook his head once. 'I always knew it would go to Rafael since I never intend—' He stopped and drew in a breath. 'Rafael has claimed to be in love with many girls, but this was the first time he'd asked for the ring.'

'And you were angry because it was me?'

His jaw clenched. 'You could have waited until the race was over,' he accused, his voice rough with emotion.

'Marco—'

'He'd have had the August hiatus to get over you; he would've mended his broken heart in the usual way—ensconced on a yacht in St Tropez or chasing after some Hollywood starlet in LA. Either way, he would've arrived back on the circuit, smiled at you, and called you *pequeña* because he'd forgotten your name. Instead he's in a hospital bed, fighting for his life!'

'But I couldn't lie,' she shot back. 'He didn't want me—not

really. And I'm not on the market for a relationship. Certainly not after—' She pulled herself up short, but it was too late.

He stood and pulled her up, caught her shoulders in a firm grip. 'After what?'

'Not after my poor track record.'

'You mean what happened with your previous lover?'

She nodded reluctantly. 'Derek proposed just before I broke up with him. I'd known for some time that it wasn't working, but I convinced myself things would work out. When I declined his proposal a week later he accused me of leading him on. He said I was only refusing him because I wanted to sell myself to the highest bidder.'

Derek had repeated that assertion to every newspaper and team boss who would listen, and Sasha's career had almost ended because of it. She pushed the painful memories away.

'Rafael knew there was no way I'd get involved with him romantically.'

Marco's grip tightened, his gaze scouring her face as if he wanted to dig out the truth. Sasha forced herself to remain still, even though the touch of his hands on her branded her—so hot she wanted to scream with the incredibly forceful sensation of it.

'Do you know the last thing I said to him?' he rasped.

Her heart aching for him, she shook her head.

'I told him to stop messing around and grow up. That he was dishonouring our mother's memory by treating life like his own personal playground.' His eyelids veiled his gaze for several seconds and his jaw clenched, his emotions riding very near the surface. 'If anything happens to him—'

'It won't.'

Without thought, she placed her hand on his arm. Hard muscles flexed beneath her fingers. His eyes returned to her face, then dropped to her mouth. Sharp sensation shot through her belly, making her breath catch.

Sasha felt an electric current of awareness zing up her arm—a deeper manifestation of the intense awareness she felt whenever he was near. *Comfort*, she assured herself. *I'm offering him com-*

fort. That's all. This need to keep touching him was just a silly passing reaction.

'He'll wake up and he'll get better. You'll see.'

Face taut and eyes bleak, he slowly dropped his hands. 'I have to go,' he said.

She stepped back, her hands clenching into fists behind her back to conceal their trembling. 'You're returning to the hospital?'

He shook his head. 'I'm going to Madrid.'

Her belly clenched with the acute sense of loss. 'For how long?' she asked lightly.

'For however long it takes to reassure my father that his precious son isn't dying.'

The state-of-the-art crash helmet was no match for the baking North Spanish sun. Sasha sat in the cockpit of the Espiritu DSI, the car that had won Rafael the championship the year before. Eyes shut, she retraced the outline of the Belgian race track, anticipation straining through her.

Sweat trickled down her neck, despite the chute pumping cold air into the car. When she'd mentally completed a full circuit she opened her eyes.

They burned from lack of sleep, and she blinked several times to clear them. She'd been up since before dawn, the start of her restless night having oddly coincided with the moment Marco's helicopter had lifted off the helipad. For hours she'd lain tangled up in satin sheets, unable to dismiss the look on Marcus's anguished face from her mind. Or the heat of his touch on her body.

Firming her lips, she forcibly cleared her mind.

She wrapped fireproof gloved hands around the wheel and pictured the Double S bends at Eau Rouge, and the exact breaking point at La Source. Keeping her breathing steady, she finally achieved the mental calm she needed to block out the background noise of the mechanics and the garage. She emptied every thought from her mind, the turmoil of the past few days reduced to a small blot. She welcomed the relief of not having to dwell on anything except the promise of the fast track in front of her.

Her eyes remained steady on the mechanic's *STOP/GO* sign, her foot a whisper off the accelerator.

When the sign went up, she launched out of the garage onto the track. Adrenalin coursed through her veins as the powerful car vibrated beneath her. Braking into the first corner, she felt G-forces wrench her head to the left and smiled. This battle with the laws of physics lent an extra thrill as she flew along the track, the sense of freedom making her oblivious to the stress on her body as lap after lap whizzed by.

'You're being too hard on your tyres, Sasha.'

Luke's voice piped into her earphones and she immediately adjusted the balance of the car, her grip loosening a touch to help manoeuvre the curves better.

'That's better. In race conditions you'll need them to go for at least fifteen laps. You can't afford to wear them out in just eight. It's early days yet, but things look good.'

Sasha blinked at the grudging respect in Luke's voice.

'How does the car feel?'

'Er…great. It feels great.'

'Good. Come in and we'll take a look at the lap times together.'

She drove back into the garage and parked. Keeping her focus on Luke as he approached her, she got out and set her helmet aside.

He showed her the printout. 'We can't compare it with the performance of the DSII, but from these figures things are looking very good for Spa in three weeks' time.'

Reading through the data, Sasha felt a buzz of excitement. 'The DSII is great at slow corners, so I should be able to go even faster.'

Luke grinned. 'When you have the world's best aerodynamicist as your boss, you have a starting advantage. We'll have a battle on the straight sections, but if you keep up this performance we should cope well enough to keep ourselves ahead.'

Again she caught the changed note in his voice.

Although she'd tried not to dwell on it, throughout the day, and over the following days during testing, Sasha slowly felt the changing attitude of her small team. They spoke to her with less condescension; some even bothered to engage her in conversation before and after her practice sessions.

And the first time Luke asked her opinion on how to avoid the under steering problem that had cropped up, Sasha forced herself to blink back the stupid tears that threatened.

Marco heard the car drive away as he came down the stairs. He curbed the strong urge to yank the door open and forced himself to wait. When he reached the bottom step he sat down and rested his elbows on his knees, his BlackBerry dangling from his fingers.

Light footsteps sounded seconds before the front door opened.

Sasha stood silhouetted against the lights flooding the outer courtyard, the outline of her body in tight dark trousers and top making sparks of desire shoot through his belly.

Clenching his teeth against the intensity of it, he forced himself to remain seated, knowing she hadn't yet spotted him in the darkened hallway. Her light wrap slipped as she turned to shut the door, and he caught a glimpse of one smooth shoulder and arm. Her dark silky hair was tied in a careless knot on top of her head, giving her neck a long, smooth, elegant line that he couldn't help but follow.

He found himself tracing the lines of her body, wondering how he'd ever thought her boyish. She was tall, her figure lithe, but there were curves he hadn't noticed before—right down to the shapely denim-clad legs.

Shutting the door, she tugged off her boots and kicked them into a corner.

She turned and stumbled to a halt, her breath squeaking out in alarm. 'Marco! Damn it, you *really* need to stop skulking in dark hallways. You nearly scared me to death!'

'I wasn't skulking.' He heard the irritation in his voice and forced himself to calm down. 'Where have you been? I called you several times.'

She pulled the wrap tighter around her shoulders, her chin tilting up in silent challenge. 'I went for a drink with the team.

They're all flying out tomorrow morning and I wanted to say goodbye. I know that wasn't part of the deal—me socialising with the team—but they kept asking and it would have been surly to refuse.'

Annoyance rattled through him. The last thing he wanted to discuss was his team, or the deal he'd made with Sasha Fleming. *Dios*, he wasn't even sure why he'd come back here. He should be by his brother's bedside—even if the doctors intended to keep him in his induced coma until the swelling on his brain reduced.

'And you were having such a great time you decided not to answer your phone?'

'I think it's died.'

'You *think*?'

'You're annoyed with me. Why?'

Sasha asked the question in that direct way he'd come to expect from her. No one in his vast global organisation would dare to speak to him that way. And yet…he found he liked it.

Rising, he walked towards her. A few steps away, the scent of her perfume hit his nostrils. Marco found himself craving more of it, wanting to draw even closer. 'Why bother with a phone if you can't ensure it works?'

'Because no one calls me.'

Her words stopped him in his tracks. For a man who commanded his multi-billion-euro empire using his BlackBerry, Marco found her remark astonishing in the extreme. 'No one calls you?'

'My phone never rings. I think *you* were the last person to call me. I get the occasional text from Tom, or Charlie, my physio, but other than that…zilch.'

Marco's puzzlement grew. 'You don't have any friends?'

'Obviously none who care enough to call. And, before you go feeling sorry for me, I'm fine with it.'

'You're fine with being lonely?'

'With being *alone*. There's a difference. So, is there another reason you're annoyed with me?'

She raised her chin in that defiant way that drew his gaze to her throat.

He shoved his phone into his pocket. 'I'm not annoyed. I'm tired. And hungry. Rosario had gone to bed when I arrived.'

'Oh, well, that's good. Not the tired and hungry part. The not annoyed part.' She bit her lip, her eyes wide on his as he moved even closer. 'And about Rosario...I hope you don't mind, but I told her not to wait up for me.'

Marco shook his head. 'So where did you go for this drink?' He strove to keep his voice casual.

'A bodega just off Plaza Mayor in Salamanca.'

He nodded, itching to brush back the stray hair that had fallen against her temple. 'And did you enjoy your evening out?'

Her shrug drew his eyes to her bare shoulder. 'Leon is beautiful. And I was glad to get out of the villa.'

Her response struck a strangely discordant chord within him. 'You don't like it here?'

'I don't mind the proximity to the track, but I was tired of knocking about in this place all by myself.'

Marco stiffened. 'Do you want to move to the hotel with the rest of the team?'

She thought about it. Then, 'No. The crew and I seem to be gelling, but I don't want to become overly familiar with them.'

Marco found himself breathing again. 'Wise decision. Sometimes maintaining distance is the only way to get ahead.'

'*You* obviously don't practise that dogma. You're always surrounded by an adoring crowd.'

'X1 Premier Racing is a multi-million-spectator sport. I can't exist in a vacuum.'

'Okay. Um...do you think we can turn the lights on in here? Only we seem to be making a habit of having conversations in the dark.'

'Sometimes comfort can be found in darkness.'

Facing up to reality's harsh light after his own crash ten years ago had made him wish he'd stayed unconscious. Angelique's smug expression as she'd dropped her bombshell had certainly made him wish for the oblivion of darkness.

Sasha gave a light, musical laugh. The sound sent tingles of pleasure down his spine even as heat pooled in his groin. His eyes fell to her lips and Marco experienced the supreme urge to kiss her. Or to keep enjoying the sound of her laughter.

'What's so funny?' he asked as she reached over his shoulder and flipped on the light switch.

'I was thinking either you're very hungry or you're very tired, because you've gone all cryptic on me.'

He *was* hungry. And not just for food. A hunger—clawing and extremely ravenous—had taken hold inside him.

Pushing aside the need to examine it, he followed her as she headed towards the kitchen. The sight of her bare feet on the cool stones made his blood thrum faster as he studied her walk, the curve of her full, rounded bottom.

'I could do with a snack myself. Do you want me to fix you something?'

Walking on the balls of her feet made the sway of her hips different, sexier. He tried to stop himself staring. He failed.

'You cook?' he asked past the strain in his throat.

'Yep. Living on my own meant I had to learn, starve or live on takeaways. Starving was a bore, and Charlie would've had conniptions if he'd seen me within a mile of a takeaway joint. So I took an intensive cookery course two years ago.'

She folded her wrap and placed it on the counter, along with a small handbag. Only then did he see that her top was held up by the thinnest of straps.

Opening the fridge, she began to pull out ingredients. 'Roast beef sandwich okay? Or if you want something hot I can make pasta carbonara?' she asked over her shoulder.

Marco pulled up a seat at the counter, unable to take his eyes off her. 'I'm fine with the sandwich.'

Her nod dislodged more silky hair from the knot on her head. 'Okay.' Long, luxurious tresses slipped down to caress her neck.

She moved around the kitchen, her movements quick, efficient. In less than five minutes she'd set a loaded plate and a bottle of mineral water before him. He took a bite, chewed.

'This is really good.'

Her look of pleasure sent another bolt of heat through him.

He waited until she sat opposite him before taking another bite. 'So, how long have you lived on your own?'

'Since…' She hesitated. 'Since my father died four years ago.'

She looked away, but not before he caught shadows of pain within the blue depths.

'And your mother? Is she not around?'

She shook her head and picked up her sandwich. 'She died when I was ten. After that it was just Dad and me.'

The sharp pain of losing his own mother surfaced. Ruthlessly, he pushed it away.

'The team are wondering how Rafael is,' Sasha said, drawing him away from his disturbing thoughts.

'Just the team?'

She shrugged. 'We're all concerned.'

'Yes, I know. His condition hasn't changed. I've updated Russell. He'll pass it on to the team.'

He didn't want to talk about his brother. Because speaking of Rafael would only remind him of why this woman who made the best sandwich he'd ever tasted was sitting in front of him.

'How is your father holding up?'

He didn't want to talk about his father either.

Recalling his father's desolation, Marco shoved away his plate. 'He watched his son crash on live TV. How do you think he's doing?'

A flash of concern darkened her blue eyes. 'Does he…does he know about me?' she asked in a small voice.

'Does he know the cause of his son's crash is the same person taking his seat?' He laughed. 'Not yet.'

He wasn't sure why he'd kept that information from his father. It certainly had nothing to do with wondering if his brother's version of events was completely accurate, despite Rafael's voice ringing in his head… *She's the one, Marco.*

Sasha's gaze sought his, the look into them almost imploring. 'I didn't cause him to crash, Marco.'

Frustrated anger seared his chest. 'Didn't you?'

She shook her head and the knot finally gave up its fight. Dark, silky tresses cascaded over her naked shoulders and everything inside Marco tightened. It was the first time he'd seen it down, and despite the fury rolling through him the sudden urge to sink his fingers into the glossy mass, feel its decadent luxury, surged like fire through his veins.

'Then what did? Something must have happened to make him imagine that idiotic move would stick.'

Her lips pursed. The look in her eyes was reluctant. Then she sighed. 'I saw him just before the race. He was arguing with Raven.'

Marco frowned. 'Raven Blass? His physio?'

She nodded. 'I tried to approach him but he walked away. I thought I'd leave him to cool off and talk to him again after the race.'

Marco's muttered expletive made her brows rise, but he was past caring. He strode into the alcove that held his extensive wine collection. 'I need a drink. White or red?'

'I shouldn't. I had a beer earlier.' She tucked a silky strand behind one ear.

Watching the movement, he found several incredibly unwise ideas crowding his brain. Reaching out, he grabbed the nearest bottle. 'I don't like drinking alone. Have one with me.'

Her smile caused the gut-clenching knot to tighten further. 'Is the great Marco de Cervantes admitting a flaw?'

'He's admitting that his brother drives him *loco*.' He grabbed two crystal goblets.

'Fine. I was going to add another twenty minutes to my work-out regime to balance out the incredible *tapas* I had earlier. I'll make it an even half-hour.'

Marco's gaze glided over her. 'You're hardly in bad shape.'

Another sweet, feminine laugh tumbled from her lips, sparking off a frenzied yearning.

'Charlie would disagree with you. Apparently my body mass index is *way* below acceptable levels.'

Marco uncorked the wine, thinking perhaps Charlie needed his eyes examined. 'How long is your daily regime?'

'Technically three hours, but Charlie keeps me at it until I'm either screaming in agony or about to pass out. He normally stops once I'm thoroughly dripping in sweat.'

His whole body froze, arrested by the image of a sweat-soaked Sasha, with sunshine glinting off her toned body.

Dios, this was getting ridiculous. He should not be feeling like this—especially not towards the woman who was the every epitome of Angelique: ruthlessly ambitious, uncaring of anything that got in her way. Sasha had nearly destroyed his brother the way Angelique had destroyed Marco's desire ever to forge a lasting relationship.

And yet in Barcelona he'd found himself thinking of Sasha... admitting to himself that his sudden preoccupation with her had nothing to do with work. And everything to do with the woman herself. The attraction he'd felt in Budapest was still present... and escalating.

Which was totally unacceptable.

He took a deep breath and wrenched control back into his body. While his brother was lying in a coma, the only thing he needed to focus on was winning the Constructors' Championship. And teaching Sasha Fleming a lesson.

He poured bold red Château Neuf into one glass and set it in front of her. 'I've seen the testing reports. You'll need to find another three-tenths of a second around Eau Rouge to give yourself a decent chance or you'll leave yourself open to overtaking. Belgium is a tough circuit.'

She took a sip and his gaze slid to the feline-like curve of her neck. Clenching fingers that itched to touch, he sat down opposite her.

'The DSII will handle the corners better.'

His eyes flicked over her face, noting her calm. 'You don't seem nervous.'

Another laugh. A further tightening in his groin.

Madre di Dios. It had been a while since he'd indulged in good, old-fashioned, no-holds-barred sex. Sexual frustration had a habit of making the unsavoury tempting, but this...this yearning was insane.

Mentally, he scanned through his electronic black book and

came up with several names. Just as fast he discarded every one of them, weariness at having to disentangle himself from expectation dampening his urge to revisit old ground.

Frustration built, adding another strand of displeasure to his already seething emotions.

'Believe me, I get just as nervous as the next racer. But I don't mind.'

'Because winning is everything, no matter the cost?' he bit out.

Her eyes darkened. 'No. Because nerves serve a good purpose. They remind you you're human; they sharpen your focus. I'd be terrified if I wasn't nervous. But eighteen years of experience also helps. I've been doing this since I was seven years old. Having a supportive father who blatantly disregarded the fact that I wasn't a boy helped with my confidence too.'

'Not a lot of parents agree with their children racing. You were lucky.'

She smiled. 'More like pushy. I threw a tantrum every time he threatened to leave me with my nanny. I won eventually. Although I get the feeling he was testing me to see how much I wanted it.'

'And you passed with flying colours.' He raised his glass to her. 'Bravo.'

Unsettlingly perceptive blue eyes rested on him. 'Oops, do I detect a certain cynicism there, Marco?'

He clenched his teeth as his control slipped another notch. 'Has anyone told you it's not nice to always go for the jugular?'

Her eyes widened. 'Was that what I was doing? I thought we were having a get-to-know-each-other conversation. At least until you went a little weird on me.'

'*Perdón*. Weird wasn't what I was aiming for.' He took a large gulp of his wine.

'First an admission of a flaw. Now an apology. Wow—must be my lucky night. Are you feeling okay? Maybe it would help to talk about whatever it is that spooked you?'

Perhaps it was the mellowing effect of the wine. Perhaps it was the fact that he hadn't had an engaging conversation like this in a while. Marco was surprised when he found himself laughing.

'I have no memory of ever being spooked. But, just for curiosity's sake, which hat will you be wearing for this little heart-to-heart? Diplomat or psychologist?'

Her gaze met his squarely. 'How about friend?' she asked.

His laughter dried up.

She wanted to be his friend.

Marco couldn't remember the last time anyone had offered to be his friend. Betrayal had a habit of stripping the scales from one's eyes. He'd learnt that lesson well and thoroughly.

He swallowed another gulp of wine. 'I respectfully decline. Thanks all the same.'

A small smile curved her lip. 'Ouch. At least you didn't laugh in my face.'

'That would have been cruel.'

One smooth brow rose. 'And you don't do cruel? You've come very close in the past.'

'You were a threat to my brother.'

'*Were?* You mean you're not under that impression any more?'

Realising the slip, he started to set her straight, then paused. *You can't control what happens in life...Rafael will resent you for controlling his life...* 'I'm willing to suspend my judgement until Rafael is able to set the picture straight himself.'

Her smile faded. 'You don't trust me at all, do you?'

He steeled himself against his fleeting tinge of regret at the hurt in her voice.

'Trust is earned. It comes with time. Or so I'm told.'

So far no one had withstood the test long enough for Marco to verify that belief. Sasha Fleming had already failed that test. She was only sitting across from him because of what he could give her.

She hid her calculating nature well, but he knew it was there, hiding beneath the fiercely determined light in her eyes.

'Well, then, here's to earning trust. And becoming friends.'

Marco didn't respond to her toast because part of him regretted the fact that friendship between them would never be possible.

CHAPTER SIX

'THIS way, Sasha!'

'Over here!'

'Smile!'

The Children of Bravery awards took place every August at one of the plushest hotels in Mayfair. Last year Sasha had arrived in a cab with Tom, who had then gone on to ignore her for the rest of the night.

Tonight flashbulbs went off in her face the moment Marco helped her out of the back of his stunning silver Rolls-Royce onto the red carpet.

Blinking several times to help her eyes adjust, she found Tom had materialised beside her. Before he could speak, Marco stepped in front of him.

'Miss Fleming won't be needing you tonight. Enjoy your evening.'

The dismissal was softly spoken, wrapped in steel. With a hasty nod, a slightly pale Tom dissolved back into the crowd.

'That wasn't very nice,' she murmured, although secretly she was pleased. Her nerves, already wound tight at the thought of the evening ahead, didn't need further negative stimulus in the form of Tom. 'But thank you.'

'*De nada,*' he murmured in that smooth deep voice of his, and her nerves stretched a little tighter.

When he took her arm the feeling intensified, then morphed into a different kind of warmth as another sensation altogether enveloped her—one of feeling protected, cherished…

She applied mental brakes as her brain threatened to go into meltdown. Forcing herself away from thoughts she had no business thinking, she drew in a shaky breath and tried to project a calm, poised demeanour.

'For once I agree with the paparazzi. *Smile.* Your face looks frozen,' Marco drawled, completely at ease with being the subject of intense scrutiny.

He seemed perfectly okay with hundreds of adoring female fans screaming his name from behind the barriers, while she could only think about the ceremony ahead and the memories it would resurrect.

Pushing back her pain, she forced her lips apart. 'That's probably because it is. Besides, you're one to talk. I don't see you smiling.'

One tuxedo-clad shoulder lifted in a shrug. 'I'm not the star on show.' He peered closer at her. 'What's wrong with you? You didn't say a word on the way over here and now you look pale.'

'That's because I don't *like* being on show. I hate dressing up, and make-up makes my face feel weird.'

'You look fine.' His gaze swept over her. 'More than fine. The stylist chose well.'

'She didn't choose this dress. I chose it myself. If I'd gone with her choice I'd be half naked with a slit up to my cro—' She cleared her throat. 'Why did you send me a stylist anyway?'

When she'd opened the door to Marco's Kensington penthouse apartment to find a stylist with a rack of designer gear in tow, Sasha had been seriously miffed.

'I didn't want to risk you turning up here in baggy jeans and a hippy top.'

'I'd never have—!' She caught the gleam of amusement in his eyes and relaxed.

Another photographer screamed her name and she tensed.

'Relax. *You* chose well.' His gaze slid over her once more. 'You look beautiful.'

Stunned, she mumbled, 'Thank you.'

She smoothed a nervous hand over her dress, thankful her new contract had come with a lucrative remuneration package that meant she'd been able to afford the black silk and lace floor-length Zang Toi gown she wore.

The silver studs in the off-the-shoulder form-fitting design flashed as the cameras went off. But even the stylish dress, with its reams of material that trailed on the red carpet, couldn't stem the butterflies ripping her stomach to shreds as the media screamed out for even more poses. Nor could it eliminate the wrenching reason why, on a night like this, she couldn't summon a smile.

'Stop fidgeting,' he commanded.

'That's easy for you to say. Anyway, why are you here? I don't need a keeper.' Nor did she need the stupid melting sensation in her stomach every time his hand tightened around her arm.

'I beg to differ. This event is hosting many sport personalities, including other drivers from the circuit. Your track record—pardon the pun—doesn't stand you in good stead. The one thing you *do* need is a keeper.'

'And you're it? Don't you have better things to do?'

When he'd pointed out after they'd landed this morning that it was more time-efficient for her to stay with him in London, than to come to the ceremony from her cottage in Kent, she hadn't bargained on the fact that he'd appoint himself her personal escort for the evening.

His rugged good looks lit up in sharp relief, courtesy of another photographer's flash, but he hardly noticed how avidly the media craved his attention. Nor cared.

'The team has suffered with Rafael's absence. It'll be good for the sponsors to see me here.'

The warmth she'd experienced moments ago disappeared. She felt his sharp gaze as she eased her arm from his grasp.

'How long do we have to stay out here?' The limelight was definitely a place she wasn't comfortable in. However irrational, she always feared her deepest secret would be exposed.

'Until a problem with the seating is sorted out.'

She swivelled towards him. 'What problem with the seating?'

Relief poured through her as he steered her away from the

cameras and down the red carpet into the huge marble-floored foyer of the five-star hotel.

The crowd seemed to pause, both men and women alike staring avidly as they entered.

Oblivious to the reaction, Marco snagged two glasses of champagne and handed one to her. 'Some wires got crossed along the line.'

Sasha should have been used to it by now, but a hard lump formed in her throat nonetheless. 'You mean I was downgraded to nobody-class because my surname is Fleming and not de Cervantes?'

He gave her a puzzled look. 'Why should your name matter?'

'Come on. I may have missed school the day rocket science was taught, but I know how this works.' Even when the words weren't said, Sasha knew she was being judged by her father's dishonour.

'Your surname has nothing to do with it,' Marco answered, nodding greetings to several people who tried to catch his eye. 'When the awards committee learned I would be attending, they naturally assumed that I would be bringing a plus one.'

A sensation she intensely disliked wormed its way into her heart. 'Oh, so I was bumped to make room for your date. Not because…?'

He raised a brow. 'Because?'

Shaking her head, Sasha took a hasty sip of her bubbly. 'So why didn't you? Bring a date, I mean?' When his brow rose in mocking query, she hurried on. 'I know it's certainly not for the lack of willing companions. I mean, a man like you…' She stumbled to a halt.

'A man like me? You mean The Ass?' he asked mockingly.

Heat climbed into her cheeks but she refused to be cowed. 'No, I didn't mean that. The other you—the impossibly rich, successful one, who's a bit decent to look at….' Cursing her runaway tongue, she clamped her mouth shut.

'*Gracias*…I think.'

'You know what I mean. Women scale skylights, risk life and limb to be with you, for goodness' sake.'

'Skylight-scaling is a bit too OTT for me. I prefer my women to use the front door. *With* my invitation.' His gaze connected with hers.

Heat blazed through her, lighting fires that had no business being lit. His broad shoulders loomed before her as he bent his head. As if to… As if to… Her gaze dropped to his lips. She swallowed.

Chilled champagne went down the wrong way.

She coughed, cleared her throat and tried desperately to find something to say to dispel the suddenly charged atmosphere. His eyelids descended, but not before she caught a flash of anguish. Stunned, she stared at him, but when he looked back up his expression was clear.

'To answer your question, this is a special event to honour children. It's not an event to bring a date who'll spend all evening checking out other women's jewellery or celebrity-spotting.'

'How incredibly shallow! Oh, I don't mean you date shallow women—I mean… Hell, I've put my foot in it, haven't I?'

The smile she'd glimpsed once before threatened to break the surface of his rigid demeanour. 'Your diplomatic hat is slipping, Sasha. I think we should go in before you insult me some more and completely shatter my ego.'

'I don't think that's possible,' she murmured under her breath. 'Seriously, though, you should smile more. You look almost human when you do.'

The return of his low, deep laugh sang deliciously along her skin, then wormed its way into her heart. When his hand arrived in the small of her back to steer her into the ballroom a whole heap of pleasure stole through her, almost convincing her the butterflies had been vanquished.

The feeling was pathetically short-lived. The pictures of children hanging from the ceiling of the chandeliered ballroom punched a hole through the euphoric warmth she'd dared to bask in. Her breath caught as pain ripped through her. If her baby had lived she would have been four by now.

'Are you sure you're okay?' Marco demanded in a low undertone.

'Yes, I'm fine.'

Unwilling to risk his incisive gaze, she hurried to their table and greeted an ex-footballer who'd recently been knighted for his work with children.

Breathing through her pain, it took a moment for her to realise she was the subject of daggered looks and whispered sniggers from the other two occupants of the table.

Feeling her insides congeal with familiar anger, she summoned a smile and pasted it on her face as the ex-footballer's trophy wife leaned forward, exposing enough cleavage to sink a battleship.

'Hi, I'm Lisa. This is my sister, Sophia,' she said.

Marco nodded in greeting and introduced Sasha.

Sophia flashed Marco a man-gobbling smile, barely sparing Sasha a glance.

A different form of sickness assailed Sasha as she watched the women melt under Marco's dazzling charisma. Eager eyes took in his commanding physique, the hard beauty of his face, the sensual mouth and the air of authority and power that cloaked him.

He murmured something that made Sophia giggle with delight. When her gaze met Sasha's, it held a touch of triumph that made Sasha want to reach out and pull out her fake hair extensions. Instead she kept her smile and turned towards the older man.

If fake boobs and faker lashes were his thing, Marco was welcome to them.

Marco clenched his fist on his thigh and forced himself to calm down. He'd never been so thoroughly and utterly ignored by a date in his life.

So Sasha wasn't technically his date. So what? She'd arrived with him. She would leave with him. Would it hurt her to try and make conversation with *him* instead of engaging in an in-depth discussion of the current Premier League?

Slowly unclenching his fist, he picked up his wine glass.

Sasha laughed. The whole table seemed to pause to drink it in—even the two women who had so rudely ignored her so far.

By the time the tables were cleared of their dinner plates he'd had enough.

'Sasha.'

She smiled an excuse at the older man before turning to him. 'Yes?'

At the sight of her wide, genuine smile—the same one she'd worn when she'd offered her friendship at *Casa de Leon*—something in his chest contracted. He forced himself to remember the reason Sasha Fleming was here beside him. Why she was in his life at all.

Rafael. The baby brother he'd always taken care of.

But he isn't a child any more…

Marco suppressed the unsettling voice. 'The ceremony's about to start. You're presenting the second award.'

Her eyes widened a fraction, then anxiety darkened their depths.

'Yes, of course. I…I have my speech ready. I'd better read it over one more time, just in case…' Her hands shook as she plucked a tiny piece of paper from her bag.

Without thinking, he covered her hand with his. 'Take a deep breath. You'll be fine.'

Eyes locked onto his, she slowly nodded. 'I… Thanks.'

The MC took to the stage and announced the first award-giver. Sasha smiled and clapped but, watching her closely, Marco caught a glimpse of the pain in her eyes. Forcing himself to concentrate on the speech, he listened to the story of a four-year-old who'd saved her mother's life by ringing for an ambulance and giving clear, accurate directions after her mother had fallen down a ravine.

The ice-cold tightening his chest since he'd stepped from the car increased as he watched the little girl bound onto the stage in a bright blue outfit, her face wreathed in smiles. Forcing himself not to go there, not to dwell in the past, he turned to gauge Sasha's reaction.

She was frozen, her whole body held taut.

Frowning, he leaned towards her. 'This is ridiculous. Tell me what's wrong. *Now.*'

She jumped, her eyes wide, darkly haunted with unshed tears. Her smile flashed, only this time it lacked warmth or substance.

'I told you, I'm fine. Or I would if I'd remembered to bring a tissue.'

Wordlessly, he reached into his tuxedo jacket and handed her his handkerchief, a million questions firing in his mind.

Accepting it, she dabbed at her eyes. 'If I look a horror, don't tell me until I come back from the stage, okay?' she implored.

It was on the tip of his tongue to trip out the usual platitudes he gave to his dates. Instead he nodded. 'Agreed.'

Marco watched her gather herself together. A subtle roll of her shoulders and a look of determination settled over her features. By the time she rose to present the award her smile was fixed in place.

Watching the lights play over her dark hair, illuminate her beautiful features and the generous curve of her breasts, Marco felt the familiar tightening in his groin and bit back a growl of frustration.

'As most of you know, Rafael de Cervantes was supposed to present this award to Toby this evening. Instead he's skiving off somewhere in sunny Spain.'

Laughter echoed through the room.

'No, seriously, just as Toby said a prayer before rushing into his burning home to save his little sister and brother, so we should all take a moment to say a prayer for Rafael's speedy recovery. Toby fought for his family to live. Not once did he give up. Even when the rescuers told him there was no hope for his little brother he ignored them and rescued him. Why? Because he'd promised his mother he'd take care of his siblings. And he never once wavered from that promise. There are lessons for all of us in Toby's story. And that's never to give up. No matter how small or big your dreams, no matter how tough or impossible the way forward seems, never give up. I'm delighted to present this award to Toby Latham, for his outstanding bravery against all odds.'

Sasha's voice broke on the last words. Although she tried to hide it, Marco caught the strain in her face and the pain behind her smile even as thunderous applause broke out in the ballroom.

Automatically Marco followed suit, but inside ice clenched his heart, squeezing until he couldn't breathe. It was always like this when he allowed himself to remember what Angelique had taken from him. What his weakness had cost him. He'd failed to take care of his own.

Never again, he vowed silently.

Sasha stepped down from the stage and made her way back to her seat. Despite the rushing surge of memories, he couldn't take his eyes off her. In fact he wanted to jump up, grab her hand and lead her away from the ballroom.

She reached the table and smiled at him. 'Thank God I didn't fall on my face.'

Sliding gracefully into the seat, she tucked her hair behind one ear. In that moment Marco, struggling to breathe and damning himself to hell, knew he craved her.

Impossibly. Desperately.

Sasha caught the expression on Marco's face and her heart stopped.

'What's the matter? Oh, my God, if you tell me I have food caught in my teeth I'll kill you!' she vowed feverishly.

Desperately blinking back the threatening tears, she tried to stem the painful memories that looking into Toby Latham's face had brought. She couldn't afford to let Marco see her pain. The pain she'd let eat her alive, consume her for years, but had never been able to put to rest.

She heard sniggers from across the table but ignored them, her attention held hostage by the savagely intense look in Marco's eyes.

'Your teeth are fine,' he replied in a deep, rough voice.

'Then what? Was my speech that bad?' Caught in the traumatising resurgence of painful memories, she'd discarded her carefully prepared notes and winged it.

'No. Your speech was...*perfecto*.'

Her heart lurched at his small pause. Before she could question him about it the MC introduced the next guest. With no choice but to maintain a respectful silence, she folded her shaking hands in her lap.

Frantically, she tried to recall her speech word for word. Marco was obviously reacting to something she'd said. Had she been wrong to mention Rafael? Had her joke been too crass? A wave of shame engulfed her at the thought.

She waited until the next award had been presented, then leaned over. 'I'm sorry,' she whispered into his ear.

His head swivelled towards her. His jaw brushed her cheek, sending a thousand tiny electric currents racing through her.

'What for?' he asked.

'I shouldn't have made that crack about Rafael skiving off. It was tasteless—'

'And exactly what Rafael himself would've done had the situation been reversed. Everyone's been skirting around the subject, either pretending it's not happening or treating it with kid gloves. You gave people the freedom to acknowledge what had happened and set them at ease. I'm no longer the object of pitying glances and whispered speculation. It is I who should be thanking you.'

'Really?'

'*Sí,*' he affirmed, his gaze dropping to her mouth.

'Then why did you look so…*off*?'

His eyes darkened. 'Your words were powerful. I was touched. I'm not made of stone, Sasha, contrary to what you might think.'

The reproach in his voice shamed her.

'Oh, I'm sorry. It's just… I thought…'

'Forget it.'

He gave a tight smile, turned away and addressed Sophia, who flashed even more of her cleavage in triumph.

As soon as the last award was given, Sophia turned to Marco. 'We're going clubbing.' She named an exclusive club frequented by young royals. 'We'd love you to join us, Marco,' she gushed.

Sasha gritted her teeth but stayed silent. If Marco wanted

to party with the Fake Sisters it was his choice. All the same, Sasha held her breath as she waited for his answer, hating herself as she did so.

'Clubbing isn't my scene, but thanks for the offer.'

'Oh, we don't have to go clubbing. Maybe we can do something...*else*?'

Sasha stood and walked away before she could hear Marco's response.

She'd almost reached the ballroom doors when she felt his presence beside her. The wave of relief that flooded her body threatened to weaken her knees. Sternly, she reminded herself that Marco's presence had nothing to do with her personally. He was here for the team's sake.

'Are you sure you'd rather not be out with the Fa... Sophia? She seemed very eager to show you a good time. Seriously, I can take a taxi back.'

His limo pulled up. He handed her inside, then slid in beside her. 'I prefer to end my evening silicone-free, *gracias*.'

She laughed. 'Picky, picky! Most men wouldn't mind.'

Perfect teeth gleamed in the semi-darkness of the limo. 'I am not most men. No doubt you'll add *that* to my list of flaws?'

His eyes dropped to her chest, abruptly cutting off her laughter.

'You had better not be examining me for silicone. I'll have you know these babies are natural.'

'Trust me, I can tell the difference,' he said, in a low, intense voice.

She swallowed hard. The thought that she was suddenly treading unsafe waters descended on her. Frantically, she cast her mind around for a safe subject.

'So you don't like clubbing?'

'It's not how I choose to spend an evening, no.'

'Let me guess—you're the starchy opera type?'

'Wrong again.'

She snapped her fingers. 'I know—you like to stay indoors and watch game shows.'

Low laughter greeted her announcement. Deep inside, a tiny part of Sasha performed a freakishly disturbing happy dance.

Encouraged, she pressed on. 'Telemetry reports and aerodynamic calculations?'

'Now you're getting warm.'

'Ha! I knew you were a closet nerd!'

He cast her a wry glance. 'I prefer to call it passion.'

She shrugged. 'A passionate nerd who surrounds himself with a crowd but keeps his distance.'

He stiffened. 'You're psychoanalysing me again.'

'You make it easy.'

'And *you* make baseless assumptions.'

'Good try, but you can't freeze me out with that tone. You're single-minded to the point of obsession. I wiki-ed you. You have more money than you could ever spend in ten lifetimes and yet you don't let anyone close. You have the odd liaison, but nothing that lasts more than a few weeks. According to your girlfriends, you never stay over. And there's a time limit on every relationship.'

'You shouldn't believe everything you read—especially in the tabloid press.'

'Tell me which part is false,' she challenged.

His gaze hardened. 'I'll tell you which part is right—every relationship ends. For ever is a concept made up to sell romance novels.'

'Didn't you have a long liaison once, when you were still racing? What was her name…? Angela? Ange—?'

'Angelique,' he bit out, his face frozen as if hewn from rock. 'And she wasn't a liaison. We were engaged.'

'She must be the reason, then.'

Cold eyes slammed into her. 'The reason?'

'For the way you are?'

'Did Derek Mahoney turn you into the intrusive woman you are today?' he fired back, his tone rougher than sandpaper. 'Because I'd like to find him and throttle the life out of him.'

Sasha knew she should let it go. But somehow she couldn't.

'Yes. No.' She sighed and looked out of the window at Kensington's nightlife. 'Damn, I wish I smoked.'

An astounded breath whistled from his lips. 'Why would you wish that?'

'Because trying to have a conversation with you is exhausting enough to drive anyone to drink. But since I have to be up at the crack of dawn tomorrow, and I've reached my one-glass drink limit, smoking would be the other choice—if I smoked.' Abandoning the view, she turned back to him. 'Where was I?'

A mirthless smile lifted one corner of his mouth. 'You were dissecting my life and finding it severely deficient.'

'Mockery? Is that your default setting?'

He lowered his gaze to her lips and her insides clenched so hard she feared she'd break in half. The limo turned a sharp corner. She grabbed the armrest to steady herself. Too late she realised the action had thrust her breasts out. Marco's gaze dropped lower. Heat pooled in her belly. Her breasts ached, feeling fuller than they'd ever felt.

He leaned closer. Her heart thundered.

'No, Sasha,' he said hoarsely. '*This* is my default setting.'

Strong hands cupped her cheeks, held her steady. Heat-filled eyes stared into hers, their shocking intensity igniting a fire deep inside her.

Sasha held her breath, almost afraid to move in case…in case…

He fastened his mouth to hers, tumbling her into a none-too-gentle kiss that sent the blood racing through her veins. He tasted of heat and wine, of tensile strength and fiery Latin willpower. Of red-blooded passion and intoxicating pleasure. And he went straight to her head.

Sasha felt a groan rise in her throat and abruptly shut it off. She wasn't *that* easy. Although right now, with Marco's mouth wreaking insane havoc on her blood pressure, *easy* was deliciously tempting.

His tongue caressed hers and the groan slipped through, echoing in the dim cavern of the moving car. One hand slipped to her nape, angling her head. Although he didn't need to. She was willingly tilting her head, all the better to deepen the pressure and pleasure of his kiss. Her mouth opened, boldly inviting him in.

His moan made her triumphant and weak at the same time. Then she lost all thought but of the bliss of the kiss.

Lost all sense of time.

Until she heard the thud of a door.

Their lips parted with a loud, sucking noise that arrowed straight to the furnace-hot apex of her thighs.

Marco stared down at her, his breath shaking out of his chest. *'Dios,'* he muttered after several tense, disbelieving seconds.

You can say that again. Thankfully, the words didn't materialise on her lips. Her eyes fell to his mouth, still wet from their kiss, and the heat between her legs increased a thousandfold.

Get a grip, Sasha. She reined herself in and pulled away as reality sank in. She'd kissed Marco de Cervantes—fallen into him like a drowning swimmer fell on a life raft.

'We're here,' he rasped, setting her free abruptly to spear a hand through his hair.

'Y-yes,' she mumbled, cringing when her voice emerged low and desire-soaked.

With one last look at her, he thrust his door open and helped her out.

They entered the exclusive apartment complex in silence, travelled up to the penthouse suite in silence. Sasha made sure she placed herself as far from him as possible.

After shutting the apartment door he turned to her. Sasha held her breath, guilt rising to mix with the desire that still churned so frantically through her.

'I have an early start—'

'Sasha—'

Marco gestured for her to go first.

Sasha cleared her throat, keeping her gaze on his chest so he wouldn't see the conflicting emotions in her eyes. 'I have an early start tomorrow. So…um…goodnight.'

After a long, heavy pause, he nodded. 'I think that's a good idea. *Buenos noches.*'

All the way down the plushly carpeted hallway she felt his

gaze on her. Even after she shut the door behind her his presence lingered.

Dropping her clutch bag, she traced her fingers over her lips. They still tingled, along with every inch of her body. Resting her head against the door, she sucked in a desperate breath.

One hand drifted over her midriff to her pelvis, where desire gripped her in an unbearable vice of need. A need she had every intention of denying, no matter how strong.

Wanting Marco de Cervantes was a mistake. Even if there was the remotest possibility of a relationship between them it would be over in a matter of weeks. And she knew without a shadow of a doubt that it would also spell the end of her career.

And her experience with Derek had taught that no man—no matter how intensely charismatic, no matter how great a kisser—was worth the price of her dreams.

CHAPTER SEVEN

'Coffee…I smell coffee,' she mumbled into the pillow, the murky fog of her brain teasing her with the seductive aroma of caffeine. 'Please, God, let there be coffee when I open my eyes.'

Carefully she cracked one eye open. Marco stood at the foot of her bed, in a dark green T-shirt and jeans, a steaming mug in his hand.

'If I demand to know what you're doing in my bedroom so early, will you withhold that coffee from me?'

There was no smile this morning, just an even, cool stare, but awareness drummed beneath the surface of her skin nonetheless.

'It's not early. It's eight o'clock.'

With a groan, she levered herself up, braced her back against the headboard. 'Eight o'clock is the crack of dawn, Marco.' She held out her hand for the cup. He didn't move. 'Please,' she croaked.

With an uncharacteristically jerky movement he rounded the bed and handed it to her. Sasha tried not to let her eyes linger on the taut inch of golden-tanned skin that was revealed when he stretched. Her brain couldn't handle anything so overwhelming. Not just yet.

She took her first sip, groaned with pleasure and sagged against the pillow.

'You're not a morning person, are you?'

'Oops, my secret is out. I think whoever decreed that anything was important enough to start before ten o'clock in the morning should be hung, drawn and quartered.' She cradled the warm mug in her hand. 'Okay, I guess now I'm awake enough to ask what you're doing in my room.'

'I knocked. Several times.'

She grimaced. 'I sleep like the dead sometimes.' She took another grateful sip and just stopped herself from moaning again. Moans were bad. 'How did you know to bring me coffee?'

'I know everything about you,' he answered.

Her heart lurched, but she managed to keep her face straight. Marco didn't know about her baby. And she meant to keep it that way.

'I forgot. You have mad voodoo skills.'

His eyes strayed up from where he'd been examining the vampire on her T-shirt. 'No voodoo. Just mad skills. As to why I'm here—I have a meeting in the city in forty-five minutes—'

'On a Saturday?' She caught his wry glance. 'Oh, never mind.'

'I wanted to discuss last night before I left.'

Her breath stalled in her chest. 'Yes. Last night. We kissed.'

A sharp hiss issued from his lips. Then, '*Sí*, we did.'

She bravely met his gaze, even as her heart hammered. 'Before you condemn me for it, you need to know I don't make a habit of that sort of thing.'

His very Latin shrug drew her eyes to the bold, strong outline of his shoulders. 'And yet it happened.'

'We could blame the wine? Oh, wait, you barely touched your glass all evening.'

'How would you know? You were neck-deep in discussing the Premier League.'

She sighed. 'What can I say? I love my footie. Which club do you support?'

'Barcelona.'

She grimaced. 'Of course. You seem the Barcelona type.'

He shook his head. 'I don't even want to know what that means.'

Silence encased them. She took a few more sips of her coffee, instinctively sensing she'd need the caffeine boost to withstand what was coming.

Marco raised his head and looked at her. The tormented gleam in his eyes stopped her breath. 'What happened last night will not happen again.'

Despite telling herself the very same thing over and over last night, she felt a sharp dart of disappointment and hurt lance through her. She feigned a casual tone. 'I agree.'

'You belong to my brother,' he carried on, as if she hadn't spoken.

'I belong to no one. I'm my own person.'

His gaze speared hers. 'It can't happen again.'

Again the uncomfortable dart of pain. 'And I agreed with you. Are you trying to convince me or yourself?'

He shook his head. 'You know, I've never met anyone so forthright.'

'I believe in being upfront. I'm nobody's yes-woman. You need to know that right now. I kiss whomever I want. But kissing you was a mistake. One that I hope will not jeopardise my contract.'

His gaze hardened. 'You value being a racing driver more than personal relationships?'

'I haven't had a successful run with relationships but I'm a brilliant driver. I think it's wise to stick to doing what I do best. And I'd prefer not to lose my job because you feel guilty over a simple kiss. I also understand if you have some reservations because of your brother. Really, it's no big deal. There's no need to beat yourself up over it.'

Running out of oxygen, she clamped her mouth shut.

This was yet another reason why she hated mornings. At this time of day the natural barrier between her brain and her mouth was severely weakened.

Throw in the fruitless soul-searching she'd done into the wee hours, and the resultant sleep-deprivation, and who knew what would come of out her mouth next?

He shoved a forceful hand through his hair. '*Dios*, this has nothing to do with your contract. If you were mine to take I'd have no reservations. None. The things I would do to you. *With* you.'

He named a few.

Her mouth dropped open.

Lust singed the air, its fumes thick and heavy. Her fingers clenched around her mug. Silently, desperately, she willed it away. But her body wasn't prepared to heed her. Underneath her T-shirt her nipples reacted to his words, tightening into painful, needy buds.

'Wow! That's…um…super, *super*-naughty.'

Hazel eyes snapped pure fire at her. 'And that's just for starters,' he rasped.

Her breath strangled in her chest.

In another life, at another time…

No! Even in a parallel universe having anything to do with Marco would be bad news.

'I hear a *but* somewhere in there. Either you still think I'm poison or it's something else. Tell me. I can take it.'

He gave a jerky nod of his head in a move she was becoming familiar with. 'Last night, at the awards, you spoke of Rafael like a friend.'

'Because that's what he is. Just a friend.'

His jaw clenched. 'You're asking me to take your word over my brother's?'

'Not really. I'm saying give us both the benefit of the doubt. See where it takes you.'

He shook his head. 'As long as Rafael sees you as his there can be nothing between us.'

Despite the steaming coffee in her hand, she felt a chill spread through her. 'The message has been received, loud and clear. Was there something else?'

For a full minute he didn't answer. Then, 'I don't want you to think that the kiss has bought you any special privileges.'

'You mean like expecting you to bring me coffee every morning?' she replied sarcastically, a surprisingly acute pain scouring its acidic path through her belly.

'My expectations from you as a driver haven't changed. In fact nothing has changed. Understood?'

Setting down her mug on the bedside table, she hugged her

knees. 'All this angst over a simple kiss, Marco?' The need to reduce the kiss to an inconsequential blip burned through her, despite her body's insistence on reliving it.

He prowled to the window and turned to face her. 'Women have a habit of reading more into a situation than there actually is.' His raised hand killed her response. 'While taking pains to state the contrary. But I want to be very clear—I don't *do* relationships.'

Her breath fractured in her lungs. 'I'm not looking for one,' she forced out.

His whole body stiffened. 'Then it stands to reason that there shouldn't be a problem.'

She hugged her knees tighter. 'Again I sense a *but*.'

'*But*...for some reason you're all I think about.'

The statement was delivered with joyless candour. Yet her heart leapt like a puppet whose string had been jerked. And when his eyes met hers and she saw the heat in them something inside her melted.

He strode back towards the bed, shoving clenched fists into his pockets. She stared up at him, her pulse racing. 'And you're annoyed about that?'

His gaze raked her face slowly. Then slid to her neck, her breasts, and back up again. Molten heat burned in his eyes. 'Livid. Frustrated. Puzzled. Intensely aroused.'

Of their own volition her eyes dropped below his belt-line. Confronted with the evidence, she felt a deep longing melt between her legs. She swallowed as heat poured through her whole being.

Looking away, she muttered, 'Don't do that.'

A strained sound escaped his throat. 'I was just about to demand the same of you.'

'I'm not doing anything. You, on the other hand—you're...' She sucked in a desperate breath.

'I'm what?' he demanded, his voice low, ferocious.

'You're all brooding and...and fierce...and angry...and... aroused. You're cursing your desire for me and yet your eyes are promising all sorts of rampant steaminess.' Her eyes darted back to the bulge in his trousers and a lump clogged her throat. 'I…I think you should leave.'

'You don't sound very sure about that.'

'*I am.* I don't want you. And even if I did you're off-limits to me, remember? So you can't…can't present me with…*this*!'

A pulse jerked in his jaw. 'I never said the situation wasn't without complications.'

'Well, the solution is easy. You hired me to do a job so let me get on with it. We don't have to see each other until the season ends and we win the Constructors' Championship. We'll stand on the top podium and douse ourselves in champagne. Then we'll go our separate ways until next season starts.'

'And you will have fulfilled this promise you made?'

Surprise zapped through her. He remembered. 'Partly, yes,' she replied, before thinking better of it.

His gaze turned speculative. 'To whom did you make the promise?'

She dragged her eyes from his, the sudden need to spill everything shocking her with its intensity. But she couldn't. Marco didn't trust her. And she wasn't prepared to trust him with the sacred memory of her father.

She shook her head. 'It's none of your business. Are you going to leave me alone to get on with it?'

His mouth firmed into a hard line. 'The team has too much riding on this for me to take my eye off the ball at this juncture. So do our sponsors. Once you have proved yourself—'

'Yes, I've heard it all before.' She couldn't stop the bitterness from spilling out. 'Prove myself. Don't bewitch anyone on the team. *Especially* not the boss. Message received and understood. Perhaps you could take your frustrations elsewhere, then, and spare me the thwarted lust backlash?'

He stiffened with anger. '*Dios.* Has no one ever told you that the difference between attractive feistiness and maddening shrew is one bitchy comment too many?'

'No one has dared,' she threw back.

'Well, take it from me. You need to stop throwing blind punches and learn to pick your fights.' He strode towards the

door. 'Romano will drive you to your appointment and bring
you back here.'

'That's not necessary. I've hired a scooter.'

He whirled to face her. 'No. Romano will drive you.' His tone
brooked no argument.

'Seriously, Marco, you need to dial back the caveman stuff—'

'And *you* need to take greater responsibility for your welfare.
If you come off your scooter and break an arm or a leg the rest
of the season is finished. I thought you wanted the drive? Or
do you think you're invincible on those little piles of junk you
like to travel on?'

She bit back a heated retort. Marco was right. All her hard
work and sacrifice would amount to nothing if she couldn't ensure she turned up to her races with her bones intact.

'Fine. I'll use the car.'

Pushing back the covers, she slid her feet over the edge and
stood. The air thickened once more as Marco tensed.

Sasha refused to look into his face. His brooding, tempting
heat would weaken her sorely tested resolve.

'I need to get ready for the shoot.'

He made a sound she couldn't decipher. She squeezed her
thighs together and fingered the hem of her T-shirt.

'Your breakfast will be delivered in half an hour.' He moved
towards the door. 'Oh, and Sasha…?'

Unable to stop herself, she looked. Framed in the doorway,
his stature was impressively male and utterly arresting. 'Yes?'
she rasped.

'Unless you want things to slide out of control, don't wear
that T-shirt in my presence again. You may not be mine, but I'm
not a saint. The next time I see you in it I may feel obliged to
take advantage of its instruction.'

His words hit her with the force of a tsunami. By the time he
shut the door, a hundred different images of Marco using his
teeth on her had short-circuited her brain.

The photo shoot was horrendously tedious. Several hours of
sitting around getting her hair and make-up done, followed by

a frenzied half-hour of striking impossible poses, then back to repeating the whole process again.

Sasha returned to the hotel very near exhaustion, but she had gained a healthy respect for models. She also now understood why men like Marco dated them. The sample pictures the photographer had let her keep showed an end result that surprised her.

After pressing the button for the lift, she fished the pictures out of her satchel, shocked all over again by how different she looked—how a few strokes of a make-up brush could transform plain to almost...*sexy*. Or was it something else? All day she'd been unable to dismiss last night's kiss from her mind. Her face burned when she reached the picture of her licking her tingling lips. She'd been recalling Marco's moan of pleasure as he'd deepened their kiss.

So really it was Marco's fault...

Opening the door to the suite, she stopped in her tracks as strains of jazz music wafted in from the living room. Following the sound, she entered the large, opulent room to find Marco lounging on the sofa, an electronic tablet in his hand and a glass of red wine on a table beside him.

'I thought you were going to be late?' The words rushed out before she could stop them. Her suddenly racing pulse made her dizzy for a few seconds.

His gaze zeroed in on her. 'I wrapped things up early.'

'And you couldn't find anyone in your little black book to spend the evening with?'

The thought that he hadn't gone out and vented his sexual frustration on some entirely willing female sent a bolt of elation through her, which she tried—unsuccessfully—to smash down.

She couldn't read the hooded look in his eyes as he set aside the gadget.

'It's only seven-thirty. The night is still young,' he replied.

Something crumpled into a small, tight knot inside her, and the sharp pang she'd felt that morning returned. 'That's just typical. You're going to call some poor woman out of the blue and expect her to be ready to drop everything to go out with you, aren't you?' she mocked.

One corner of his mouth quirked. 'Luckily, the women I know are kind enough to *want* to drop everything for me.'

She snorted. 'Come off it. We both know kindness has nothing to do with it.'

As she'd seen first-hand at the awards ceremony, women would crawl over hot coals to be with Marco. And many more would do so regardless of his financial status or influence. With a body and face like his, he could be penniless and still attract women with a snap of his fingers. As for that lethal, rarely seen smile, and the way he kissed—

Her thoughts screeched to a halt as he stood and came towards her.

'Maybe not,' he conceded, with not a hint of arrogance in sight. 'How was the shoot?'

The question wrenched her from her avid scrutiny of his body. 'Aside from the free shoes, it was a pain in the ass,' she replied.

'Of course,' he agreed gravely. Then without warning he reached out and plucked the pictures from her fingers. 'Maybe you'll even get around to wearing them instead of going barefoot or wearing those hideous boots—'

He stopped speaking as he stared at the pictures. Awareness crawled across her skin as he slowly thumbed through them, lingering over the one where she was draped over the bonnet of the not-yet-released prototype of his latest car, the Cervantes Triunfo. Eventually he returned to *that* one. And looked as if he'd stopped breathing.

'Marco…'

She stretched out her hand to retrieve the pictures. He ignored her, his attention fixed on the picture, his skin drawn tight over the chiselled bones of his face.

'Marco, I don't want to keep you. I have plans of my own.'

His head snapped up. 'What plans?' he demanded, his tone rough and tight.

Sasha couldn't think how to answer. Her whole mind was

paralysed by the way his eyes blazed. Shaking her head, she tried to turn away. He grabbed her arm in a firm hold.

No! Too hot. Too irresistible. Too much.

'Let me go,' she murmured, her voice scraped raw with desire.

'What plans?' he gritted out.

'Are you sure you want to know? You may not approve.'

His hand tightened on her arm, his eyes darkening into storm clouds that threatened thunder and lightning. 'Then think carefully before you speak.'

She sighed. 'Fine. You've busted me. I was going to beg your chef to make me that T-bone steak and salad he made for us yesterday, followed by chocolate caramel delight for dessert— I'll think about the calories later. Afterwards I intend to have a sweltering foursome with Joel, LuAnn and Logan.'

The hand that had started to relax suddenly tightened, harder than before.

'Excuse me?' Marco bit out, his voice a thin blade of ice slicing across her skin.

Reaching into the handbag slung over her shoulder, she pulled out the boxed set of her favourite TV vampire show.

He released her and reached for it. After scrutinising it, he threw it down onto the sofa along with the pictures.

'Take a piece of advice for free, *pequeña*. It's a mistake to keep goading me. The consequences will be greater than you ever bargained for.' His voice was soft. Deadly soft.

Sasha felt a shiver go through her. Most people mistakenly assumed partaking in one of the most dangerous sports in the world meant X1 Premier Racing drivers were fearless. Sasha wasn't fearless. She had a healthy amount of fear and respect for her profession. She knew when to accelerate, when to pull back the throttle, when to pull over and abandon her car.

Right now the look on Marco's face warned her she was skidding close to danger. She heeded the warning. Lashing out because of the maelstrom of emotions roiling inside her would most likely result in far worse consequences than she'd endured with Derek.

'Understood. Let me go.'

Surprise at her easy capitulation lit his eyes. Abruptly he released her.

'I need a shower. I guess you'll be gone when I come out. Enjoy your evening.'

Shamelessly, she fled.

Marco watched her go, frustration and bewilderment fighting a messy battle inside him.

He prided himself on knowing and understanding women. After Angelique, his determination never to be caught out again had decreed it. Women liked to think they were complicated creatures, but when it came down to it their needs were basic, no matter how much they tried to hide it. Hell, some—like Angelique—even spelled it out.

'I want fame, Marco. I want excitement! I can't be with a man who's a has-been.'

The memory slid in, reminding him why he now ensured the women he associated with knew there was no rosy future in store for them and had no surprises waiting to trap him.

A reality devoid of surprises suited him just fine.

His eyes followed Sasha's tall, slim figure down the hallway.

She surprised him, he admitted reluctantly. She also infuriated him. She made his blood boil in a way that was so basic, so...*sexual*—even without the benefit of those pictures...

Dios! With a growl, he whirled towards the window. When he'd gone to her room to set things straight this morning the last thing he'd expected was for her to reassure him that it had been no big deal.

Despite being totally into the kiss—as much as he'd been—she'd walked away from him last night. A situation he'd never encountered before.

Was it because she didn't really want him? Or was she merely waiting for his brother to wake up so she could resume where they'd left off?

Acid burned through his stomach at the thought. But even the corrosive effect couldn't wash away the underlying sexual need that seared him.

He'd rushed through his meeting with every intention of calling one of the many willing female acquaintances on his BlackBerry. But once he'd returned, his need to go out again had waned. He withdrew from examining why too closely.

He turned back from the window and his eyes fell on the pictures on the sofa. To the one of her draped all over his car...

Blindly he stumbled towards his jacket and dug around for his phone. Two minutes later reservations were made. By the time his Rolls collected him from the foyer, Sasha Fleming had been consigned to the furthest corner of his mind.

Marco stood outside the door ninety minutes later, caught himself listening for sounds from inside, and grimaced in disbelief. He'd spent the last hour or so wining and dining a woman whose name he couldn't now remember.

He'd stared at his date's in-your-face scarlet lips and thought of another set of lips. Plump, freshly licked lips, captured in perfect celluloid. Lips that had responded to his kiss in a way that had sent the most potent pulse of excitement through him.

Forbidden lips.

In the end he'd thrown down his napkin and extracted several large notes. 'You'll have to forgive me. I'm terrible company tonight. I shouldn't have disturbed your evening.'

The practised pout had reappeared. 'You know I'll forgive you anything, Marco.'

Candy? Candice? had leaned forward in another carefully calculated pose, designed to showcase her body to its best advantage.

'Listen, I have an idea. I know how much you like your coffee. When I was filming in Brazil last month I absolutely fell in love with the coffee and brought some back with me. Why don't we skip dessert and go back to my place and I'll give you a taste?'

Barely containing rising distaste, he'd shaken his head. 'Sorry, I'll take a rain check.'

He'd led her out amid soft protests and further throaty promises of the delights of her cafetière. But coffee, or sex with Candy/Candice had been the last thing on his mind.

His sudden hunger for chocolate caramel had become over-powering.

'Take my car. I'll walk,' he'd said.

And now here he stood, skulking outside his own apartment like a hormonal teenager on his first date.

He entered and approached the living room.

She was curled up on the sofa, a bowl of popcorn in her lap. Her head snapped towards him. As if she'd been listening out for him too. The thought pleased him more than it should have.

The striking blue of her eyes paralysed him.

'You're still awake.' *Excelente, Marco. First prize for stating the obvious.*

She blinked. 'It's only nine-fifteen.' Her eyes followed him as he shrugged off his jacket and dropped it on the sofa. When her gaze lingered on his chest he felt the blood surge stronger than before.

He watched her fingers dance through the bowl of popcorn, the movement curiously erotic. His heart hammered harder. 'You didn't have the chocolate caramel after all?'

'Charlie's disapproving face haunted me. Popcorn is healthier.' She looked away. 'So, how was your date?' she asked, her voice husky.

He wrenched his gaze from her fingers. 'You really want to know?'

Her sensual lips firmed and she shook her head.

The need to gauge her true feelings drew him closer. 'Jealous?'

She inhaled sharply. 'I thought we weren't doing this?'

His eyes fell to her lips. 'Maybe I've changed my mind.'

'Well, change it back. Nothing has changed since this morning. I can't handle your…baggage. And I don't want a relationship. Of any sort.'

Marco opened his mouth to tell her he didn't want anything from her either. But he knew he was lying. His very presence in this room belied that.

Forbidden or not, he wanted her with a compulsive need that unnerved and baffled him. But the fact that he wanted her didn't mean he would have her. He was known for his legendary control. He sat down next to her, caught her scent, and simply willed himself not to react.

Forcing his body to relax, he nodded towards the television. 'You have a thing for vampires?'

'Doesn't everyone?' she replied breathlessly.

He wanted to look at her. But he denied himself the urge and kept his gaze fixed ahead. 'What's the story about?'

She hesitated, fidgeted and sat forward. From the corner of his eye he saw her lick her lips. Fiery heat sang through his veins.

'Oh, you know—it's the usual run-of-the-mill storyline. Two brothers in love with the same girl.'

Something tightened in his chest and his stomach muscles clenched. 'I see.'

'You don't have to watch it.' She shifted backwards, out of his periphery.

'Why not? I'm intrigued.' The two male protagonists faced off on the screen, fangs bared. 'What are they doing now?'

Again she hesitated. 'They're about to fight to the death for her.'

His muscles pulled tighter. Blood surged through his veins and he forcibly relaxed the clenched fist on his thigh.

'Which one are you rooting for?' he asked, the skin on his nape curiously tight as he waited for her answer.

It occurred to him how absurd the conversation was. How absurd it was to be so wound up by a TV show. But every second he waited for her answer felt like an eternity.

'Neither.'

Illogically, his insides hollowed. 'You don't care if either one of them dies?' The words grated his throat.

'That's not what I said. I said neither because I know they won't kill each other. They might tear chunks out of each other, but ultimately they love each other too much to let a woman come between them. No matter how difficult, or how heart-wrenching it is to watch, I know they'll work it out. That's why I love the show. Popcorn?'

The bowl appeared in front of him.

He declined and nodded at the screen as a female character walked on. 'Is she the one?'

Sasha laughed. 'Yep. LuAnn—*femme fatale extraordinaire.* With those huge brown eyes and that body she can have any man she wants. On *and* off the screen.'

'She may look innocent onscreen but off-screen is another matter.'

It was her gasp that did it. That and her scent, mingled with the strangely enticing aroma of popcorn.

Control failed and his eyes met Sasha's stunning blue. Marco wondered if she knew how enthralling they were. How captivating. How very easily she could give LuAnn a run for her money.

'You've met her?'

'Briefly. At one of Rafael's parties.'

Her eyes returned to the screen. 'As much as I'm dying to know the details of your no-doubt salacious meeting, I don't really want the illusion spoiled. Do you mind?'

Again Marco was struck by Sasha's contrast to the other women he'd dated. They would have been bowled over by his mention of a celebrity, dying to know every single detail. Her refreshingly indifferent attitude made him relax a little more.

When he found himself munching on popcorn another bolt of surprise shot through him.

When was the last time he'd relaxed completely like this? Shared an enjoyable evening with a woman that hadn't ended in sex if he'd wanted it to?

He glanced at Sasha. Her eyes were glued to the screen, her lower lip caught between her teeth. Heat ratcheted through him. Correction—an evening that wasn't going to end in sex because sex was forbidden?

He reached for another mouthful of popcorn and his hand brushed hers. Her breath caught but she didn't look away from the screen. When he reluctantly forced his gaze away from her, he saw LuAnn caught in a heated clinch with Joel.

As a thirty-five-year-old man, who knew that sex onscreen was simulated, he shouldn't have found the scene erotic. Especially not with those damned fangs thrown in.

Nevertheless, when Sasha's breath caught for a second time he turned to her, his heart pounding so loudly in his ears he couldn't hear anything else.

'You should be watching the screen, not me.'

Her husky murmur thrummed along his nerve-endings and made a beeline for his groin.

'I was never much of a spectator. I prefer to be a participant.'

Dios! He was hard—so hard it was a toss-up as to whether the feeling was pain or pleasure. The logical thing to do was to get up, walk away.

Yet he couldn't move. Couldn't look away from this woman his body ached for but his mind knew he couldn't have.

Her eyes found his. 'Marco...'

Again it was a husky entreaty.

His fingers brushed her cheek. 'Why can't I get you out of my head? I took a beautiful woman to dinner but I can barely remember what she looked like now. I ate but hardly tasted the food. All I could think about was you.'

'Do you want me to apologise?'

'Would you mean it?'

Her pink tongue darted out, licked, darted back in. He groaned in pain.

'Probably not. But I may have an explanation for you.'

A few feet away the TV belted out the closing sequence of the show. Neither of them paid any attention. His forefinger traced her soft skin to the corner of her mouth, the need to taste her again a raging fever flaming through his veins. 'I'm listening.'

She shrugged. 'Maybe you share a trait with your brother after all. Deny you something and you want it more?'

Marco didn't need to think about it to answer. 'No. The difference between Rafael and me is that he wouldn't have hesitated to take—consequences be damned. He sees something he wants and he takes it.'

'Whereas you agonise about it endlessly, then deny yourself anyway? It's almost as if you're testing yourself—putting yourself through some sort of punishment.'

Her eyes darkened when he froze. She moved her head and

her lips came closer to his finger. Marco couldn't speak, needing every single ounce of self-control to keep his shock from showing. He *deserved* to put himself through punishment for what he'd done. He'd lost the most precious thing in life—a child—because he'd taken his eye off the ball.

'Maybe you should learn to bend a little…take what is being offered? What is being offered freely.'

An arrow of pain shot through the haze of desire engulfing him. He gave a single shake of his head and inhaled. 'I stopped believing in *free* a long time ago, Sasha. There are always consequences. The piper always expects payment.'

'I don't believe that. Laughter is free. Love is free. It's hate that eats you up inside. Bitterness that twists feelings if you let them. And, no, I'm not waxing philosophical. I've experienced it.'

'Really?' he mocked, dropping his hand. When his senses screeched in protest he merely willed the feeling away. 'To whom did you make your promise?' he asked, the need to know as forceful as the need raging through his veins.

Wariness darkened her eyes. Then her shoulders rolled. 'My father.'

'What did you promise him?'

'That I'd win the Drivers' Championship for him.'

'Out of some misguided sense of duty, no doubt?' he derided.

Anger blazed through her eyes. 'Not duty. *Love.* And it's about as misguided as your bullheaded need to coddle Rafael.'

'There's a difference between responsibility and your illusionary love,' he rebutted, irate at this turn of the conversation.

'I suffer no illusions. My father loved me as unconditionally as I loved him.'

Tensing, he sat back in the seat. 'Then you were lucky. Not everyone is imbued with unconditional love for his or her child. Some even use their unborn children as bartering tools.'

Her breath caught. 'Did you…? Are you saying that from experience?'

A cold drench of reality washed over him at how close he'd come to revealing everything.

Surging to his feet, he stared into her face. 'I was merely making a point. As much as I want you, Sasha, I'll never take you. The consequences would be too great.'

CHAPTER EIGHT

THE consequences would be too great.

Sasha tried to block out the words as she adjusted the traction control on her steering wheel. The tremor in her fingers increased and she clenched her fists tighter around the wheel.

Shears, Marina Bay, Raffles Boulevard. Watch out for Turn Ten speed bump—Padang, pit lane exit, look after the tyres...

Her heart hammered, excitement and adrenaline shooting through her as she went through the rigorous ritual of visualising every corner of the race. At her third attempt, fear rose to mingle with her emotions.

She'd secured pole position for the first time in her racing career, but despite the team's euphoria afterwards she'd sensed a subtle waning of their excitement as speculation as to whether she could do the job trickled in. Sasha had seen it in their faces, heard it in Luke's voice this morning when he'd grilled her over race strategy for the millionth time. Even Tom had weighed in.

Consequences...responsibility...last chance...

Sweat trickled down her neck and she hastily sipped at her water tube. She couldn't afford dehydration. Couldn't afford to lose focus. In fact she couldn't afford to do anything less than win.

Beyond the bright lights of the circuit that turned night into day at the Singapore Grand Prix thousands of fans would be watching.

As would Marco.

He hadn't spoken to her since that night on his sofa in London, but he'd attended every race since the season had resumed and Sasha knew he was somewhere above her, in the exclusive VIP suite of the team's motor home, hosting the Prime Minister, royalty and a never-ending stream of celebrities.

Some time during the sleepless night, when she'd been looking down at the race track from her hotel room, she'd wondered whether he'd even bother to grace the pit with his presence if she made it onto that final elusive step on the podium. Or whether he would be too preoccupied with entertaining his latest flame—the blonde daughter of an Italian textile magnate who never seemed far from his side nowadays.

She tried desperately to block him from her mind. Taking pole position today—a dream she'd held for longer than she could remember—should be making her ecstatic. She was one step further towards removing the dark stain of her father's shame from people's minds. To finally removing herself from Derek's malingering shadow.

Yet all she could think about was Marco and their conversation in London.

She clenched her teeth in frustration and breathed in deeply.

Luke's voice piped through her helmet, disrupting her thoughts.

'Adjust your clutch—'

She flicked the switch before he'd finished speaking. The sheer force of her will to win was a force field around her. Finally she found the zen she desperately craved.

Focusing, she followed the red lights as they lit up one by one. Adrenaline rushed faster, followed a second later by the drag of the powerful car as she pointed it towards the first corner.

She made it by the skin of her teeth, narrowly missing the front wing of the number two driver. Her stomach churned through lap after gruelling lap, even after she'd established a healthy distance between her and the car behind.

What seemed like an eternity later, after a frenzied race, including an unscheduled pitstop that had raised the hairs on her arms, she heard the frenzied shouts of her race engineer in her ear.

'You won! Sasha, you won the Singapore Grand Prix!'

Tears prickled her eyes even as her fist pumped through the air. Her father's face floated through her mind and a sense of peace settled momentarily over her. It was broken a second later by the sound of the crowd's deafening roar.

Exiting the car, Sasha squinted through the bright flashes of the paparazzi, desperate to see familiar hazel eyes through the sea of faces screaming her name.

No Marco.

A stab of disappointment hollowed out her stomach. With a sense of detachment, she accepted the congratulations of her fellow drivers and blinked back tears through the British national anthem.

Dad would be proud, she reminded herself fiercely. *He* was all that mattered. Plastering a smile on her face, she accepted her trophy from the Prime Minister.

This was what she wanted. What she'd fought for. The team—*her* team—were cheering wildly. Yet Sasha felt numb inside.

Fighting the alarming emptiness, she picked up the obligatory champagne magnum, letting the spray loose over her fellow podium winners. Brusquely she told herself to live in the moment, to enjoy the dream-come-true experience of winning her first race.

Camera flashes blinded her as she stepped off the podium. When it cleared Tom stood in front of her, a huge grin on his face.

'I *knew* you could do it! Prepare yourself, Sasha. Your world's about to rock!'

The obligatory press conference for the top three winning drivers took half an hour. When she emerged, Tom grabbed her arm and steered her towards the bank of reporters waiting behind the barriers.

'Tom, I don't really want—'

'You've just won your first race. *"I don't really want"* shouldn't feature in your vocabulary. The world's your oyster.'

But I don't want the world, she screamed silently. *I want Marco. I want not to feel alone on a night like this.*

Feeling the stupid tears build again, Sasha rapidly blinked them back as a microphone was thrust in her face.

'How does it feel to be the first woman to win the Singapore Grand Prix?'

From deep inside she summoned a smile. 'Just as brilliant as the first man felt when he won, I expect.'

Beside her she heard Tom's sharp intake of breath.

Behave, Sasha.

'Are you still involved with Rafael de Cervantes?' asked an odious reporter she recognised from a Brazilian sports channel.

'Rafael and I were never involved. We're just friends.'

'So now he's in a coma there's nothing to stop you from switching *friendships* to his brother, no?'

Tom stepped forward. 'Listen, mate—'

Sasha stopped him. 'No. It's fine.' She faced the reporter. 'Marco de Cervantes is a world-class engineer and a visionary in his field. His incredible race car design is the reason we won the race today. It would be an honour for me to call him my friend.' She tagged on another smile and watched the reporter's face droop with disappointment.

Tom nodded at a British female reporter. 'Next question.'

'As the winner of the race, you'll be the guest of honour at the rock concert. What will you be wearing?'

Mild shock went through her at the question, followed swiftly by a deepening sense of hollowness. The X1 Premier Rock Concert had become a fixture on every A-List celebrity's calendar. No doubt Marco would be there with his latest girlfriend.

'It doesn't matter what I'll be wearing because I'm not going to the concert.'

Sasha dashed into the foyer of her six-star hotel, grateful when the two burly doormen blocked the chasing paparazzi. She heaved in a sigh of relief when she shut her suite door behind her.

The ever-widening chasm of emptiness she couldn't shake threatened to overwhelm her. Quickly she stripped off her clothes and showered.

The knock came as she was towelling herself dry. For a second she considered not answering it.

A sense of *déjà vu* hit her as she opened the door to another perfectly coiffed stylist, carting another rack of clothes.

'I think you've got the wrong suite.'

The diminutive Asian woman in a pink suit simply bowed, smiled and let herself in. Her assistant sailed in behind her, clutching a large and stunningly beautiful bouquet of purple lilies and cream roses.

'For you.' She thrust the flowers and a long oblong box into Sasha's hand.

Stifling a need to scream, Sasha calmly shut the door and opened the box. On a red velvet cushion lay the most exquisite diamond necklace she'd ever seen. With shaking fingers, she plucked the card from the tiny peg.

Pick a dress, then they'll leave. Romano is waiting downstairs.

Sasha stared at Marco's bold scrawl in disbelief. When she looked up, the women smiled and started pulling clothes off the hangers.

'No—wait!'

'No wait. Twenty minutes.'

'But...where am I going?' she asked.

The stylist shrugged, picked up a green-sequinned dress barely larger than a handkerchief, and advanced towards her. Sasha stepped back as the tiny woman waved her hand in front of her.

'Off.'

With a sense of damning inevitability...and more than a little thrill of excitement...she let herself be pulled forward. 'Okay, but definitely not the green.'

The stylist nodded, trilled out an order in Mandarin, and advanced again with another dress.

Twenty minutes later Sasha stepped from the cool, air-conditioned car onto another red carpet. This time, without

Marco, she was even more self-conscious than before. On a warm, sultry Singapore night, the cream silk dress she'd chosen felt more exposing than it had in the safety of her hotel room. At first glance she'd refused to wear the bohemian mini-dress because...well, because it had no back. But then the stylist had fastened the draping material across her lower back and Sasha had felt...*sexy*—like a woman for the first time in her life.

Her hair was fastened with gold lamé rope, her nails polished and glittering. The look was completed with four-inch gold stilettos she'd never dreamt she'd be able to walk in, but she found it surprisingly easy.

Romano appeared at her side, his presence a reminder that somewhere beyond the wild flashes of the paparazzi's cameras Marco was waiting for her.

All the way from her hotel she'd felt the emptiness receding, but had been too scared to acknowledge that Marco had anything to do with it. Now she couldn't stop a smile from forming on her face as the loud boom of fireworks signalled the start of the rock concert.

The VIP lounge teemed with rock stars and pop princesses. She tried to make small talk as she surreptitiously searched the crowd for Marco. Someone thrust a glass of champagne in her hand.

Half an hour later, when a Columbian platinum-selling songstress with snake hips asked who her designer was, Sasha started to answer, then stopped as an ice-cold thought struck her. Was Marco even here? Had she foolishly misinterpreted his note and dressed up only to be stood up?

The depths of her hurt stunned her into silence.

She barely felt any remorse as the pop star flounced off in a huff. Blindly she turned for the exit, humiliation scouring through her.

'Sasha? You're heading for the stage, right?' Tom grabbed her arm and stopped her.

'The...the stage?'

'Your favourite band is about to perform. Marco had me fly them out here just for you.'

'He *what*?' A different kind of *stun* stopped her heart.

'Come on—you don't want them to start without you.'

A thousand questions raced through her brain, but she didn't have time to voice a single one before she was propelled onto the stage and into the arms of the band's lead singer.

Torn between awe at sharing the stage with her favourite band, and happiness that she hadn't misinterpreted Marco's note after all, Sasha knew the next ten minutes were the most surreal of her life. Even seeing herself super-sized on half a dozen giant screens didn't freak her out as much as she'd imagined.

She exited the stage to the crowd's deafening roar. Tom beamed as he helped her down the stairs.

'Have you seen Marco?' Sasha attributed her breathlessness to her onstage excitement—not her yearning to see Marco de Cervantes.

Tom's smile slipped and his gaze dropped. 'Um, he was around a moment ago...'

She told herself not to read anything into Tom's answer. 'Where is he?'

'Sasha...' He sighed and pointed towards the roped-off area manned by three burly bodyguards.

At first she didn't see him, her sight still fuzzy from the bright stage lights.

When she finally focused, when she finally saw what her mind refused to compute, Sasha was convinced her heart had been ripped from her chest.

Each step she took out of the concert grounds felt like a walk towards the opening mouth of a yawning chasm. But Sasha forced herself to keep going, to smile, to acknowledge the accolades and respect she finally had from her team.

Even though inside she was numb and frozen.

The knock came less than ten minutes later.

Marco leaned against the lintel. The buttons of his shirt were *still* undone; his hair was unkempt. As if hands—*female hands*—had run through it several times. He stood there, arrogantly imposing, larger than life.

She hated him more than she could coherently express. And yet the sight of him kicked her heart into her throat.

'What do you want?' she blurted past the pain in her throat.

His gaze, intense and unnerving, left her face to take in the bikini she'd changed into. 'Why did you leave the concert?'

'Why aren't you back there, being pawed by your Italian sexpot?'

'You left because you saw me with Flavia?'

'You know what they say—two's company, three's a flash mob. Now, if you'll excuse me...' She grabbed her kaftan from the bed and the box containing the diamond necklace.

'Here—take this back. I don't want it.'

'It's yours. Every member of the team receives a gift for the team's win. This is yours.'

Her mouth dropped open. 'You're kidding me?'

'I'm not. Where are you going?'

She stared at the box, not sure how to refuse the gift now. 'For a swim—not that it's any of your business.'

'A swim? At this hour?'

'Singapore is the longest race on the calendar. It's even longer when you're leading and trying to defend your position. If I don't warm up and do my stretching exercises my muscles will seize up. That's what I'd planned to do before... Whatever—will you please get out of my way?'

His gaze dropped to her legs. A hoarse sound rumbled from his throat. A look entered his eyes—one that made her excited and afraid at the same time.

'Marco, I said—'

'I heard you.' Still, he didn't move away. Instead, he extracted his phone and issued a terse command in Spanish, his gaze on her the whole time.

Sasha dropped the box on the bed and took a deep calming breath, willing her skin to stop tingling, her heartbeat to slow down. Her senses were too revved up, ready to unleash the full power of her conflicted feelings for this man.

'Let's go.' He finally moved out of the doorway.

'I'm not going anywhere with you until you tell me what you're doing here,' she responded.

He speared a hand through his hair, mussing up the luxurious strands even more. 'Does it matter why I'm here, Sasha? Are you happy to see me?' he demanded in a low, charged tone.

She hated the fire that raced through her veins, stinging her body to painful life in a way even her first race win hadn't been able to achieve.

'Less than half an hour ago you had another woman all over you. Last time I checked, my name wasn't Sloppy Seconds Sasha.'

He swore under his breath. 'You know, you're the most difficult, infuriating woman I know.'

Despite the raspy vehemence in his tone, she smiled. 'Thank you.'

He took her arm and led her to the lift. 'It wasn't a compliment.'

'I know. But I'll take it as one.' She tried not to breathe too deeply of his scent as he stepped in beside her.

The lift whisked them upwards. From the corner of her eye she saw him turn his phone off and shove it into his pocket.

The doors opened onto a space that was so beautiful Sasha couldn't speak for several seconds. In the soft breeze potted palm trees swayed. Strategically placed lights gave the space an exotic but intimate feel that just begged to be enjoyed. Several feet away an endless, boomerang shaped infinity pool poised over the tip of the hotel's tower glimmered blue and silver.

Then she noticed what was missing. 'It's empty.' There wasn't a single soul on the sixtieth-floor skydeck.

'*Sí.*'

The way he responded had her turning to face him.

'You had something to do with it?'

A simple nod.

'Why?'

His shook his head in disbelief. 'That's the hundredth question you've asked since I knocked on your door. I didn't want your swim to be interrupted.'

She kicked away her slippers, her temperature rising another notch when his gaze dropped to her bare feet. 'This pool is three times the size of an Olympic pool. It's hardly cramped.'

His gaze turned molten. 'I wanted privacy.' He released the last button on his shirt and it fell open to reveal a golden washboard torso.

Heat piled on. Beneath the Lycra bikini, her nipples tightened, and her stomach muscles quivered with a need so strong she could barely breathe. 'I see. Will you snarl at me if I ask why?'

'Yes,' he snarled.

Striding to her, he drew the hem of her kaftan over her head and tossed it over his shoulder. Then he took her hair tie, raked his fingers through the strands and secured her hair on top of her head.

Fresh waves of desire threatened to drown her. 'Marco…'

'How many laps do you need to be less tense?'

'Tw—twenty.' She couldn't drag her eyes from the beauty of his face, from the sensual, inviting curve of his mouth.

'Twenty laps it is, then.' He shrugged off his shirt, then released his belt.

Her eyes widened. 'What are you doing?'

'What does it look like?'

'Um…'

Without warning he leaned forward and sniffed the skin between her neck and shoulder. 'You're covered in *eau de* Sleazy Rock Star. I smell of cloying Italian perfume. What say we wash the scent of other people off our skin, and then we'll talk, *si*?

'Marco…'

He swore under his breath. 'Go, Sasha. I need to cool off, or *Dios* help me, I won't be responsible for my actions.'

She went, with the heaviness of his hot gaze scorching her skin.

Pausing at one end of the pool, she stretched her arms over her head. At his sharp intake of breath, she let a sensual smile curve her lips.

The water was a welcome but temporary relief from the sensations arcing between them. He dived in after her a second later, quickly caught up with her and matched her stroke for stroke. When she swam faster, to escape the frenzied need clawing inside, he kept up with her.

His presence made every stroke of water against her skin feel like a caress. At the last lap he increased his pace and heaved himself out of the water. She clung to the side, her lungs heaving, and watched the play of water on his magnificent body as he returned to the poolside.

'Out,' he commanded tersely, his hand holding out a towel like a bull-baiting matador.

She rose out of the pool, careful not to look at the wet clinginess of his boxers. He folded the towel around her, his movements brisk as he rubbed the moisture off her. Then he swung her into his arms and carried her to the enclosed cabana a few feet away.

Two silk-covered loungers stood side by side, separated by a table laid out with several platters of food, from local delicacies to caviar on blinis. In a sterling silver tub a linen-draped bottle of vintage champagne chilled on ice.

Marco set her down on the lounger and picked up the bottle.

Sasha forced her gaze from the play of muscles and looked at the table. 'There's enough here to feed an army.' Reaching for a small plate, she dished out grilled prawns and fragrant rice.

'You don't like caviar?'

She grimaced. 'It smells funny and tastes disgusting. I don't know why people eat the stuff.' She took a mouthful of her food and felt the explosion of textures on her tongue. Thankfully she managed to swallow without choking. 'Now, *this* is heavenly.' She took another mouthful and groaned.

Marco took his seat across from her and held out one glass of champagne, his gaze never leaving hers. What she glimpsed in the heated depths made her heart quicken.

'Marco—'

'Eat. We'll talk when you're done.'

How can I eat? she wanted to ask. Especially when his eyes followed her every move. But words refused to form on her lips.

It was as if he'd cast some sort of spell on her. Maybe he was a vampire after all, she thought hysterically.

The thought should have lightened her mood, made it easier for her to cope, but all it did was cause a fevered shudder to race down her spine.

Clawing in a desperate breath, she set the plate aside. 'Let's talk now. You invited me to the concert, then ignored me to make out with your girlfriend. What else is there to talk about?'

'Flavia's not my girlfriend, and I wasn't making out with her. She was congratulating me on the team's win, just like a lot of people have done tonight.'

'She was *all* over you. And you didn't seem to mind.'

'I was...preoccupied.'

She snorted. 'Evidently.'

'*Para el amor de Dios!* I was waiting in the VIP room for *you*! The Prime Minister turned up when I was about to come and meet you. I tried to get away as quickly as possible, only to find you were more interested in plastering yourself all over your favourite rock star. It was very evident you didn't have a bra on, but tell me—were you even wearing panties under that dress?'

A harsh flush of anger tinged his cheekbones. This was the angriest she'd ever seen Marco. The reason why stopped her breath.

'You were jealous?'

His jaw clenched. 'Do you mean was that what I expected when I had the band flown over for you? No. Did I want to break every bone in his pathetically thin body? *Sí.* For starters.'

The air thickened around them.

A thousand different questions rushed into her mind. One emerged.

'I'm not stupid, Marco, I know where this is going. But what about the consequences? The ones that made you avoid me for the past three weeks?'

He abandoned his glass and rested his hands on his knees, his eyes never leaving hers. 'Seeing you in another man's arms has simplified my decision. For the sake of my sanity, and to avoid murder charges, no more staying away,' he rasped.

'Right. Well, I'm happy for you and your sanity. But what about what *I* want?'

His eyes dropped to her lips. 'If you know where this is going then you know how badly I want to kiss you. Come here.'

Her mouth, the subject of his very intense scrutiny, tingled so badly she had to curb the urge to bite it. 'I meant what I said in London. I don't want a relationship.'

A hard look passed through his eyes. 'I don't want a relationship either.'

'What about *your* clause?'

'I'm not a racing driver and I don't work for the team so I'm exempt. Come here, Sasha.'

'No. Aren't you twisting the rules?'

'No. I can quote them verbatim for you later. Right now I want you to come over here and kiss me.'

Her breath shortened. 'What if I don't want to?'

His gaze darkened. 'Then I'll return to the concert, find your reedy rock star and decorate the VIP lounge with him.'

A roar went up a few miles away. The throb of the rock concert echoed superbly the blood surging through her veins as Marco continued to watch her.

'I hope you won't expect me to bail you out of jail.'

He shrugged. 'I live in hope for a lot of things, *querida*. At this moment I'm hoping you'll stop arguing and crawl into my lap. Would it help if I said that not a day went by these past three weeks when you didn't feature in my thoughts?' He lifted a winged brow.

'Maybe that helps. A little…'

Without warning he reached across the table and scooped her up. Settling her in his lap, he freed her hair and sighed in pleasure as the heavy tresses spilled into his hands. Then he lowered her until her back rested on the upraised lounger.

Despite her bikini's relative modesty, Sasha had never felt more exposed in her life. Especially when Marco took his time to trail his fierce gaze over her, missing nothing as he scoured her body, and followed more slowly with one long, lazy finger.

'You're doing it again.' Her voice was smoky with lust, her flesh alight wherever he touched.

'What?' he murmured, his eyes resting at the apex of her thighs.

Beneath her bottom the hard ridge of his erection pressed into her flesh, its heat making her skin tighten in feverish anticipation.

'The thing with your eyes. And your hands. And your body.'

'If you want me to stop you'll have to kiss me.'

'Maybe I don't want you to stop. Maybe this is what I'll allow before I decide this is a very bad idea.'

His finger paused on her belly. 'You think this is a bad idea?'

A thread of uncertainty wheedled through her desire. 'My last involvement left a lot of bruises.'

He tensed. 'Derek physically hurt you?'

'No, but he influenced a lot of people against me. You included.'

He shook his head. 'I make up my own mind. If you truly don't want this, say the word and I'll stop.'

The thought of denying herself made her heart lurch painfully.

Her body moved closer of its own volition. He hissed out a breath, the skin around his mouth tightening as he visibly reined in control. 'If you intend to stop that's not a great idea, *querida.*'

Sasha had had enough. Marco had spent far too much of his life controlling everything. For once she yearned to see him lose his cool, to crack the shell of tightly reined-in emotion. She wriggled again.

His gaze connected with hers. The dark hunger in its depths made her breath catch. Giving in to the urge, she slipped her hand over his nape and urged his head down.

He took control of her lips in a kiss so driven, so desperate, she cried out against his mouth. He fisted one hand in her hair to hold her still, his other hand sliding over her bottom to drag her closer.

Sasha went willingly, her body a fluid vessel of rampant desire that craved only him. Every single doubt that crowded in her brain drowned under ever-increasing waves of sensation.

She might be risking everything to experience a few hours of pleasure, but Sasha could no more push Marco away than she could voluntarily stop breathing. She would deal with regret in the morning.

Losing herself in the kiss, she boldly thrust her tongue against his. His body jerked, making a tiny fizz of pleasure steal through her.

When his fingers squeezed her buttock, she moaned.

He pulled back. 'You like that?' he rasped, his gaze heavy and hooded.

She nodded and licked her lips, already missing the feel of his mouth against hers.

'Tell me what else you'd like, *mi tentación*.' He released the tie of her bikini top and trailed his mouth over her skin.

'You…not to be so overdressed…' she gasped out.

Another roar from the concert ripped through the night air. Momentarily she remembered where they were.

'On the other hand, maybe that's not so bad—'

'We won't be disturbed.'

The finality of the statement, along with the graze of his teeth over one Lycra-clothed nipple, melted the last of her reservations. Giving her feelings free rein, she slid her hand over his shoulders, touching the smooth skin of his nape before exploring his damp, luxurious hair.

Her urgency fed his. With renewed vigour he kissed her again, pulling off the wet cloth and tossing it aside. Reversing their positions, he eased her onto the lounger, then tugged off her bikini bottoms.

In the soft, ambient light of the enclosed cabana his skin gleamed golden, the dark silky hairs on his chest making her fingers tingle to touch.

'I want to touch you all over.' The heated words had slipped out before she could stop them.

His face contorted in a pained grimace. Tugging off his boxers, he stretched out next to her. Leaning down, he ran his tongue over her mouth. 'I believe I mentioned the near insanity that has plagued me these past weeks? Touching me all over is not a good idea right now.'

Her breath rasped through her chest. Breathing had become increasingly difficult. 'Oh. Then I guess it's not a good time to mention I also intend biting a few strategic places?'

A heartfelt groan preceded a few heated Spanish words muttered against her lips. 'Do me a favour, *mi tentadora*. Keep your thoughts to yourself for the time being. You have my word. I'll let you vocalise your every want later.'

Swooping down, he captured one exposed nipple in his mouth, his fierce determination to shut her up working wonders. Words deserted her as sensation took over. Liquid heat pooled at the apex of her thighs, the flesh of her sex swelling and pulsating with the strength of her need. By the time he transferred his attention to her other nipple Sasha was incoherent with desire.

Marco traced his lips lower, ruthlessly turning her inside out with pleasure, but when she felt his mouth dip below her navel she froze.

Sensing her withdrawal, he raised his head. 'You don't want this?'

'I *do*.' So much so the force of her need shocked her. 'I do… But you don't have to if…' Her words fizzled out at the searing heat in his eyes.

'I've spent endless nights imagining the taste of you, Sasha.' He parted her legs wider, licked the sensitive skin inside her thigh, his eyes growing darker at her breathless groan. 'But I've always preferred reality to dreams.'

He put his mouth on her, slowly worked his tongue over the millions of nerve-endings saturated with pleasure receptors. Sasha screamed, and came in a rush of pleasure so intense her whole body quivered with it.

Before the last of her orgasm had faded away Marco was surging over her. His kiss was less frantic but no less demanding. And, just like the engine of a finely tuned car, her body responded to his demands, anticipation firing her blood like nothing had ever done in her life.

Tension screamed through Marco's body as he raised himself from the intoxicating kiss. The sound of Sasha's orgasm echoed in his head like a siren's call, promising him pleasure beyond measure. He couldn't remember ever being so fired up about sex—so impatient he'd nearly forgotten protection.

Luckily sanity prevailed just in time.

Sasha moved restlessly beneath him, her sultry gaze steady on his as he parted her thighs.

Every single night of the past three weeks he'd woken with an ache in his groin and a sinking sensation that he was fighting a losing battle. He'd congratulated himself on staying away, but he'd known deep down it was a hollow victory.

Truth was he'd never wanted a woman as much as he wanted Sasha. He'd stopped trying to decipher what made her so irresistible. She just *was*. He'd also made discreet enquiries and verified that she'd spoken the truth—she hadn't been involved with Rafael.

So just this once he was going to take. Sasha Fleming had worked her way under his skin like no other woman had and now this was the inevitable conclusion. Her underneath him, her thighs parted, her sultry gaze steady on his. Just as he'd dreamed...

With a groan he sank into her.

'Thank God!' she cried. 'For a second there I thought you were about to change your mind.'

As if to stop him taking that route, her muscles clamped tight around him.

Another groan tore from his throat. 'I thought I told you to shut up?' He pulled back and surged into her once more, pleasure such as he'd never known rocking through him.

'I am... I will... Just please don't stop.' Raking her nails down his back, she clamped her hands around his waist.

As if he could even if he wanted to. He was past the point of no return, his need so great he was almost afraid to acknowledge its overwhelming scope. Instead he lost himself in her pleasure, in the hitched sounds and feminine demands of her body as she welcomed him into her sweet warmth.

'*Dios*, you feel incredible,' he rasped as sensation piled upon sensation.

Inevitably the bough broke. Ecstasy rode through him, blinding him to everything else but the glorious satisfaction of unleashed passion.

With her cry of bliss he followed off the peak, the muscles in his body tightening with the force of his orgasm as he emptied himself into her.

He collapsed on top of her, her soft, sweat-slicked body a cushion to his hardness. He remained there until their breathing calmed then, rolling onto the lounger, he tucked her against his side.

As the last of the haze faded away he felt the first inevitable twinge of regret. He'd succumbed to temptation. Now the piper would expect payment. And for the first time in his life Marco was afraid at just how much he was willing to pay.

CHAPTER NINE

'WHAT—?' Sasha jerked awake.

The solid body curved around hers and the arm imprisoning her kept her from falling off the lounger. Opening her eyes, she encountered Marco's accusing gaze.

'You fell asleep.'

The wide expanse of muscled chest scrambled her brain for a few seconds, before a few synapses fired a thought. She'd had sex with Marco. Wild, unbelievable, pleasure-filled sex. After which—

'You fell *asleep*,' he incised a second time, affront stamped all over his face.

'Uh…I'm sorry…'

'I get the feeling you don't mean that.'

'And I get the feeling I'm not following this conversation at all.' Before she could stop it a wide yawn broke through.

His glare darkened.

'Did I not please you?' He seemed genuinely puzzled, and a little unsure. One hand curved under her nape to tilt her face up to his.

Thoughts of their lovemaking melted her insides. 'Of course you did,' she said, struggling to keep from blushing at recalling her cries of pleasure. Lifting her hands, she framed his face. 'I've never felt more pleasure than I did with you.'

'It was so good you fell asleep straight after?'

'Take it as a compliment. You wore me out.'

His lids veiled his eyes. 'This is a first, I admit.'

'Wearing a woman out?' she asked, stunned.

'Of course not. The falling asleep part.'

Laughter bubbled up from deep within her, delight filling her. Leaning up, she pressed her lips against his in a light kiss.

Marco took over and turned it into a long, deep kiss.

By the time he was done with her she struggled to breathe. And he...he was fully engorged, his erection a forceful presence against her belly. Emboldened by the thought that she could arouse him again so quickly, she caressed her fingers down his side, eliciting a shuddered groan from him that released a wanton smile from her.

'Like I said, I'm sorry. How can I make it up to you?' She slid her hand between them and gripped him tight. His lips parted on another groan. She caressed up and down, marvelling at the tensile strength of him.

His mouth trailed over her face to the juncture between her neck and shoulder. Erotic heat washed through her.

When her grip tightened, his breath shuddered out. '*Sí, mi querida*, that's the right way to make it up to me.'

His hips bucked against her hold, heat and strength pulsing through her fingers. Liquid heat gathered between her thighs. She was unbelievably turned on by the pleasure she gave him.

At yet another caress he suddenly reared up and flipped her over. 'You're getting carried away.'

She slid her thighs either side of him and lowered herself until her wet heat touched him. The feel of his strong hands sliding down her back to capture her bottom made her shiver with delight.

'Then me being on top wasn't the best idea, was it?'

His predatory gaze swept over her, lingering on her breasts, making them peak even more painfully.

'It's time you learned that I can control you from whichever position I'm in,' he breathed.

He surged into her, filling her so completely stars exploded behind her closed lids. He captured her nape, forced her down and took her mouth in a scorching kiss. His tongue seeking the deep cavern of her mouth, he took her over completely, escalating the desire firing through her until Sasha was aflame with a pleasure so intense it frightened the small part of her brain that could still function.

Sasha hung on as he clamped one hand in the small of her back to hold her still. His pace was frantic, frightful in its demand and exquisite in its delivery of pleasure. She whimpered when he freed her mouth, only to blindly seek his for herself before she could draw another breath. Sensation spiralled out of control as bliss gathered with stunning speed.

'Open your eyes. Let me see your eyes when you come for me.'

She obeyed. Then wished she hadn't when the heat in his eyes threatened to send her already flaming world out of control.

'Marco...'

'*Sí*, I feel it too.'

She believed him. The sheen of sweat coating his skin, the unsteady hand that caressed down her face before recapturing her nape, the harsh pants that escaped his lungs all attested to the fact that he was caught in this incredible maelstrom too.

Pleasure scythed through her heart, arrowed down into her pelvis, forcing her to cry out one last time as her orgasm exploded through her.

Beneath her, still controlling their pleasure, Marco thrust into her release, groaning at the sensation of her caressing convulsions, then found his own satisfaction.

Their harsh breaths mingled, hearts thundering as the breeze cooled their sweat-damp skin. Far away, another burst of fireworks lit up the sky.

Inside the cabana, the intensity of their shared pleasure sparked a threat of fear through her.

To mask her feelings, she hid her face in his shoulder. 'I'd love to compose a sonnet to you right now. But I have no words.'

A short rumble of laughter echoed through his heated chest. 'Sonnets are overrated. Your screams of pleasure were reward enough.'

Sasha sighed, put her head on his chest and tried to breathe. The alarm that had taken root in that small part of her brain grew. Something had happened between their first and second lovemaking.

Then she'd felt safe enough to fall asleep in Marco's arms.

Now... Now she felt exposed. Her emotions felt raw, naked. Unbidden, tears prickled her eyes. She scrambled to hide her composure but Marco sensed her feelings.

Pushing her head gently off his shoulder, he stared into her face. 'You're crying. Why?'

How could she explain something she had no understanding of?

When she tried to shrug he shook his head. 'Tell me.'

'I'm just feeling a little overwhelmed. That's all.'

After a second he nodded and brushed a hand down her cheek. '*Sí*. This is your first victory. That feeling can never be equalled.'

For several heartbeats Sasha didn't follow his meaning. When she realised he was talking about the race, and not the roiling aftermath of their lovemaking, her heart lurched.

Panic escalating, she grasped the lifeline. 'I wish my father had been there.'

Marco nodded. 'He would've been proud of you.'

Surprise widened her eyes. 'You knew my father?'

'Of course. He was the greatest driver never to win a championship. I've seen every single race of his. Clearly you inherited his talent.'

The unexpected compliment made her feel even more tearful. She tried to move away but he caught her back easily, lowered his head and kissed his way along her arm. When she shivered, he shook out a cashmere throw and pulled it over them, one muscular leg imprisoning both of hers.

She was grateful for the cover—not least because the familiar feeling of humiliation had returned. 'You know what happened to him, then?'

'He bet on another car to win and deliberately crashed his car.' The cold conviction in his voice sent an icy shiver down her spine, bleeding away the warmth she'd felt in his arms.

This time she moved away forcefully. Standing, she grabbed

her kaftan and slid it over her head, even though it did little to cover her nakedness.

'The allegations were false!'

Marco folded his arms behind his head. 'Not according to the court that found him guilty.'

'He never managed to disprove the claims. But *I* believed him. He would *never* have done that. He loved racing too much to crash deliberately for money.'

'I was on the board that reviewed the footage, Sasha. The evidence was hard to refute.'

Shock and anger twisted in her gut. '*You* were one of those who decided he was guilty?'

He lowered his feet to the floor. 'He didn't do much to defend himself. It took him weeks to even acknowledge the charges.'

'And that makes him automatically guilty? He was devastated! Yes, he should have responded to the allegations earlier, but the accusations broke his heart.'

Her voice choked as memories rushed to the fore. Her father broken, disgraced by the sport he'd devoted his life to. It had taken Sasha weeks to convince her father to fight to clear his name. And in those precious weeks his reputation in the eyes of the public had been sullied beyond repair. By the time Jack Fleming had taken the stand his integrity had been in tatters.

'So he gave up? And let you carry the weight of his guilt?'

'Of course not!'

'Why did you promise him the championship?'

Sasha floundered, pain and loss ripping through her. 'He started drinking heavily after the trial. The only time he stopped was when I had a shot at the Formula Two Championship. When I crashed and had to stay a while in hospital he started drinking again.'

'You were in hospital? And the father you claim loved you *unconditionally* wasn't there for you?'

Hazel eyes now devoid of passion taunted her.

Tears prickled her eyes but she refused to let them fall. In her darkest, most painful moments after losing her baby she'd asked herself the same question.

Blinking fiercely, she raised her chin. 'Whatever point you're trying to make, Marco, make it without being a total bastard.'

He sighed and ran a hand over his chin.

She stayed at the other end of the cabana, her arms curved around her middle.

'Did you hire another lawyer to appeal?'

'Of course we did. He... Dad died before the second trial.'

His gaze softened a touch. 'How did he die?'

'He drove his car off a bridge near our cottage.' Pain coated her words. 'Everyone thinks he did it because he was guilty. He was just...devastated.'

'And you feel guilty for this?'

She plucked at the hem of her kaftan. 'If I hadn't got involved with Derek I'd have won a championship earlier. Maybe that would've saved my father...'

Marco's hand slashed through her words. 'Your life is your own. You can't live it for someone else. Not even your father.'

'Who's got their psychoanalysing hat on now?'

His brow lifted. 'You can dish it out but you can't take it?'

Sasha tried to stem the wave of guilt that rose within her. After his trial she'd suggested her father not come to her races, because she'd watched him slide deeper into depression after attending every one.

'Whatever he was, he wasn't a cheat. And I intend to honour his memory.'

Marco rose from the lounger, completely oblivious to his sheer masculine beauty and the effect it had on her tangled emotions. Sasha wanted to burrow into him, to return to the warm cocoon of his arms. But she forced herself to stay where she was.

'Come here.'

She shook her head. 'No. I don't like you very much right now.'

His smile made a mockery of her words as he strolled towards her. 'That's not true. You can't keep your eyes off me. Just like I can't take mine off you.'

'Marco...'

He cupped her jaw and lifted her face to his. Her heart stuttered, then thundered. 'You made your promise out of guilt—'

'No, I want to win the Championship.'

'Sometimes the best deal is to walk away.'

'I don't intend to. So don't stand in my way.'

He brought his mouth within a whisper of hers. Sasha swayed towards him, her willpower depleting rapidly.

'Determination is a quality I admire, *querida*. But remember I won't tolerate anything that stands in the way of *my* desires.'

Tugging her firmly into his arms, he proceeded to make her forget everything but him. Including the fact that he'd never believed her father's innocence.

Marco attended the next two races, flying back each time from Spain, where Rafael was still in a coma. When she won in Japan he took the whole team to celebrate, after which he took Sasha to his penthouse for a private celebration of their own.

After a tricky, hair-raising start, Korea secured her yet another victory. But one look at Marco's taut expression when she emerged from the press conference told her there would be no team celebrations this time.

'Marco?'

'We're leaving. Now.'

He whisked her away from the Yeongam Circuit in his helicopter, his possessive fingers tense around hers all through the flight to a stunning beach house on the outskirts of Seoul City, where he proceeded to strip off her race suit and her underclothes.

'You know that by dragging me away like that in front of the team you've blown this thing between us wide open, don't you?' she asked, in the aftermath of another pulse-melting session in his bed.

His lovemaking had been especially intense, with an edge that had bordered on the frenzied. And, as much as she'd loved it, he'd left her struggling for breath, in danger of being swept away by the force of his passion.

He brushed a damp curl from her cheek and studied her face. 'Does it bother you?'

She gave the matter brief thought. 'There was speculation even before we were together. Paddock gossip can make the tabloid press look like amateurs.'

He pulled back slightly, his earlier tension returning. 'That doesn't answer my question.'

'They knew I was a good driver before I started sleeping with you. They just didn't want to acknowledge it because of who I am. I only care about what they think of me as a driver. What they think of me personally doesn't matter. It never has.'

'You're a fighter,' he said, his expression reflective.

'I've had to fight for what I've achieved.' She cast him a droll look. 'As you well know.'

When he didn't smile back, a cloud appeared on the horizon of her happy haze. 'It bothers you that I don't care what other people think about me?'

'Single-mindedness has its place.'

'I smell a *but* in there somewhere.'

His gaze because suspiciously neutral. 'Following a single dream is risky. When it's taken from you you'll have nothing.'

'*When?* Not *if*? Are you trying to tell me something?'

'Nothing lasts for ever.'

'You must be jet-lagged again, because you've gone all cryptic on me. I'm three races away from securing the Constructors' Championship for you. Unless I don't finish another single race, and our nearest rival wins every one, it's pretty much a done deal.'

He got out of bed and pulled on his boxer shorts. For a man who embraced nudity the way Marco did, the definitive action sent a shiver of unease down her spine.

'Done deals have a way of coming undone.'

Her anxiety escalated. 'Enough with the paradoxes. What's going on, Marco?'

Marco strode to the champagne chilling in a monogrammed silver bucket, filled up a glass and brought it back to her.

Returning to the cabinet, he poured a whisky for himself and downed it in one go.

He slammed the glass down and spun towards her. '*Madre di Dios*, you nearly crashed today!'

Her fingers tightened around the delicate stem of her glass as the full force of his smouldering temper hit her. Her car had stalled at the start of the race, leaving her struggling to retain pole position. Her rivals hadn't hesitated in trying to take advantage of the situation. She'd touched tyres with a couple of cars and nearly lost a front wing.

'I found myself in a slightly hairy situation. I dealt with it.' She glanced at him. 'Were you worried?'

'That my lover would end up in a mangled heap of metal just like my brother did mere weeks ago? What do you think?' he ground out.

She trembled at the harshness in his tone even while a secret part of her thrilled that he'd been worried about her. 'I know what I'm doing, Marco. I've been doing it almost all my life.'

He speared a hand into her hair, tilting her face up to his. 'Rafael knew what he was doing too. Look where he ended up. You can't do it for ever. You do realise that, don't you?'

The question threw her, for Sasha had been deliberately avoiding any thoughts of the future. Even the end of the racing season didn't bear thinking about. If by some sheer stroke of bad luck she lost the Constructors' Championship then she was out of a job.

If she won her professional future would be secured for another year. But what about her personal future?

The reality was that she'd fallen into Marco's bed expecting little more than a one-night stand. But with each day that passed she was being consumed by the magic she experienced there. With no thought to the future…

'Yes,' she finally whispered. 'I realise nothing lasts for ever.'

'*Bueno,*' he breathed, as if her answer had satisfied him.

He shucked his boxers in one smooth move. 'Are you going to drink that? Only, after watching you nearly crash, I feel an urgent need to re-affirm life with you again. Repeatedly.'

She passed him the glass and opened her arms.

It wasn't until their breaths were gasping out in the aftermath of soul-shattering orgasms that she tensed in disbelief.

'Marco!'

'What?' He raised his head, a swathe of hair falling seductively over one eye.

'We didn't… We forgot…' Frantically she calculated dates.

He let loose a single epithet. '*Dios.* Please tell me you're on the Pill?' he rasped.

His voice was a choked sound that chilled her.

Reassured with the dates, she nodded, then noticed his pallor. 'Hey, it's okay. Even if the Pill doesn't work it's the wrong time of the month.'

'Are you sure?' he demanded.

Frowning, Sasha laid a hand on his cheek, which had grown cold and clammy. 'I'm sure. Relax.'

Marco eased away from Sasha, steeling himself against her throaty protest as he left the bed. Pulling on a robe, he went into his study. His laptop was set up on his desk, his folders neatly arranged by his assistant. He bypassed it, threw himself into the leather sofa and scrubbed a hand down his face.

He hadn't meant to lose it with Sasha like that earlier.

But seeing her come within a whisker of crashing had set him on a knife-edge of fear and rage he hadn't been able to completely dismiss. Now his loss of control had made him forget his one cardinal rule—contraception. *Always.*

He hadn't slipped once in ten years. Until tonight. Thank goodness Sasha was as against accidentally conceiving a child as he was…

Grimly reining in the control that seemed to be slipping from him, he strode to his desk and picked up the top folder. A sliver of guilt rose inside him but he quashed it.

Enough. He'd done what needed to be done. He refused to feel guilty for protecting what was important to him. Nothing mattered except keeping his family safe.

He picked up the phone and called his brother's doctors. Once he'd been updated on Rafael's condition, he placed another call.

Fifteen minutes later he slammed down the lid of his laptop and pushed away from the desk, at peace with his decision.

Feeling a sense of rightness, he returned to the bedroom and slid into bed, his need for Sasha overcoming the wish to let her rest. With a soft murmur she wound her supple body around his. The sense of rightness increased, making his head spin.

'I missed you. Where have you been?'

Another wave of guilt hit him—harder than before. Inhaling the seductive scent of her, he pushed away the disturbing feeling. 'I needed to take care of something.' Bending his head, he placed his lips against the smooth skin of her neck. His body stirred, transmitting its persistent message.

'Um. And have you?' she murmured.

'*Sí.*' His voice emerged gruffer than he wished. 'It's all taken care of.'

CHAPTER TEN

SASHA watched Marco turn the page of his newspaper, a frown creasing his brow before it smoothed out again. Watching him had become something of a not-so-secret pleasure in the last few weeks. On cue, she experienced the slow drag of desire in her belly as her gaze drifted over the sensual curve of his lips, the unshaven rasp of his jaw and the strong column of his throat to the muscled bare torso which she'd caressed to her heart's content last night and this morning.

As if sensing her gaze, his eyes met hers over the top of the paper. One brow lifted. 'You want to go back to bed?'

He laughed at her less-than-convincing shake of the head. The remnants of breakfast lay scattered on the table, long forgotten as they basked in the South Korean sun.

'I didn't know you could read Korean,' she said, eager for something to distil the suffocating heat of the desire that was never far from the surface.

Marco smiled and folded away the paper. 'It's Japanese. I never quite mastered Korean.'

'Wow. You're freely admitting *another* flaw? Shocking!'

He shrugged. 'It was down to a choice of which was the most useful.'

She wrinkled her nose. '*Useful?* Do you ever do anything just for pleasure?'

His droll look made her colour rise higher.

'Besides sex,' she mumbled.

'Sex with you is all the pleasure I crave, *mi corazón*.'

'You have other interests, surely? Everyone does.'

His throaty laugh made her pulse pound harder. 'What did you have in mind?'

'Some culture. An exhibition. Something other than...' Flustered, she waved her hand towards the severely rumpled bed beyond the sliding doors leading into the master suite, trying not to think of all the *other* places—the highly polished teak floor, the wooden bench in his outdoor bathroom, the hammock overlooking the stunning beach—where Marco had pleasured her during the long night.

Leaning over, he slid a hand around her nape and pulled her in for a hot kiss. 'I'd much rather spend the day with you in my bed. But if you insist—'

'I insist.'

Because Sasha had woken up this morning with a fearful knowledge deep in her heart. She was in danger of developing feelings for Marco de Cervantes. Feelings that she dared not name. Feelings that threatened to overwhelm her the more time she spent locked in his embrace.

At least away from this place, real life would impede long enough to knock some sense into her. To remind her that she couldn't afford to lose her head over a man like Marco—a man whom she knew deep down grappled with his guilt for being attracted to her. After all, hadn't it taken him three weeks to decide he could be with her?

He was also a man who believed her father to be guilty of fraud, a small voice added.

A sharp pang pierced through the concrete she'd packed around her pain. She hadn't been able to raise the subject with Marco since that night in Singapore. Somehow knowing he'd painted her father with the same brush of guilt as everyone else hurt so much more. Which made her a fool. Why should he believe any differently? Just because they were sleeping together it didn't mean the taint of her name had disappeared.

'You have fifteen minutes to get ready.'

She roused herself to find Marco ending a call. 'Ready for what?'

He tossed his phone on the table and brushed his knuckle along her jaw. Sparks of pleasure lit along her skin.

'You want culture, *mi encantadora*. Korea awaits.'

'Oh, my God,' Sasha whispered as her bare feet touched the wet flagstones that led to the ancient lake temple, unable to tear her gaze away from the magnificent vista before her.

'I'm finding that I don't like you using that expression unless it relates directly to me, *pequeña*,' Marco complained, releasing her hand as she leapt onto the next flagstone.

'Are you jealous?' she asked on a laugh.

He raised a mocking brow. 'Of your insane adoration of old temples and ancient monuments?' He rolled up his trouser cuffs and stepped on to the flagstones, bringing his warmth and addictive body up close and personal. 'Not a chance. But I suggest you alter your phraseology, because every time you say *Oh, my God* in that sexy tone I want to flatten you against the nearest surface and have my way with you.'

He grinned at her gasp and his head started to descend.

'No.' She pulled away reluctantly.

He frowned. *'Qué diablos?'*

'Shh, we're in a holy place,' she whispered. 'No kissing. And no swearing.'

She giggled at his muted growl and skipped over the rest of the flagstones until she stood in front of the temple.

'Wow.'

'*Wow* I can live with.'

'You'll have to. I have no other words.'

From where they stood the small temple seemed to float on the water, its curved eaves reminiscent of a bird in flight. In the light of the dying sun huge pink water lilies glowed red, their rubescent petals unfurled to catch the last of the sun's rays.

'It's all so beautiful. So stunning.' With reverent steps Sasha approached the temple doors. 'Can we go in?'

He nodded. 'It's not normally open to visitors. But on this occasion...'

Unbidden, a lump rose to her throat. 'Thank you.'

'*De nada.* Go—explore to your heart's content.'

With legs that felt shaky, and a heart that hammered far too hard to be healthy, Sasha paused to wipe her feet, then entered the temple.

Like every single place Marco had taken her to since he'd summoned his car after breakfast, the temple was breathtakingly exquisite. The *shoji* scrolls lining the walls looked paper-thin and fragile, causing her to hold her breath in case she damaged the place in any way. Examining one, she wished she had a translator to explain the three lines of symbols to her.

'"Peace through wisdom. Wisdom through perspicacity,"' Marco murmured from behind her. 'This temple was originally Japanese. It changed owners a few times before the Shaolin monks took over in the fourth century.'

'It puts everything into perspective, doesn't it?'

'Does it?'

'You said nothing lasts for ever. This temple proves some things do.'

For a long moment he didn't answer. His hooded gaze held hers, but in the gathering dusk she couldn't read the expression in his eyes.

'Come, it is time to leave. Romano will think you've kidnapped me.'

'What? Little ol' me?'

He laughed—a sound she was finding she liked very much. 'Romano knows you have a black belt in Jujitsu.'

'I'd still think twice before I tried to drop-kick a man of his size. So you're safe with me.'

'*Gracias.*' He threaded his fingers through hers, then signalled to Romano to bring the car round.

She waited until they were in the car before leaning over to press her lips to his. 'Thank you for showing me Seoul.'

His hand tightened around her waist and pulled her closer. 'The tour isn't over yet. I have one last treat for you.'

Pleasure unfurled through her. 'Really?'

'The night is just beginning. I know a little place where, if you're really nice to the staff, they'll name a dish after you.

Will you allow me to show it to you?' He picked up her hand and kissed the back of it.

Watching the dark head bent over her hand, Sasha experienced that irrational fear again. Only this time it was ten times worse. Her heart hammered and her pulse raced through her veins as the reason for her feelings whispered softly through her mind.

No. She *wasn't* falling for Marco de Cervantes. Because that would be stupid.

And reckless.

Marco didn't do relationships. And she'd barely survived being burned once.

His lips caressed the sensitive skin of her wrist.

At her helpless sigh, he smiled. 'On second thoughts, a Michelin-star-chef-prepared meal on the beach sounds very appealing.'

Resisting temptation was nearly impossible. But Sasha forced herself to speak. 'It's not fair to dangle the opportunity to have a dish named after me and then withdraw it. Now it's on my lust-have list.'

He reached out and cupped her breast. 'I have only one thing on *my* lust-have list.'

'You're insatiable,' she breathed, unable to stop her moan when his thumb passed over her nipple.

Bending his head, he brought his lips close to hers. 'Only for you do I have this need,' he muttered thickly. 'And, *por favor*, I won't have it denied.' He drew closer until their breaths mingled.

'What about dinner…the dish…?' she whispered.

'You'll have it,' he vowed. 'Just…later.'

With a muted groan, he closed the gap, sealing them in a hot cocoon of fevered need so intense it stopped her breath.

The cocoon held them intimately all the way through their torrid lovemaking in Marco's bed and in the shower afterwards, where he explored every inch of her body as if seeing it for the first time.

His phone rang as they dressed for dinner. At first she thought it was a business call. Then she noticed his ashen pallor.

Their cocoon had been shattered.

'Who was that?' she asked, even though part of her knew the answer.

'It was the hospital. Rafael's suffered another bleed.'

'What the hell are you doing under there? Freebasing engine oil?'

Sasha froze at the voice she hadn't heard in six long sleepless nights and forced herself to breathe. 'Hand me the wrench.'

'Didn't the staff tell you no one's allowed in here?' The harsh censure in his voice grated on her already severely frayed nerves.

'They probably *tried*.'

'You didn't listen, of course?'

'I don't speak Spanish, remember? Are you going to hand me the wrench or not?'

His designer-shod feet moved, then a wrench appeared underneath the body of the 1954 Fiat 8V Berlinetta.

'Not that one. The retractable.'

The right wrench reappeared. 'Thanks.'

She hooked the wrench on to the bolt and pulled. Nothing happened.

'Come out from under there.'

'No.'

'Sasha…' His voice held more than a hint of warning.

Her mouth compressed. She didn't want to see his face, didn't want to breathe his scent. In fact she wanted to deny herself everything to do with Marco. To deny that every single atom of her being yearned to wheel herself from under the car and throw herself into his arms.

She gripped the wrench and yanked harder, reminding herself of how almost a week ago he'd ordered Romano to bring her to *Casa de Leon* and walked away.

As if Seoul had never happened.

'We need to talk.'

Her heart clenched. 'So talk.'

An expensively cut suit jacket landed a few feet from her head, followed a millisecond later by Marco's large, tightly packed frame.

'What are you doing?' she squeaked, holding herself rigid as his shoulder brushed hers.

He ignored her, taking his time to study the axle she'd been working on. 'Hand me the wrench and move over.'

'Why? Because you think you're bigger and stronger than me?'

'I *am* bigger and stronger than you.'

'Sexist pig.'

'Simple truth.'

'I see you still live in the Dark Ages.'

'Only when it comes to protecting what's mine.'

Realising he wasn't going to go away, she shrugged. 'Fine. Knock yourself out.'

His gaze sharpened. 'No arguments, *querida*? That's how it works between us usually, isn't it? I say something, then you argue my words to death until I kiss you to shut you up?'

'I don't crave arguments—or your kisses, if that's what you're implying. In fact I'd love nothing better than for you to leave me alone,' she suggested. 'You've managed it quite successfully for almost a week.'

Silently he held out his hand. She slapped the wrench into his palm. With a few firm twists he loosened the bolt on the axle.

'Show-off,' she quipped. 'What do you want?'

'I thought you'd want an update on Rafael.' His gaze stayed intense on hers.

'I thought he was off-limits?'

'If I still believed you and he were involved I wouldn't have taken you to my bed.'

'Okay. So how is he?'

'He's doing better. The doctors managed to stop the bleed. They expect him to wake up any day now.'

Licking her lips carefully, she nodded. 'That's great news.'

'*Sí.*'

The intensity in his eyes sent a bolt of apprehension through her. Without warning, his gaze dropped to her lips. Belatedly Sasha realised she was licking them. She stopped. But the quickening was already happening. The cramped space underneath the car became smaller. The air grew thinner.

'You didn't have to come back here to tell me that. A simple phone call would've sufficed. I'll pack my things and leave this afternoon.'

He stiffened. 'Why would you do that?'

'Rafael will need you when he comes home. I can't be here.'

'Of course you can. I want you here.'

Despite the thin hope threading its way through her, she forced herself to speak. 'That wasn't the impression I got from your six-day silence.'

He sucked in a weary breath and for the first time she noticed the lines of strain around his eyes.

'I didn't expect to be away this long. I'm sorry.'

When her mouth dropped open in surprise at the ready apology he grimaced.

'I know. I must be losing my touch.' He glanced around, his strained look intensifying. 'How did you get in here? The door is combination locked.'

'Rosario let me in. She recognises stir-craziness when she sees it. So—twenty-five vintage cars locked away in a garage? Discuss.'

He inhaled sharply, then flung the wrench away. 'I refuse to have this conversation underneath a car, with grease dripping on me.'

'You should've thought of that before you crawled down here.'

'*Dios*, I've missed your insufferable attitude.' He paused. 'This is your chance to tell me you've missed me too.'

The stark need to do just that frightened her. 'Are you sure you don't want me to leave? I can go home for a few days before the team leaves for Abu Dhabi next week. Maybe it's for the best.'

'And maybe you need to shut up. Just for one damn moment,' he snarled, then grabbed her arm and turned her into his body.

The heat of his mouth devoured hers. Fiery sensation was instantaneous. Sasha held nothing back. Her fingers gripped his nape, luxuriating in the smooth skin before spearing upward to spread through his hair. His deep groan echoed hers. Willingly, she let her mouth fall open, let his tongue invade to slide deliciously against hers.

His hand snaked around her waist and veered downwards, bringing her flush against his heated body. Need flooded her. To be this close again with him, to feel him, to be with him, made her body, her heart sing.

She wanted to be close. Closer. Physically and emotionally. Because… Because…

Infinitely glad he'd shed his jacket, she explored the large expanse of his shoulders.

When the demands of oxygen forced them apart his gaze stayed on her. One hand cupped her bottom. Against her belly she felt the ripe force of his erection.

'You do realise we're making out under a car, don't you?' she asked huskily.

'It's the only thing stopping me from pulling you on top of me and burying myself inside you. Tell me you missed me.'

'I missed you.'

'Bueno.' He fastened his mouth to hers once more.

By the time he freed her and pulled them from underneath the car her brain had become a useless expanse seeking only the pleasure he could provide. When he undressed her, led her to the back door of a 1938 Rolls-Royce, she was a willing slave, ready to do his every bidding.

Snagging an arm around her waist, he speared a hand through her hair and tilted her face to his. 'You have no idea how long I've wanted to do this.'

'What?' she breathed.

His mouth swooped, locked on the juncture where her shoulder met her neck, where her pulse thundered frantically.

Her blood surged to meet his mouth. When his teeth grazed her skin she cried out. The eroticism of it was so intense that liquid heat pooled between her legs, where she throbbed, plumping up for the studied and potent possession only he could deliver.

He took his time, tasted her, his mouth playing over the delicate, intensely aroused skin. Just when she thought it couldn't

get any more pleasurable his tongue joined in. Ecstasy lashed at
her insides, creating a path of fire from her neck to her breasts,
to her most sensitive part and down to her toes. Nowhere was
safe from the utter bliss rushing through her.

Finally, satisfied, he lifted his head. He took a step forward,
then another, until the edge of the car seat touched her calves.
With his gentle push she fell back onto the wide seat.

He followed immediately, his warmth surrounding her. In
his arms she felt delicate, cared for, as if she mattered. As if
she was precious. Which was silly. For Marco this was just sex.
But for her...

She shut her mind off the painful train of thought. 'I thought
you wanted me on top?'

His teeth gleamed in a slow, feral smile. 'In good time, *mi
tentación*. We have a long way to go. Now, don't move.'

He cupped her breasts, toying with the nipples, torturing her
for so long she wriggled with pleasure.

'I said don't move,' he gritted through clenched teeth, the
harsh stamp of desire tautening his face.

'You expect me to just lie here like a ten-dollar hooker?'

Despite the intense desire threatening to swallow them whole,
laughter rumbled through his chest. 'Never having been graced
with the attentions of a ten-dollar hooker, I can't answer that.
But if you don't stop tormenting me with your body I won't be
responsible for my actions.'

'Oh, *now* you're just threatening me with a good time.'

'*Dios*, woman. Your mouth...'

'You want to kiss it?' It was more of a plea than a question.
Her head rose off the seat in search of his.

He pulled away. 'It's a weapon of man's destruction.'

She groaned. 'You can always kiss me to shut me up. I can't
promise I won't blow you away, though.'

He mumbled something low and pithy under this breath. And
then he kissed her.

A long while later, stretched out alongside Marco's warm
length on the back seat of the car, she finally acknowledged
her feelings.

She was happy. It was a happiness doomed to disaster and a short lifespan, but no matter how delusional she wanted it to last a little while longer.

Glancing down, she noticed Marco's wallet had dropped onto the floor of the car. Spying a picture peeking out, she picked up the wallet and peered closer.

The long, unruly hair was unfamiliar, as was the small go-kart in the background. But the determination and fierce pride in those hazel eyes looked familiar.

'This picture of you is adorable. Now I know what your children will look like.' She tried not to let the pain of that thought show on her face. 'I bet they'll be racers just like you and Rafael.'

Marco stiffened, his eyes growing cold and bleak. 'There won't be any children.'

The granite-like certainty in his voice chilled her soul. 'Why do you say that?'

For a long, endless moment he didn't answer. Then he took the wallet from her. Reaching for his trousers, he opened the car door, stepped out and pulled them on.

'Come with me.'

Despite already missing his arms around her, she sat up. 'Where are we going?'

The look in his eyes grew bleaker. 'Not far. Put your clothes on. I don't want to get distracted.'

She was all for distracting him if it meant he wouldn't look so cold and forbidding. But she did as he said.

Marco led her to the far side of the garage. Keying in a security code, he threw open the door and stepped inside, pulling her behind him.

With a flick of a switch, light bathed the room. Sasha looked around and gasped at the contents of many glass cabinets.

'These are all yours?' she whispered. Walking forward she opened the first cabinet and lifted the first trophy.

'*Sí.*' Marco's voice was husky with emotion. 'I started racing when I was five.'

There were more trophies than she could count, filling four huge cabinets. 'I know.'

He walked to the farthest cabinet and picked up the lone trophy standing in a case by itself. 'This was my last trophy.'

'You never told me why you gave up racing,' she murmured.

When he tensed even more, she went to him and grasped his balled fists.

'Tell me what happened.'

His eyes bored into hers, as if judging her to see if he could trust her with his pain. After an eternity his hand loosened enough to grasp hers.

'I got my first contract to race when I was eighteen. By twenty-one I'd won two championships and acquired a degree in engineering. I was on the list of every team, and I had the choice of picking which team to drive for. A week after I signed for my dream team I met Angelique Santoro. I was twenty-four, and foolishly believed in love at first sight. And even by then I'd had my fill of paddock bunnies. She was…different. Smart, sexy, exciting—far older than her twenty-five years. All I wanted to do was race and be with her. She convinced me to sack my manager and take her on instead. Six months later we were engaged and she was pregnant.'

A shiver of dread raced over Sasha. Deep inside her chest a ball of pain, buried but not forgotten, tightened.

There won't be any children.

'You didn't want the baby?' she whispered in horror.

He laughed. A harsh, tortured sound that twisted her heart. 'I wanted it more than I'd ever wanted anything in my life.'

Sasha frowned. 'But…what happened?'

'I rearranged my whole life around that promise of a family. I designed the *Casa de Leon* track so I could train there, instead of going away to train at other tracks. My parents moved here. My mother was ecstatic at becoming a grandparent.'

The note of pain through his voice rocked her.

'Angelique wasn't satisfied?'

'She wholeheartedly agreed with everything. Until I crashed.'

Her hand tightened around his. 'I don't understand. Your crash was serious, yes, but nothing you couldn't come back from.'

'I was in a coma for nine days. The team hired someone else to replace me when the doctors told my parents and Angelique it was unlikely I'd race again.'

'They must have been devastated for you.'

'My parents were.'

Sadness touched her soul. 'I'm sorry. I can't imagine what you must have gone through.'

He slid a finger under her chin and lifted her face to his, an echo of pain in his eyes. 'Nor would I want you to. But this…' he pulled her closer, his gaze softening a touch '…this helps.'

With a smile, she lifted her mouth to his. 'I'm glad.'

Their kiss was gentle, a soothing balm on his turbulent revelations.

When they parted, she glanced again at the trophies. 'Is that why you don't let anyone in here? Because it reminds you that your racing career is over?'

'When I accepted that part of my life was over I locked them away.' He pulled her away from the cabinet.

'Wait. You said your parents were devastated? What about Angelique?'

He stiffened again, his gaze turning hooded as he thrust his hands into his pockets. 'When it turned out I was destined for a job designing cars instead of racing them, she lost interest,' he said simply, but his oblique tone told a different story.

'That's not all, is it?'

Pain washed over his face before he could mask it. 'Before I crashed Angelique was almost three months pregnant. When I woke from my coma she was no longer pregnant.'

Sasha's horrified gasp echoed through the room. 'She had an abortion?'

His eyes turned almost black with pain. '*Sí*. Two months later she married my ex-team boss.'

A wave of horror washed over her. 'Are you even sure she was pregnant in the first place?' Considering how heartless the woman had been, Sasha wouldn't be surprised if she'd faked the pregnancy.

Marco's movements were uncharacteristically jerky as he

reached for his wallet. Beneath the photo, a small grey square slid out. In the light of the trophy room Sasha saw the outline of a tiny body in a pre-natal scan.

Tears gathered in her eyes and fell before she could stop them. With shaking hands she took the picture from him, the memory of her own loss striking into her heart so sharply she couldn't breathe.

'I was there the day this was taken. The thing was, all along I suspected Angelique was capable of that. She was extremely ruthless—driven to the point of obsession. But since she channelled all that into being my manager I chose to see it as something else.'

'Love?' she suggested huskily.

His jaw tightened. 'I blinded myself to her true colours. My mother tried to warn me, but I wouldn't listen to her. I almost cut her out of my life because of Angelique.' He sucked in a harsh breath. 'I lost my child…she lost her grandchild…because I chose to bury my head in the sand. She was devastated, and I don't think she really got over the damage I did to our family.'

Brushing a hand across her cheek, she asked, 'Why do you keep this?'

Marco took the scan and placed it back in his wallet. 'I failed to protect my daughter. This reminds me never to fail my family again.'

CHAPTER ELEVEN

MARCO left again the next day and didn't return for another two. When he returned Sasha met him in the hallway. His dragged her into his study and proceeded to kiss her with brutal need.

His confession in the garage had afforded her a glimpse into the man he was today. She now truly understood why he was so ferociously protective of Rafael. And why she couldn't afford for him to find out the true depth of her feelings.

Taking a deep breath, she forced herself to vocalise what she'd been too afraid to say over the phone the night before.

'Marco, I think I should leave. You can stay in Barcelona and not keep flying back here to see me. I can use the race track back home to train.'

His face clouded in a harsh frown. 'What the hell are you talking about?' Roughly he pulled her into his arms and kissed her again. 'You're not going anywhere.'

She tried to pull back but he held her easily. 'But—'

His smile was strained through tiredness. 'Rafael woke briefly last night. Only for a few minutes. But he appeared lucid, and he recognised me.' The relief in his voice was palpable.

Sasha smiled. 'I'm glad. But I think that's even more of a reason for you to stay in Barcelona. What if he wakes again when you're not there?'

Setting her free, he stabbed a hand through his hair. 'He's been moved to a private suite and I've set up video conferencing so I have a live feed into his room. Nothing will happen to him without my knowledge. I've also hired extra round-the-clock staff for when he comes home—including that nurse who was fired from the hospital in Budapest. So, you see, I'm not a total ass.'

'I know you're not. But you're splitting yourself in two when it's really Rafael who needs you most now.'

'Maybe I want to put my needs ahead of Rafael's for once in my life.' He threw his hands up in the air. 'What exactly do you want from me, Sasha?'

She was unprepared for the question. But she had one of her own burning at the back of her mind.

'What do *you* want from *me*? What is the real reason you want me to stay here? Am I here just so you can have sex on tap or is this something more…?' She faltered to a halt, too afraid to voice the words traipsing through her mind.

His eyes narrowed. 'I hardly think this is the time to be having a *where is this relationship going?* conversation.'

'Is there ever a right time? Besides, you don't *do* relationships, remember?'

He shrugged off his jacket and flung it onto a nearby chair. 'I want you here with me. Isn't that enough?' he rasped.

Another question she wasn't prepared for. Not because she didn't know the answer. It was because she knew the answer was *no*. Wanting was no longer enough. She was in love with Marco: with the boy whose heart had been shredded by a heartless woman and the formidable man who'd loved his unborn child so completely he'd closed his heart to any emotion.

She loved him. And it scared the hell out of her. The urge to retreat stabbed through her. Marco's obvious reluctance to discuss their relationship frightened her. But looking at him, his face haggard, his hands clenched on the desk in front of him, she knew she couldn't leave. Not just yet. Not when he was so worried about Rafael.

'I'll stay,' she said.

Naked relief reflected in his eyes. *'Gracias.'* He pulled her into his arms. 'Don't mention leaving again. Even the mere thought makes me want to hurl something.'

She hated herself for the thrill of pleasure that surged through her. 'It was for your own good—even if you don't want to see it.' And not just for Marco's sake. She had to find the strength to walk away. Because the longer she stayed, the more she risked losing everything.

'If you want suggestions on what's good for me, I have several ideas—' He stopped and cursed when his phone started ringing.

'Before you start hurling things, I'll remove myself to the garage. Your '65 Chevelle Impala's chrome finish needs polishing.'

'It also has extra wide front seats, if I recall.'

Desire weakened her. 'Marco…'

'Fine. But before you go—'

He plastered his lips against hers and proceeded to show her just how foolish her decision to leave had been.

By the time Sasha stumbled from the study she knew her heart was in serious trouble.

Marco threw himself into his seat two days later and barely stopped himself from punching a hole in the wall behind him.

Even though she'd changed her mind about leaving, Marco had sensed a withdrawal in Sasha he couldn't shake. It was almost as if Rafael's impending emergence from his coma had put a strain between them.

But why? If there was nothing between them Sasha should be happy that Rafael was recovering. Unless…? The thought that Sasha had feelings for Rafael after all sent a wave of anger and jealousy through him.

No. He dismissed the thought.

She'd listened to him bare his soul, held him in her arms as he'd relived Angelique's betrayal. Sasha had shed tears for him; he refused to believe the raw pain he'd seen in her eyes wasn't real.

But he couldn't deny something was wrong.

Only when they made love, when he held her afterwards, did he feel he had the real Sasha back. Even now, mere hours before she was due to leave for London, she'd locked herself away in his garage, hell-bent on restoring his vintage cars to even more pristine condition than they'd originally been in. While he sat here, grappling with confusion and a hunger so relentless he was surprised he didn't spontaneously combust from want.

No. It was more than want. This craving for Sasha, whether she was within arm's reach or he was in Barcelona, went beyond anything he'd ever known. The few times he'd contemplated whether it would be better if she wasn't at the villa at all he'd felt a wrench so deep it had shaken him.

Angelique had never made him feel like this, even though at the time he'd thought he would never yearn for another woman the way he'd yearned for her.

What he felt for Sasha was different...deeper...purer...

Marco stiffened, the breath trapped in his chest as he tried to get to grips with his feelings. But the more he tried to unravel the unfamiliar feeling, the more chaotic and frantic it grew.

He glanced out of his study window towards his garage. The feeling that she was slipping through his fingers wouldn't fade. But he couldn't deal with it now. There were too many loose ends left to tie up.

As if on cue, his phone rang. With a muttered curse, he picked it up.

All the way to his suite Sasha forced herself to breathe. Despite the cold lump of stone in her stomach, she needed to do this. She couldn't continue to string things along any longer.

She entered the suite and heard the shower running. Without pausing, she crossed the room and slid open the door.

Water streamed off Marco's naked, powerful body. The need that slammed through her threatened to weaken her resolve. It took several seconds before she could speak.

'Marco, I...I've decided...I'm not coming back here after the next race.'

He whirled about, looked stricken for a moment, then his jaw clenched. 'I thought we had this conversation already.'

Even now, with the wrenching pain of losing him coursing through her, she couldn't resist the intense pull of desire that watching the water cascade over his body brought.

She steeled herself against it. 'I tried to talk. You laid down the law.'

He snapped a towel off the heated rack and stepped from the shower. 'You timed it perfectly, didn't you?'

'Excuse me?'

'Your exit strategy. At first I didn't want to believe it, but now it makes perfect sense.'

She frowned. 'Perfect sense... What are you talking about?'

'You can drop the pretence. I had a call twenty minutes ago. From Raven Blass.'

Her eyes widened in surprise. 'Raven? Why—?'

'She's in Barcelona. She wants to see Rafael. I gave the hospital permission to let her see him, but funnily enough she was more worried about how *you* would feel about her visit.'

'Marco—'

'Apparently you're very *territorial* about Rafael. She said something about warning Rafael to stay away from her the day he crashed?'

'That wasn't how it was—'

He tied the towel around his trim waist. 'What was the plan? Use me as a stopgap until Rafael was on his feet, then go back to him?'

'Of course not!'

'You started withdrawing from me the moment I told you Rafael was about to wake up. Well, I'm glad to have been of service. But if you have any designs on my brother, kill them now. He won't like soiled goods.'

She flinched and bit back her gasp. For a moment he appeared to regret his words, then his expression hardened again.

'Wow. Okay, I guess your mind's made up.'

'I mean it, Sasha. Come anywhere near Rafael and I'll crush you like a bug.'

Pain congealed into a crushing weight in her chest. 'I suspected this, and I see I was right. Rafael will always come first with you—no matter how much you protest about putting yourself first. I just hope you don't have to give up something you really want one day.'

He frowned. 'There's nothing I want more than my family safe.'

'Well, that says it all, doesn't it?'

Whirling, she hurried from the room, cursing the stupid tears that welled up in her eyes.

In her room, she grabbed her suitcase and stuffed her belongings into it. She was snapping it shut when her door flew open.

'What are you doing?'

'Leaving. *Obviously.*'

'Your flight is not for another four hours.'

She picked her case off the bed. 'Oh? And what? You want one last shag for old times' sake?'

His eyes darkened in a familiar way even as his jaw clenched.

A stunned laugh escaped her. 'Let me get this straight. You want more sex with me even though I'm "soiled goods" you wouldn't let your own brother touch?'

Dull colour swam into his cheeks. 'Don't put it like that.'

'You know when I said you weren't an ass? I was stupendously wrong! You're the biggest ass in the universe.' She stalked towards the door.

'Sasha—'

'And to think I fooled myself into thinking I was in love with you. You don't deserve love. And you certainly don't deserve mine!'

Had she looked back as she sped through the door, pleased with herself for not breaking down in front of him, she would have seen his stunned face, his ashen pallor.

Sasha flew home to Kent after the Indian Grand Prix, one step closer to cementing the Constructors' Championship.

Returning home for the first time in months felt bittersweet. Glancing round the familiar surroundings of the home she'd grown up in, she wanted to burst into tears. Pictures of her father graced the mantel. A wooden cabinet in the dining room held their trophies. They weren't as numerous as Marco's, but she was proud of every single one of them. Unlike Marco, who'd chosen to hide his away the way he'd chosen to close off his heart…

But had he? He'd shown her that he would fight to the death to protect his family. Didn't that prove it was *her* who wasn't worth fighting for? The thought hurt more than she could bear.

With an angry hand she dashed away the tears. She refused to dwell on him. Her only goal now was finishing the season. She couldn't summon the appropriate enthusiasm for next year.

Wearily, she trudged to the kitchen and put on the kettle. Mrs Miller, her next door neighbour, had texted to let her know the fridge was fully stocked.

Sasha opened the fridge, caught a whiff of cheese and felt her stomach lurch violently. She barely made it to the bathroom seconds before emptying the contents of her stomach. Rinsing her mouth, she decided to forgo the tea in favour of sleep. Dragging herself to the shower, she washed off the grime of her transatlantic flight and fell into bed.

The stomach bug she suspected she'd caught in India, along with half of the team, didn't go away immediately, but by the time she arrived in Brazil three and a half weeks later she was in full health.

And three points away from securing the championship.

São Paolo was vibrant and exhilarating. The pit was abuzz with the excitement of the season's final race, and Team Espiritu even more so with a potential championship win only a few short hours away.

Sasha had taken the coward's way and hidden in her hotel room until the last minute, in case she bumped into Marco. In Abu Dhabi she'd declined his invitation to an after-race party on his sprawling yacht. It seemed he was back to entertaining dignitaries and A-list celebrities with barely a blink in her direction.

Whereas she…she just wanted the season to be over.

The joy had gone out of racing.

With a sharp pang she realised Marco had been right—her guilt about her father had blinded her to the fact that she didn't need to prove to anyone that she was good enough. Nor did she need to defend Jack Fleming's integrity. With her deeper integration and final acceptance into the team she'd discovered that most people remembered Jack Fleming as the great driver he'd been. Her guilt lingered, but she would deal with that later.

First she had to get through the press interviews before and after the race.

She spotted Tom heading her way as she was pulling on her jumpsuit. She winced at the sensitivity of her breasts as the Velcro tightened over them.

She paused, then suddenly was scrambling madly for dates, calculating frantically and coming up short every time. Panic seized her.

'Are you all right? You've gone pale. Here—have some water.'

Tom poured water into a plastic cup and handed it to her. His attitude had undergone a drastic change since she'd become involved with Marco. Snarkily, Sasha wondered whether he'd go back to being insufferable once he found out she and Marco were no longer together.

'It's the heat,' she replied, setting the cup aside. 'I'm fine,' she stressed when he continued to peer at her in concern.

'Okay. Your last interview is with local TV.' He rolled his eyes. 'It's that smarmy one who interviewed you in Singapore. I'd cut him out of the schedule, but since we're on his home turf we don't have any choice. Don't worry. If he looks as if he's straying into forbidden territory I'll stop him.'

He went on to list the other interviewers, but Sasha was only half listening. She'd finally worked out her period dates and breathed a sigh of relief. She'd had her last albeit brief period just before she'd left Leon. And her cycle was erratic at the best of times.

Reassured, she followed Tom around to the paddock and spoke to the journalists.

The race itself was uneventful. With her eight-second lead unchallenged after the first six laps she cruised to victory, securing the fastest lap ever set on the Interlagos circuit. She managed to keep a smile plastered on her face all through the celebrations and the myriad interviews that followed, sighing with relief as she entered the team's hospitality suite for her last interview.

Despite having done dozens of interviews, she still suffered an attack of nerves whenever a camera was trained on her. And, unlike nerves during a race, interview nerves never worked to her advantage.

'Don't worry, Miss Fleming. It will be all right.'

The note of insincerity in the interviewer's thick accent should have been her first warning.

The first few questions were okay. Then, 'How does it feel to be dating the team boss? Has it earned you any advantages?'

From the corner of her eye she saw Tom surge from his seat. Her 'no comment' made him relax a little.

'After winning the Constructors' Championship, surely your seat for next year is secured?'

'No comment.'

He shrugged. 'How about your ex, Derek Mahoney? Have you heard he's making a comeback to racing?'

Sasha tensed. 'No, I haven't heard.'

'He gave us an interview this morning. And he mentioned something quite interesting.'

Icy dread crept up her spine. 'Whatever it is, I'm sure it has nothing to do with me.'

'On the contrary, it has everything to do with you.'

Her interviewer rubbed his chin in a way that was probably supposed to make him appear smart. It only confirmed the slimeball he really was.

'You see, Mr Mahoney claims you were pregnant with his child when you broke up, and that you deliberately crashed to lose the baby because you didn't want a child to hamper your career. What's your response to that?'

The room swayed around her. Vaguely she heard Tom shouting at the cameraman to stop filming. Inside she was frozen solid, too afraid to move. The buzz in the room grew louder. Someone grasped her arm and frogmarched her into another room. The sole occupant, a waitress cleaning a table, looked from her to the TV and quickly made herself scarce.

'Sasha... I... God, this is a mess,' Tom stuttered. 'Will you be all right? I need to secure that footage...'

'Please, go. I...I'll be fine,' she managed through frozen lips.

He hurriedly retreated and she was alone.

Dropping her head between her thighs, she tried to breathe evenly, desperately willing herself not to pass out. The TV hummed in the background but she didn't have the strength to walk over to turn it off.

Oh, God, how had Derek found out? Not that it mattered now. Her secret was out. Out there for the whole world to pore over...

Tears welled in her eyes. Derek was all about causing maximum damage. But she'd never dreamed he'd sink this low.

The door flew open and Marco walked in.

Her gaze collided with his, and every single thing she'd told herself over the last three weeks flew out of the door.

He'd lost weight. The gap at the collar of his light blue shirt showed more of his collarbones and his jacket hung looser. But he was just as arresting, just as breathlessly beautiful, and her heart leapt with shameless joy at the sight of him.

'I need to talk to you,' he said tautly, his gaze roving intensely over her before capturing hers again.

She licked her dry lips. 'I...I need to tell you...' How could she tell him? She'd never vocalised her pain, never told another human being.

'What is it?' He came over and took her hands. 'Whatever it is, tell me. I can handle it.'

That gave her a modicum of strength. 'You promise?'

'*Sí.* I have a few things I need to tell you too, *mi corazón*. The things I said in Leon...' He paused and shook his head, a look of regret in his eyes. 'You were right. I'm an ass.'

'I didn't...' *I didn't mean it*, she started to confess, but her eyes had strayed to the TV. There, like a vivid recurring nightmare, her interview was being replayed.

Seeing her distraction, Marco followed her gaze.

Just in time to hear the interviewer's damning question.

Marco dropped her hands faster than hot coals and surged to his feet. '*No!* It's a lie. Isn't it, Sasha? *Isn't it?*' he shouted when she couldn't speak.

'I...'

He paled, his cheekbones standing out against his stark face as he stepped back from her.

'Marco, please—it wasn't like that.' She finally found her voice. But it was too late.

He'd taken several more steps backwards, as if he couldn't stand to breathe the same air as her.

'Did you race knowing you were pregnant?' he insisted, his voice harsh.

'Not the day Derek's talking about—'

'But you *did* race knowing you were pregnant?'

'I suspected I was—'

'Dios mío!'

'I'd already lost the baby when I crashed. That was *why* I crashed! Racing was all I knew. After the doctor told me I'd lost the baby I didn't know what else to do.'

'So you got straight back in your car? You didn't even take time to mourn the loss of your child?' he condemned in chilling tones.

Somehow she found the strength to stand and face him. 'The doctor said it wasn't my fault. The pregnancy wasn't viable to begin with. But I still cried myself to sleep every night for years afterwards. If you're asking if I carry a picture of a scan to punish myself with, or as an excuse to push people away, then no, I don't. She lives in my heart—'

"She?" His voice was a tortured rasp, his fists clenching and unclenching and his throat working as he paled even more.

Tears spilled from her eyes and she nodded. 'Mine was a girl too. She lives in my heart and that's where I choose to remember her. You say you don't live in the past, but that's exactly what you're doing. You're judging *me* by what happened to you ten years ago.'

He inhaled sharply. 'And you've proved to me just how far you'll go. I told you about Angelique, about my child, and you said nothing. Because a small thing like a lost pregnancy is less important to you than your next race, isn't it?'

She swayed as pain clamped her chest in a crushing vice. 'You know why I wanted to race!'

'I was a fool to believe you were trying to preserve the memory of your father. You were really just seeking to further your own agenda.'

Pain arrowed through her. 'Don't pretend you don't think he was guilty.'

'I said he was *found* guilty. I didn't say I agreed with the verdict.'

'But—'

He slashed a hand through her words. 'I had my lawyers investigate the case. Some of the testimony didn't add up. If your father had spent less time feeling sorry for himself and more time getting his lawyers to concentrate on his case he'd have realised that. That's one of the things I came here to tell you.'

Tears stung the backs of her eyes, her throat clogging with unspoken words. 'Marco, please—can't we talk about this?'

He gave a single, finite shake of his head. 'I'm not interested in anything you have to say. I'm only grateful I never made you pregnant. I don't think I could survive another child of mine being so viciously denied life for the sake of ruthless ambition.'

Her insides froze as his words cut across her skin.

With one last condemning look he headed towards the door. Panic seized her. 'Marco!'

He stilled but didn't turn around, one hand on the doorknob. 'What else did you come to say to me?'

The cold malice in his eyes when he turned around made her heart clench.

'I sold the team six weeks ago. In Korea. The paperwork was finalised today. As of one hour ago your contract is null and void.'

CHAPTER TWELVE

SHE was pregnant with Marco's child. Sasha had been certain of it almost as soon as Marco had walked out on her in São Paolo. Taking the pregnancy test once she'd returned home had only established what she'd known in her heart.

There was no doubt in her mind that she would tell him he was about to become a father. The only problem was when.

He'd made his feelings clear. Her own emotions were too raw for her to face another showdown with Marco. She doubted he would believe whatever she had to tell him anyway.

Gentle fingers stroked over her belly. The doctor had confirmed today that she was almost three months pregnant. Her fingers stilled. Angelique had terminated Marco's child at three months. Sadness welled inside her as she recalled Marco's face when he'd shown her his scan.

Making up her mind before she lost the courage, she dug out her phone. Her fingers shook as she pressed the numbers.

'*Si?*' came the deep voice.

'Marco, it's me.'

Taut silence.

'I know you don't want to speak to me...but there's something I need to tell you.'

'I'm no longer in the motor racing business, so you're wasting your time.' The line went dead.

Sasha stared at the phone, anger and pain churning through her. '*Ass.*'

She threw the phone down, vowing to make Marco beg before she let him anywhere near his child.

Two days later Sasha was standing at her fridge stacking groceries when she heard the agonisingly familiar sound of helicopter rotorblades. The aircraft flew directly over her small cottage before landing in a field half a mile away.

Even though she forced herself to finish her task, every sense was attuned to the knock that came less than five minutes later.

Heart hammering, she opened her door to find Marco standing there, tall, dark and windswept.

'You know you'll have my neighbours dining out on your spectacular entrance for years, don't you? What the hell are you doing here anyway? I recall you wanting nothing to do with me.'

Hazel eyes locked on hers, the look in them almost imploring. 'Invite me in, Sasha.'

'I don't invite heartless bloodsuckers into my home. You can stay right where you are. Better yet, jump back into your vampire-mobile and leave.'

'I'm not leaving until you hear what I have to say. I don't care what your neighbours think, but I get the feeling *you* do. There's a blue-haired one staring at us right now.' Brazen, he waved at Mrs Miller, who shamelessly waved back and kept right on staring at them.

Firming her lips, Sasha stepped back and waved him in. 'You think you're very clever, don't you?'

Expecting a quick comeback, she turned from shutting the door to find him staring at her, a tormented grimace on his face.

'No, I don't think I'm clever at all. In fact, right now, I'm the stupidest person I know.'

Her mouth dropped open.

His grimace deepened. 'Yes, I know. Shocker.'

'Marco...' She stopped and finally did what she'd been dying to do since he knocked on her door. She let her eyes devour him. Let her heart delight in the sheer magnificent sight of him. He went straight to her head. Made her sway where she stood.

He stared right back at her, a plethora of emotions she was

too afraid to name passing over his face. He opened his mouth a couple of times but, seemingly losing his nerve to speak, cast his gaze around her small living room, over the pictures and racing knick-knacks she and her father had accumulated over the years.

Finally he dug into his jacket pocket. 'This is for you.'

Sasha took the papers. 'What are these?'

'Signed affidavits from two former drivers who swear your father wasn't involved in the fraud. He was the fall guy.'

Hands shaking, she read through the documents. 'How...? Why...?' Tears clogged her throat, making the words difficult to utter. Finally she could clear her father's name.

'The how doesn't matter. The why is because you deserve to know.'

She didn't realise she was crying until the first teardrop landed on her hand. Sucking in a sustaining breath, she swiped at her cheeks. 'I...I really don't know what to say. After what happened...' She glanced down at the papers again and swallowed. 'Thank you, Marco,' she said huskily.

'De nada,' he replied hoarsely.

'You didn't have to deliver it in person, though.'

His watchful look intensified. 'I didn't. But I needed the excuse to see you.'

'Why?' she whispered, too afraid to hope.

He swallowed. 'Rafael woke up—really woke up yesterday.'

Her heart lurched. 'Is he okay?'

Marco nodded. 'I went to see him this morning. He told me what happened in Budapest.'

Sasha sighed. 'I know it was stupid, but I lost it when I found out what Rafael was doing.'

'You mean deliberately using your friendship to make Raven jealous?'

She nodded. 'I think she was smitten with Rafael when she first joined the team. That changed when she found out he'd dated most of the women in the paddock. She refused to have anything to do with him after that.'

Marco pursed his lips. 'And he, of course, found it a challenge when she kept refusing him. Why didn't you tell me?' he demanded.

'You told me the significance of your mother's ring. I didn't think you needed to know Rafael was intending to use it to...'

'Get lucky?' He grimaced, then sobered. 'He's over that now, I think. He's seems different—more...mature. I think the accident was a wake-up call for him.'

His eyes locked on her, their expression so bleak it broke her heart.

'For me too. You were right.'

'I was?'

He moved towards her suddenly. '*Sí*. I was living in the past. I knew it even before you left Leon. I knew it when I came to see you in São Paolo. Hearing Rafael tell me what I already knew—how great you are, how much of a friend you'd been to him...' He stopped and swallowed. 'Did I mention I'm the stupidest person I know right now?'

'Um, you may have.'

'What I said in São Paolo was unforgivable...' His anxious gaze snared hers. 'I was in shock, but I never should've said what I did. I'm sorry you lost your baby. I think you would've made a brilliant mother.'

'You do?'

'*Sí*. I saw how the Children of Bravery Awards affected you. You held it together despite your pain. Watching you on stage with the kids made me wish my child had had a mother like you. At least then she would've had a chance.'

Tears filled her eyes. 'Oh, Marco...' She could barely speak past the lump in her throat.

Another grimace slashed his face. 'I've made you cry again.' He sat next to her and gently brushed away her tears. 'This wasn't what I intended by coming here.'

'Why did you come here, Marco?'

He sucked in a huge breath. 'To tell you I love you. And to beg your forgiveness.'

'You love me?'

He gave a jerky nod. 'It ripped me apart to learn I'd had your love and lost it because I'd been so stupid. When you called two days ago—'

'When you hung up on me?'

'I panicked. The hospital had just called about Rafael. I thought you knew and were calling to ask to see him.' He frowned. 'Why *did* you call?'

'I had something to tell you. When you hung up on me I wrote a letter instead.'

'A letter?'

'Well, it was more like a list.'

She'd done it to stop herself from crying—something she couldn't seem to stop doing lately.

Reaching into her pocket, she pulled it out and held it towards him. 'Here.'

He stared at the paper but didn't take it, his face ashen. 'Is forgiveness anywhere on that list, by any chance?'

Her gaze sharpened on him. 'Forgiveness?'

'Yes. Forgiveness of judgemental bastards who don't know the special gift of love and beauty and goodness when it's handed to them.'

'Er...' She glanced down at the list, her thundering heartbeat echoing loudly in her ears. 'No. But then I've only had two days to work on it.'

Dropping down on his haunches, he cupped her face in his hands. 'Then consider this a special request, *por favor*. I know I have a lot of grovelling to do for judging you harshly from the beginning.'

'You were hurting. And you were right. I *was* acting out of guilt.'

'No. You were doing whatever it took for you to move on—whereas I let one stumbling block shatter me. I resented you for that.'

'The blows you were dealt were enough to knock anyone sideways.'

'But I let it colour my judgement. I told myself I had recovered, that I didn't care, but I did. Do you know that until you came to Leon I hadn't entered that garage in over ten years? You opened my eyes to what a barren life I'd led until then.'

'Look at the letter, Marco.'

He inhaled sharply and stood. 'No. If you're going to condemn me I'd rather hear it from you.'

'You might want to sit down.'

He stuffed his fingers into his coat pockets, but not before she caught the trembling of his hands.

'Just tell me.'

'Fine. But if you faint from shock don't expect me to help you. You're too big—'

When he made an incoherent sound racked with pain, she unfolded the paper.

Anxiety coursed through her. He'd said he loved her, but what if Marco truly didn't want another child? What if the loss of his unborn child had been too great a pain for him ever to move on from?

'Sasha, *por favor.*'

'That's the second time you've said please in the last five minutes,' she whispered.

When his eyes grew dark, she read aloud. *'"Marco, you were an ass for hanging up on me but I think you should know—"'* She looked up from the sheet. *'"You're going to become a father."'*

For a full minute he didn't move. Didn't breathe, didn't blink. Then he stumbled into the chair. His hands visibly shook when he reached out and cupped her cheek. 'Sasha. Please tell me this isn't a dream,' he rasped.

'This isn't a dream. I'm pregnant with your child.'

A look of complete reverence settled over his face before his eyes dropped to her still-flat stomach.

'Are you okay? Is everything all right?' he demanded.

'You mean with the baby?'

'With both of you.'

'Yes. I saw the doctor. Everything is fine. Does that mean you want the baby?'

'*Mi corazón*, you've given me a second chance I never would've been brave enough to take on my own. I may have burned my bridges with you, but, yes, I want this baby.' His eyes dropped to her stomach, and lingered. *'Por favor*, can I touch?'

Sweet surprise rocked through her. 'You want to touch my belly?'

'If you'll allow me?'

'You know the baby isn't any larger than your thumb right now, don't you?'

'Sí, but my heart wants what it wants. Please?'

Renewed tears clogged her throat as she nodded and unbuttoned her jeans.

Warm fingers caressed her belly. Watching his face, she felt the breath snag in her chest at the sheer joy exhibited there. Then his eyes locked on hers and his fingers slid under her sweater, heating her bare flesh.

Her heart kicked, the fierce love she felt for this man and for her baby making her throat clog with tears. Reluctantly she withdrew from his seductive warmth. 'Marco, I haven't finished reading the letter.'

A look of uncertainty entered his eyes. 'I know what a hard bargain you can drive. Is there any room for negotiation?'

'You need to hear what's in it first.'

He gave a reluctant nod, his joy fading a little.

"'If it's a boy I would like to name him after my father. One of his names, at least."'

A quick nod met her request. 'It will be so.'

"'I want our child to be born in Spain. Preferably in Leon."'

He swallowed hard. 'Agreed.'

She looked up from the paper. *"'I'd like to stay there after the baby's born. With you."'*

His eyes widened and he stopped breathing. 'You want to stay in Leon? With me?'

Her heart in her throat, she nodded. 'Our child deserves two parents who don't live in separate countries.'

Disappointment fleeted over his face. 'You're right.'

'Our child also deserves parents who love each other.'

Pain darkened his eyes. 'I intend to do everything in my power to earn your love again, Sasha.'

She shrugged, her heart in her throat. 'You'll need to focus your energies on other things, Marco. Because I love you.'

He sucked in a breath. 'You…love me…?'

'Yes,' she reiterated simply. 'I knew in Leon, even though I'd convinced myself it wouldn't work.'

'I didn't exactly make it easy. I felt my life unravelling and I got desperate.'

Shock rocked through her. 'Was that why you sold the team?'

He grimaced. 'Rafael's accident and your near-collision in Korea convinced me it was time to get out of racing. But I managed to bulldoze my way through that too. I also may have left a tiny detail out regarding your firing.'

'Oh?'

'The sale contract included a stipulation that you were to have first refusal of the lead driver's seat. If you wanted it.'

Lifting loving hands, she cradled his face. 'Didn't you read Tom's press release last week?'

'What press release?'

'I've retired from motor racing.'

He frowned. 'What about your promise to your father?'

'He would've been proud that I helped you win the Constructors' Championship. But what he really wanted was for me to be happy.'

'And are you?'

'Tell me you love me again and I'll let you know.'

'I am deeply, insanely in love with you, Sasha Fleming, and I can't wait to make you mine.'

She flung the letter away and slid her arms around his neck. 'Then, yes, I'm ecstatically happy.'

EPILOGUE

'Happy birthday, *mi preciosa.*'

Sasha turned from where she'd been watching another stunning Leon sunset and tucked the blanket around their two-month-old baby.

'*Shh.* You'll wake him.'

Marco joined her at the crib. With a look of complete adoration on his face, he brushed a finger down his son's soft cheek. 'Jack Alessandro de Cervantes can sleep through a hurricane—just like his mother.' He pressed a kiss on his son's forehead, then held out his hand to her. 'Come with me.'

'Marco, you're not giving me another present? You've already given me six—oh, never mind.' By now she knew better than to dissuade her husband when he was on a mission. Today his mission was to shower her with endless gifts.

'*Sí,* now you're learning.'

As Marco led her to their bedroom she glanced down at the large square diamond ring he'd slid next to her seven-month-old wedding ring this morning. Not a week went by without Marco giving her a gift of some sort. Last week he'd presented her with the most darling chocolate Labradoodle puppy, and then grumbled when she'd immediately fallen in love with the dog.

'I hope it's not another diamond. There's only so much bling a girl can wear before she's asking for a mugging.'

'It's not a diamond. This present is much more...personal.'

He shut the door behind them, settled his hands on her hips and pulled her closer, his hazel eyes growing dramatically darker. 'The kind of *personal* that happens when you wear this T-shirt.'

'Why do you think I'm wearing it?'

He gave a low, sexy laugh. '*Dios*, you're merciless.'

'Only when it comes to you. Turning you on gives me a huge buzz.'

Stretching up, she wrapped her arms around his neck, luxuriating in their long kiss until she reluctantly pulled away.

At his protest, she shook her head. 'I have something to show you before we get too carried away.'

Reaching towards her bedside table, she handed him a single piece of heavily embossed paper.

He read through the document before glancing up at her. 'It's finalised?'

Happiness burst through her chest. 'Yes. The mayor's office sent over confirmation this afternoon. I'm officially patron of the De Cervantes Children's Charity. My programme to help disadvantaged kids who're interested in racing is a go!'

His devastating smile held pride even as he sighed. 'Between that and you being spokeswoman for women motor racers, I see my cunning plan to keep you busy in my bed having babies fast disappearing.'

Her smack on his arm was rewarded with a kiss on her willing mouth.

He sobered. 'Are you sure you don't want to go back to racing? You know you'd have my support in that too.'

Sasha blinked eyes prickling with tears and pressed her mouth against his. 'Thank you, but that part of my life is over. The chance to work with children is another dream come true. As for making more babies with you—it's my number one priority. Right up there with loving you for ever.'

His eyes darkened. 'I love you too, *mi corazón*.'

'Enough to take advantage of the instruction on my T-shirt?'
she asked saucily.

With a growl, he tumbled her back onto the bed and proceeded
to demonstrate just how good he was at taking instruction.

* * * * *

LET'S TALK
Romance

For exclusive extracts, competitions
and special offers, find us online:

f facebook.com/millsandboon

🐦 @MillsandBoon

📷 @MillsandBoonUK

Get in touch on 01413 063232

For all the latest titles coming soon, visit
millsandboon.co.uk/nextmonth

Want even more
ROMANCE?

Join our bookclub today!

MILLS & BOON
MODERN
Power and Passion

Prepare to be swept off your feet by sophisticated, sexy and seductive heroes, in some of the world's most glamourous and romantic locations, where power and passion collide.

Julia James

Heiress's
**PREGNANCY
SCANDAL**

MILLS & BOON

Jennie Lucas

Obsession the
**SHEIKH'S ROYAL
BRIDE**

MILLS & BOON

Kim Lawrence

**A WEDDING
at the
ITALIAN'S DEMAND**

MILLS

Sharon Kendrick

The
**SHEIKH'S
SECRET BABY**

MILLS & BOON

Eight Modern stories published every month, find them all at:

millsandboon.co.uk/Modern

MILLS & BOON
True Love

Romance from the Heart

Celebrate true love with tender stories of heartfelt romance, from the rush of falling in love to the joy a new baby can bring, and a focus on the emotional heart of a relationship.

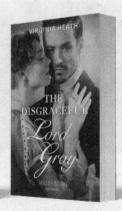

MILLS & BOON
Desire

Indulge in secrets and scandal, intense drama and plenty of sizzling hot action with powerful and passionate heroes who have it all: wealth, status, good looks... everything but the right woman.

MILLS & BOON

HEROES

At Your Service

Experience all the excitement of a gripping thriller, with an intense romance at its heart. Resourceful, true-to-life women and strong, fearless men face danger and desire - a killer combination!

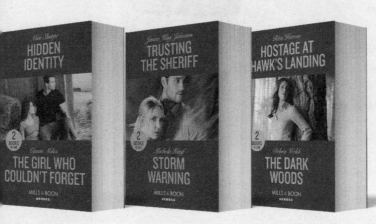

JOIN US ON SOCIAL MEDIA!

Stay up to date with our latest releases, author news and gossip, special offers and discounts, and all the behind-the-scenes action from Mills & Boon...

 millsandboon

 millsandboonuk

 millsandboon

It might just be true love...